Legends

Legends

A NOVEL OF DISSIMULATION

Robert Littell

W F HOWES LTD

This large print edition published in 2005 by
W F Howes Ltd
Units 6/7, Victoria Mills, Fowke Street
Rothley, Leicester LE7 7PJ

1 3 5 7 9 10 8 6 4 2

First published in the United Kingdom in 2005
by Gerald Duckworth & Co. Ltd

A CIP catalogue record for this book is available
from the British Library

ISBN 1 84505 793 7

Typeset by Palimpsest Book Production Limited,
Polmont, Stirlingshire
Printed and bound in Great Britain
by Antony Rowe Ltd, Chippenham, Wilts.

This is a work of fiction. Any similarity to persons living or dead is purely coincidental . . . the same is true for events.

For my muses:

Marie-Dominique and Victoria

For my muses:

Marie-Dominique and Victoria

1993: THE CONDEMNED MAN CATCHES A GLIMPSE OF THE ELEPHANT

They had finally gotten around to paving the seven kilometers of dirt spur connecting the village of Prigorodnaia to the four-lane Moscow-Petersburg highway. The local priest, surfacing from a week-long binge, lit beeswax tapers to Innocent of Irkutsk, the saint who in the 1720s had repaired the road to China and was now about to bring civilization to Prigorodnaia in the form of a ribbon of macadam with a freshly painted white stripe down the middle. The peasants, who had a shrewder idea of how Mother Russia functioned, thought it more likely that this evidence of progress, if that was the correct name for it, was somehow related to the purchase, several months earlier, of the late and little lamented Lavrenti Pavlovich Beria's sprawling wooden dacha by a man identified only as the *Oligarkh*. Next to nothing was known about him. He came and went at odd hours in a glistening black Mercedes S-600 sedan, his shock of silver hair and dark glasses a fleeting apparition behind its tinted windows. A local woman hired to do laundry was said to have seen him angrily flick cigar ashes from the crow's-nest rising like a turret from the dacha before turning back to issue instructions to someone. The woman, who was terrified of the dacha's new-fangled electric washing machine and scrubbed the laundry in a shallow reach of the river, had been too far away to make out more than a few words – 'Buried, that's what I want, but alive . . .' – but they and the *Oligarkh*'s feral tone had dispatched a chill down her spine that made her shudder every time she recounted the story. Two peasants cutting firewood on the other side of the river had caught a glimpse of the *Oligarkh* from a distance, struggling on aluminum crutches along the path behind his dacha that led to the dilapidated paper factory disgorging dirty white smoke from its giant stacks fourteen hours a day, six days a week, and beyond that to the village cemetery and the small Orthodox church with the faded paint peeling away from its onion domes. A pair of Borzois rollicked in the dirt ahead of the *Oligarkh* as he thrust one hip forward and dragged the leg after it, then repeated the movement with the other hip. Three men in Ralph Lauren jeans and *telnyashki,* the distinctive striped shirts that paratroopers often continued to wear after they quit the army, trailed after him, shotguns cradled in the crooks of their arms. The peasants had been sorely tempted to try for a closer look at the stubby, hunch-shouldered newcomer to their village, but abandoned the idea when one of them reminded the other what the Metropolitan come from Moscow to celebrate Orthodox Christmas two Januaries earlier had proclaimed from the ambo:

If you are stupid enough to dine with the devil, for Christ's sake use a long spoon.

The road crew, along with giant tank-treaded graders and steamrollers and trucks brimming with asphalt and crushed stone, had turned up during the night while the aurora borealis was still flickering like soundless cannon fire in the north; it didn't take much imagination to suppose a great war was being fought beyond the horizon. Casting elongated shadows in the ghostly gleam of head-lights, the men pulled on tar-stiff overalls and knee-high rubber boots and set to work. By first light, with forty meters of paved road behind them, the aurora and the stars had vanished, but two planets were visible in the moonless sky: one, Mars, directly overhead, the other, Jupiter, still dancing in the west above the low haze saturated with the amber glow of Moscow. When the lead crew reached the circular crater that had been gouged in the dirt spur the day before by a steam shovel, the foreman blew on a whistle. The machines ground to a halt.

'Why are we stopping?' one of the drivers, leaning out the cab of his steamroller, shouted impatiently through the face mask he'd improvised to filter out the sulfurous stench from the paper factory. The men, who were paid by the meter and not the hour, were anxious to keep moving forward.

'At any moment we are expecting Jesus to return to earth as a Russian czar,' the foreman called back lazily. 'We don't want to miss it when he comes across the river.' He lit a thick Turkish cigarette from the embers of an old one and strolled down to the edge of the river that ran parallel to the road for several kilometers. It was called the Lesnia, which was the name of the dense woods it meandered through as it skirted Prigorodnaia. At 6:12 a cold sun edged above the trees and began to burn off the mustard-thick September haze that clung to the river, which was in flood, creating a margin of shallow marshes on either side; long blades of grass could be seen undulating in the current.

The fisherman's dinghy that materalized out of the haze couldn't make it as far as the shore and the three occupants were obliged to climb out and wade the rest of the way. The two men wearing paratrooper shirts pulled off their boots and socks and rolled their jeans up to their knees. The third occupant didn't have to. He was stark naked. A crown of thorns, with blood trickling where the skin had been torn, sat on his head. A large safety pin attached to a fragment of cardboard had been passed through the flesh between his shoulder blades; on the cardboard was printed: 'The spy Kafkor.' The prisoner, his wrists and elbows bound behind him with a length of electrical wire, had several weeks growth of matted beard on his face, and purple bruises and what

4

looked like cigarette burns over his emaciated body. Stepping cautiously through the slime until he reached solid ground, looking disoriented, he regarded his image in the shallow water of the river while the paratroopers dried their feet with an old shirt, then pulled on their socks and boots and rolled down their pants.

The spy Kafkor didn't appear to recognize the figure gaping at him from the surface of the river.

By now the two dozen crewmen, mesmerized by the arrival of the three figures, had abandoned all interest in road work. Drivers swung out of their cabs, the men with rakes or shovels stood around shifting their weight from one foot to the other in discomfort. No one doubted that something dreadful was about to happen to the naked Christ, who was being prodded up the incline by the paratroopers. Nor did they doubt that they were meant to witness it and spread the story. Such things happened all the time in Russia these days.

Back on the stretch of freshly paved road, the team's ironmonger wiped his sweaty palms on his thick leather apron, then retrieved a lunch box from the bullock-cart piled with welding gear and scrambled up the slope to get a better view of the proceedings. The ironmonger, who was short and husky and wearing tinted steel-rimmed eyeglasses, flicked open the lid of the lunch box and reached into it to activate the hidden camera set up to shoot through a puncture in the bottom of a thermos. Casually balancing the thermos on his knees, he began to rotate the cap and snap photographs.

Below, the prisoner, suddenly aware that every member of the road crew was gazing at him, seemed more distressed by his nakedness than his plight – until he caught sight of the crater. It was roughly the size of a large tractor tire. Thick planks were stacked on the ground next to it. He froze in his tracks and the paratroopers had to grasp him by the upper arms and drag him the last few meters. The prisoner sank to his knees at the lip of the crater and looked back at the workers, his eyes hollow with terror, his mouth open and gulping air with rattling gasps through a parched throat. He saw things he recognized but his brain, befuddled with chemicals released by fear, couldn't locate the words to describe them: the twin stacks spewing plumes of dirty white smoke, the abandoned custom's station with a faded red star painted above the door, the line of white-washed bee hives on a slope near a copse of stunted apple trees. This was all a terrible dream, he thought. Any moment now he would become too frightened to continue dreaming; would force himself through the membrane that separated sleep from wakefulness and wipe the sweat from his brow and, still under the spell of the nightmare, have trouble falling back to sleep. But the ground felt damp and cold under his knees and a whiff of sulfurous air stung his lungs and the cold sun playing on his skin seemed to stir the cigarette burns to pain, and the pain brought home to him that what had happened, and what was about to happen, were no dream.

A Mercedes made its way slowly down the dirt road from the village, followed closely by a chase vehicle, a metallic gray Land Cruiser filled with bodyguards. Neither car had license plates, and the workers watching the scene play out understood this to mean that the people in them were too important to be stopped by the police. The Mercedes half turned so that it was astride the road and stopped a dozen meters from the kneeling prisoner. The rear window wound down the width of a fist. The *Oligarkh* could be seen peering out through dark glasses. He removed the cigar from his mouth and studied the naked prisoner for a long while, as if he were committing him and the moment to memory. Then, with a look of unadulterated malevolence on his face, he reached out with one of his crutches and tapped the man sitting next to the driver on the shoulder. The front door opened and the man emerged. He was of medium height and thin, with a long pinched face. He wore suspenders that kept his trousers hiked high on his waist, and a midnight blue Italian suit jacket draped cape-like over a starched white shirt, which was tieless and buttoned up to a very prominent Adam's apple. The initials 'S' and 'U–Z' were embroidered on the pocket of the shirt. He strode to the chase car and plucked a lighted cigarette from the mouth of one of the bodyguards.

7

Holding it away from his body between his thumb and third finger, he walked over to the prisoner. Kafkor raised his eyes and saw the cigarette and recoiled, thinking he was about to be branded with the burning tip. But S U-Z, smiling faintly, only reached down and wedged it between the lips of the prisoner. 'It is a matter of tradition,' he said. 'A man condemned to death is entitled to a last cigarette.'

'They . . . damaged me, Samat?' Kafkor whispered huskily. He could make out the shock of silver hair on the figure watching from the back seat of the Mercedes. 'They locked me in a basement awash in sewage, I could not distinguish night from day, I lost track of time, they woke me . . . with loud music when I fell asleep. Where, explain it to me if there exists an explanation, is the why?' The condemned man spoke Russian with a distinct Polish accent, emphasizing the open Os and stressing the next to last syllable. Terror tortured his sentences into baroque grammatical configurations. 'The endmost thing I would tell to nobody is what I am not supposed to know.'

Samat shrugged as if to say, The matter is out of my hands. 'You arrive too close to the flame, you must suffer burning, if only to warn others away from the flame.'

Trembling, Kafkor puffed on the cigarette. The act of smoking, and the smoke cauterizing his throat, appeared to distract him. Samat stared at the ash, waiting for it to buckle under its own weight and fall so they could get on with the execution. Kafkor, sucking on the cigarette, became aware of the ash, too. Life itself seemed to ride on it. Defying gravity, defying sense, it grew longer than the unsmoked part of the cigarette.

And then a whisper of wind coming off the river dislodged the ash. Kafkor spit out the butt. '*Poshol ty na khuy*,' he whispered, carefully articulating each of the Os in '*Poshol*.' '*Go impale yourself on a prick*.' He rocked back on his heels and squinted in the direction of the copse of stunted apple trees on the slope above him. 'Look!' he blurted out, vanquishing terror only to confront a new enemy, madness. 'Up there!' He sucked in his breath. 'I see the elephant. It can be said that the beast is revolting.'

At the Mercedes, the back door on the far side swung open and a frail woman dressed in an ankle-length cloth coat and peasant galoshes stumbled from the car. She wore a black pillbox hat with a thick veil that fell over her eyes, making it difficult for someone who didn't know her to divine her age. 'Jozef—' she shrieked. She stumbled toward the prisoner about to be executed, then, sinking to her knees, she turned to the man in the back of the car. 'What if it should begin to snow?' she cried.

The *Oligarkh* shook his head. 'Trust me, Kristyna – he will be warmer in the ground if the hole is covered with snow.'

'He is the same as a son to me,' the woman

sobbed, her voice fading to a cracked whimper. 'We must not bury him before he has had his lunch.'

Still on her knees, the woman, shuddering with sobs, started to crawl through the dirt toward the crater. In the back of the Mercedes, the *Oligarkh* gestured with a finger. The driver sprang from behind the wheel and, pressing the palm of his hand to the woman's mouth, half carried, half dragged her back to the car and folded her body into the back seat. Before the door slammed shut she could be heard sobbing: 'And if it does not snow, what then?'

Closing his window, the *Oligarkh* watched the scene unfold through its tinted glass. The two paratroopers took a grip on the prisoner's arms and lifted him into the crater and set him down on his side, curled up in a fetal position in the round hole. Then they began covering the crater with the thick planks, kicking the ends into the ground so that the tops of the planks were flush with the dirt road. When that was done they dragged a section of metal webbing over the planks. All the while nobody spoke. On the slope the workers, puffing on cigarettes, looked away or stared at their feet.

When the paratroopers finished covering the crater, they backed off to admire their handiwork. One of them waved to the driver of a truck. He climbed behind the wheel and backed up to the crater and worked the lever that elevated the flatbed to spill tarmacadam onto the road. Several workers came over and spread the macadam with long rakes until a thick glistening coating covered the wooden planks and they were no longer visible. They stepped away and the paratroopers signaled for the steamroller. Black fume billowed from its exhaust pipe as the rusty machine lumbered to the edge of the crater. When the driver seemed to hesitate, the horn of the Mercedes sounded and one of the bodyguards standing nearby pumped an arm in irritation. 'It is not as if we have all day,' he shouted above the bedlam of the steamroller's engine. The driver threw it into gear and started across the crater, packing down the tarmacadam. When he reached the other side, he backed over it again and then swung out of the cab to inspect the newly paved patch of highway. Suddenly, he tore off his improvised face mask and, bending, vomited on his shoes.

Barely making a sound, the Mercedes backed and filled and swung past the chase car and started up the dirt spur toward the sprawling wooden dacha at the edge of the village of Prigorodnaia, soon to be connected to the Moscow-Petersburg highway – and the world – by a ribbon of macadam with a freshly painted white stripe down the middle.

1997: MARTIN ODUM HAS A CHANGE OF HEART

C lad in a washed out white jumpsuit and an old pith helmet with mosquito netting hanging from it to protect his head, Martin Odum cautiously approached the rooftop beehives from the blind side so as not to obstruct the flight path of any bees straggling back to the frames. He worked the bellows of his smoker, spewing a fine white cloud into the nearest of the two hives; the smoke alerted the colony to danger, rousing the 20,000 bees inside to gorge themselves on honey, which would calm them down. April really was the cruelest month for bees, since it was touch and go whether there would be enough honey left over from the winter to avoid starvation; if the frames inside were too light, he would have to brew up some sugar candy and insert it into the hive to see the queen and her colony through to the warm weather, when the trees in Brower Park would be in bud. Martin reached inside with a bare hand to unstick one of the frames; he had worn gloves when he handled the hives until the day Minh, his occasional mistress who worked in the Chinese restaurant on the ground floor below the pool parlor, informed him that bee stings stimulated your hormones and increased your sex drive. In the two years he had been keeping bees on a Brooklyn roof top, Martin had been stung often enough but he'd never observed the slightest effect on his hormones; on the other hand the pinpricks seemed to revive memories he couldn't quite put his finger on.

Martin, who had dark hollows under his eyes that didn't come from lack of sleep, pried the first frame free and gingerly brought it out into the midday sunlight to inspect the combs. Hundreds of worker bees, churring in alarm, clung to the combs, which were depleted but still had enough honey left in them to nourish the colony. He scraped burr comb from the frame and examined it for evidence of American foulbrood. Finding none, he carefully notched the frame back into the hive, then backed away and pulled off the pith helmet and swatted playfully at the handful of brood bees that were trailing after him, looking for vengeance. 'Not today, friends,' Martin said with a soft laugh as he retreated into the building and slammed the roof door shut behind him.

Downstairs in the back room of the one-time pool parlor that served as living quarters, Martin stripped off the jumpsuit and, throwing it on the unmade Army cot, fixed himself a whiskey, neat. He selected a Ganaesh Beedie from a thin tin filled with the Indian cigarettes. Lighting up, dragging on the eucalyptus leaves, he settled into the swivel chair with the broken caning that scratched at his back; he'd picked it up for a song at a Crown Heights garage sale the day he'd rented the pool parlor and glued Alan Pinkerton's unblinking eye on the downstairs street door above the words 'Martin Odum – Private Detective.' The fumes from the Beedie, which smelled like marijuana, had the same effect on him that smoke had on bees: it made him want to eat. He pried open a tin of sardines and spooned them onto a plate that hadn't been washed in several days and ate them with a stale slice of pumpernickel he discovered in the icebox, which (he reminded himself) badly needed to be defrosted. With a crust of pumpernickel, he wiped the plate clean and turned it over and used the back as a saucer. It was a habit Dante Pippen had picked up in the untamed tribal badlands of Pakistan near the Khyber Pass; the handful of Americans running agents or operations there would finger rice and fatty mutton off the plate when they had something resembling plates, then flip them over and eat fruit on the back the rare times they came across something resembling fruit. Remembering a detail from the past, however trivial, gave Martin a tinge of satisfaction. Working on the back of the plate, he deftly peeled the skin off a tangerine with a few scalpel-strokes of a small razor sharp knife. *'Funny how some things you do, you do them well the first time,'* he'd allowed to Dr Treffler during one of their early sessions.

'Such as?'

'Such as peeling a tangerine. Such as cutting a fuse for plastic explosive long enough to give you time to get out of its killing range. Such as pulling off a brush pass with a cutout in one of Beirut's crowded souks.'

'What legend were you using in Beirut?'

'Dante Pippen.'

'Wasn't he the one who was supposed to have been teaching history at a junior college? The one who wrote a book on the Civil War that he printed privately when he couldn't find a publisher willing to take it on?'

'No, you're thinking of Lincoln Dittmann, with two ts and two ns. Pippen was the Irish dynamiter from Castletownbere who started out as an explosives instructor on the Farm. Later, posing as an IRA dynamiter, he infiltrated a Sicilian Mafia family, the Taliban mullahs in Peshawar, a Hezbollah unit in the Bekaa Valley of Lebanon. It was this last mission that blew his cover.'

'I have a hard time keeping track of your various identities.'

'Me, too. That's why I'm here.'

'Are you sure you have identified all of your operational biographies?'

'I've identified the ones I remember.'

'Do you have the feeling you might be repressing any?'

'Don't know. According to your theory, there's a possibility I'm repressing at least one of them.'

'The literature on the subject more or less agrees—'

'I thought you weren't convinced that I fit neatly into the literature on the subject.'

15

'*You are* hors genre, *Martin, there's no doubt about it. Nobody in my profession has come across anyone quite like you. It will cause quite a stir when I publish my paper—*'

'*Changing the names to protect the innocent.*'

To Martin's surprise she'd come up with something that could pass for humor. '*Changing the names to protect the guilty, too.*'

There are other things, Martin thought now (continuing the conversation with Dr Treffler in his mind), no matter how many times you do them, you don't seem to do them better. Such as (he went on, anticipating her question) peeling hard-boiled eggs. Such as breaking into cheap hotel rooms to photograph married men having oral sex with prostitutes. Such as conveying to a Company-cleared shrink the impression that you didn't have great expectations of working out an identity crisis. Tell me again what you hope to get out of these conversations? he could hear her asking. He supplied the answer he thought she wanted to hear: In theory, I'd like to know which one of my legends is me. He could hear her asking, *Why in theory?* He considered this for a moment. Then, shaking his head, he was surprised to hear his own voice responding out loud: 'I'm not sure I have a need to know – in practice, I might be better able to get on with my dull life if I don't know.'

Martin would have dragged out the fictitious dialogue with Dr Treffler, if only to kill time, if he hadn't heard the door buzzer. He padded in bare feet through the pool parlor, which he'd converted into an office, using one of the two tables as a desk and the other to lay out Lincoln Dittmann's collection of Civil War firearms. At the top of the dimly lit flight of narrow wooden stairs leading to the street door, he crouched and peered down to see who could be ringing. Through the lettering and Mr Pinkerton's private eye logo he could make out a female standing with her back to the door, scrutinizing the traffic on Albany Avenue. Martin waited to see if she would ring again. When she did, he descended to the foyer and opened the two locks and the door.

The woman wore a long raincoat even though the sun was shining and carried a leather satchel slung over one shoulder. Her dark hair was pulled back and twined into a braid that plunged down her spine to the hollow of her back – the spot where Martin had worn his hand gun (he'd recut the holster's belt slot to raise the pistol into an old shrapnel wound) in the days when he'd been armed with something more lethal than cynicism. The hem of her raincoat flared above her ankles as she spun around to face him.

'So are you the detective?' she demanded.

Martin scrutinized her the way he'd been taught to look at people he might one day have to pick out of a counterintelligence scrapbook. She appeared to be in her mid or late thirties – guessing the ages of women had never been his strong suit.

Spidery wrinkles fanned out from the corners of her eyes, which were fixed in a faint but permanent squint. On her thin lips was what from a distance might have passed for a ghost of a smile; up close it looked like an expression of stifled exasperation. She wore no makeup as far as he could see; there was the faint aroma of a rose-based perfume that seemed to come from under the collar on the back of her neck. She might have been taken for handsome if it hadn't been for the chipped front tooth.

'In this incarnation,' he finally said, 'I'm supposed to be a detective.'

'Does that mean you've had other incarnations?'

'In a manner of speaking.'

She shifted her weight from one foot to the other. 'So are you going to invite me in or what?'

Martin stepped aside and gestured with his chin toward the steps. The woman hesitated as if she were calculating whether someone living over a Chinese restaurant could really be a professional detective. She must have decided she had nothing to lose because she took a deep breath and, turning sideways and sucking in her chest, edged past him and started up the stairs. When she reached the pool parlor she looked back to watch him emerging from the shadows of the staircase. She noticed he favored his left leg as he walked.

'What happened to your foot?' she asked.

'Pinched nerve. Numbness.'

'In your line of work, isn't a limp a handicap?'

'The opposite is true. No one in his right mind would suspect someone with a limp of following him. It's too obvious.'

'Still, you ought to have it looked at.'

'I've been seeing a Hasidic acupuncturist and a Haitian herbalist, but I don't tell one about the other.'

'Have they helped you?'

'Uh-huh. One of them has – there's less numbness now – but I'm not sure which.'

The ghost of a smile materialized on her lips. 'You seem to have a knack for complicating simple things.'

Martin, with a cold politeness that masked how close he was to losing interest, said, 'In my book that beats simplifying complicated things.'

Depositing her satchel on the floor, the woman slipped out of her raincoat and carefully folded it over the banister. She was wearing running sneakers, tailored trousers with pleats at the waist and a man's shirt that buttoned from left to right. Martin saw that the three top buttons were open, revealing a triangle of pale skin on her chest. There was no sign of an undergarment. The observation made him suck in his cheeks; it occurred to him that the bee stings might be having some effect after all.

The woman wheeled away from Martin and wandered into the pool parlor, her eyes taking in the faded green felt on the two old tables, the moving company cartons sealed with masking tape

19

piled in a corner next to the rowing machine, the overhead fan turning with such infinite slowness that it seemed to impart its lethargic rhythm to the space it was ventilating. This was obviously a realm where time slowed down. 'You don't look like someone who smokes cigars,' she ventured when she spotted the mahogany humidor with the built in thermometer on the pool table that served as a desk.

'I don't. It's for fuses.'

'Fuses as in electricity?'

'Fuses as in bombs.'

She opened the lid. 'These look like paper shotgun cartridges.'

'Fuses, paper cartridges need to be kept dry.'

She threw him an anxious look and went on with her inspection. 'You're not crawling in creature comforts,' she noted, her words drifting back over her shoulder as she took a turn around the wide floorboards.

Martin thought of all the safe houses he had lived in, furnished in ancient Danish modern; he suspected the CIA must have bought can openers and juice makers and toilet bowl brushes by the thousands because they were the same in every safe house. And because they were safe houses, none of them had been perfectly safe. 'It's a mistake to possess comfortable things,' he said now. 'Soft couches, big beds, large bath tubs, the like. Because if nothing is comfortable you don't settle in; you keep moving. And if you keep moving, you have a better chance of staying ahead of the people who are trying to catch up with you.' Flashing a wrinkled smile, he added, 'This is especially true for those of us who limp.'

Looking through the open door into the back room, the woman caught a glimpse of crumpled newspapers around the Army cot. 'What's with all the newspapers on the floor?' she asked.

Hearing her speak, Martin was reminded how satisfyingly musical an ordinary human voice could be. 'I picked up that little trick from *The Maltese Falcon* – fellow named Thursby kept newspapers around his bed so no one could sneak up on him when he slept.' His patience was wearing thin. 'I learned everything I know about being a detective from Humphrey Bogart.'

The woman came full circle and stopped in front of Martin; she studied his face but couldn't tell if he was putting her on. She was having second thoughts about hiring someone who had learned the detective business from Hollywood movies. 'Is it true detectives were called gumshoes?' she said, eyeing his bare feet. She backed up to the pool table covered with muzzle-loading firearms and powder horns and Union medals pinned to a crimson cushion, trying to figure out what fiction she could come up with that would get her out of there without hurting his feelings. At a loss for words, she absently ran her fingers along the brass telescopic sight on an antique rifle. 'My father collects guns from the Great Patriotic War,' she remarked.

'Uh-huh. That makes your father Russian. In America we call it World War Two. I'd appreciate it if you wouldn't touch the weapons.' He added, 'That one's an English Whitworth. It was the rifle of choice of Confederate sharpshooters. The paper cartridges in the humidor are for the Whitworth. During the Civil War Whitworth cartridges were expensive, but a skilled sniper could hit anything he could see with the weapon.'

'You some sort of Civil War buff?' she asked.

'My alter ego is,' he said. 'Look, we've made enough small talk. Bite the bullet, lady. You must have a name.'

Her left palm drifted up to cover the triangle of skin on her chest. 'I'm Estelle Kastner,' she announced. 'The precious few friends I have call me Stella.'

'*Who are you?*' Martin persisted, quarrying for deeper layers of identity than a name.

The question startled her; there was clearly more to him than met the eye, which raised the prospect that he might be able to help her after all. 'Listen, Martin Odum, there are no shortcuts. You want to find out who I am, you're going to have to put in time.'

Martin settled back against the banister. 'What is it you hope I can do for you?'

'I hope you can find my sister's husband, who's gone AWOL from his marriage.'

'Why don't you try the police? They have a missing person's bureau that specializes in this sort of thing.'

'Because the police in question are in Israel. And they have more pressing things to do than hunt for missing husbands.'

'If your sister's husband went missing in Israel, why are you looking for him in America?'

'We think that's one of the places he might have headed for when he left Israel.'

'We?'

'My father, the Russian who calls World War Two the Great Patriotic War.'

'What are the other places?'

'My sister's husband had business associates in Moscow and Uzbekistan. He seems to have been involved in some kind of project in Prague. He had stationary with a London letterhead.'

'Start at the start,' Martin ordered.

Stella Kastner hiked herself up on the edge of the pool table that Martin used as a desk. 'Here's the story,' she said, crossing her legs at the ankles, toying with the lowest unbuttoned button on her shirt. 'My half-sister, Elena, she's my father's daughter by his first wife, turned religious and joined the Lubavitch sect here in Crown Heights soon after we immigrated to America, which was in 1988. Several years ago the rabbi came to my father and proposed an arranged marriage with a Russian Lubavitcher who wanted to immigrate to Israel. He didn't speak Hebrew and was looking for an observant wife who spoke Russian. My father had mixed feelings about Elena leaving Brooklyn, but it was my sister's dream to live in

Israel and she talked him into giving his consent. For reasons that are too complicated to go into, my father wasn't free to travel so it was me who accompanied Elena when she flew to Israel. We took a *sharoot*' – she noticed Martin's frown of confusion – 'that's a communal taxi, we took it to the Jewish settlement of Kiryat Arba on the West Bank next to Hebron. Elena, who changed her name to Ya'ara when she set foot in Israel, was married an hour and a quarter after the plane landed by the rabbi there, who had emigrated from Crown Heights ten years before.'

'Tell me about this Russian your sister married sight unseen.'

'His name was Samat Ugor-Zhilov. He was neither tall nor short but somewhere between the two, and thin despite the fact that he asked for seconds at mealtime and snacked between meals. It must have been his metabolism. He was the high strung type, always on the move. His face looked as if it had been caught in a vise – it was long and thin and mournful – he always managed to look as if he were grieving over the death of a close relative. The pupils of his eyes were seaweed-green, the eyes themselves were utterly devoid of emotion – cold and calculating would be the words I'd use to describe them. He dressed in expensive Italian suits and wore shirts with his initials embroidered on the pocket. I never saw him wearing a tie, not even at his own wedding.'

'You would recognize him if you saw him again?'

24

'That's a strange question. He could cover his head like an Arab – as long as I could see his eyes, I could pick him out of a crowd.'

'What did he do by way of work?'

'If you mean work in the ordinary sense of the term, nothing. He'd bought a new split-level house on the edge of Kiryat Arba for cash, or so the rabbi whispered in my ear as we were walking to the synagogue for the wedding ceremony. He owned a brand new Japanese Honda and paid for everything, at least in front of me, with cash. I stayed in Kiryat Arba for ten days and I came back again two years later for ten days, but I never saw him go to the synagogue to study Torah, or to an office like some of the other men in the settlement. There were two telephones and a fax machine in the house and it seemed as if one of them was always ringing. Some days he'd lock himself in the upstairs bedroom and talk on the phone for hours at a stretch. The few times he talked on the phone in front of me he switched to Armenian.'

'Uh-huh.'

'Uh-huh what?'

'Sounds like one of those new Russian capitalists you read about in the newspapers. Did you sister have children?'

Stella shook her head. 'No. To tell you the awful truth, I'm not positive they ever consummated the marriage.' She slid to the floor and went over to the window to stare out at the street. 'The fact is

I don't fault him for leaving her. I don't think Elena – I never got used to calling her Ya'ara – has the vaguest idea how to please a man. Samat probably ran off with a bleached blonde who gave him more pleasure in bed.'

Martin, listening listlessly, perked up. 'You make the same mistake most women make. If he ran off with another woman, it's because he was able to give her more pleasure in bed.'

Stella turned back to gaze at Martin. Her eyes tightened into a narrower squint. 'You don't talk like a detective.'

'Sure I do. It's the kind of thing Bogart would have said to convince a client that under the hard boiled exterior resided a sensitive soul.'

'If that's what you're trying to do, it's working.'

'I have a question: Why doesn't your sister get the local rabbi to testify that her husband ran out on her and divorce him in absentia?'

'That's the problem,' Stella said. 'In Israel a religious woman needs to have a divorce handed down by a religious court before she can go on with her life. The divorce is called a *get*. Without a *get*, a Jewish woman remains an *agunah*, which means a chained woman, unable to remarry under Jewish law; even if she remarries under civil law her children will still be considered bastards. And the only way a woman can obtain a *get* is for the husband to show up in front of the rabbis of a religious court and agree to the divorce. There's no other way, at least not for religious people. There are dozens of Hasidic husbands who disappear each year to punish their wives – they go off to America or Europe. Sometimes they live under assumed names. Go find them if you can! Under Jewish law the husband is permitted to live with a woman who's not his wife, but the wife doesn't have the same right. She can't marry again, she can't live with a man, she can't have children.'

'Now I'm beginning to see why you need the services of a detective. How long ago did this Samat character skip out on your sister?'

'It'll be two months next weekend.'

'And it's only now that you're trying to hire a detective?'

'We didn't know for sure he wasn't coming back until he didn't come back. Then we wasted time trying the hospitals, the morgues, the American and Russian embassies in Israel, the local police in Kiryat Arba, the national police in Tel Aviv. We even ran an ad in the newspaper offering a reward for information.' She tossed a shoulder. 'I'm afraid we don't have much experience tracking down missing persons.'

'You said earlier that your father and you thought Samat might head for America. What made you decide that?'

'It's the phone calls. I caught a glimpse once of his monthly phone bill – it was several thousand shekels, which is big enough to put a dent in a normal bank account. I noticed that some of the calls went to the same number in Brooklyn.

27

I recognized the country and area code – I for America, 718 for Brooklyn – because it's the same as ours on President Street.'

'You didn't by any chance copy down the number?'

She shook her head in despair. 'It didn't occur to me . . .'

'Don't blame yourself. You couldn't know this Samat character was going to run out on your sister.' He saw her look quickly away. 'Or did you?'

'I never thought the marriage would last. I didn't see him burying himself in Kiryat Arba for the rest of his life. He was too involved in the world, too dynamic, too attractive—'

'You found him attractive?'

'I didn't say I found him attractive,' she said defensively. 'I could see how he might appeal to certain women. But not my sister. She'd never been naked in front of a man in her life. As far as I know she'd never seen a naked man. Even when she saw a fully clothed man she averted her eyes. When Samat looked at a woman he stared straight into her eyes without blinking; he undressed her. He claimed to be a religious Jew but I think now it may have been some kind of cover, a way of getting into Israel, of disappearing into the world of the Hasidim. I never saw him lay tefillin, I never saw him go to the synagogue, I never saw him pray the way religious Jews do four times a day. he didn't kiss the mezuzah when he came into the house the way my sister did. Elena and Samat lived in different worlds.'

'You have photographs of him?'

'When he disappeared, my sister's photo album disappeared with him. I have one photo I took the day they were married – I sent it to my father, who framed it and hung it over the mantle.' Retrieving her satchel, she pulled a brown envelope from it and carefully extracted a black and white photograph. She stared at it for a moment, the ghost of an anguished smile deforming her lips, then offered it to Martin.

Martin stepped back and held up his palms. 'Did Samat ever touch this?'

She thought a moment. 'No. I had the film developed in the German Colony in Jerusalem and mailed it to my father from the post office across the street from the photo shop. Samat didn't know it existed.'

Martin accepted the photo and tilted it toward the daylight. The bride, a pale and noticeably overweight young woman dressed in white satin with a neck-high bodice, and the groom, wearing a starched white shirt buttoned up to his Adam's apple and a black suit jacket flung casually over his shoulders, stared impassively into the camera. Martin imagined Stella crying out the Russian equivalent of 'Cheese' to pry a smile out of them, but it obviously hadn't worked; the body language – the bride and groom were standing next to each other but not touching – revealed two strangers at a wake, not a husband and wife after a wedding ceremony. Samat's face had all but disappeared behind a shaggy black beard and mustache. Only his eyes, storm-dark with anger, were visible. He was obviously irritated, but at what? The religious ceremony that had gone on too long? The prospect of marital bliss in a West Bank oubliette with a consenting Lubavitcher for cellmate?

'How tall is your sister?' Martin inquired.

'Five foot four. Why?'

'He's slightly taller, which would make him five foot six or seven.'

'Mind if I ask you something?' Stella said.

'Ask, ask,' Martin said impatiently.

'How come you're not taking notes?'

'There's no reason to. I'm not taking notes because I'm not taking the case.'

Stella's heart sank. 'For God's sake, why? My father's ready to pay you whether you find him or not.'

'I'm not taking the case,' Martin announced, 'because it'd be easier to find a needle in a field of haystacks than your sister's missing husband.'

'You could at least try,' Stella groaned.

'I'd be wasting your father's money and my time. Look, Russian revolutionaries at the turn of the century grew beards like your sister's husband. It's a trick illegals have used since Moses dispatched spies to explore the enemy order of battle at Jericho. You live with the beard long enough, people identify you with the beard. The day you want to disappear, you do what the Russian revolutionaries did – you shave it off. Your own wife couldn't pick you out of a police lineup afterward. For argument's sake, let's say Samat was one of those gangster capitalists you hear so much about these days. Maybe things got too hot for your future ex-brother-in-law in Moscow the year he turned up in Kiryat Arba to marry your half sister. Chechen gangs, working out of that monster of a hotel across from the Kremlin – it's called the Rossiya, if I remember right – were battling the Slavic Alliance to see who would control the lucrative protection rackets in the capital. There were shootouts every day as the gangs fought over territories. Witnesses to the shootouts were gunned down before they could go to the police. People going to work in the morning discovered men hanging by their necks from lampposts. Maybe Samat is Jewish, maybe he's an Armenian Apostolic Christian. It doesn't really matter. He buys a birth certificate certifying his mother is Jewish – they're a dime a dozen on the black market – and applies to get into Israel. The paperwork can take six or eight months, so to speed things up your brother-in-law has a rabbi arrange a marriage with a female Lubavitcher from Brooklyn. It's the perfect cover story, the perfect way to disappear from view until the gang wars in Moscow peter out. From his split level safe house in a West Bank settlement, he keeps in touch with his business partners; he buys and sells stocks, he arranges to export Russian raw materials in exchange for Japanese computers or American jeans. And then one bright morning, when things in Russia have calmed down, he decides he's had enough of his Israeli dungeon. He doesn't want his wife or the rabbis or the state of Israel asking him where he's going, or looking him up when he gets there, so he grabs his wife's photo album and shaves off his beard and, slipping out of Israel, disappears from the face of the planet earth.'

Stella's lips parted as she listened to Martin's scenario. 'How do you know so much about Russia and the gang wars?'

He shrugged. 'If I told you I'm not sure how I know these things, would you believe me?'

'No.'

Martin retrieved her raincoat from the banister. 'I'm sorry you wasted your time.'

'I didn't waste it,' she said quietly. 'I know more now than when I came in.' She accepted the raincoat and fitted her arms into the sleeves and pulled it tightly around her body against the emotional gusts that would soon chill her to the bone. Almost as an afterthought, she produced a ballpoint pen from her pocket and, taking his palm, jotted a 718 telephone number on it. 'If you change your mind . . .'

Martin shook his head. 'Don't hold your breath.'

The mountain of dirty dishes in the sink had grown too high even for Martin. His sleeves rolled up to the elbows, he was working his way through the first stack when the telephone sounded in the pool parlor. As usual he took his sweet time answering; in his experience it was the calls you took that complicated your life. When the phone continued ringing, he ambled into the pool room and, drying his hands on his chinos, pinned the receiver to an ear with a shoulder.

'Leave a message if you must,' he intoned.

'Listen up, Dante –' a woman barked.

A splitting headache surged against the backs of Martin's eye sockets. 'You have a wrong number,' he muttered, and hung up.

Almost instantly the telephone rang again. Martin pressed the palm with the phone number written on it to his forehead and stared at the telephone for what seemed like an eternity before deciding to pick it up.

'Dante, Dante, you don't want to go and hang up on me. Honestly you don't. It's not civilized. For God's sake, I know it's you.'

'How did you find me?' Martin asked.

The woman on the other end of the line swallowed a laugh. 'You're on the short list of ex-agents we keep track of,' she said. Her voice turned serious. 'I'm downstairs, Dante. In a booth at the back of the Chinese restaurant. I'm faint from the monosodium glutamate. Come on down and treat yourself to something from column B on me.'

Martin took a deep breath. 'They say that dinosaurs roamed the earth sixty-five million years ago. You're living proof that some of them are still around.'

'Sticks and stones, Dante. Sticks and stones.' She added, in a tight voice, 'A word of advice: You don't want to *not* come down. Honestly you don't.'

The line went dead in his ear.

Moments later Martin found himself passing the window filled with plucked ducks hanging from meat hooks and pushing through the heavy glass door into Xing's Mandarin Restaurant under the pool parlor. Tsou Xing, who happened to be his landlord, was holding fort as usual on the high stool behind the cash register. He waved his only arm in Martin's direction. 'Hello to you,' the old man called in a high pitched voice. 'You want to eat in or take out, huh?'

'I'm meeting someone . . .' He surveyed the dozen or so clients in the long narrow restaurant and saw Crystal Quest in a booth near the swinging doors leading to the kitchen. Quest was better known to a generation of CIA hands as Fred because of an uncanny resemblance to Fred Astaire; a story had once made the rounds claiming that the president of the United States, spotting her at an intelligence briefing in the Oval Office, had passed a note to an aide demanding to know why a drag queen was representing the CIA. Now Quest, a past master of tradecraft, had positioned herself with her back to the tables, facing a mirror in which she could keep track of who came and went. She watched Martin approach in the mirror.

'You look fit as a flea, Dante,' she said as he slid onto the banquette facing her. 'What's your secret?'

'I sprang for a rowing machine,' he said.

'How many hours do you put in a day?'

'One in the morning before breakfast. One in the middle of the night when I wake up in a cold sweat.'

'Why would someone with a clean conscience wake up in a cold sweat? Don't tell me you're still brooding over the death of that whore in Beirut, for God's sake.'

Martin brought a hand up to his brow, which continued to throb. 'I think of her sometimes but that's not what's bothering me. If I knew what was waking me up, maybe I'd sleep through the night.'

Fred, a lean woman who had risen through the ranks to become the CIA's first female Deputy Director of Operations, was wearing one of her famous pantsuits with wide lapels and a dress shirt with frills down the front. Her hair, as usual, was cropped short and dyed the color of rust to conceal the gray streaks that came to topsiders who worried themselves sick, so Fred always claimed, over Standard Operating Procedure: Should you start with a hypothesis and analyze data in a way that supported it, or start with the data and sift through it for a useful hypothesis?

'What's your pleasure, Dante?' Fred asked, pushing aside a half eaten dinner, fingering her frozen daiquiri, noisily crunching chips of ice between her teeth as she regarded her guest through bloodshot eyes.

Martin signaled with a chopstick and then worked it back and forth between his fingers. At the bar, Tsou Xing poured him a whiskey, neat. A slim young Chinese waitress with a tight skirt slit up one thigh brought it over.

Martin said, 'Thanks, Minh.'

'You ought to eat something, Martin,' the waitress said. She noticed him toying with the chopstick. 'Chinese say man with one chopstick die of starvation.'

Smiling, he dropped the chopstick on the table. 'I'll take an order of Peking duck with me when I leave.'

Fred watched the girl slink away in the mirror. 'Now that's what I call a great ass, Dante. You getting any?'

'What about you, Fred?' he asked pleasantly. 'People still screwing you?'

'They try,' she retorted, her facial muscles drawn into a tight smile, 'in both senses of the word. But nobody succeeds.'

Snickering, Martin extracted a Beedie from the tin and lit it with one of the restaurant's matchbooks on the table. 'You didn't say how you found me.'

'I didn't, did I? It's more a case of we never lost you. When you washed up like a chunk of jetsam over a Chinese restaurant in Brooklyn, alarums, not to mention excursions, sounded in the battleship-gray halls of the shop. We obtained a copy of the lease the day you signed it. Mind you, nobody was surprised to find you'd slipped into the Martin Odum legend. What could be more logical? He'd actually been raised on Eastern Parkway, he went to PS 167, Crown Heights was his stamping ground, his father had an electric appliance store on Kingston Avenue. Martin even had a school chum whose father owned the Chinese restaurant on Albany Avenue. Martin Odum was the legend you worked up on my watch, or have you misplaced that little detail? Now that I think of it, you were the last agent I personally ran before they kicked me upstairs to run the officers who ran the agents, although, even at one remove, I always considered that I was the person playing you. Funny part is I have no memory of Odum being a detective. You must have decided the legend needed embroidering.'

Martin assumed that they had bugged the pool parlor. 'Being a detective beats having to work for a living.'

'What kind of cases do you get?'

'Mahjongg debts. Angry wives who pay me for photographs of errant husbands caught in the act. Hasidic fathers who think their sons may be dating girls who don't keep kosher. Once I was hired by the family of a Russian who died in Little Odessa, which is the part of Brooklyn where most of the Russians who wind up in America live, because they were convinced the Chechens who ran the neighborhood crematorium were extracting gold teeth from the late lamented before cremating their bodies. Another time I was hired by a colorful Little Odessa political figure to bring back the Rottweiler that'd been kidnapped by his ex-wife when he fell behind on alimony payments.'

'You get a lot of work in Little Odessa.'

'I keep nodding when my clients can't come up with the right word in English and wind up speaking Russian to me. They seem to think I understand them.'

'Did you find the dog?'

'Martin Odum always gets his dog.'

She clanked glasses with him. 'Here's looking at you, Dante.' She sipped her daiquiri and eyed him over the rim of the glass. 'You don't by any chance do missing husbands?'

The question hung in the air between them. Martin sucked on his Beedie for a moment, then said, very casually, 'What makes you ask?'

She drummed a forefinger against the side of her Fred Astaire nose. 'Don't play Trivial Pursuit with me, Pippen.'

'Up to now I've steered clear of missing husbands.'

'What about as of now?'

Martin decided that his apartment wasn't bugged after all; if it had been, Fred would have known he'd turned down Stella Kastner. 'Missing husbands are not my cup of tea, mainly because ninety-nine times out of a hundred they have settled comfortably into new identities involving new women. And it is extremely difficult, as in statistically impossible, to find people who have their heart set on never returning to their old women.'

A weight seemed to lift from Fred's padded shoulders. She scooped another cube of ice from her daiquiri and ate it. 'I have a soft spot for you, Dante. Honestly I do. In the eighties, in the early nineties, you were legendary for your legends. People still talk about you, though they refer to you by different names, depending on when they knew you. 'What's old Lincoln Dittmann up to these days?' a topsider asked me just last week. Agents like you come along once or twice a war. You floated on a cloud of false identities and false backgrounds that you could reel off, complete with what zodiac signs and which relatives were buried in what cemetery. If I remember correctly, Dante Pippen was a lapsed Catholic – he could recite rosaries in Latin that he'd learned as an altar boy in County Cork, he had a brother who was a Jesuit priest in the Congo and a sister who worked in a convent-hospital in the Ivory Coast. There was the Lincoln Dittmann legend, where you'd been raised in Pennsylvania and taught history at a junior college. It was filled with anecdotes about a high school prom in Scranton that was raided by the police or an uncle Manny in Jonestown who made a small fortune manufacturing under-wear for the Army during World War Two. In that incarnation you had visited every Civil War battle-field east of the Mississippi. You lived so many identities in your life you used to say there were times when you forgot which biographical details were real and which were invented. You plunged into your cover stories so deeply, you documented them so thoroughly, you lived them so intently, the disbursing office got confused about what name to use on your paycheck. I'll tell you a dark secret, Dante: I not only admired your tradecraft, I envied you as a person. Everyone enjoys wearing masks, but the ultimate mask is having alternate identities that you can slip into and out of like a change of clothing – aliases, biographies to go with them, eventually, if you are really good, personalities and languages that go with the biographies.'

With his Beedie, Martin playfully made the sign of the cross in the air. *'Ave Maria, Gratia Plena, Dominus Tecumi, Benedicta Tu In Mulieribus.'*

Snickering, Fred waved at Xing in the mirror. 'Would it be asking too much to get a check?' she called. She smiled sweetly at Martin. 'I presume you've gotten the message I came all this way to deliver. Steer clear of missing husbands, Dante.'

'Why?'

The question irritated Fred. 'Because I am telling you to steer clear, damn it. On the off chance you were to find him, why, we'd have to go back and take a hard look at certain decisions we made concerning you. In the end you turned out to be a rotten apple, Dante.'

He didn't have the foggiest idea what she was talking about. 'Maybe there were lines I couldn't cross,' he said, trying to keep the conversation going; hoping to discover why he woke up nights in a cold sweat.

'We didn't hire your conscience, only your brain and your body. And then, one fine day, you stepped out of character – you stepped out of all your *characters* – and took what in popular idiom is called a moral stand. It slipped your mind that morality comes in a variety of flavors. At Langley, we held a summit. The choices before us were not complicated: We could either terminate your employment or terminate your life.'

'What was the final vote?'

'Would you believe it was fifty-fifty? Mine was the tiebreaker. I came down on the side of those who wanted to terminate your employment, on condition you signed up at one of our private asylums. We needed to be sure—'

Before Fred could finish the sentence, Minh turned up carrying a small saucer with a check folded on it. She set it down between the two. Fred snared it and glanced at the bottom line, then peeled off two tens from a wad of bills and flattened them on the saucer. She weighed them down with a salt cellar. She and Martin sat silently, waiting for the waitress to remove the salt cellar and go off with the money.

'I really did have a soft spot for you,' Fred finally said, shaking her head at a memory.

Martin appeared to be talking to himself. 'I needed help remembering,' he murmured. 'I didn't get any.'

'Count your blessings,' Fred shot back. She slid off the banquette and stood up. 'Don't do anything to make me regret my vote, Dante. Hey, good luck with the detecting business. One thing I can't abide is Chechens who swipe gold teeth before cremating the corpus delicti.'

They were speeding up the Brooklyn-Queens Expressway toward La Guardia Airport to catch the shuttle back to Washington when the telephone on the dashboard squawked. The Operations Directorate wallah doubling as a chauffeur snatched it out of the cradle and held it to his ear. 'Wait one,' he said and passed the phone over his shoulder to Crystal Quest, dozing against a door in the back.

'Quest,' she said into the receiver.

She straightened in the seat. 'Yes, sir, I did. Dante and I go back a long way – I'm sure the fact that I delivered the message in person convinced him we were not playing pickup sticks.' She listened for a moment. Up front the wallah surmised that the tinny bursts resonating from the earpiece were conveying exasperation in both tone and content.

Quest scratched at her scalp through her rust colored hair. 'I am definitely not going soft, Director – soft is not my style. I ran him when he

42

was operational. Fact that he came in from the cold, as that English spy writer put it, doesn't change anything. As far as I'm concerned, I'm still running him. As long as he doesn't remember what happened – as long as he keeps his nose out of this Samat business – there's no reason to revisit that decision.' She listened again, then said, coldly, 'I take your point about unnecessary risks. If he steps over the fault—'

The man on the other end of the phone finished the sentence for her; the wallah at the wheel could see his boss in the rear view mirror nodding as she took aboard an order.

'Count on it,' Quest said.

The line must have gone dead in her ear – the Director was notorious for ending conversations abruptly – because Quest leaned forward and dropped the telephone onto the passenger seat. Sinking back against the door, staring sightlessly out of the window, she started muttering disjointed phrases. After a while the words began taking on a sense. 'Directors come and go,' she could be heard saying. 'The ones who wind up in Langley through their ties to the White House aren't the keepers of the flame – we are. We man the ramparts while the Director busts his balls working the Georgetown dinner circuit. We run the agents who put their lives on the line prowling the edge of empire. And we pay the price. Field agent drinks too much, controlling officer gets a hangover. Field agent turns sour, we curdle. Field agent dies, we break out the sackcloth and ashes and mourn for forty days and forty nights.' Quest sighed for her lost youth, her femaleness gone astray. 'None of which,' she continued, her voice turning starchy, 'would prevent us from terminating the son of a bitch if it looked as if he might compromise the family's jewel.'

Martin's bedside alarm went off an hour before first light. In case Fred had managed to plant a microphone after all, he switched on the radio and turned up the volume to cover his foot falls and the sound of doors closing. Still in his tracksuit, he climbed to the roof and worked the bellows of his smoker, sending the colony of bees in the second of the two hives into a frenzy of gorging on honey. Then he reached into the narrow space between the top of the frames and the top of the hive to extract the small packet wrapped in oilcloth. Back downstairs, Martin opened the refrigerator and stuck a plastic basin under the drip notch. In the faint light that came from the open refrigerator, he unfolded the oilcloth around the packet and spread out the contents on his cot. There were half a dozen American and foreign passports, a French Livret de Famille, three internal passports from East European countries, a collection of laminated driver's licenses from Ireland and England and several East Coast states, an assortment of lending library and frequent flyer and Social Security cards, some of them brittle with age. He collected the identity papers and distributed them evenly between the cardboard lining and the top of the shabby leather valise with stickers from half a dozen Club Med resorts pasted on it. He filled the valise with shirts and underwear and socks and toilet articles, folded Dante Pippen's lucky white silk bandanna on top, then changed his clothing, putting on a light three-piece suit and the sturdy rubber soled shoes he'd worn when he and Minh had hiked trails in the Adirondacks the year before. Looking around to see what he'd forgotten, he remembered the bees. He quickly scribbled a note to Tsou Xing asking him to use the spare front door key he'd left in the cash register to check the beehives every other day; if there wasn't enough honey in the frames to see the bees through until spring, Tsou would know how to brew up sugar candy with the ingredients under the sink and deposit it in the hives.

Carrying the valise and an old but serviceable Burberry, Martin made his way to the roof. He locked the roof door behind him and stashed the key under a loose brick in the parapet. Looking up at the Milky Way, or what you could see of it from a roof in the middle of Brooklyn, he was reminded of the Alawite prostitute Dante had come across in Beirut during one particularly hairy mission. Leaning on the parapet, he surveyed Albany Avenue for a quarter of an hour, watching the darkened windows across the street for the slightest movement of curtains or Venetian blinds or a glimpse of embers glowing on a cigarette. Finding no signs of life, he crossed the roof and studied the alleyway behind the Chinese restaurant. There was motion off to the right where Tsou Xing parked his vintage Packard, but it turned out to be a cat trying to work the lid off a garbage pail. When Martin was sure the coast was clear, he backed down the steel ladder and then carefully descended the fire escape to the first floor. There he untied the rope and lowered the last section to the ground (through runners that he'd greased every few months; for Martin, tradecraft was the nearest thing he had to a religion). He tested the quality of the stillness for another few minutes before letting himself down into Tsou Xing's backyard heaped with stoves and pressure cookers and refrigerators that could one day be cannibalized for spare parts. He slipped the note for Tsou under the back door of the restaurant, crossed the yard to the alleyway and headed down it until he came to Lincoln Place. Two blocks down Lincoln, on the northeast corner of Schenectady, he ducked into a phone booth that reeked of turpentine. The first faint smudges of metallic gray were visible in the east as he checked the number written on his palm. Feeding a coin into the slot, he dialed it. The phone on the other end rang so many times that Martin began to worry he'd dialed the wrong number. He hung up and double checked the number and dialed again. He started counting how many times it rang and then gave up and just listened to it ring, wondering what to do if nobody answered. He was about to hang up – he would go to ground in a twenty-four hour diner on Kingston Avenue and try again in an hour – when someone finally came on the line.

'Do you have any idea what time it is?' a familiar voice demanded.

'I have decided I can't live without you. If you still want me, I think we can work something out.'

Estelle Kastner caught her breath; she understood he was afraid the conversation was being overheard. 'I'd given up on you,' she admitted. 'When can you come over?'

He liked her style. 'How about now?'

She gave him an address several blocks down President Street between Kingston and Brooklyn. 'It's a big private house. There's a door around the side – the light over it will be on. I'll be waiting for you in the vestibule.' On the off chance the phone really was tapped, Estelle added, 'I've never had a relationship with someone whose sign isn't compatible with mine. So what are you?'

'Leo.'

'Come on, you're not a Leo. Leo's are cock sure of themselves. If I had to guess, I'd say you have the profile of a Capricorn. Capricorns are impulsive, whimsical, stubborn as a mule in the good sense – once you start something, you finish it. Your being a Capricorn suits me fine.' She cleared her throat. 'What made you change your mind. About calling?'

She caught Martin's soft laughter and found the sound curiously comforting. She heard him say, 'I didn't have a change of mind, I had a change of heart.'

'Fools rush in,' she remarked, quoting from an old American song she played over and over on the phonograph, 'where angels fear to tread.' She could hear Martin breathing into the phone. Just before she cut the connection, she said, more to herself than to him, 'I have a weakness for men who don't use aftershave.'

1994: MARTIN ODUM GETS ON WITH HIS LIVES

'Could you say something so I can check the voice level?'

'What should I say?'

'Anything that comes into your head.'

'". . . the silent cannons bright as gold rumble lightly over the stones. Silent cannons, soon to cease your silence, soon unlimber'd to begin the red business."'

'That's fine. Remember to speak directly into the microphone. All right, here we go. For the record: We're Thursday, the sixteenth of June, 1994. What follows is a tape recording of my first session with Martin Odum. My name is Bernice Treffler. I'm the director of the psychiatric unit at this private hospital in Bethesda, Maryland. If you want to break at any time, Mr Odum, wave a hand. What were those lines from, by the way?'

'One of Walter Whitman's Civil War poems.'

'Any reason you call him Walter instead of Walt?'

'I was under the impression that people who knew him called him Walter.'

'Are you a fan of Whitman's?'

'Not that I'm aware of. I didn't know I knew the lines until I said them.'

'Does the Civil War interest you?'

'It doesn't interest me, Martin Odum, but it interested – how can I explain this? – it interested someone close to me. In one of my incarnations, I was supposed to have taught a course in a junior college on the Civil War. When we were working up the legend—'

'I'm sorry. The CIA people I've treated up to now have all been officers working at Langley. You're my first actual undercover agent. What is a legend?'

'It's a fabricated identity. Many Company people use legends, especially when they operate outside the United States.'

'Well, I can see my vocabulary is going to expand talking to you, Mr Odum. Go on with what you were saying.'

'What was I saying?'

'You were saying something about working up a legend.'

'Uh-huh. Since in my new incarnation I was supposed to be something of an expert on the subject, the person I was becoming had to study the Civil War. He read a dozen books, he visited many of the battlefields, he attended seminars, that sort of thing.'

'He, not you?'

'Uh-huh.'

'Was there a name assigned to this particular, eh, legend?'

'Dittmann, with two t's and two n's. Lincoln Dittmann.'

'Do you have a headache, Mr Odum?'

'I can feel one starting to press against the back of my eyes. Could you crack a window? It's very stuffy in here . . . Thanks.'

'Would you like an aspirin?'

'Later, maybe.'

'Do you get headaches often?'

'More or less often.'

'Hmmm. What kind of person was this Lincoln Dittmann?'

'I'm not sure I understand the question.'

'Was he different, say, from you? Different from Martin Odum?'

'That was the whole point – to make him different so he could operate without anyone mistaking him for me or me for him.'

'What could Lincoln Dittmann do that you couldn't?'

'To begin with, he was an extraordinary marksman, much more skilled than me. He would take his sweet time to be sure he got the kill, one shot to a target. He would crank in corrections for windage and distance and then slowly squeeze (as opposed to jerk) the trigger. I'm too high-strung to kill in cold blood unless I'm goaded into action by the likes of Lincoln. The few times in my life that I aimed at a human target, my mouth went dry, a pulse pounded in my temple, I had to will my trigger finger not to tremble. When a born-again sniper like Lincoln shot at a human target, the only thing he felt was the recoil of the rifle. What else? I was more proficient in tradecraft – I could melt into a crowd when there wasn't one, so they said. Lincoln stood out in a crowd like a sore thumb. He was obviously more cerebral than me, or my other legend, for that matter. He was a better chess player, not because he was smarter than me, it's just that I was too impatient, too restless to figure out the implications of any particular gambit, to work out what would happen eight or ten moves down the tube. Lincoln, on the other hand, was blessed with incredible patience. If an assignment required stalking someone, Lincoln was the agent of choice for the job. And then there was the way we each looked at the world.'

'Go on.'

'Martin Odum is a basically edgy individual – there are days when he jumps at his own shadow. He's afraid to set foot in a place he's never been to before, he's apprehensive when he meets someone he doesn't already know. He lets people – women, especially – come to him. He has a sex drive but he's just as happy to abstain. When he makes love, he goes about it cautiously. He pays a lot of attention to the woman's pleasure before he takes his own.'

'And Dittmann?'

'Nothing fazed Lincoln – not his own shadow, not places he hadn't been to, not people he didn't already know. It wasn't a matter of his being fearless; it was more a question of his being addicted to fear, of his requiring a daily fix.'

'What you're describing is very similar to a split personality.'

'You don't get it. It's not a matter of *splitting* a personality. It's a matter of creating distinct personalities altogether who . . . Excuse me but why are you making notes when this is being recorded?'

'The conversation has taken a turn for the fascinating, Mr Odum. I'm jotting down some initial impressions. Were there other dissimilarities between Dittmann and Odum; between Dittmann and you?'

'Creating a working legend didn't happen overnight. It took a lot of time and effort. The details were worked out with the help of a team of experts. Odum smokes Beedies, Dittmann smoked Schimelpenicks when he could find them, any thin cigars when he couldn't. Odum didn't eat meat, Dittmann loved a good sirloin steak. Odum is a Capricorn, Dittmann didn't know what his Zodiac sign was and couldn't have cared less. Odum washes and shaves every day but never uses aftershave lotions. Dittmann washed when he could and doused himself with Vetiver between showers. Odum is a loner; the handful of people who know him joke that he prefers the company of bees to humans, and there's a grain of truth to that. Dittmann was gregarious; unlike Odum he was a good dancer, he liked night clubs, he was capable of drinking large quantities of cheap

alcohol with beer chasers without getting drunk.
He did dope, he solved crossword puzzles in ink,
he played Parcheesi and Go. When it came to
women, he was an unconditional romantic. He
had a soft spot for females' – Martin remembered
a mission that had taken Lincoln to a town on
the Paraguayan side of Three Border – 'who were
afraid of the darkness when the last light has been
drained from the day, afraid of men who removed
their belts before they took off their trousers, afraid
life on earth would end before dawn tomorrow,
afraid it would go on forever.'

'And you—'

'I don't do dope. I don't play board games. I
don't do crossword puzzles, even in pencil.'

'So Odum and Dittmann are antipodes? That
means—'

'Lincoln Dittmann would know what antipodes
means. And in a corner of one lobe of my brain
I have access to what he knows.'

'What does this *access* consist of?'

'You're not going to believe this.'

'Try me.'

Martin said, very softly, 'There are moments when
I hear his voice whispering in my ear. That's how I
came up with those Walter Whitman lines.'

'Lincoln Dittmann whispered them to you.'

'Uh-huh. Other times I know what he would do
or say if he were in my shoes.'

'I see.'

'What do you see?'

'I see why your employer sent you to us. Hmmm. I'm a bit confused about something. You talk about Lincoln Dittmann in the past tense, as if he doesn't exist anymore.'

'Lincoln's as real as me.'

'The way you talk about Martin Odum, it almost seems as if he's a legend, too. Is he?'

When Martin didn't answer she repeated the question. 'Is Martin Odum another of your fabricated identities, Mr Odum?'

'I'm not sure.'

'Are you telling me you really don't know?'

'I thought that's what you were supposed to help me find out. One of the legends must be real. The question is which.'

'Well, this is certainly going to be more interesting than I expected. You have a very original take on MPD.'

'What the heck is MPD?'

'It stands for Multiple Personality Disorder.'

'Is what I have fatal? Why are you smiling?'

'Multiple Personality Disorder is far more likely to be functional than fatal, Mr Odum. It permits patients who suffer from it to survive.'

'Survive what?'

'That's what we're going to try to work our way back to. Let me give you the short course on MPD. My guess is that somewhere along the line something happened to you. In the overwhelming majority of cases, the trauma took place in childhood – sexual assaults are high on the list of childhood traumas, but not the only things on the list. I had one case about four years ago where a patient turned out to have been traumatized because he played with matches and started a fire that resulted in the death of his baby sister. The trauma short-circuited the patient's narrative memory. This particular patient developed seven distinct adult personalities, each with its own set of emotions and memories and even skills. He switched from one to another whenever he came under any stress. None of the seven alter personalities – what you would call legends, Mr Odum – remembered the original childhood personality or the trauma associated with that personality. So you see, switching between personalities – almost always accompanied by a headache, incidentally – was a survival mechanism. It was his way of erecting a memory barrier, of shielding himself from an extremely frightening childhood experience, and it's in this sense that MPD is considered to be functional. It allows you to get on with your life—'

'Or your lives.'

'Very good, Mr Odum. Or your lives, yes. My instinct tells me you certainly don't fit neatly into the literature on the subject, inasmuch as you developed your alter personalities out of operational necessity, as opposed to a psychological necessity. When your psyche decided it needed to disappear behind a memory barrier, you had a series of personalities crafted and waiting to be

56

stepped into. It's in this sense that you can be said to fit into the Multiple Personality profile.'

'How different were your patient's seven personalities?'

'In my patient's case, as in the majority of MPD cases, they were quite distinct, involving diverse habits, talents, interests, values, dress codes, mannerisms, body language, ways of expressing themselves. They even made love differently. The alter personalities had different names and several of them even had different ages. One of them was unable to communicate verbally while another spoke a language – in his case Yiddish – that the others didn't understand.'

'How is it possible for one personality to speak a language that another of his personalities doesn't understand?'

'It's a perfect example of how compartmented what you call legends can be in the brain.'

'Were the seven personalities aware of each other's existence?'

'Some were, some weren't. This aspect can vary from case to case. More often than not several of the personalities seem to be aware of the existence of several other of the personalities – they think of them the way you would think of friends who you know exist but haven't seen in awhile. And there is what we call a *trace* personality – in your case it would appear to be Martin Odum – who serves as a repository of information about all of the other personalities except the *host* personality that experienced the trauma. This would account for the sensation you have that, as you said a moment ago, in a corner of your brain you have access to the specialized knowledge or talents of another alter personality, or as you would put it, another legend.'

'I have a question, Dr Treffler.'

'Listen, since we're going to be working together for some time, how about if we move on to a first name basis. Call me Bernice and I'll call you Martin, okay?'

'Sure. Bernice.'

'What's your question, Martin?'

'I seem to be able to distinguish three operational identities. There's Martin Odum. There's Lincoln Dittmann. And there's one I haven't introduced you to – the Irishman, Dante Pippen. Today of all days, Dante would be out on a pub crawl in Dublin, seeing how many of the city's pubs he could drink in before the sun set.'

'What's so special about today?'

'It's Bloomsday, for pete's sake. All the action in *Ulysses* takes place ninety years ago today – 16 June, 1904.' Martin shut his eyes and angled his head. ' "Bloom entered Davy Byrne's. Moral pub. The publican doesn't chat. Stands a drink now and then." On top of everything, it was a Tuesday, like today. In Ireland, that's the kind of thing you don't let pass without praying at what Dante liked to call licensed tabernacles.'

'Hmmm.'

'So here's my question: Is one of my three legends genuine? Or is there a fourth personality lurking in the shadows who's the original me?'

'Can't respond to that one yet. Either premise could be correct. There could be a fourth legend, even a fifth. We won't know until we start to break down the memory barriers, brick by brick, to get to the identity that recognizes himself as the original you.'

'For that to happen, the childhood trauma will have to surface?'

'Is that a question or a statement of fact?'

'Question.'

'I'm going to enjoy working with you, Martin. You're very quick. You're not frightened, at least not to the point where you'd walk away from this adventure. The answer to your question is: To get to what you call the original you, you're almost certainly going to have to experience pain. How do you feel about pain?'

'Not sure what to answer. Martin Odum may feel one way about it, Lincoln Dittmann and Dante Pippen, another.'

'On that delightful note, what do you say we call it a day?'

'Uh-huh.' As an afterthought, Martin asked, 'Could I take you up on that aspirin?'

1997: MARTIN ODUM DISCOVERS THAT NOT MUCH IS SACRED

From Lower Manhattan, as the crow flies, Crown Heights is a mere four miles across the river but a world away. Since race riots raged in its streets in the early 1990s, this particular section of Brooklyn had enjoyed a degree of extraterritoriality. Riding in squad cars with the mantra 'Courtesy Professionalism Respect' visible on the doors not spattered with mud, police officers patrolled the neighborhood during daylight hours, but only for the most flagrant crimes would they abandon the relative safety of their vehicles. Depending on which street you were on, in some cases which sidewalk, different mafias ruled. On the streets south of Eastern Parkway off Nostrand Avenue, the Lubavitchers, solemn men in black suits and black hats, busied themselves reading the Torah in neighborhood shuls and obeying its 613 commandments while they waited for the Messiah, who was expected to turn up any day now; by the weekend at the very latest. Because the end of the world was nigh, Lubavitchers were enthusiastic about mortgages, the longer the better; but they hesitated buying anything they couldn't immediately consume, they didn't get involved in fights they couldn't finish before darkness fell. One block farther down President, on Rogers Avenue, the Lubavitchers gave way to African-Americans crowded into tenements; ghetto blasters with the volume turned up drowned out the occasional shrieks of addicts who needed a hit but didn't have the cash to pay for it. The West Indian ghetto, with its tidy streets and social clubs and block parties that had young people strolling in the gutter until dawn, began a few blocks farther south, on Empire Boulevard. Where the denizens of the different ghettos rubbed shoulders, tensions ran high. Everyone understood it only needed a spark to set off a conflagration.

Martin, an outsider in all of the Crown Heights ghettos, knew enough to keep his head down and avoid looking anyone in the eye when he walked the streets. The sun was up and toasting the crispness out of the air as he made his way down Schenectady, past a large 'Rent Strike' sign whitewashed onto a storefront window, past several broken shopping carts with small placards saying they were the property of Throckmorton's Minimarket on Kingston Avenue, kindly return. His leg with the pinched nerve was starting to ache as he turned onto President, a wide residential street with trees and two-story homes on either side. He stepped off the sidewalk to make way for three Lubavitch women, one more anemic than the other, all of them wearing long skirts and kerchiefs over their shaven heads. They didn't so much as glance in his direction but went on prattling to each other in a language Martin couldn't identify. As he neared Kingston, he came abreast of an ambulance with a Jewish Star of David painted on the door, parked in front of a brownstone that had been converted into a synagogue; two pimply young men, with embroidered skull caps on their heads and long sideburns curling down to their jaws, sat in the front seats listening to Bob Dylan on the tape deck.

. . . Everything from toy guns that spark
To flesh-colored Christs that glow in the dark
It's easy to see without looking too far
That not much is really sacred.

Once across Kingston Avenue, Martin began to search for the house numbers. Two thirds of the way down the block, he found the big house that Estelle Kastner had described; a narrow flagstone walkway led to the side door with the light burning over it. He continued past the house without stopping and turned right on Brooklyn Avenue, and then right again on Union Street, all the while watching the streets for the telltale signs that he was being followed, either by someone on foot or in a car. He felt a certain nostalgia for the good old days in the boondocks when he would have had a sweeper or two trailing after him to make sure he was clean, and tidy up behind him if he wasn't. Nowadays, he was obliged to make do with rudimentary tradecraft precautions. Streets and alleyways and intersections, the lobbies of buildings with their banks of elevators, the toilets in the backs of restaurants and the windows in the backs of the toilets that looked out on alleyways – he took it all in as if his life might one day depend on remembering what he saw.

Halfway down Union he climbed the front steps of a brownstone and stabbed at the bell. An old man in an undershirt flung open an upstairs window and shouted down, 'What'cha want?'

'Looking for a family, name of Grossman,' Martin called back.

'You're barking up the wrong block,' the man yelled. 'The Jewish, they live on President Street. Union is still thanks to God reasonably Roman.' With that he pulled his head back into the house and slammed the window shut.

Martin stood on the stoop for a moment, feigning confusion as he surveyed the street in either direction. Then he doubled back the way he'd come and made his way along President Street to the flagstones that led to the side entrance with the light over it. He was about to knock on the 'No Peddlers' sign when the door was pulled open. Stella, wearing tight jeans with a man's shirt tucked into them, stood inside, squinting up at him. The same three top buttons of her shirt were unbuttoned, revealing the same triangle of pale chest. Strangely, Martin found her more attractive than he remembered. He noticed her hands for the first time; the nails were neither painted nor bitten, the fingers themselves were incredibly long and extremely graceful. Even her chipped front tooth, which had struck him as downright ugly when they met the day before, seemed like an asset.

'Well, if it isn't the barefoot gumshoe, Martin Odum, Private Eye,' Stella said with a mocking grin. She let him in and slipped his valise under a chair. 'In that raincoat,' she said, taking it from him and hanging it on a vestibule hook, 'you look like a foreign correspondent from a foreign country. I saw you limp past ten minutes ago,' she announced as she led him up a flight of stairs and into a windowless walk-in closet. 'I concluded that your leg must be hurting. I concluded also that you're paranoid someone might be following you. I'll bet you didn't call me from home – I'll bet you called from a public phone.'

Martin grinned. 'There's a booth on Lincoln and Schenectady that smells like a can of turpentine.'

A booming voice behind Martin exclaimed, 'My dear Stella, when will you learn that some paranoids have real enemies. I was watching from an upstairs window when he limped down President Street. Our visitor has the haunted look of someone who would circle the block twice before visiting his mother.'

Martin spun around to confront the corpulent

figure wrapped in a terrycloth robe and crammed into a battery-powered wheelchair. Scratching noisily at an unshaven cheek with the nicotine-stained fingers of one hand, working a small joystick with the other, the man piloted himself into the closet, elbowed the door closed behind him and backed up until his back was against the wall. The naked electric bulb, dangling from the ceiling, illuminated his sallow face. Studying it, Martin experienced a twinge of recognition: in one of his incarnations he'd come across a photograph of this man in a counterintelligence scrapbook. But when? And under what circumstances?

'Mr Martin Odum and me,' the man growled in the grating voice of a chain-smoker, 'are birds of a feather. Tradecraft is our Kabala.' He scraped a kitchen match against the wall and sucked a foul smelling cigarette into life. 'Which is how come I meet you in this safe room,' he plunged on, taking in with a sweep of his arm the shelves filled with household supplies, the mops and brooms and the vacuum cleaner, the piles of old newspapers waiting to be recycled. 'Both of us know there are organizations that can eavesdrop on conversations over the land lines, it does not matter if the phones are on their hooks.'

Stella made a formal introduction. 'Mr Odum, this is my father, Oskar Alexandrovich Kastner.'

Kastner removed a pearl-handled Tula-Tokarev from the pocket of his terrycloth robe and set the handgun down on a shelf. Martin, who understood

65

the value of gestures, accepted Kastner's decision to disarm with a nod.

All the tradecraft talk had tripped a memory. Suddenly Martin recalled which counterintelligence scrapbook he'd been studying when he came across the face of Stella's father: it was the one filled with mug shots of Soviet defectors. 'Your daughter told me you were Russian,' Martin said lazily. 'She didn't say you were KGB.'

Kastner, nodding excitedly, gestured toward a plastic kitchen stool and Martin scraped it over and settled onto it. Stella leaned back against a folded stepladder, half sitting on one of its steps. 'You are a quick wit, Mr Martin Odum,' Kastner conceded, his bushy brows dancing over his heavy lidded eyes. 'My body has slowed down but my brain is still functioning correctly, which is how come I am still cashing my annuity checks. It goes without saying but I will anyhow say it: I checked you out before I sent Stella over to test the temperature of the water.'

'There aren't that many people in the neighborhood you could have checked me out with,' Martin observed, curious to identify Kastner's sources.

'Your name was suggested to me by someone in Washington, who assured me you were overqualified for any job I might propose. To be on the safe side, I made discreet inquiries – I talked with a Russian in Little Odessa whose ex-wife stole his Rottweiler when he missed some alimony payments. The person in question compared you to a long distance runner. He told me once you started something you finished it.'

Martin put two and two together. 'Oskar Kastner can't be your real name,' he said, thinking out loud. 'A KGB defector living in Brooklyn under an assumed name – there will surely be an elaborate cover story to go with the pseudonym – means that you, like the other Soviet defectors, must be in the FBI's witness protection program. According to your daughter, you came here in 1988, which means the CIA has long since wrung you dry and probably doesn't return your calls if you make any. Which suggests that your friend in Washington who gave you my name is your FBI handler.'

So that was how Crystal Quest had gotten wind of Stella's visit to the pool parlor! Someone in the FBI had heard that an ex-CIA type was playing detective in Crown Heights and passed Martin's name on to Kastner. The FBI clerks who keep tabs on people in the protection program would have circulated a routine 'contact' report when a former KGB officer announced his intention of employing a former CIA officer – even if the case in question had nothing to do with CIA operations. Somewhere in the labyrinthian corridors of Langley, a warning buzzer would have gone off; it had probably been the one wired to Quest's brain.

Did this mean that Kastner's missing son-in-law had some connection to past or present CIA

67

operations? Martin decided it was an angle worth considering.

'He is pretty rapid for a long distance runner,' Kastner was telling his daughter. 'My FBI friend said you were discharged from the CIA in 1994. He did not explain why, except to say it had nothing to do with stealing money or selling secrets or anything unpleasant like that.'

'I'm relieved you're both on the same side,' Stella ventured from her perch on the ladder.

Martin batted a palm to disperse Kastner's cigarette smoke. 'Why didn't you ask the FBI to try and find your missing son-in-law?'

'First thing I tried. They stretched some rules and searched the computer database for missing persons who had turned up dead. Unfortunately none of them fit Samat's description.'

Martin smiled. *'Unfortunately?'*

Kastner's craggy features twisted into a scowl. 'I speak American with an accent – Stella never stops correcting me – but I pick my words as if my life depended on their accuracy.'

'I can vouch for Kastner's accent,' Stella said with a laugh.

'You call your father Kastner?'

'Sure. You've already figured out that's not his real name – it's the name the FBI gave him when he came into the witness protection program. Calling my father Kastner is a running joke between us. Isn't it, Kastner?'

'It reminds us who we're not.'

Martin turned to Stella. 'Meeting your father explains a lot.'

'Such as?' she demanded.

'It explains how you played along so quickly when I phoned this morning; you understood that I thought the phone might be tapped. You are your father's daughter.'

'She was raised to be discreet when it comes to telephones,' Kastner agreed with evident pride. 'She knows enough tradecraft to pay attention to people who are window shopping for objects they do not seem likely to buy. Women and fishing rods, for example. Or men and ladies undergarments.'

'You really didn't need to go around the block twice,' Stella told Martin. 'I promise you I wasn't followed when I came to see you. I wasn't followed on the way home either.'

'That being the case, how come the folks I used to work for are trying to discourage me from getting involved with missing husbands?'

Kastner manipulated the joystick; the wheelchair jerked toward Martin. 'How do you know they know?' he asked quietly.

'A woman named Fred Astaire whispered in my ear.'

Kastner said, 'I can see from the look in your eyes that you do not consider this Fred Astaire person to be a friend.'

'It takes a lot of energy to dislike someone. Occasionally I make the effort.'

Stella was following her own thoughts. 'Maybe

69

your pool parlor was bugged,' she suggested. 'Maybe they hid a microphone in that Civil War rifle of yours.'

Martin shook his head. 'If they had bugged my loft, they would have heard me refuse to take the case and not gone out of their way to lean on me.'

Tilting his large head, Kastner thought out loud: 'The tip could have come from the FBI – someone there might have routinely informed my CIA conducting officer if it looked as if you might become involved with me. But you probably figured that out already.'

Martin was mightily relieved to hear him reach this conclusion. It underscored his credibility.

Kastner stared at Martin, his jaw screwed up. 'Stella told me you refused to take the case. Why did you modify your mind?'

Stella kept her eyes on Martin as she spoke to her father. 'He didn't modify his mind, Kastner. He modified his heart.'

'Respond to the question, if you please,' Kastner instructed his visitor.

'Let's chalk it up to an unhealthy curiosity – I'd like to know why the CIA doesn't want this particular missing husband found. That and the fact that I don't appreciate having an unpleasant woman who munches ice cubes tell me what I can or cannot do.'

'I like you,' Kastner burst out, his face breaking into a lopsided smile. 'I like him,' he informed his daughter. 'But he would not have gone very far in our *Komitet Gosudarstvennoi Bezopasnosti*. He is too much of a loner. We did not trust the loners. We only recruited people who were comfortable serving as cogs in the machine.'

'Which Directorate?' Martin asked.

The bluntness of Martin's question made Stella wince; in her experience, people talking about intelligence matters usually beat around the bush. 'In the USA, Kastner,' she told her father, who was visibly flustered, 'they call this talking turkey.'

Kastner cleared his throat. 'The Sixth Chief Directorate,' he said, adapting to the situation. 'I was the second deputy to the man who ran the Directorate.'

'Uh-huh.'

The Russian looked at his daughter. 'What does it mean, uh-huh?'

'It means he is familiar with the Sixth Chief Directorate, Kastner.'

In fact, Martin had more than a passing acquaintance with this particular Directorate. At one point in the late eighties, Lincoln Dittmann had recruited a KGB officer in Istanbul. Lincoln had made his pitch when he heard on the grapevine that the officer's younger brother had been arrested for being out of step during a military drill; the instructor had acused him of sabotaging the parade to discredit the glorious Red Army. Lincoln had arranged to smuggle the disenchanted KGB officer and his family out of Istanbul in return for a roll of microfilm filled with Sixth Chief Directorate documents. The material provided the CIA with its first inside look into the operations of this up to then secret section. It had been carved out of the KGB Directorate structure back in the sixties to keep track of economic crimes. In 1987, when what the Soviets called 'cooperatives' and the world referred to as 'free market enterprises' were legalized by Comrade Gorbachev, the Sixth Chief Directorate shifted gears to keep track of these new businesses. As the economy, crippled by inflation and corruption at the most senior levels of government, began to stall, gangster capitalism thrived; cooperatives had to buy protection – what the Russians called *krysha* or *a roof* – from the hundreds of gangs sprouting in Moscow and other cities if they wanted to stay in business. When the Sixth Chief Directorate found it couldn't crush the gangs and protect the emerging market economy, it simply stopped trying and joined in the free-for-all looting of the country. Martin remembered Stella's saying that her father had immigrated to America in 1988. If he had been getting rich on the looting, he would have stayed and skimmed off his share. Which meant he was one of those die-hard socialists who blamed Gorbachev and his 'restructuring' for wrecking seventy years of Soviet communism. In short, Kastner was probably the rarest of birds, an ardent, if disheartened, Marxist condemned to live out his days in capitalist America.

'You are thinking so hard, smoke is emerging

from your ears,' Kastner said with a laugh. 'What conclusion have you reached?'

'I like you, too,' Martin declared. 'I like your father,' he told Stella. 'Fact is, he wouldn't have lasted long in the CIA. He is far too idealistic for a shop that prides itself on the virtuosity of its pragmatists. Unlike your father, Americans aren't interested in constructing a Utopia, for the simple reason they believe they're living in one.'

Stella seemed stunned. 'I like that you like Kastner, and for the right reasons,' she said softly.

Kastner, his nerves frayed, swiveled his wheelchair to one side and then the other. 'It remains for us to put our heads together and figure out why the lady with the pseudonym Fred Astaire does not want my son-in-law, Samat, to be discovered.'

Martin permitted a rare half-smile onto his lips. 'To do that I'm going to have to *discover* Samat.'

Stella disappeared to brew up some tea and hurried back minutes later carrying a tray with a jar of jam and three steaming cups on it. She found her father and Martin, their knees almost touching, deep in conversation. Martin was smoking one of his wafer-thin Beedies. Her father had started another cigarette but held it at arm's length so the smoke wouldn't obscure Martin.

'. . . somehow managed to falsify the records so the Party would not know his mother was Jewish,' Kastner was explaining. 'His father was an Armenian doctor and a member of the Party – at one point he was accused of being an enemy of the people and sent to Siberia, where he died. The post-Stalinist program to rehabilitate people falsely accused of crimes counted in Samat's favor when he applied to the Forestry Institute; the state had killed his father so it felt it had to compensate the son.'

Martin nodded. 'I seem to recall reading about your famous Forestry Institute that taught everything except forestry.'

Kastner set aside his cigarette in a saucer and stirred a spoonful of jam into one of the cups. Blowing noisily across it, he sipped at the scalding tea. 'It was the secret institute for our space program,' he said. 'In the seventies, it was the best place in the Soviet Union to study computer science. Samat went on to do advanced studies at the State Planning Agency's Higher Economic School. When he graduated near the top of his class, he was drafted into the KGB. Because of his computer skills, he was posted to the Sixth Chief Directorate.'

'You knew him personally?'

'He was assigned to several cases I worked on. He became an expert on money laundering techniques – he knew everything there was to know about off-shore banks and bearer-share business operations. In 1991, when Yeltsin ousted Gorbachev and took power, one of the things he did was break up our Committee for State Security into its component parts, at which point a great many KGB officers found themselves suddenly unemployed and scrambling to make a living. Samat was one of them.'

'You were in America by then. How do you know all this?'

'Your Central Intelligence Agency encouraged me to keep in touch with the Sixth Directorate. They wanted me to recruit agents in place.'

'Did you succeed?'

Kastner flashed a pained smile. Martin said, 'I take back the question. So we're up to where Samat, with the KGB closing down its shop, starts looking at the help wanted ads. What kind of job did he land?'

'He ended up working for one of the rising stars in the private sector, someone who had his own model of how to make the transition from socialism to market-oriented capitalism. His solution was gangster capitalism. He was one of the gangsters the Sixth Chief Directorate kept track of when I was there. Samat, with his knowledge of money laundering techniques, quickly worked his way up to become the organization's financial wizard. He was the one who brought the shell game to Russia. You have seen the Negroes playing the shell game on street corners down on Rogers Avenue. They fold your ten-dollar bill until it is the size of a walnut and put it under a sea shell and move it around with two other shells. When they stop your ten-dollar bill has disappeared. Samat did the same thing but on a much larger scale.'

'And this is the Russian Lubavitch who wanted to marry your daughter and live in Israel?'

Kastner nodded heavily. 'At one point the CIA asked me to try and recruit Samat. They arranged for me to talk with him on the telephone when he was in Geneva. I spoke of a secret account that could be his if he came over. I named a sum of money that would be deposited in this account. He laughed and replied that the sum of money they were suggesting was the loose change in his pocket. He told me the CIA could not afford to pay him a tenth of what he was earning. When Samat returned to Russia he made sure everyone knew the CIA had attempted to recruit him. There was even a satiric article published in *Pravda* describing the clumsy approach by a defector.'

'When did Samat get in touch with you about marrying your daughter?' Martin asked.

'It was not Samat who contacted Kastner,' Stella said. 'Samat's employer, who happened to be Samat's uncle – his father's brother – is the one who got in touch with Kastner.'

Martin looked from one to the other. 'And who was Samat's employer?'

Kastner cleared his throat. 'It was Tzvetan Ugor-Zhilov, the one known as the *Oligarkh*.'

'*The* Tzvetan Ugor-Zhilov who was on the cover of *Time* magazine in the early nineties?'

'There is only one Tzvetan Ugor-Zhilov,' Kastner remarked with some bitterness.

'You knew that Samat was working for Tzvetan Ugor-Zhilov when you agreed to the marriage?'

Kastner looked at his daughter, then dropped his eyes. It was obviously a sore subject between them. Stella answered for her father. 'It was not an accident that Tzvetan Ugor-Zhilov contacted Kastner – the two of them were acquainted from the days when the Sixth Chief Directorate was keeping track of the new cooperatives.'

'In the early nineteen-eighties,' Kastner explained, 'Ugor-Zhilov was a small-time hoodlum in a small pond – he ran a used-car dealership in Yerevan, the capital of Armenia. He had a KGB record: He'd been arrested in the early seventies for bribery and black market activities and sent to a gulag in the Kolyma Mountains for eight years. Read Solzhenitsyn's *Ivan Denisovich* and you will get a glimpse of what each day of Ugor-Zhilov's eight years was like. By the time he made his way back to Armenia and scraped together enough money to open the used-car business, he was bitterly anti-Soviet; bitterly anti-Russian, also. He would have faded from our radar screen if he hadn't set his sights on bigger fish in bigger ponds. He came to Moscow and in a matter of months cornered the used-car market there. One by one he bought out his competitors. Those who would not sell wound up dead or maimed. The punishment handed out by the *Oligarkh* was what you Americans call cruel and unusual – he believed that it was good for business if his enemies had reason to dread him. When I spoke to Samat in Geneva, he passed on a story that Ugor-Zhilov had actually buried someone alive and had a road paved over him – and this while several dozen workers looked on. The story of the execution may or may not be true – either way it served its purpose. Few Russians were reckless enough to challenge the *Oligarkh.*'

'You seem to know an awful lot about Tzvetan Ugor-Zhilov,' Martin observed.

'I was the conducting officer in charge of the investigation into the *Oligarkh*'s affairs.'

Martin saw where the story was going. 'I'll take a wild guess – he paid off the Sixth Directorate.'

Kastner didn't respond for a moment. 'You have to put yourself in our shoes,' he said finally. 'We were honest cops and we went after him in a straightforward manner. But he bought the minister in the Kremlin who ran the KGB, then he bought my colleague who was the head of the Sixth Chief Directorate, and then he turned to me and put a thick packet of money on the table, this at a time when we sometimes went several months without drawing a salary because of the economic chaos. What was I to do? If I accepted I would be on his payroll. If I refused I would seriously compromise my life expectancy.'

'So you defected to America.'

Kastner plucked his cigarette from the saucer and inhaled deeply, then sniffed at the smoke in the air. 'It was the only solution,' he said.

'Knowing what you knew about uncle Ugor-Zhilov, why did you agree to let your daughter marry his nephew Samat?'

Stella came to her father's defense. 'Kastner agreed because he didn't have a choice.'

Kastner said, very quietly, 'You do not understand how things worked after communism collapsed. One morning there arrived in my mailbox downstairs here on President Street a letter typed on expensive bonded paper. It was not signed but I immediately understood where it came from. The writer said that his nephew was obliged to leave Russia, and quickly. It said that the best place for him to go would be Israel. It was a time when Jews were queuing up by the tens of thousands for visas at the Israeli embassy in Moscow; the Israeli Mossad, fearful that what was left of the KGB apparatus would try to infiltrate agents into Israel, was screening the Jewish applicants very carefully. And carefully meant slowly. Ugor-Zhilov obviously knew that my daughter Elena had joined the Lubavitch sect soon after we settled in Crown Heights. He knew that the Lubavitchers had a lot of influence when it came to getting Jews into Israel – they could arrange for the Israeli immigration authorities to speed things up if there was a Lubavitch marriage involved, especially if the newlyweds planned to live in one of the Jewish settlements on the West Bank, which the Israeli government at the time was eager to populate.'

Martin felt claustrophobic in the airless closet;

he had a visceral revulsion for closed spaces without windows. 'Something doesn't make sense here,' he said, eyeing the door, mastering an urge to throw it open. 'How could Tzvetan Ugor-Zhilov send a letter to you if you were in the FBI's witness protection—'

Martin's mouth sagged open; the answer to his question came to him before Kastner supplied it.

'It was *because* he was able to send a letter to me,' Kastner said, 'despite my being in the FBI program, that it was out of the realm of possibility to refuse him. Tzvetan Ugor-Zhilov is one of the richest men in all of Russia; one of the fifty richest men in the world, according to that article in *Time*. He has a long arm, long enough to reach someone who has been given a new identity and lives on President Street in Crown Heights.' He glanced at Stella and the two exchanged grim smiles. 'Long enough,' Kastner continued, 'to reach his two beautiful girls, also. When the *Oligarkh* asks for a favor, it is not healthy to refuse if you are confined to a wheel chair and have nowhere else to defect to.'

Martin remembered the words from the Bob Dylan song he'd heard in the street and he repeated them aloud: '*Not much is really sacred.*'

'Not true,' Kastner burst out. 'Many things are still sacred. Protecting my daughters is at the top of the list.'

'Kastner could not be expected to anticipate how Samat would mistreat Elena,' Stella put in. 'It was not his fault—'

Kastner cut her off. 'Whose fault was it if not mine?' he said despondently.

'Aren't you running a risk by hiring me to find this Samat?'

'I only want him to give my Elena the religious divorce so she can marry again. What he does with his life after that is his affair. Surely this is not an unreasonable request.' Kastner worked the joystick, backing the wheelchair into the wall with a light thud. He shrugged his heavy shoulders as if he were trying to rid himself of a weight. 'In terms of money, how do we organize this?'

'I pay my way with credit cards. When the credit card people ask me for money, I will ask you to pay my expenses. If I find Samat and your daughter gets her *get*, we'll figure out what that's worth to you. If I don't find him, you'll be out of pocket my expenses. Nothing more.'

'In your pool parlor you spoke of the problem of searching for a needle in a field of haystacks,' Stella said. 'Where on earth do you begin looking for it?'

'Everyone is somewhere,' Martin informed her. 'We'll start in Israel.'

Stella, startled, said, 'We?'

Martin nodded. 'First off, there's your sister – she'll trust me more if you're with me when I meet her. Then there's Samat. Someone on the run can easily change his appearances – the color and length of his hair, for instance. He could even pass himself off as an Arab and cover his head

81

with a kaffiyeh. I need to have someone with me who could pick him out of a crowd if she only saw his seaweed-green eyes.'

'That more or less narrows it down to me,' Stella agreed.

1997: MINH SLEEPWALKS THROUGH ONE-NIGHT STANDS

Dressed in loose-fitting silk pants and a high-necked silk blouse with a dragon embroidered on the back, Minh was clearing away the last of the dirty lunch dishes when Tsou Xing poked his head through the kitchen doors and asked her if she would run upstairs and check Martin's beehives. He would do it himself, he said, but he was expecting a delivery of Formosan beer and wanted to count the cartons before they stored them in the cellar to make sure he wasn't being short changed. Sure, Minh said. No problem. She opened the cash register and retrieved Martin's keys and headed for the street, glad to have a few minutes to herself. She wondered if Tsou suspected that she had slept with Martin. She thought she'd spotted something resembling a leer in his old eyes when Tsou raised the subject of their upstairs' neighbor earlier that week; he had been speaking in English but had referred to Martin using the Chinese word for *hermit*. Where you think *yin shi* goes when he goes? Tsou had asked. Minh had hunched her muscular shoulders into a shrug. It's not part of my job to keep track of the customers, she'd replied testily. No reason climb on high horse, Tsou had said, whisking a fly from the bar with the back of his only hand. Not a crime to think you could know, okay? And he had smiled so wickedly that the several gold teeth in his mouth flashed into view. Well, I don't know and I couldn't care less, Minh had insisted. Pivoting on a heel, she had stalked off so Tsou would get the message: She didn't appreciate his sticking his nose into her love life, or lack of same.

Now Minh rubbed her sleeve across the private-eye logo on Martin's front door to clean the rain stains off of it, then let herself in and, taking the steps two at a time, climbed to the pool parlor. Actually, she did wonder where Martin had gone off to; wondered, too, why he hadn't left a message for her as well as Tsou. She attributed it to Martin's shyness; he would have been mortified if he thought Tsou had gotten wind of their relation-ship, assuming you could call their very occasional evenings together a relationship. She meandered through the pool parlor, brushing her fingers over his Civil War guns and the folders on his desk and the unopened cartons that contained heaven knows what. Soon after he'd moved in she had asked him if he wanted help opening them. He'd kicked at one of the cartons and had said he didn't need to open them, he knew what was inside. The reply struck her as being very in character.

When Minh thought about it, which was more often than she liked to admit, the fact that she really wasn't sure where she stood with *yin shi* exasperated her. He always seemed happy enough to see her but he never went out of his way to initiate meetings. Minh had been raised in lower Manhattan's Chinatown, a cauldron simmering with refugees of one sort or another, so she knew one when she saw one; the thing that betrayed them was they seemed to be alone even in a crowd. She herself was in the country illegally, a refugee from Taiwan. Minh was not even her real name, a detail she'd never revealed to Martin for fear he might be shocked. Sometimes she had the weird feeling that Martin, too, was some kind of refugee – though from what, she had no clue. *Yin shi* lived what she thought of as a boring life, ordering up the same dishes three or four nights a week, attending to his hives on the roof, making love to her when she turned up at his door. For excitement, he broke into hotel rooms to photograph husbands committing adultery, though when he described what he did for a living he managed to make even that sound boring. The single time she had raised the subject of boredom he had astonished her by admitting that he relished it; boring himself to death, he'd insisted, was how he planned to spend the rest of his life.

At the time Minh had thought it was one of those things you say to sound clever. Only later did it dawn on her that he'd meant every word; that boring yourself to death was a way of committing suicide in slow motion.

Stepping into the back room, Minh straightened the sheets and blanket on the cot, emptied the water from the plastic basin on the floor, closed the refrigerator door, put away the dishes that Martin had finally gotten around to washing. She retrieved Martin's faded white jumpsuit and, rolling up the cuffs and the sleeves, slipped into it and zipped up the front. She put on the pith helmet with the mosquito netting hanging from it and took a look at herself in the cracked mirror over the bathroom sink. The outfit was not what you would call feng shui. Taking Martin's smoke gun from under the sink, she made her way up the stairs to the roof. The sun, high overhead, was burning off the last drops of rain that had fallen the previous night. Vapor rose from shallow puddles as she crossed the roof to the hives. Martin had bought them and the equipment, and even the first queen bees, from a catalogue when he got it into his head to raise bees. In the beginning he had pored over the instruction book that came with the hives. Then he'd dragged a chair up to the roof and had spent hours staring at the colonies, trying to figure out if there was a flight pattern to the swarm's movements, a method to its apparent madness. Minh had never seen him do anything with such intensity. When he'd begun inspecting and cleaning the frames he'd worn gloves, but he discarded them when Minh happened to mention the Chinese belief that bee stings stimulated your hormones and increased your sex drive. Not that the subsequent stings on his hands had changed anything – it was invariably Minh who made the first move toward the cot in the back of the loft, pulling Martin into the room, onto the cot, peeling off her clothing and then his. He made love to her cautiously, as if (she finally realized) he, not she, were fragile; as if he were afraid to let emotions surface that he might not be able control.

Minh was crouching in front of the first hive, preparing the smoker, ruminating on how making love with Martin had been like sleepwalking through a string of one-night stands that were physically satisfying but emotionally frustrating, when the dumdum bullet plunged into the frames. There was an instant of absolute silence, as if the 20,000 residents of the hive – those that had survived the impact – had been reduced to a state of catatonic bewilderment. Then a raging yellowish-brown football-sized swarm burst out of the hive with such ferocity it knocked Minh over backward. The pith helmet and veil flew off to one side and the bees attacked her nostrils and her eyes, planting their darts with savage vengeance. She clenched her fingers into fists and hammered wildly at the layers of bees encrusting her skin, crushing them by the hundreds until her knuckles were covered with a sticky residue. There was no longer a sun overhead, only a thick carpet of rioting insects ricocheting off one another as they fought for a turn at the intruder who had wrecked their hive.

Her face and lids swelling, Minh slumped back onto the hot tarpaper of the roof, swatting weakly at the bees the way Tsou had whisked at the fly on the bar. As the pain gave way to numbness, she heard a voice that sounded remarkably like her own telling Martin that, hey, you really shouldn't wear gloves. Sure there's a reason why. According to the Chinese, bee stings can stimulate your . . .

1997: OSKAR ALEXANDROVICH KASTNER DISCOVERS THE WEIGHT OF A CIGARETTE

The two men in Con-Ed uniforms parked their repair truck in the narrow alley between President and Carroll and made their way on foot to the only back garden on the block protected by a chainlink fence. One of the men muttered something into a walkie-talkie, listened for a response and nodded to his colleague when he heard it. The second man produced a key, opened the door in the fence and used the same key to switch off the alarm box inside. The two, walking soundlessly on crepe soled shoes, climbed the stairs to the porch. Using a second key, they let themselves into the kitchen at the rear of the house and punched the code into the alarm there. They stood motionless for several minutes, their eyes fixed on the ceiling. When they heard the muffled scrape of a wheelchair rolling along a hallway over their heads, the two men produced pistols fitted with silencers and started up the back staircase. Reaching the first floor, they could hear a radio playing in the front room. Gripping their pistols with both hands, angling the barrels up, they worked their way along the hall to the closed door and flattened themselves against the wall on either side of it. One of the men tapped the side of his nose to indicate he had gotten a whiff of foul smelling cigarette smoke; their quarry was inside the room. Baring his teeth in a tight smile, his companion grasped the knob and flung open the door and the two of them, hunched over to keep their profiles low, burst into the room.

Oskar Alexandrovich Kastner, sitting in his wheelchair next to the window, was oiling the firing mechanism on a Soviet PPSh 41, a Second World War automatic weapon in mint condition. Smoke coiled up from a cigarette burning in an ashtray. Kastner's heavy lidded eyes blinked slowly as he took in the intruders. One appeared much older than the other but the younger man, gesturing to the other to shut the door, seemed to be in charge.

'*Vy Russky?*' Kastner inquired.

'*Da. Ya Russky,*' replied the younger Con-Ed man. '*I gdye vasha doch?*'

Kastner eyed the pearl-handled Tula-Tokarev on the table, a 1930s pistol that he always kept charged, but he knew he could never reach it. '*Ya ne znayu,*' he replied. He was not about to tell them that Stella was on her way to Israel, accompanied by a CIA agent turned detective who lived over a Chinese restaurant. He wondered how the two killers had broken through the chainlink fence and gotten into the kitchen without tripping the alarms. 'You took your time getting here,' Kastner growled in English. 'Nine years.' He set the PPSh down and, working the joystick, maneuvered the wheelchair so that his back was to the intruders.

'*Kto vas poslal?*' he asked.

'*Oligarkh,*' the younger gunman said with a ruthless snicker.

Gazing out the window, Kastner caught sight of two small Lubavitch boys, dressed in black like their fathers, hurrying down the street. He knew from Elena that they expected the Messiah to appear at any moment and redeem mankind. Maybe this Messiah had turned up and the boys were actually angels on their way to welcome him. He himself would surely end up where angels fear to tread, as that song Stella played on the Victrola put it. Kastner gasped when he felt the needle prick the skin of his back next to the shoulder blade. In his day the KGB specialists in wetwork had favored a tasteless, colorless rat poison that thinned the blood and brought breathing to an abrupt halt. The *Oligarkh*'s hit men would surely be using something more sophisticated and less traceable; perhaps one of those newfangled adrenalin-like substances that caused widespread gastric bleeding and, eventually, death, or, better still, a clotting agent that blocked a coronary artery and triggered what doctors called a myocardial infarction and laymen referred to as a heart attack. On the off-chance that one of the angels might ask him to identify himself, Kastner tried to recollect what his name had been before the FBI assigned the pseudonym Oskar. It irritated him that he was unable to remember what his mother had called him as a child. If he could suck on his cigarette, it would surely calm his nerves long enough for the name to come back to him. Moving languidly, as if he were underwater, Kastner reached for the ashtray. With great concentration he managed to pinch the cigarette between his thumb and two fingers, only to discover that it was too heavy to lift.

1987: DANTE PIPPEN BECOMES AN IRA BOMBER

Assembled in a windowless storage room in a basement of Langley filled with empty watercoolers, the eight people around the conference table started, as always, with the family name and in short order narrowed the list down to one that had an Irish ring to it, but then spent the next half hour debating how it should be spelled. In the end the chairman, a station chief who reported directly to Crystal Quest, the new Deputy Director of Operations, turned to the agent known as Martin Odum, who had been following the discussion from a chair tilted back against the wall; as Martin's 'Odum' legend had been burned and he would be the person employing the new identity, it would save time if he settled on the spelling. Without a moment's hesitation, Martin opted for Pippen with three p's. 'I've been reading newspaper stories about a young black basketball player at the University of Central Arkansas named Scottie Pippen,' Martin explained. 'So I thought Pippen would have the advantage of being easy to remember.'

'Pippen it is,' announced the chairman and he turned to the selection of a Christian name to go with Pippen. The junior member of the Legend Committee, a Yale-educated aversion therapist, sarcastically suggested that they might want to go whole hog and use Scottie as the Christian name. Maggie Poole, who had read medieval French history as an Oxford undergraduate and liked to salt her conversation with French words, shook her head. 'You're all going to think I am off the wall but I came up with a name in my dreams last night that I consider *parfait*. Dante, as in Dante Alighieri?' She looked around the table expectantly.

The only other woman on the committee, a lexicographer on loan from the University of Chicago, groaned. 'Problem with Dante Pippen,' she said, 'is it wouldn't go unnoticed. People tend to remember a name like that.'

'But don't you see, that's exactly what makes it an excellent choice,' exclaimed Maggie Poole. 'Nobody thumbing down a list of names would suspect Dante Pippen of being a *pseudonyme* precisely because it stands out in a crowd.'

'She has a point,' agreed the committee's doyen, a gargoyle-like CIA veteran who had started out creating legends for OSS agents during World War Two.

'I will admit I don't *dislike* the sound of Dante,' ventured the aversion therapist.

The chairman looked at Martin. 'What do you think?' he asked.

Martin repeated the names several times. Dante. Dante Pippen. 'Uh-huh. I think it suits me. I can live with Dante Pippen.'

Once the committee had decided on a name, the rest of the cover story fell neatly into place.

'Our Dante Pippen is obviously Irish, born, say, in County Cork.'

'Where in County Cork?'

'I once vacationed in a seaport called Castletownbere,' said the aversion therapist.

'Castletownbere, Cork, has a good ring to it. We'll send him there for a week of R and R. He can get a local map and the phone book, and fix in his head the names of the streets and hotels and stores.'

'Castletownbere is a fishing port. He would have worked on a salmon trawler as a *teenager*.'

'Then when the economy turned bad, he would have gone off to try his luck in the New World, where he will have picked up a lot about the history of the Irish in America – the potato famine of 1840 that brought the first Irish immigrants to our shores, the Civil War draft riots, that sort of thing.'

'If he comes from Castletownbere, he must be Catholic. For the price of a generous donation, we can probably get the local Castletownbere church to slip his name into its baptism records.'

'One fine day, like many, if not most, Irish men, he would have become fed up with the church.'

'A lapsed Catholic, then,' said the chairman,

jotting the biographical detail down on his yellow pad.

'A *very* lapsed Catholic,' Martin piped up from his place along the wall.

'Just because he's lapsed doesn't mean his family will have lapsed.'

'Why don't we give him a brother and a sister who are in the church but can't be traced because they are no longer living under the name Pippen. Brother such and such. Sister such and such.'

'The brother could be a Jesuit priest in the Congo, converting the natives to Jesus at the bitter end of some crocodile infested river.'

'And the sister – let's put her in a convent hospital in the back country of the Ivory Coast.'

'She will have taken a vow of *silence,* which means she couldn't be interviewed even if someone got to her.'

'Is Dante Pippen a smoker or nonsmoker?

The chairman turned to Martin, who said, 'I've been trying to cut down. If Dante Pippen is supposed to be a nonsmoker, it'll give me an incentive to go cold turkey.'

'Nonsmoker it is, then.'

'Be careful you don't put on weight. The CIA takes a dim view of overweight agents.'

'We ought to hire one or two – being *obese* would be a perfect cover.'

'Even if our Dante Pippen's a lapsed Catholic, he would still have gone to Catholic school as a child. He would have been taught to believe that the seven sacraments – Baptism, Confirmation, Eucharist, Confession, Anointing of the Sick, Matrimony and Holy Orders – could see you through a lifetime of troubles.'

The chairman scribbled another note on his pad. 'That's a good point,' he said. 'We'll get someone to teach him rosaries in Latin – he could slip them into the conversation to lend credibility to the new identity.'

'Which brings us to his occupation. What exactly does our Dante Pippen do in life?'

The chairman picked up Martin Odum's 201 Central Registry folder and extracted the bio file. 'Oh, dear, our Martin Odum can be said to be a renaissance man only if one defines renaissance narrowly. He was born in Lebanon County, Pennsylvania, and spent the first eight years of his life in a Pennsylvania backwater called Jonestown, where his father owned a small factory manufacturing underwear for the U.S. Army during World War Two. After the war the underwear business went bankrupt and the elder Odum moved the family to Crown Heights, Brooklyn, to start an electrical appliance business. Crown Heights is where Martin was brought up.'

'Being brought up in Brooklyn is not the most auspicious beginning for a renaissance man, even defined narrowly,' quipped Maggie Poole. She twisted in her seat toward Martin. 'I'm not ruffling your feathers, am I?'

Martin only smiled.

'Yes, well,' the chairman continued, 'our man majored in commerce and minored in Russian at a Long Island state college but never seems to have earned a degree. During vacations he climbed the lower alps in the more modest American mountain ranges. At loose ends, he joined the army to see the world and wound up, God knows why, toiling for military intelligence, where he focused on anticommunist dissidents in the satellite states of Eastern Europe. Do I have that right, Martin? Ah, here's something positively intriguing. When he was younger he worked in the private sector with explosives—'

Maggie Poole turned to Martin. 'What *précisément* did you do with explosives?'

Martin rocked his chair off the wall onto its four legs. 'It was a summer job, really. I worked for a construction company demolishing old buildings that were going to be replaced, then blasting through bedrock to make way for the subbasement garages. I was the guy who shouted through a bullhorn for everyone to clear the area.'

'But do you know anything about dynamite?'

'I picked up a bit here and a bit there hanging around the dynamiters. I bought some books and studied the subject. By the end of the summer I had my own blasting license.'

'Did you fabricate dynamite or just light the fuses?'

'Either, or. When I first came to work for the Company,' Martin said, 'I spent a month or two making letter bombs, then I got promoted to rigging portable phones so that we could detonate them from a distance. I also worked with pentaerythritol tetranitrate, which you know as PETN, an explosive of choice for terrorists. You can mix it with latex to give it plasticity and mold it to fit into anything – a telephone, a radio, a teddy bear, a cigar. You get a big bang out of relatively small amounts of PETN, and in the absence of a detonator, it's extremely stable. PETN isn't readily available on the open market but anyone with a blasting license, which Martin Odum has, can obtain the ingredients for roughly twenty dollars the pound. The explosive, incidentally, can pass through any airport X-ray machine in operation today.'

'Well, that opens up some intriguing possibilities,' the chairman informed the others.

'He could have done a stint as an explosive specialist at a shale quarry in Colorado, then been fired for something or other—'

'Stealing PETN and selling it on the open market—'

'Sleeping with the boss's wife—'

'*Homosexualité*, even.'

Martin piped up from the wall. 'If you don't mind, I draw the line at having homosexuality in my legend.'

'We'll figure out why he was fired later. What we have here is an Irish Catholic—'

'Lapsed. Don't forget he's lapsed.'

'—a lapsed Irish Catholic who worked with explosive in the private sector.'

'Only to be fired for an as yet undetermined offense.'

'At which point he became a free-lance explosive *expert*.'

'We may have a problem here,' said the chairman, tapping a forefinger on one page of Martin Odum's 201 folder. 'Our Martin Odum is circumcised. Dante Pippen, lapsed or not, is an Irish Catholic. How do we explain the fact that he's circumcised.'

The committee kicked around several possibilities. It was Maggie Poole who invented a suitable fiction. 'In the unlikely event the question should come up, he could say he was talked into it by his first American girlfriend, who thought she would have less chance of catching a venereal disease from him if he were circumcised. Pippen could say the operation was performed in a New York clinic. It shouldn't be too difficult to plant a medical record at a clinic to backstop the story.'

'Moving on, could he have been a member, at one point, of the IRA?'

'An IRA dynamiter! Now that's creative. It's not something the Russians or East Europeans could verify because the IRA is more secretive than the KGB.'

'We could give him an arrest record in England. Arrested, questioned about an IRA bombing or two, released for lack of evidence.'

'We could even plant small items in the press about the arrests.'

'We are mining a rich vein,' declared the chairman, his eyes bulging with enthusiasm. 'What do you think, Martin?'

'I like it,' Martin said from his seat. 'Crystal Quest will like it, too. Dante Pippen is exactly the kind of legend that will open doors.'

1989: DANTE PIPPEN SEES THE MILKY WAY IN A NEW LIGHT

When the battered Ford reached the fertile rift known as the Bekaa Valley, the Palestinians knotted a blindfold over Dante's eyes. Twenty minutes later the two-car motorcade passed through a gate in a perimeter fence and pulled to a stop at the edge of an abandoned quarry. The Palestinians tugged Dante from the back seat and guided him through the narrow dirt streets to the mosque on the edge of a Lebanese village. In the antechamber, his shoes and the blindfold were removed and he was led to a threadbare prayer carpet near the altar and motioned to sit. Ten minutes later the imam slipped in through a latticed side door. A corpulent man who moved, as heavy men often do, with surprising suppleness, he settled onto the carpet facing Dante. Arranging the folds of his flowing white robe like a Noh actor preoccupied with his image, he produced a string of jade worry beads and began working them through the stubby fingers of his left hand. In his early forties, with a crew cut and a neatly trimmed beard, the imam rocked back and forth in prayer for several moments. Finally he raised his eyes and, speaking English with a crisp British accent, announced, 'I am Dr Izzat al-Karim.'

'I suspect you know who I am,' Dante replied.

The corners of the imam's mouth curled into a pudgy grin. 'Indeed I do. You are the IRA dynamiter we have heard so much about. I may say that your reputation precedes you—'

Dante dismissed the compliment with a wave of his hand. 'So does your shadow when the sun is behind you.'

The imam's jowls quivered in silent laughter. He held out a pack of Iranian Bahman cigarettes, offering one to his visitor.

'I have stopped smoking,' Dante informed his host.

'Ah, if only I could follow your example,' the imam said with a sigh. He tapped one of the thin cigarettes against the metal tray on a low table to tamp down the tobacco and slipped it between his lips. Using a Zippo lighter with a picture of Muhammad Ali on it, he lit the cigarette and slowly exhaled. 'I envy you your strength of character. What was the secret that enabled you to give up cigarettes?'

'I convinced myself to become a different person, so to speak,' Dante explained. 'One day I was smoking two tins of Ganaesh Beedies a day. When I woke up the next morning I was someone else. And this someone else was a nonsmoker.'

The imam let this sink in. 'I wear the black turban of the sayyid, which marks me as a descendant of the Prophet Muhammad and his cousin Ali. I have two wives and I am about to take a third. Many people – my wives, my children, my fighters – count on me. It would be awkward for everyone if I were to become someone else.'

'If I had as many wives as you,' Dante remarked, 'I'd probably start smoking again.'

'Whether you smoke or abstain,' the imam replied, his voice as soft as the cooing of a pigeon, 'you will only live as long as God gives you to live. In any case, longevity is not what inspires a religious man like myself.'

'What does inspire a religious man like yourself?' Dante heard himself ask, though he knew the answer; Benny Sapir, the Mossad spy master who had briefed Dante Pippen in a Washington safe house before the mission, had even imitated the imam's voice delivering stock answers to religious questions.

'The thought of the angel Gabriel whispering the verses of the Holy Koran into the ear of the Prophet inspires me,' the imam was saying. 'Muhammad's description, in what you call *The Book of the Ladder* and we call *The Miraj*, of his ascent to the nine circles of heaven and his descent into hell, guided by the angel Gabriel, keeps me up nights. The Creator, the Maker, the All-Merciful, the All-Compassionate, the All-Sublime, the All-Mighty inspires me. The one true God inspires me. Allah inspires me. The thought of spreading His word to the infidel, and killing those who do not accept it, inspires me.' He held his cigarette parallel to his lips and studied it. 'And what is it that inspires you, Mr Pippen?'

Dante grinned. 'The money your organization deposited in my account in the Cayman Islands inspires me, Dr al-Karim. The prospect of monthly installments, paid in exchange for services rendered, inspires me. No need to shake your head in disapproval. It comes as no surprise to me that you find our several inspirations discordant, yours, of course, being the nobler of the two, and mine, by far the more decadent. Since I don't believe in your God, or any God, for that matter – I am what you would call a very lapsed Catholic – I think that your particular inspiration is as ephemeral as the contrails I saw on my drive down from Beirut. One moment they were there, sharp and precise, each with a silver Israeli jet fighter streaking through the crystal Lebanese sky at the cusp, the next they were thickening and drifting and eventually dissipating in the high winds.'

The imam considered this. 'I can see you are not a timid man, Mr Pippen. You speak your mind. A Muslim who permitted himself to say what you have said would be putting his limbs, perhaps even his life, in jeopardy. But we must make allowances for a *very* lapsed Catholic, especially one who has come all this way to teach our fedayeen how to devise bombs to blow up the Israeli occupiers of

Lebanon and Palestine.' He leaned toward Dante. 'Our representative in Paris who recruited you said you were born in an Irish town with the curious name of Castletownbere.'

Dante nodded. 'It's a smudge on the map on the southern coast of the Beara Peninsula in County Cork. Fishing port. I worked on one of the salmon trawlers before I went off to seek my fortune where the streets are paved with gold.'

'And were they paved with gold, Mr Pippen?'

Dante laughed under his breath. 'At least they were paved, which is more than you can say for some parts of the Beara Peninsula. Or the Bekaa Valley, for that matter.'

'Am I correct in thinking there was an expensive restaurant in Castletownbere called The Warehouse?'

'There was a pricy restaurant for the occasional tourist, but it wasn't named The Warehouse. It was called The Bank because it was in the old bank, one flight up on Main Street. Still had the bank vault in the back when I was there. I seem to remember a Mary McCullagh ran it in the sixties. I went to school with one of her daughters, a pretty little thing we called Deidre of the Sorrows because she made so many of us sorry when we discovered we couldn't sweet talk her into bed.'

'You were arrested by Scotland Yard following the explosion of a bomb on a bus near Bush House, the BBC building in London.'

'Is that a question or a statement of fact?'

'A statement of fact that I'd like you to corroborate, Mr Pippen.'

'I was killing time in London when the bus blew,' Dante said, his eyes blinking innocently. 'The coppers barged into a licensed tabernacle and more or less picked up anyone who spoke the King's English with an Irish accent. They were obliged to release me after forty-eight hours for want of evidence. Bloody bastards never even apologized.'

'Did you blow up the bus, Mr Pippen?'

'I did not. But the two who did learned which side was up from yours truly.'

The imam smiled thinly. Glancing at a wall clock with a silhouette of Ayatollah Khomeini on its face, he pushed himself to his feet and started to leave. At the door, he turned back. 'I seldom have the chance to speak with an Occidental nonbeliever, Mr Pippen, especially one who is not in awe of me. Talking with you is going to be an enlightening experience. One must know the enemy before one can defeat him. I invite you to visit me in my study after your afternoon classes, every day of the week except Friday. I will offer you mint tea and honey cakes, you can reciprocate by offering me insights into the secular mentality.'

'The pleasure will—' Dante started to say but the imam had already vanished through the latticed door, which squeaked back and forth on its hinges, evidence of his passage.

Dante was taken to his living quarters, a room in the back of one of the low brick houses with flat roofs at the edge of the village beyond the perimeter of the Hezbollah camp. At sunup an elderly woman with a veil over the lower part of her face appeared with what passed for breakfast: a steaming pot of green tea to wash down the chalk-dry biscuits covered with an oily paste made from crushed olives. Dante's bodyguard, who trailed after him everywhere, including to the outhouse, led him down the dirt path to the lip of the quarry. Several young boys in dusty striped robes were already tossing stones at a troop of goats to steer them away from the perimeter fence and up a nearby slope. A yellow Hezbollah flag decorated with a hand holding aloft a rifle flapped from the pole atop the brick building where the explosives and the fuses were stored. High overhead the contrails of Israeli jets on their dawn patrols crisscrossed the sky. Dante's students, nineteen fedayeen, all in their late teens or early twenties and wearing identical baggy khaki trousers and blouses and thick web belts under their robes, waited at the bottom of the quarry. An older man with an orange and white kaffiyah draped over his shoulders squatted on the rocky ground, setting out cartons filled with pentaerythritol tetranitrate, commonly known as PETN, along with latex, coils of electric wire and plungers powered by automobile batteries. 'I, Abdullah, will translate for you,' the man informed Dante when he reached the floor of the quarry. 'Please to speak slow in consideration of my English, which is curdled like last week's goat milk.'

Dante inspected the cartons, then kicked at the coils of wire and the plungers. 'We will need modern detonators that can be tripped by radio-controlled devices from distant locations,' he informed Abdullah.

'How far will be the distance to these locations?' Abdullah inquired.

Dante pointed to the goats disappearing over the top of the slope. 'We will mix the PETN and the latex in a manner that I will demonstrate,' he said, 'and conceal the charges here in the quarry. Then we will climb to the top of that hill and detonate the explosives from there.' Dante pointed to the hill and imitated the boom of the explosion. Abdullah translated for the fedayeen and they all turned to stare at the hill. They talked excitedly among themselves, then looked at their instructor, nodding respectfully at his expertise.

During the first several sessions, Dante concentrated on the PETN and the latex, showing the Hezbollah fighters how to mix the two and then mold the clay-like explosive to fit any receptacle. He filled a portable radio with explosives one day, then turned it on to demonstrate that it still functioned, which was important if you wanted to get the radio past military checkpoints or airport security. Another time he packed the plastique into one of those new-fangled satellite telephones and explained, with Abdullah translating, the advantages: If it was done correctly, you could actually telephone the target and identify his voice before setting off the charge and decapitating him.

In the beginning, the young men were afraid to touch the explosive charges until they saw Dante juggling a clump of it from one hand to the other to demonstrate how stable it was. Abdullah, meanwhile, took Dante's hand-written list to Dr al-Karim and then set off for Beirut in the Ford with a purse-full of the imam's precious American dollars to purchase the battery-operated transmitters and receivers that would go into the construction of remote detonators.

The first afternoon that Dante turned up in Dr al-Karim's study, he found the imam seated well back from a table, leaning over his abundant stomach and typing away with two fingers on an IBM electric typewriter. From behind the building came the low hum of the gasoline-powered generator. '*Assalamu aleikum* – Peace be upon you. I would offer you a cigarette if you smoked cigarettes,' the imam said, swiveling to face his visitor, waving him toward a wooden kitchen chair. 'Can I assume you do not mind if I light up?'

'Be my guest.'

The imam appeared to be puzzled. 'How is it possible for me to be your guest in *my* house?'

'It was a meaningless figure of speech,' Dante conceded.

'I have observed that Americans often come up

with meaningless cliches when they do not know what to say.'

'I won't make the same mistake twice.'

The woman who brought Dante breakfast appeared from the next room and set out plates filled with small honey-coated cakes and two glasses filled with mint leaves and boiling water. Nibbling on one of cakes as he waited for the mint tea to cool, Dante took in the Spartan furnishings of the imam's study: framed photographs of the training camp's fedayeen graduating classes (slightly askew, as if someone had dusted them and left them askew to show they'd been cleaned), a poster depicting the golden-domed Mosque of Omar in Jerusalem tacked to one wall, the Kalashnikov in a corner with a clip in it and a spare clip taped to the stock, the glass bowl on a low table with a single goldfish circling round and round as if it were looking for the exit, the copies of *Newsweek* stacked on the floor near the door. Dr al-Karim scraped his chair around the table and, settling his bulk onto it facing his guest, warmed both his hands on the glass of mint tea.

Speaking softly, selecting his words carefully, the imam said: 'There was a time when people held me in high esteem.'

'Judging from what I've seen, they still do.'

'How long, Mr Pippen, will this last? How long do you think one can go on preaching that the destruction of your principal enemy is inevitable without it transpiring; without losing the credibility

111

that is indispensable to continue as the spiritual leader of a community? This is the predicament I find myself in. I must continue to hold out hope that our sacrifices will be rewarded not only with martyrdom but with certain victory over the Israeli occupiers of Lebanon and Palestine, and the Jews who are conspiring to take over the world. But in time even the simplest of the fedayeen, sent to combat the enemy, observes through binoculars that the Israelis still occupy their sandbagged fortresses in the south of Lebanon, that the wakes of their patrol boats still crisscross the waters off our coast, that the contrails of their jet aircraft still stain the sky over our heads.'

'Do *you* believe victory is inevitable?' Dante asked.

'I am convinced that the Jews will one day be seen, like the Christian Crusaders before them, as a footnote in the long flow of Arab history. This is written. Will it happen in my lifetime? Will it happen in the lifetime of my children?' Dr al-Karim sipped at the tea, then, licking his lips to savor the taste of the mint, he leaned forward. 'I can buy time, Mr Pippen, if your talents provide me with some incremental measure of success. Our Hezbollah fighters, armed with conventional weapons, are unable to inflict casualties on the better armed Israeli soldiers occupying the zone in southern Lebanon. We attack them with mortars or artillery, fired from the heart of some Lebanese village so that the Israelis are unable to riposte.

Very occasionally, we manage to wound or kill one or two of them. For every one we kill, we lose twenty or thirty fedayeen when our enemies, with remarkably accurate intelligence, descend from their fortresses to raid our bases here in the Bekaa Valley, or closer to the front lines. They always seem to know where we are, and in what strength.' The imam shook his head. 'We are like waves lapping against boulders on a shore – I cannot recruit and train and send into combat fighters by telling them that the boulders will, in a century or two, be washed smooth and reduced in size.'

'I suppose that's why you retained my services,' Dante said.

'Is it true that you can mold your explosives to fit almost any receptacle?'

'Absolutely.'

'And detonate them from a great distance by radio command, as opposed to electrical wires stretched along the ground?'

Dante nodded emphatically. 'Hard wire on the gruond is more reliable, but radio-detonated explosions are more creative.'

'Precisely how do radio-detonated explosions work?'

'You need a transmitter – a cordless phone, a wireless intercom, a radio paging system – and a receiver, both tuned to the same frequency. The transmitter sends not just a signal but also an audio tone – known as electronic pulses – which are modulated by the transmitter and demodulated by the receiver. The receiver picks up the transmission, demodulates the audio tone, closes the electric circuit, which sends current to the blasting cap which, in turn, detonates the explosive charge.'

'With your expertise, could we disguise the explosives in what appears to be ordinary roadside rocks and explode them from, say, a hilltop a kilometer away as an Israeli patrol passes?'

'Child's play,' Dante declared.

The imam slapped his knee in elation. 'God willing, we will bloody the Israelis, Mr Pippen. God willing, the waves lapping against the shore will demolish the boulders in my lifetime. And when we have finished with the near enemy, we will turn our attention to the distant enemy.'

'The Israelis are obviously the near enemy,' Dante said. 'But who is the distant enemy?'

Dr al-Karim looked Dante in the eye. 'Why, you, Mr Pippen, are the distant enemy. You and your American civilization which considers smoking dangerous for the health while everything else – extramarital sex, pornography, carnal secularism, materialism – is permissible. The Israelis are an outpost of your corrupt civilization. The Jews are your surrogates, dispatched to steal our land and colonize our countries and demoralize our souls and humiliate our religion. When we have defeated them we will turn our attention to the ultimate enemy.'

'I can see how you might attack what you call

114

the near enemy,' Dante replied. 'But how will you war against a distant enemy who can obliterate you the way he would a mosquito caught in flagrante delicto on the back of his wrist?'

The imam sat back in his chair, a knowing smile flickering on his pudgy face. 'We will use the vast amounts of money we earn from selling you petrol for your gas-guzzling cars to hire the talents of people like you, Mr Pippen. American heads are already poisoned by Hollywood films and glossy magazines such as *Playboy* or *Hustler*. We will poison their bodies. We will hijack their planes and crash them into their buildings. We will construct, with your help, the poor man's bomb – valises filled with germs or chemicals – and explode it in their cities.'

Dante reached for the glass of mint tea and touched his lips to it. 'I'd best be immigrating back to Ireland, then,' he said lightly.

'I can see that you do not take what I say seriously. No matter.' The imam pushed back his sleeve, glanced at his wristwatch and rose to his feet. 'You will sleep fitfully tonight as you turn over in your mind what I have told you. Questions will occur to you. I invite you to come back tomorrow and pose them, Mr Pippen. God willing, we will pick up the conversation where we left it off.'

Dante stood up. 'Yes. I will return. Thank you.'

In the days that followed, Dante used what Abdullah had brought from Beirut to show his students how to assemble remote control detonators and set off explosive charges in the quarry from the top of the nearby hill. When Dr al-Karim's people supplied the first molded rock made out of plaster of paris, Dante filled it with PETN and rigged a remote detonator. The students set the molded rock down at the side of the road and tethered a lame goat ten meters from it. Then everyone trooped up the hill. The imam himself, hearing of the experiment, showed up at the lip of the quarry to watch. Dante waved to him and Dr al-Karim, surrounded by four bodyguards, raised a palm in salute. One of the young fedayeen wired the small transmitter to a car battery. Everyone turned to stare at the goat at the bottom of the quarry. 'Okay, Abdullah,' Dante said. 'Let her rip.' Reaching for the small radio, Abdullah rotated the switch until there was an audible click and then depressed it. Far below, in the quarry, a dry cough of a blast stirred up a swell of dust. When it cleared, the goat had vanished. Where it had stood, the ground was saturated with blood and entrails.

'God is great,' Abdullah murmured.

'PETN is greater,' Dante remarked.

When Dante entered the imam's study that afternoon, Dr al-Karim came bounding around the desk to congratulate him. 'You have earned your wages, Mr Pippen,' he said, throwing a pulpy arm over Dante's shoulder. 'My fighters are eager to use your remote control device against the Jews.'

The two settled onto kitchen chairs. Dr al-Karim produced his jade beads and began threading them through his fingers with great dexterity as Dante explained that he needed another ten days, no more, no less, to make the imam's fedayeen ready for combat.

'We have waited this long,' the imam said. 'Another ten days will not inconvenience us.'

The conversation drifted on to the two-year-old Syrian occupation of parts of Lebanon; the month before Dante's arrival, Damascus had installed surface-to-air missiles in the Bekaa, a move that Hezbollah did not appreciate since it was bound to attract Israeli attention to the valley. Dr al-Karim wanted to know whether President Bush would put pressure on the Israelis to pull back from the buffer zone in southern Lebanon. Dante said he was far from being an expert in such matters, but he doubted it. He, in turn, wondered whether the Iranians would put pressure on the Syrians to end their virtual occupation of Lebanon now that the civil war had quieted down. The imam replied that the death the week before of Iran's Ayatollah Khomeini had created a vacuum in the Islamic world and predicted that it would be a long time before the Shiites found someone with enough charisma to take his place. Dante asked jokingly if the imam aspired to the job. Dr al-Karim took the question seriously. He stopped manipulating his worry beads and placed a finger along the side of a nostril. 'I aspire to serve God and lead my people to victory over the Jews,' he said. 'Nothing more.'

'Tell me something, Dr al-Karim—' Dante hesitated.

The imam's head bobbed. 'Only ask, Mr Pippen.'

'I notice that you often speak of the Jews, not the Israelis. I'm curious to know if Hezbollah isn't confusing the two. What I'm getting at is this: Are you anti-Israeli or anti-Jewish?'

'In as much as Isra'il is an enemy state,' the imam replied without hesitation, 'we are, of course, anti-Israeli.' He started manipulating his worry beads again. 'But make no mistake, we are also anti-Jewish. Our common history goes back to the Prophet Muhammad. The Jews never recognized the legitimacy of Islam as the true religion, and the Koran as the word of God.'

'Your critics say this attitude more or less puts you in the same boat as Adolf Hitler.'

The imam shook his head vigorously. 'Not at all, Mr Pippen. Our critics miss an essential point. Hitler was anti-Semite. There are enormous differences between being anti-Jewish and anti-Semite.'

'I'm afraid you're losing me . . .'

'Anti-Semites, Mr Pippen, believe that once a Jew, always a Jew. For Hitler, even a Jew who converted to Christianity remained a Jew. It follows that for the Nazis in particular and for anti-Semites in general, there was no solution except what they called the Final Solution, namely the extermination of the Jews. Being anti-Jewish,

118

on the other hand, implies that there is a solution short of extermination; a way for Jews to save themselves from extermination.'

'And what might that be?'

'The Jew can convert to Islam, at which point Islam will have no quarrel with him.'

'I see.'

'What do you see, Mr Pippen?'

'I see that I shouldn't have started this conversation in the first place. I am a hired gun. You pay me for services rendered, not my opinions on your opinions.'

'Quite right, quite right. Though if my answers don't interest you, I will admit to you that your questions interest me.'

Abdullah materialized outside the window, tapping a fingernail against a pane. When the imam went over to the window, Abdullah pointed to the car winding its way up the dirt road toward the Hezbollah camp.

'I had almost forgotten,' Dr al-Karim said, turning back to Dante. 'I am expecting a visitor. The Syrian commander in the Bekaa stops by every once in awhile to see what we are up to. He will stay through prayers and the evening meal tomorrow. It might be wise if you keep out of sight, as I have not informed him of your presence and the Syrians do not take kindly to foreigners in the valley.'

'How about if I disappear in the direction of Beirut,' Dante asked. 'It's been almost three weeks since I arrived. As tomorrow is Friday and my students will be in the mosque praying, I was going to ask you for a day off.'

'And what will you do on this day off of yours?'

'In my entire life I have never gone this long without a swill of beer. I will take my warm body off to a bar and drink a barrel of it.'

'Why not? Beirut has quieted down. And you have earned a day of rest. I will send Abdullah and one of my bodyguards to keep you out of harm's way.'

'An Irishman does not go to a licensed tabernacle to keep out of harm's way, Dr al-Karim.'

'Nevertheless, out of harm's way is where we must keep you until you have completed your work here. What you do after that is your affair.'

The following afternoon the battered Ford that had transported Dante to the Bekaa three weeks earlier threaded its way through a tangle of secondary roads in the direction of Beirut. The bodyguard, sporting baggy khakis and cradling a Kalashnikov with notches cut into the stock for each of his kills, sat up front bantering in Arabic with the driver, a coal-black Saudi with matted dreadlocks. Dante, wearing a coarse brown Bedouin burnoose, a black-and-white checkered kaffiyah and dark sunglasses, shared the backseat with Abdullah, who climbed out of the car at each Syrian checkpoint to wave, with an imperious snap of the wrist, the letter

120

bearing Dr al-Karim's seal and signature in the face of the soldiers who were (so Abdullah swore) completely illiterate. Dante, lost in thought, stared through his reflection in the window, barely noticing the dusty villages with the swarms of barefoot boys playing soccer in the unpaved streets, the crowded open-air souks with giant dish antennas for sale on one side and donkeys and camels tethered to a nearby fence, the tiled butcher shops with young boys fanning the flies off the carcasses hanging from hooks. At the outskirts of Beirut, the Ford passed through the first of the militia barricades but (as Abdullah explained in halting English) the pimply gunmen there, though literate, were more interested in the twenty-dollar bills folded into Dr al-Karim's letter than the letter itself or the passengers in the car.

With the presence of the Syrian army, the warring factions that had slaughtered each other in the streets of Beirut since the mid 1970s had more or less gone to ground; Muslim and Christian emissaries were rumored to be meeting at Taif, in Saudi Arabia, to formalize the cease-fire accord but armed militias still patrolled the city, which sprawled like a mutilated virago at the edge of the Mediterranean, its shell-ridden buildings mute testimony to the brutal fifteen-year civil war. As the sun dipped into the sea and darkness enveloped Beirut, the whetted crack of distant gunfire reverberated through the city; Abdullah, visibly edgy, muttered something about old scores being settled before the formal cease-fire came into effect. Careful not to stray from the Muslim-controlled areas of Beirut, he guided the driver to the port area and deposited Dante on a corner opposite the burnt-out shell of a neighborhood mosque. A narrow street angled off downhill toward the docks. 'We will wait for you here,' Abdullah told Dante. 'Please to be returned by the hour of ten so we can be returned to the camp by the midnight.'

On the narrow street, broken neon lights sizzled over a handful of bars that catered to the seamen from the ships docked at the quays or tied to giant buoys in the harbor. Waving cheerfully at his keepers, Dante skipped down the sidewalk and, ducking to get under a broken neon tube dangling from its electric cord, shouldered past the thick rug that served as a door into the first bar, set up in a mercantile building that had been gutted by a direct hit from a mortar. The charred rafters that held up the jury-rigged sloping roof had been whitewashed, but they still stank from the fire. Dante found a place at the makeshift bar between two Turkish sailors holding each other up and a Portuguese purser wearing a rumpled blue uniform.

'So now, what will your pleasure be?' the barman called, a distinct Irish lilt to his gruff voice.

Dante punched a hole in the cigarette smoke that obscured his view and spoke through it. 'Beer and lots of it,' he called back, 'the warmer the better.'

The bartender, a thick man with a shock of tousled rusty hair spilling over his eyes and a priest's white shirt buttoned up to his neck, plucked a large bottle of Bulgarian beer from a carton at his feet. He flicked off the metal cap with a church key, stopped the throat of the bottle with the ball of his thumb and shook the beer to put some life into it, then set it on the counter in front of Dante. 'And will your lordship be wanting a mug to drink from?' he inquired with a laugh.

'Do you charge for it?' Dante asked.

'Oh, for Christ's sake, why would we want to do that? You're paying such an outrageous price for the goddamned beer, we supply the mug at no extra cost to yourself.' He slid a freshly washed mug down the bar to Dante. 'Now what ship did you say you were off?'

'I didn't say,' Dante shot back. 'It's the H.M.S. *Pinafore*.'

The smile froze on the bartender's face. 'H.M.S. *Pinafore*, did you say?'

Dante filled the mug, swiped away the foam with the back of a forefinger and, tilting back his head, drank off the beer in a long gulping swallow. 'Ah, that surely transforms the way a man sees the world,' he announced, starting to fill the mug again. 'H.M.S. *Pinafore*. That's what I said.'

Accepting this with a brisk nod, the bartender made his way to the far end of the bar and, blocking one ear with the tip of a finger, spoke into a telephone. Dante was halfway through his second bottle of Bulgarian beer when the woman appeared at the top of the broken wooden steps that led to what was left of the offices on the upper floor of the mercantile building. A sailor buttoning his fly trailed behind her. The woman, wisps of long dark hair falling across a face disfigured by smallpox scars, was wearing a tight skirt slit high on one thigh and a gauzy blouse through which her breasts were as visible as they would be if she'd been caught walking naked through a morning haze. All conversation ceased as she came across the room, her high heels drumming on the wooden floorboards. She stopped to take her bearings, spotted Dante and installed herself at the bar next to him.

'Will you buy me a whiskey?' she demanded in a throaty murmur.

'I'd be a horse's ass not to,' Dante replied cheerfully, and he held up a finger to get the bartender's eye and pointed to the woman. 'Whiskey for my future friend.'

'Chivas Regal,' the woman instructed the bartender. 'A double.'

Dante authorized the double with a nod when the bartender looked at him for confirmation, then turned to scrutinize the woman the way he'd been taught to look at people he might one day have to pick out of a counterintelligence scrapbook. As usual he had difficulty figuring out her age. She was Arab, that much was evident despite the thick eyeliner and the splash of bright red on her lips, and probably in her forties, but exactly where he didn't know. It occurred to him that she must be Christian, since Muslims would kill their women before they'd let them work as prostitutes.

'So what would be your name, darling?' Dante asked.

She absently combed the fingers of one hand through her hair, brushing it away from her face; two large silver hoop earrings caught the light and shimmered. 'I am Djamillah,' she announced. 'What is your name?'

Dante took a long swig of beer. 'You can call me Irish.'

'From the look of you, you have been at sea for a while.'

'What makes you think that?'

'You're dying of thirst, I can see that from the way you gulped down that disgusting Bulgarian beer. What else are you dying of, Irish?'

Dante glanced at the bartender, rinsing glasses in a sink just out of earshot. 'Well, now, Djamillah, to tell you the God awful truth, I haven't been laid in a month of Sundays. Is that a predicament you could remedy?'

The Portuguese purser, sitting with his back to Dante, could be heard snickering under his breath. Djamillah was unfazed. 'You are a direct man,' she said. 'The answer to your question, Irish, is: I could.'

'How much would it set me back?'

'Fifty dollars U.S. or the equivalent in a European currency. I don't deal in local money.'

'Bottoms up,' Dante said. He clicked glasses with her and downed what was left in the mug, grabbed the half-empty bottle of beer by the throat (in case he needed a weapon) and followed her across the room to the stairs. At the top of the stairs she pushed open a wooden door and led Dante into what must have once been the head office of the mercantile company. There was a large desk covered in glass with photographs of children flattened under it near the boarded-over oval windows, and an enormous leather couch under a torn painting depicting Napoleon's defeat at Acre. A dozen sealed cartons without markings were stacked against one wall. Locking the door behind them, Djamillah settled onto the couch and, reaching through a torn seam into the cushion, produced a folder filled with eight-by-ten aerial photographs. Dante, settling down alongside her, used his handkerchief to grip the photographs and examined them one by one. 'These must have been taken from high altitude,' he remarked. 'The resolution is excellent. They'll do nicely.'

The woman offered Dante a felt-tipped pen and he began to draw arrows to various buildings in the camp and label them. 'The recruits, nineteen fedayeen in all, live in these two low buildings inside the perimeter fence,' he said. 'Explosives and fuses are stored in this small brick building with the Hezbollah flag on the roof. Dr al-Karim lives and works in the house behind the mosque. It is easily the largest in the village so your people won't have a problem identifying it. I don't know where he sleeps but his office looks out at the mosque so it must be—' he drew another arrow and labelled it 'K's office' – 'here. I bunk in with a family in this house in the village.'

'What kind of security do they have at night?'

'I've strolled around the camp after dark several times – they have a roadblock, manned by two recruits and one of the instructors, stationed here where the road curves uphill to the village and the camp. There's bunker with a heavy machine gun on top of the hill over the quarry which is manned during the day. I've never been able to get up there at night because the gate in the perimeter fence is locked and I didn't want to raise suspicions by asking for the key.'

'We must assume it is manned at night. They'd be fools not to. The machine gun must be a priority target. What kind of communications do they have?'

'Don't know really. Never saw the radio shack, or a radio for that matter. Spotted what looked like high frequency antennas on the top of the minaret of the mosque, so whatever they have must be somewhere around there.'

'We don't want to bomb a mosque, so we'll have to take that out by hand. Does Dr al-Karim have a satellite phone?'

'Never saw one but that doesn't mean he doesn't have one.'

'When will this round of training be finished.'

'I've told Dr al-Karim I needed ten more days.'

'What happens then?'

'The graduating class goes off to the front to kill Israeli soldiers occupying the buffer zone in Lebanon. And a freshman class turns up to start a new cycle of training.'

'How many instructors and staff are in the camp?'

'Including transportation people, including the experts on small arms and martial arts, including Dr al-Karim's personal bodyguards, four that I've seen, I'd say roughly eighteen to twenty.'

Djamillah went over the photographs again, double checking the distances between buildings, the location of the gate in the perimeter fence, identifying the footpaths that crisscrossed the village and the Hezbollah camp. She produced a military map of the Bekaa to see what other forces Hezbollah might have in the general vicinity of the camp. 'When the raid begins, you must somehow get to this spot' – she pointed to a well between the village and the Hezbollah camp. She handed Dante a white silk bandanna and he stuffed it into the pocket of his trousers. 'Wear this around your neck so you can be easily identified.'

'How will I know when to expect the raid?'

'Exactly six hours before, two Israeli M-16s will fly by at an altitude high enough to leave contrails.

They'll come from north to south. When they are directly above the camp they will make ninety degree turns to the west.'

Djamillah slipped the photographs and the map back into the folder and wedged it into the seam of the cushion.

'Looks as if we've more or less covered the essentials,' Dante remarked.

'Not quite.' She stood up and began matter of factly stripping off her clothing; it was the first time in his life Dante had seen a woman undress when the act didn't seem sensual. 'You are supposed to be up here having sex with me. I think it would be prudent for you to be able to describe my clothing and my body.' She removed the blouse and the skirt and her underpants. 'I have a small scar on the inside of my thigh, here. My pubic hair is trimmed for a bikini. I have a faded tattoo of a night moth under my right breast. And on my left arm you will see the scars of a smallpox vaccination that didn't prevent me from getting smallpox, which accounts for the pockmarks on my face. When we came up here I locked the door and you put fifty dollars – two twenties and a ten – on the desk and weighed them down with the shell casing that's on the floor over there. We both took off our clothing. You asked me to suck you – that was the expression you used – but I said I don't do that. You stripped and sat down on the couch and I gave you a hand job and when you were erect I slipped on a condom and came on top of you. Please make note of the fact that I make love with my shoes on.' She began to dress again. 'Now it's your turn to strip, Irish, so that I can describe your body if I need to. Why do you hesitate? You are a professional. This is a matter of tradecraft.'

Dante shrugged and stood up and lowered his trousers. 'As you can see, I am circumcised. My first American girlfriend talked me into having it done – she seemed to think there was less chance of her catching some venereal disease from me if I were circumcised.'

'Circumcised and well endowed, as they say. Do you have any scars?'

'Physical or mental?'

She didn't think he was humorous. 'I do not psychoanalyze my clients, I only fuck them.'

'No scars,' he said dryly.

She inspected his body from foot to head, and his clothing, then gestured for him to turn around. 'You can put your clothes back on,' she finally said. She walked him to the door. 'You are in a dangerous business, Irish.'

'I am addicted to fear,' he murmured. 'I require a daily fix.'

'I do not believe you. If you did not believe in something you would not be here.' She offered her hand. 'I admire your courage.'

He gripped her hand and held it for a moment. 'And I am dazzled by yours. An Arab who risks—'

She tugged her hand free. 'I am not an Arab,' she said fiercely. 'I am a Lebanese Alawite.'

'And what the hell is an Alawite?'

'We're a sliver of a people lost in a sea of Arab Muslims who consider us heretics and detest us. We had a state once – it was under the French Mandate when the Ottoman Empire broke up after the First World War. The Alawite state was called Latakia; my grandfather was a minister in the government. In 1937, against our will, Latakia became part of Syria. My grandfather was assassinated for opposing this. These days most of the Lebanese Alawites side with the Christians against the Muslims in the civil war. Our goal is to crush the Muslims – and this includes Hezbollah – in the hope of returning Lebanon to Christian rule. Our dream is to reestablish an Alawite state, a new Latakia on the Levantine shore washed by the Mediterranean.'

'I wish you good luck,' Dante said with elaborate formality. 'What is it that Alawites believe that Muslims don't?'

'Now is not the moment for such discussions—'

'You are a professional. This is a matter of tradecraft. I might be asked what we talked about after we had sex.'

Djamillah almost smiled. 'It is our belief that the Milky Way is made up of the deified souls of Alawites who rose to heaven.'

'For the rest of my life I shall think of you when I look at the Milky Way,' he announced.

She unlocked the door and stepped aside. 'In another incarnation,' she remarked solemnly, 'it would have been agreeable to make love with you.'

'Maybe when all this is over—'

This time Djamillah did smile. 'All this,' she said bitterly, 'will never be over.'

Two days after his return from Beirut, Dante was squatting in the dirt at the bottom of the quarry, demonstrating to his nineteen apprentice bombers how to fill the body cavity of a dead dog with PETN, when there was a commotion at the gate of the perimeter fence above them. Several of Dr al-Karim's personal guards were tugging aside the razor wire. Horns blaring, two cars and a pick-up truck roared into the camp and pulled up in a swirl of dust. As the dust settled, gunmen wearing the distinctive checkered Hezbollah kaffiyah could be seen dragging someone wearing loose fitting striped pajamas and a hood over the head from the second car. Women from the village emerged from their homes and began filling the air with ululations of triumph. Lifting the hem of his burnoose, Abdullah trotted up the path until he was within earshot of the gunmen who had stayed behind to guard the vehicles and called out to them. One shouted an answer to his question and fired a clip from his Kalashnikov into the air. Abdullah turned back toward the quarry and, cupping his hands around his mouth, yelled, 'God is great. They have captured an Israeli spy.'

The apprentice bombers started talking excitedly

among themselves. Dante, suddenly edgy, barked at them to pay attention to the demonstration. The students reacted to the tone of his voice even before Abdullah, scampering back down to the group, translated the words. Dante, wearing a surgical glove on his right hand, finished pulling the intestines through the slit he'd made in the dog's stomach and began stuffing the packets of PETN wrapped in burlap, and then the radio-controlled detonator, into the cavity. Using a thick needle and a length of butcher's cord, he sewed up the slit with large stitches. Standing, peeling off the surgical glove, he addressed Abdullah. 'Tell them to position the dead dog so that its stomach is facing away from the enemy when he approaches.' One of the students raised his hand. Abdullah translated the question. 'He says you, is a dead dog more suitable than the papicr-mâché rocks we learned to plant at the side of the road?'

'Tell him the Greeks couldn't have used the Trojan horse trick twice,' Dante said. 'Tell him the same goes for the Israelis. They'll catch on very quickly to the fake rocks stuffed with explosives. So you need to invent other ruses. A dead dog lying in the middle of a road is so common that the Israeli jeeps will keep going. At which point—'

Dr al-Karim appeared above them on the rim of the quarry. He raised a bullhorn and called, 'Mr Pippen, I would like a word with you, if you please.'

Dante saluted lazily and started to climb the path. Halfway to the top he looked up and noticed that several of the Hezbollah gunmen had joined the imam. All of them had pulled their checkered kaffiyahs over their faces so that only their eyes were visible. Out of breath, Dante reached the top and approached Dr al-Karim. Two of the gunmen slammed bullets into the chambers of their Kalashnikovs. The metallic sound caused Dante to stop in his tracks. He forced a light laugh through his lips. 'Your warriors seem jittery today,' he remarked. 'What's going on?'

Without answering, Dr al-Karim turned and stalked off toward his house. Two of the gunmen prodded Dante with the barrels of their rifles. He bristled. 'You want me to follow him, all you have to do is ask. Politely.'

He trailed after the imam to the large house next to the mosque. When he reached the back of the house he found the door to Dr al-Karim's office ajar. One of the gunmen behind him gestured with his Kalashnikov. Shrugging, Dante kicked open the door with his toe and went in.

Time seemed to have stopped inside the room. Dr al-Karim, his corpulent body frozen in the seat behind the desk, his eyes hardly blinking, stared at the Israeli spy, bound with strips of white masking tape to a straight-backed kitchen chair set in the middle of the floor. Muffled groans came from the prisoner's mouth under the black hood. Dante noticed the thinness of the prisoner's wrists and ankles and jumped to the conclusion that Hezbollah had arrested a teenage boy. The imam motioned for Dante to sit in the other straight-backed chair. Four of the gunmen took up positions along the wall behind him.

'Where did we leave off our last conversation?' Dr al-Karim inquired stiffly.

'We were talking about the Greeks and Aristotle. You were condemning them for teaching that reason gives access to truth, as opposed to faith.'

'Precisely. We know what we know because of our faith in Allah and His Prophet, who guide us to the right way, the only way. It may be seen as a transgression when a lapsed Catholic like you does not accept this; normally a believer such as myself should attempt to convert you or, failing at that, expel you.' He glanced at the spy. 'When one of our own turns his – or her – back on faith, it is a mortal sin, punishable by execution.'

The imam muttered an order in Arabic. One of the gunmen came up behind the Israeli spy and tugged off the hood. Dante caught his breath. Patches of Djamillah's long dark hair were pasted to her scalp with dried blood. One of her eyes was swollen shut, her lips were badly cut, several front teeth were missing. A large hoop earring dangled from one lobe; the skin on the other lobe hung loose, the result of having had the earring wrenched off without first undoing it.

'You do not deny that you know her?' Dr al-Karim said.

Dante had trouble speaking. 'I know her in the carnal sense of the word,' he finally replied, his voice barely audible. 'Her name is Djamillah. She is the prostitute who worked the licensed tabernacle I visited in Beirut. She carted me off upstairs to what the Irish call the intensive care unit.'

'Djamillah is a pseudonym. She claims she cannot remember her real name but she is obviously lying; she is protecting members of her family against retribution. She was passing herself off as a prostitute in order to spy for the Jews. Aerial photographs of several training camps, ours included, were discovered hidden in the room she used. Some of the photographs had notations, in English, describing the camp layout. We suspect you may have provided her with these notations when you visited the bar in Beirut.'

A rasp of a whisper came from Djamillah's cracked lips; she spoke slowly, struggling to pronounce certain consonants with her mouth open. 'I told the ones . . . ones who questioned me . . . the Irishman was a client.'

'Who, then, made the notations on the photographs?' demanded the imam.

'The notations . . . were on the photographs when they . . . they were delivered to me.'

Dr al-Karim nodded once. The gunman behind Djamillah slipped two fingers through the hoop of the remaining earring and pulled down hard on it. It severed the skin on the lobe and came free in a spurt of blood. Djamillah opened her mouth to scream, but passed out before the sound could emerge from her throat.

A pitcher of water was flung in her face. Her eyes twitched open and the muted scream lodged at the back of her throat like a fish bone exploded with savage force. Dante winced and turned away. Dr al-Karim came around the desk and planted himself in front of Dante. 'Who are you?' he demanded in a low growl.

'Pippen, Dante. Free-lance, free-minded, free-spirited explosive expert of Irish origin, at your beck and call as long as you keep depositing checks in my off-shore account.'

The imam circled the prisoner, looking at her but talking to Dante. 'I would like to believe you are who you say, for your sake; for mine, as well.'

'Come on, now – she must have seen dozens, perhaps hundreds of men in the room over the bar. Any one of them could have been her contact.'

'Were you intimate with her?'

'Yes.'

'Does she have any distinguishing marks on her body?'

Dante described the small scar on the inside of her thigh, the trimmed pubic hair, the vaccination scar on her left arm, or was it her right – he wasn't sure. Ah, yes, there was also the faded tattoo of a night moth under her right breast. Dr al-Karim turned to the prisoner and, gripping the loose fitting shirt at the buttons, ripped it away from her body. He gazed at the faded tattoo under her breast, then flung the shirt closed, tucking the loose fabric under the strips of white masking tape.

137

'How much did you pay her?' the imam asked.

Dante thought a moment. 'Fifty dollars.'

'What denomination bills?'

'Two twenties and a ten.'

'You handed her two twenties and a ten?'

Dante shook his head. 'I put the bills on the desk. I weighed them down with a shell casing.'

'What was she wearing when you had sex with her?'

'Her shoes.'

'What were you wearing?'

'A condom.'

Dr al-Karim watched Dane closely. 'She, too, said you were wearing a condom – *on your circumcised penis*. I assume you can explain how an Irish Catholic from Castletownbere came to be circumcised?'

Dante rolled his eyes in frustration. 'Of course I can explain it. In a moment of intense stupidity, I let myself be talked into it by my first American girlfriend, who more or less made it a condition of sleeping with me. She'd somehow convinced herself she stood less chance of my passing on a venereal disease if I had my foreskin lopped off.'

'What was the girl's name?'

'For Christ's sake, you don't really expect me to come up with the name of every girl I slept with.'

'Where was the operation performed?'

'Ah, that I remember. On the fourth floor of an ether-reeking clinic.' Dante supplied the clinic's name and address.

The imam returned to the chair behind the desk. 'Consider yourself under house arrest,' he informed Dante. 'Clearly you are an expert in explosives. But I fear you may be working for someone other than Hezbollah. We will reexamine your curriculum vitae with a fine-toothed comb. We will send someone to Castletownbere on the Beara Peninsula, we will start with Mary McCullagh and the restaurant called The Bank and follow the trail from there. We will check to see if the New York clinic has a record of your circumcision. If you have lied about a single detail . . .' He didn't bother to finish the sentence.

As Dante rose to his feet a deep groan escaped from the prisoner. Everyone in the room turned to look at her. Her mouth agape, Djamillah hyperventilated and angled her head and, gasping for breath, fixed her one open eye on Dante. With some effort she managed to spit out, 'You are . . . one lousy lover, Irish.' And then she smiled a crooked smile and gagged on the mordant laughter seeping from the back of her throat.

Back in his low room, with armed guards posted at the door, Dante sprawled on his cot and stared at the white washed ceiling, wondering if the stains of the crushed flies might convey bulletins from the front. And he re-created her voice in his skull; he could make out the words, forced with great effort through her bruised lips. *You are one lousy lover, Irish.*

At sunset Abdullah turned up at the door of

his room. His manner had changed; it was written in his eyes that he no longer thought of Dante as a comrade in arms. 'You are instructed to come with me,' he announced, and without waiting he turned and quit the room. Two gunmen with their kaffiyahs masking their faces and only their eyes visible fell in behind Dante as he followed Abdullah through the village to the Hezbollah camp's perimeter fence. The gate in the fence had been dragged back and Abdullah signaled for Dante to follow him through it to the rim of the quarry. The nineteen apprentice bombers, along with the permanent staff and the Hezbollah gunmen who had brought the prisoner from Beirut were lined up along the rim. Across the quarry, her back to the setting sun, Djamillah was being bound to a stake by two of the gunmen. One of them hung a small khaki army satchel around her neck, then reached inside it to manipulate the wires and complete the electrical circuit. Djamillah's knees buckled under her and she collapsed into the ropes holding her to the stake. As the gunmen left her side, the satchel dangling from its straps against her chest, Dr al-Karim materialized alongside Dante. He was holding a small remote transmitter, which he offered to the Irishman. 'Would you like the honor?'

Dante looked down at the transmitter. 'She is not my enemy,' he said.

High above the Bekaa rift two Israeli jets, flying

soundlessly, their contrails catching the last smudges of sunlight, appeared from the north. When they were directly over the Hezbollah camp they banked ninety degrees to the west. As they headed toward the sea the sound of their engines engulfed the camp.

The imam gazed across the quarry at the woman tied to the stake. Then, in an abrupt gesture, he raised the transmitter and rotated the switch until there was a hollow click and depressed it. For an instant that stretched into an eternity nothing happened. Dr al-Karim, his brows knitted, was raising the transmitter to activate it again when, across the quarry, a dull blast stirred up a fume of mustard-colored smoke. When it dissipated, the woman had vanished and only the stump of the stake remained. Around the rim of the quarry the fedayeen began to wander off into the darkness that settled quickly over the Bekaa at this time of year. The imam produced the string of jade worry beads and began working them through his pudgy fingers. The gesture struck Dante as therapeutic. He noticed that Dr al-Karim's fingers and lips were trembling. Could it be that this was the first time he'd killed someone with his own hand?

'When one of our own turns her back on faith,' the imam murmured – he appeared to be talking to himself – 'it is a mortal sin, punishable by execution.'

By midnight the cold gusts that swept down from the Golan Heights most nights of the year had picked up, drowning out the sound of the heli-copters coming in high and fast and plummeting toward the ground like shot birds to land at strategic points around the Hezbollah camp. The roadblock at the spot where the Beirut highway curved up hill to the village and the camp was overrun without a shot being fired. The fedayeen noticed that the men coming toward them were wearing kafiyyahs and made the fatal mistake of taking them for Arabs. 'Assalamu aleikum,' one of the men in kafiyyahs called out; a sentry at the roadblock called back, '*Wa aleikum salam.*' It was the last word he uttered. In the bunker on top of the hill above the quarry, the fedayeen started firing their heavy machine gun into the darkness when they caught sight of figures sprinting up the slope; the attackers, equipped with night vision goggles, didn't return fire until they were close enough to lob stun grenades over the bunker's sandbags. Other teams from the helicopters, their faces blackened with charcoal, raced through the village to attack the two low buildings that served as the camp's dormitory. Most of the apprentice bombers, as well as the staffers and the visiting fedayeen, were gunned down as they tried to flee through the doors and the windows. Explosive charges planted against the small brick building blew away the Hezbollah flag on the roof and set off a string of smaller explosions as the wooden boxes filled with ammunition caught fire.

Dante, crouching inside the door of his room,

heard the two guards outside hollering into a walkie-talkie for instructions. When there was no response they both raced off in the direction of the imam's house behind the mosque, only to be killed by one of the Israeli teams blocking the narrow streets. The first casualties for the raiders came when several of them burst through the back door into Dr al-Karim's office: One of the imam's personal guards walked toward them with his hands raised over his head and then blew himself up, killing two of the attackers and wounding two more. The other raiders, streaming through doors and windows, stormed through the house, killing the bodyguards and servants and one of the imam's wives and two of his teenage sons as they dashed from room to room. They found Dr al-Karim hiding in an armoir on the top floor as his second wife and two other children cowered in a nearby bathroom fitted with gold-plated faucets on the sink and the bathtub. The imam was handcuffed and blindfolded and hauled through the streets toward one of the waiting helicopters.

When the sound of gunfire subsided, Dante knotted Djamillah's white silk bandanna around his neck and darted from the house in the direction of the water well between the village and the Hezbollah camp. Turning the corner of a narrow street, he was suddenly caught in a cross fire between some fedayeen who had taken cover on the ground floor of the school and the attackers crouching behind a low wall across the street. Dante dove behind a pickup truck as the fedayeen started firing rifle grenades. One of them exploded next to the pickup and Dante felt the tingling prick of hot shrapnel in his lower back. The sound of gunfire seemed to grow more distant as he lay on the road, staring up at the dull white stain stretching across the night sky while he waited for the pain that always trailed after the tearing of skin. Slightly delirious, he was trying to focus on the Milky Way in order to identify the star that represented the deified soul of the Alawite prostitute, Djamillah, when it finally arrived: a searing stitch of pain shot up his spinal column and he blacked out.

Dante woke to the blinding whiteness of a hospital room. Sunlight streamed through two windows and he felt its warmth on his shoulders above the bandages. He turned his head away from the sunlight and discovered Crystal Quest sitting on the next bed, munching crushed ice as she worked on a crossword puzzle. Benny Sapir, the Mossad spymaster who had briefed him in Washington, watched from the foot of the bed.

'Where the hell am I, Fred?' Dante asked weakly.
'He's come back to life,' Benny observed.
'About time,' Quest growled; she didn't want Dante to take her presence there as a manifestation of softness. 'I have other things to do in life besides holding his hand. Hey, Dante, being Irish, you ought

to know this one: Joyce's "Silence, exile, and . . ." Seven letters, starts with a "c."'

'Cunning. That was Stephen Dedalus's strategy for survival in *Portrait of an Artist*.'

'Cunning. Ha! It fits perfectly.' Fred peered over the top of the newspaper, her bloodshot eyes focusing on the wounded agent. 'You're in Haifa, Dante, in an Israeli hospital. The doctors had to pry some metal out of your lower back. The bad news is you'll wind up with a disagreeable cavity and a gimpy left leg, the result of a compressed nerve. The good news is there will be no major infirmities, and you'll be able to tuck a pistol behind your back without it producing a bulge in your clothing.'

'Did you capture the imam?'

'We collared the guy who was *masquerading* as an imam. A direct descendant of the Prophet my ass! I suppose it won't hurt if you fill him in,' she told Benny.

'Izzat Al-Karim was a pseudonym. Your imam's real name was Aown Kikodze; he was the only son of an Afghan father and his third wife, a teenage Kazakh girl who won a local beauty contest in Alma-Ata. Kikodze studied dentistry in Alma-Ata and was working as a dentist's assistant there in the early 1980s when he made hegira to Mecca, where he was discovered by Iranian talent scouts and recruited into Hezbollah. We first noticed him when he opened a mosque above a warehouse in southern Lebanon and began preaching some malarkey about the near enemy and the far enemy – nobody could make heads or tails out of what he was saying, but it came across like the Islamic version of what you Americans call fire and brimstone and he made a name for himself. Next thing you know he was sporting the black turban of a sayyid and running a Hezbollah training base. Even as we speak, my colleagues are trying to talk him into helping them with their inquiries into Hezbollah activities in the Bekaa.'

'I suspect they'll succeed,' Fred said. 'The Israelis are at war, Dante, so they don't have weak-kneed civil libertarians breathing down their necks the way we do. If he's still compos mentis when they finish with him, we get to get sloppy seconds.'

Dante turned on Benny. 'Why didn't you tell me all this when you briefed me in Washington?'

'If you'd been caught, you'd have talked. We didn't want the putative imam to know we knew he was putative.'

'Yeah, well, we lost Djamillah,' Dante said bitterly.

Crystal Quest slid off the bed and approached Dante. 'The Levant is full of girls named Djamillah. Which one are you talking about?'

'The Djamillah in Beirut, for God's sake, the Alawite who was posing as a prostitute. They executed her six hours before the helicopters arrived. I'll lay odds you don't want to hear how.'

Fred snorted. 'Oh, *that* Djamillah! Jesus, Dante, for someone in your line of work you can be awfully naive. 'Djamillah' was a legend. Her real name was Zineb. She wasn't *posing* as a prostitute; she was working as a prostitute in Dubai when she was recruited. And she wasn't an Alawite, she was an Iraqi Sunni. Thanks to some fancy footwork on our part, she believed she would be working for Saddam Hussein's *Mukhabarat*. There was an elegant logic to this false flag pitch, if I do say so myself: Saddam detests the Shiites and their Iranian mentors, and by extension, he loathes Hezbollah, which is a Shiite client of the Iranian mullahs.'

Dante could hear Djamillah's voice in his ear. *You are one lousy lover, Irish.* 'Whoever she was, she tried to save me when she could have used what she knew to save herself.' He noticed the square of white silk hanging from a hook on the back of the door. 'Do me a favor, bring me the bandanna, Fred.'

Crystal Quest retrieved the square of silk and folded it into Dante's hand. 'It's a hell of a memento,' Benny said from the end of the bed. 'You owe your life to that bandanna. When you didn't turn up at the well, our raiding party decided to write you off. One of the teams taking a last look around the camp reported seeing a man lying next to a pickup wearing a white bandanna. It saved your life.'

'My Dante Pippen cover must be blown.'

'That's the least of our problems,' Fred said with a titter. 'One thing we have an endless supply of in Langley is legends. We'll work up a brand new one for you when you're back on your feet.'

Benny said, 'Thanks to you, Dante, the operation was a great success.'

'It was a crying shame,' Dante said with sudden vehemence, and he meant it literally.

1997: MARTIN ODUM DISCOVERS THAT *SHAMUS* IS A YIDDISH WORD

L ulled by the drone of the jet engines, Martin – his right leg jutting into the aisle, his left knee jammed into the back of the seat in front of him – had dozed off halfway through the flight and had missed the sight of the coastal shoal of Israel unrolling like a fulgent carpet under the wing of the plane. The wheels grinding out of their bays woke him with a start. He glanced at Stella, who was sound asleep in the seat next him.

He touched her shoulder. 'We're almost there.'

She nodded gloomily; the closer she got to Israel, the less sure she was about tracking down her sister's runaway husband. What if she caught up with him? What then?

As a matter of simple tradecraft, they had come to Israel using different routes: She had taken a flight to London and gone by train to Paris and then flown on to Athens to catch the 2 A.M. flight to Tel Aviv: He had flown New York–Rome and spent several hours getting lost in crowds around the Colosseum before boarding a train to Venice

149

and an overnight car ferry to Patras, where he caught a bus to Athens airport and then the plane to Israel. Martin, queuing behind Stella, had winked at the woman behind the counter and asked for a seat next to the good looking girl who had just checked in.

'Do you know her?' the woman had asked.

'No, but I'd like to,' he'd replied.

The woman had laughed. 'You guys never give up, do you?'

Landing at Ben-Gurion Airport in a light drizzle, the plane taxied to the holding area and the captain, speaking in English over the intercom, ordered the passengers to remain seated for security reasons. Two lean young men, their shirttails hanging loose to hide the handguns tucked into their belts, strolled down the aisle, checking identity photos in passports against faces. One of the young men, wearing opaque sunglasses, reached Martin's row.

'Passports,' he snapped.

Stella produced hers from the side pocket of the hand bag under the seat. Martin pulled his from the breast pocket inside his vest and handed both of them to the security agent. He riffled through the pages with his thumb. Returning to the page with Martin's photograph, he looked over the top of the passport at Martin. 'Are you traveling together?'

They both said 'No' at the same time.

The young man pocketed the two passports.

'Come with me,' he ordered. He stepped aside so that Martin could retrieve his valise from the overhead rack. Then he shepherded Stella and Martin down the aisle ahead of him. The other passengers gaped at the man and woman being hustled from the plane, trying to figure out whether they were celebrities or terrorists.

An olive-green Suzuki with a thick plastic partition between the front and rear seats was waiting on the damp tarmac at the bottom of the portable stairs and Martin and Stella were motioned into the backseat. Martin could hear the locks in the back doors click shut as he settled down for what turned out to be a short ride. Stella started to say something but he cut her off with a twitch of his finger, indicating that the automobile could be bugged. Seeing her nervousness, he offered her a smile of encouragement.

The first shadows of first light were starting to graze the tarmac and fields to the east of the airport as the car made its way to a distant hangar on the far side of the main runway and parked next to a metal staircase that led to a green door high in the hangar. The locks on the back doors of the Suzuki clicked open and the driver pointed with his chin toward the staircase.

'I suppose they mean for us to go up there,' Stella ventured.

'Uh-huh,' Martin agreed.

Favoring his game leg, he led the way up the long flight of steps. At the top he tugged open the heavy gunmetal door and, holding it for Stella, followed her into an immense loft with a remarkably low ceiling. Sitting at desks scattered around the loft were twenty or so people working at computer terminals; despite the 'Positively No Admittance' sign on the outside of the door, none of them looked up when the two visitors appeared. Female soldiers in khaki shirts and khaki miniskirts steered carts through the room, picking up and distributing computer disks. A man with a gray crew cut appeared from behind a heavy curtain that served to partition off a corner of the loft. He was dressed in a suit and tie (rare for an Israeli) and wore a government-issue smile on his very tanned face.

'Look what the cat dragged in. If it isn't Dante Pippin in the flesh.'

'Didn't know that Shabak mandarins got up before the sun,' Martin ventured.

The smile vanished from the Israeli's face. 'Shabak mandarins never sleep, Dante. That's something you used to know.' He glanced at Stella, who was peeling away the rubber bands on the braid dangling down her spine so that her hair, damp from the light rain, would dry without curling. 'Step out of character,' the Shabak mandarin said to Martin, all the while taking in his companion's thin figure in tailored trousers and running shoes, 'be a gentleman and introduce us.'

'His name used to be Asher,' Martin informed Stella. 'Chances are he's recycled himself by now.

When our paths crossed he was a gumshoe for the Shabak, which is short for Sherut ha-Bitachon ha-K'lali. Is my pronunciation in the ball park, Asher? The Shabak is the nearest thing Israel has to an FBI.' Martin grinned at the Israeli. 'I haven't the foggiest idea who she is.'

The Israeli spread his hands wide. 'I didn't come down with the first snowfall, Dante.'

'If your people pulled her off the plane, it means you know who she is. Come clean, Asher. Who tipped you off?'

'A little canary.' Asher pulled back a corner of the curtain and ushered his visitors into the area that served as an office. He gestured toward a couch and settled onto a high stool facing them.

'Could that little canary of yours be a female of the species called Fred?' Martin inquired.

'How can a female be named Fred?' Asher asked innocently.

'Fred is Crystal Quest, the honcho of the CIA's dirty tricks department.'

'Is that her real name, Dante? We know the CIA's Deputy Director of Operations by another name.'

Stella looked at Martin. 'Why does he keep calling you Dante?'

Asher answered for him. 'When your traveling companion did us a favor eight years ago, Dante Pippen was his working legend. He disappeared from our radar screen before we had a chance to learn his real identity. So you can imagine our surprise when we discovered that Dante Pippen would be on the Olympus flight from Athens, traveling under the name of Martin Odum. Is Martin Odum the real you or just another one of your legends?'

'Not sure, actually.'

'People like you shouldn't breeze into Israel without touching base with the Shabak. The way I see it, it's a matter of professional courtesy. This is especially true when you're traveling with a former member of the KGB.'

Martin melted back into the couch, his eyes fixed on Stella. 'The Israelis don't get details like that wrong,' he said quietly. 'Next thing you know, you'll be telling me Stella isn't your real name.'

'I can explain,' she said.

One of the girl soldiers wearing a particularly short khaki miniskirt backed past the curtain carrying a tray with a pot of hot tea and two mugs. She set it down on the table. Asher mumbled something to her in Hebrew. Glancing at the two visitors over her shoulder as she left, the girl snickered appreciatively.

'If you can explain, explain,' Asher told Stella. He filled the two mugs and slid them across the table toward his visitors.

Martin asked Stella, 'What did you do for the KGB?'

'I wasn't a spy or anything like that,' she told him. 'Kastner was the deputy head of the Sixth Chief Directorate before he defected. The directorate's main line of work was dealing with economic

154

crimes, but it wound up housing sections that didn't have a home in any of the other directorates. The forgers, for instance, worked out of the Sixth Chief Directorate, and their budget was buried in the directorate's overall budget. The same was true for the section that drew up blueprints for weapons the Soviet Union had no intention of developing, and then let the plans fall into the hands of the Americans in the hope of making them waste their resources keeping up with us. I was teaching English to grade-school children when Kastner proposed a job in a section that was so secret only a handful of Party people outside the Kremlin knew of its existence. Its in-house name was subsection Marx – but it was named after Groucho, not Karl. At any given time there were two dozen men sitting around a long table clipping stories from newspapers and magazines and inventing anti-Soviet jokes—'

Disbelief was written all over Asher's face. 'I've heard some tall tales in my life but this beats them all.'

'Let her finish.'

Stella plunged on. 'The KGB thought of the Soviet Union as a pressure cooker, and subsection Marx as the little metal cap that you occasionally lifted to let off steam. I and some other young women would come in on Fridays and memorize the jokes that the subsection had produced during the week. We were on an expense account – over the weekend we'd go out to restaurants or Komsomol clubs or workers' canteens or poetry readings and repeat the jokes. They did a study once – they found that a good joke that started out in Moscow could reach the Kamchatka Peninsula on the Pacific coast in thirty-six hours.'

'Give us some examples of the jokes you spread,' Asher ordered, still dubious.

Stella closed her eyes and thought for a moment. 'When there were demonstrations in Poland against the stationing of Soviet troops there, I helped spread the story of the Polish boy who runs into a Warsaw police station and cries, "Quick, quick, you have to help me. Two Swiss soldiers stole my Russian watch." The policeman looks puzzled and says, "You mean two Russian soldiers stole your Swiss watch.' And the boy says, 'That's right but *you* said it, not me!"'

When neither Martin nor Asher laughed, Stella said, 'It was considered very humorous in its day.'

'Do you remember another?' Martin asked.

'One of our most successful jokes was the one about two Communist Party apparatchiks meeting on a Moscow street. One of them says to the other: "Have you heard the latest? Our Soviet scientists have managed to miniaturize nuclear warheads. Now we no longer need those expensive inter-continental ballistic missiles to wipe out America. We can put the nuclear warhead into a valise and put the valise in a locker at Grand Central Station in New York City and if the Americans give us any trouble, pfffffft, New York will be reduced to radioactive ashes." The second Russian replies:

"Nyevozmozhno. It's not possible. Where in Russia will we find a valise?"'

Stella's joke reminded Martin of a fragment from a previous legend: Lincoln Dittmann's conversation, at a terrorist training camp in Triple Border, with the Saudi who was interested in obtaining a Soviet nuclear valise-bomb. Somehow Stella's little joke didn't seem like a laughing matter. Asher obviously agreed because he was gnawing on the inside of a cheek in irritation.

Stella, exasperated, repeated, '*Where in Russia will you find a valise*! That's the punch line of a joke, for God's sake. Is it against Israeli law to laugh?'

'Asher, like his colleagues in the CIA and the KGB, lost laughter a long time ago,' Martin said. 'They're time servers, hanging on by their finger tips to a world they no longer understand. If they can hang on long enough, they'll get a government pension and end their days growing stringless green beans in some suburban backyard. The reigning emotion here is nostalgia. On the rare occasions they loosen up, they start all their sentences with: Remember the time we . . . Isn't that right, Asher?'

Asher appeared to wince at Martin's little speech. 'Okay,' he said, turning to Stella, 'for the moment let's agree that you worked for subsection Marx spreading lousy anti-Soviet jokes so the country could let off steam. Whatever brings you and Dante to the Holy Land, it's not to tell jokes.'

'Tourism,' Martin said flatly.

'Absolutely. Tourism,' Stella agreed emphatically. She reached for the mug of tea and dipped a pinky in it and carefully moistened her lips with the ball of her finger. 'We came to see the Temple Mount, we came to see Masada on the Dead Sea, we came to see the Church of the Holy Sepulcher . . .' Her voice trailed off.

'Are you plannign to visit your sister in her West Bank settlement at some point?'

Stella glanced at Martin, then turned back to Asher. 'That also, naturally.'

'And Dante is keeping you company in exactly what capacity?'

Stella raised her chin. 'I know him by the name of Martin. He is my lover.'

The Israeli eyed Martin. 'I suppose you could describe her body if you had to.'

'No problem. Up to and including the faded tattoo of a Siberian night moth under her right breast.'

Out of the corner of his eye Martin saw Stella start to undo the top buttons of her shirt; once again there was no sign of an undergarment, only a triangle of pale skin. Asher, embarrassed, cleared his throat. 'That, eh, won't be necessary, Miss Kastner. I have reason to believe Dante works as a private detective and you hired his services. What you do after working hours is your business.' Asher regarded Martin. 'So that's what spies turn into when they come in from the cold – they metamorphose into private detectives.

Sure beats cultivating stringless green beans. Tell me something, Dante, how does one go about becoming a private detective?'

'You watch old detective films.'

'He's a great fan of Humphrey Bogart,' Stella asserted, avoiding Martin's eye.

Asher watched her sip at the tea for a moment. When he spoke again his mood had changed; to Martin, he suddenly looked more like an undertaker than a cop. 'Let me offer you some sympathy with your tea, Miss Kastner,' Asher began. He slid off the stool and walked over to a table and flipped open the top dossier on a thick pile of dossiers. 'I am sorry to be the bearer of sad news,' he said, and he read from the page: 'The following is a State Department advisory forwarded by the American embassy in Tel Aviv. "Please pass this information to Estelle Kastner: her father, Oscar Alexandrovich Kastner, suffered a heart attack at his home in Brooklyn five days ago."'

Stella's eyes tightened into an anguished squint. 'Oh my God, I've got to telephone Kastner immediately,' she whispered.

Martin could tell from the dark expression on Asher's face that there was no point to putting in a phone call. 'He's dead, isn't he?'

'I'm afraid Dante's right,' Asher told Stella. His gaze fell on Martin. 'There's something the little canary wanted me to pass on to you, Dante. The body of a Chinese girl was discovered on the roof over your pool parlor. Her boss at a Chinese restaurant went looking for her when she didn't turn up for work. She'd been stung to death by bees from one of your hives. Hell of a way to go, wouldn't you say?'

'Yeah,' Martin agreed grimly. 'I would say.'

Neither Martin nor Stella said a word in the communal taxi for fear the driver or one of the other passengers might be working for the Shabak; both worried also that emotions would get the upper hand if one of them broke the comforting silence. Fifty minutes after leaving the airport they found themselves standing on a street corner in downtown Jerusalem. Heavy morning traffic flowed around them. Squads of soldiers, some of them dark skinned Ethiopians wearing green flak jackets and green berets, patrolled the streets, checking the identity papers of young men who looked as if they could be Arabs. Martin let six taxis pass before hailing the seventh. They took it to the American Colony Hotel in East Jerusalem, where a line of Palestinian taxis queued on the street outside the hotel. A young Russian, in Israel for a chess tournament, was leaning over a chess board set up on the hood of a car parked outside the hotel entrance as a television camera filmed him. He was playing against himself, slamming the pieces down on the board as he made a dozen rapid moves, muttering all the while about a flaw in black's position or the ineptness of white's attack. Spotting an opening, he gleefully thrust the white pieces forward for the kill, then looked up and announced in English that black had resigned in the face of white's dazzling attack.

'How can he play against himself and remain sane?' Stella asked.

'The advantage of playing against yourself is, unlike real life, you know what your opponent's next move will be,' Martin observed.

He waited until the first three Palestinian taxis had driven off with passengers before signaling to the fourth. 'Mustaffah, at your beck and call,' announced the young Palestinian driver as he loaded their valises into the back of a yellow Mercedes that, judging from its appearance, had been around longer than the driver. 'So to where?'

'Kiryat Arba,' Stella said.

The enthusiasm drained from Mustaffah's eyes. 'It will cost you a hundred twenty shekels or thirty dollars U.S.,' he said. 'I only take you to the main gate. The Jews will not tolerate Arab taxis inside.'

'Main gate will be fine,' Martin said as he and Stella settled onto the cracking leather of the back seat.

Mustaffah's plastic worry beads dangling from the rearview mirror tapped against the windshield as the taxi sped past fortress-like Israeli neighborhoods and bus stops swarming with religious Jews, and headed away from Jerusalem on a new highway that knifed south into the Judean Hills. On the rocky slopes on either side of the highway, knots of Palestinian men walked along dirt paths to avoid the Israeli checkpoints as they made their way into Jewish Jerusalem in the hope of finding a day's work. In the wadis, boys who had climbed onto the high branches of trees could be seen picking olives and stuffing them under their open shirts.

'You were tempting fate back at the airport,' Martin remarked. 'I'm talking about when you started to unbutton your shirt to show Asher the night moth under your breast. What would you have done if he hadn't stopped you?'

Stella inched closer to Martin until her thigh was touching his; she badly wanted to be comforted. 'I consider myself a pretty good judge of character,' she replied. 'My instinct told me he would stop me, or at the very least avert his eyes.'

'What about me?' Martin asked. 'Did you think I'd avert my eyes?'

Stella stared through the grime on the window, remembering how she had clung to Kastner when she had hugged him good-bye; he had wheeled his chair away abruptly but she had still caught sight of the tears welling in his eyes. She turned to Martin. 'Sorry. I was somewhere else. What did you say?'

'I asked whether you thought I'd avert my eyes, too, if you started to show Asher the night moth supposedly tattooed under your breast.'

'Not sure,' she admitted. 'Haven't figured you out yet.'

'What's to figure out?'

'There are parts of you my instinct can't get to.

The heart of the matter is hidden under too many moods – it's almost as if you were several different people. For one thing, I can't decide if you are interested in women. I can't decide if you want to seduce me, or not. Females need to get this detail right before they can have a working relationship with a man.'

'Not,' Martin said without hesitation. 'Trouble with women in general, and you in particular, is you're incapable of being on the receiving end of courtesy without assuming seduction is behind it.' Martin thought of Minh coaxing erections out of his reluctant flesh during their occasional evenings together; he wondered if her death on the roof above the pool parlor had really been an accident. 'Here's the deal, Stella: I'm past seduction. When I'm backed up against a wall I make war, not love.'

'That's pain speaking,' Stella whispered, thinking of her own pain. 'You ought to consider the possibility that intimacy can be a painkiller.'

Martin shook his head. 'My experience has been that you become intimate in order to have sex. Once the sex is out of the way, the intimacy only brings more pain.'

Moving back to her side of the seat, Stella burst out in irritation, 'It's typical of the male of the species to think you become intimate in order to have sex. The female of the species has a more subtle take on the subject – she understands that you have sex in order to become intimate; that intimacy is the ultimate orgasm, since it allows you to get outside of the prison of yourself; get outside your skin and into the skin, the psyche, of another human being. Sex that leads to intimacy is a jailbreak.'

Mustaffah slowed for an Israeli checkpoint, but was waved through when two soldiers peered through the window and mistook the passengers for Jews heading back to one of the settlements. The taxi sped past roadside carts brimming with oranges and zucchinis and restaurants with kabob roasting on spits and garages with cars up on cinder blocks and mechanics flat on their backs underneath them. It slowed again for a flock of sheep that scattered when Mustaffah leaned on the horn. Young Arab women with babies strapped to their backs by a shawl, older women in long robes with heavy bundles balanced on their heads trudged along the side of the road, turning their faces away to avoid the dust kicked up by the Mercedes barreling past.

Half an hour out of Jerusalem, the taxi eased to a stop outside Kiryat Arba next to a sign that read: 'Zionist Settlement – "The more they torture him, the more he will become."' Martin could see the two guards at the gate in the security fence watching them suspiciously. Both were armed with Uzis, with the ritual tzitzit jutting from under their bullet proof vests. While Stella retrieved the two valises from the trunk of the Mercedes, Martin walked around to the open passenger window to pay Mustaffah. From one of the minarets below, the recorded wail of the muezzin summoning the faithful to midday prayer drifted up to the Jewish settlement. Slipping three ten dollar bills through the window, Martin noticed that the framed license on the glove compartment had a photograph of Mustaffah, but identified him, in English, as Azzam Khouri.

'Why did you tell me your name was Mustaffah?' he asked the driver.

'Mustaffah, he was my brother killed by the Israeli army during the Intifada. We was both of us throwing stones at the Jewish tanks and they got mad and started throwing bullets back. Since, my mother calls me Mustaffah to pretend my brother is still being alive. Some days I call myself Mustaffah for the same reason. Somedays I'm not sure who I am. Today is such a day.'

The guards at the gate scrutinized the passports of the visitors. When Stella explained that she was there to see her sister, Ya'ara Ugor-Zhilov, they phoned up to the settlement, a sprawl of stone-faced apartment buildings and one-family houses spilling like lava down several once barren hills toward the Arab city of Hebron. Minutes later a battered pickup appeared at the top of the hill and slowly made its way, its spark plugs misfiring, past the playground teeming with mothers and little children to the gate. A moment later Stella and her sister were clinging to each other. Martin could see Stella talking quietly into the ear of her sister. Elena, or Ya'ara as she was now called, took a step back, shook her head vehemently, then burst into tears and fell back into her sisters arms. The driver of the pickup, a stocky, bearded man in his fifties, wearing black sneakers, a black suit, black tie and black fedora, approached Martin. He inspected him through windowpane-thick bifocals set into wire frames.

'*Shalom* to you, Mr Martin Odum,' he said with a distinct Brooklyn accent. 'I'm the rabbi Ben Zion. You need to be Stella's detective friend. I'm right, right?'

'Right on both counts,' Martin said. 'I'm a detective and I'm a friend.'

'It's me, the rabbi who married Ya'ara to Samat,' Ben Zion announced. 'If you're trying to track down Samat and get poor Ya'ara a religious divorce, I'll give you the time of day. If not, not.'

'How'd you know I was a detective? Or about my tracking down Samat?'

'A little canary told someone in the Shabak, and that someone told yours truly that two tourists who weren't touring anything but Kiryat Arba could be expected to wash up on our doorstep. Miracle of miracles, here you are.' The rabbi raised a hand to shield his eyes from the noon sun and sized up the Brooklyn detective who had found his way to Kiryat Arba. 'So you're not Jewish, Mr Odum.'

Behind them the two sisters started to walk up the hill, their arms around each other's waists. Martin said, 'How can you tell?'

Rabbi Ben Zion tossed his head in the direction

of Hebron, visible through swells of heat rising from the floor of the valley below them. 'You don't live in the middle of a sea of Arabs without recognizing one of your own when you see him.'

'In other words, it's a matter of instinct.'

'Survival instinct, developed over two thousand years.' The rabbi pitched the two valises into the back of the pickup. 'So be my guest and climb in,' he ordered. 'I'll take you to Ya'ara's apartment. We'll get there before the girls and cook up water for tea, and light a memorial candle for her father – the canary told me about the death in the family, too, but I thought it would be better if Stella broke the bad news to her sister. Ask me nicely and I'll tell you what I know about the missing husband.'

The rabbi threw the pickup into gear and, his sidecurls flying, gunned it up the hill, past the settlement post office, past the shopping center tceming with women in ankle length skirts and small boys wearing knitted yarmulke. Ya'ara, it turned out, lived in a small two-room apartment on the ground floor of one of the apartment buildings with a view of Hebron. 'When her husband abandoned her, she had no resources of her own so our synagogue took her under its wing,' the rabbi explained. He searched through a ring of keys until he came to the right one and unlocked the door. The furnishings were Spartan. There was a narrow cot in one room, with a cracked mirror bordered with plastic sea shells over it and a wooden crate turned upside down serving as a night table. A folding bridge table covered with a square of oil cloth, a motley assortment of folding chairs with a small black-and-white television set on one of them, were scattered around what served as a living room. On the sill of a waist-high book-case separating the living room from the tiny kitchen alcove were three flower pots containing plastic geraniums. Martin opened the door to the small bathroom. Women's cotton underwear and several pairs of long woolen stockings hung from a cord stretched over the bathtub. Ben Zion noticed Martin's expression as he returned to the living room. 'We bought the furniture from Arabs whose houses were bulldozed between us and Hebron so we could walk to the Cave of Machpela safely.'

Martin strolled over to the window, raised the shade and looked out at the tangle of streets and buildings that made up Hebron. 'What's the Cave of Machpela?' he called over his shoulder.

The rabbi was in the kitchen alcove, attempting to light the gas burner with a match to boil water in a kettle. 'Am I hearing you correctly? What's the Cave of Machpela? It's nothing less than the second holiest place for Jews on the planet earth, ranking immediately behind the Temple Mount or what's left of it, the Wailing Wall. Hebron – which in biblical times was also called Kiryat Arba – is where the Patriarch Abraham bought his first dunams of land in Canaan. The Cave is where Abraham is buried; his sons Isaac and Jacob, his wife, Sarah, too. It is also holy to the Palestinians, who coopted our Abraham to be one of their prophets; they built a mosque on the spot and we are obliged to take turns praying at the cave.' Lighting a burner, the rabbi slid the kettle over the grill. Shaking his head in disbelief, he struck another match and lit a *yortseit* candle for the dead and carried it back into the room. 'What is the Cave of Machpela?' he asked rhetorically, setting the candle on the table. 'Even a *shagetz* ought to know the answer to that one. We always stroll down to the cave on Fridays at sunset to welcome the Sabbath in at this holy site. You and Stella are welcome to join us – that way you can tell the Shabak you actually did some sightseeing.'

Martin decided there'd been enough small talk. 'What about Samat?'

Rabbi Ben Zion covered his mouth to smother a belch. 'What about Samat?' he repeated.

'Did he run off with another woman?'

'Let me tell you something, Mr Brooklyn detective who thinks men only leave their wives for other ladies. Samat didn't need to quit his wife to have another lady – he rented all the ladies his libido desired. When he disappeared in his Honda for two, three days running, where do you think he went? It's an open secret where he went. He went where a lot of men go when they want ladies to do things their wives won't do. In Jaffa, in Tel Aviv, in Haifa, there are what my mother, may she rest in peace, used to call houses of ill repute where you can get your ashes hauled by ladies who don't mind being naked with a man, who, for a price, are willing to do anything to satisfy a client.' The rabbi waved a hand in the general direction of the Mediterranean coast. 'Samat had sexual appetites, you could see it in his eyes, you could tell it from the way he looked at his sister-in-law Estelle when she visited Kiryat Arba. Samat also had his share of obsessions that weren't carnal. What I'm saying is, he had other axes to grind besides sex.'

In the kitchenette, the kettle began to shriek. The rabbi leaped to turn off the gas and set about preparing tea. He returned moments later carrying the kettle and four china cups, which he put on the bridge table next to the memorial candle. Leaning over the table the better to see what he was doing, Ben Zion slipped Lipton tea bags into the four cups and filled the first one with boiling water. When Martin waved it away, he took the cup himself and sank onto one of the folding chairs, his knees apart, his feet flat on the floor and tapping impatiently. Martin scraped over another chair and sat down facing him.

'Why would someone like Samat, who needed to visit houses of ill repute to satisfy his lusts, marry a religious woman whom he had never met?'

'Am I inside Samat's head to know the answer?' The rabbi blew noisily across the cup, then touched his lips to the tea to test the temperature. Deciding it was too hot to drink, he set it down on the table. 'He was a strange bird, this Samat. I am Ya'ara's rabbi. In the Jewish religion we don't confess to

170

our spiritual leaders the way Catholics do. But we confide in them. I believed Ya'ara when she said that Samat never touched her on her wedding night, or after. He never slept in the marriage bed. For all I know she may still be a virgin. When Samat was living under the same roof with her, she was absolutely convinced something was wrong with her. I tried to persuade her that the something that was wrong was wrong with him. I tried to persuade him, too.'

'Did you succeed?'

The rabbi shook his head cheerlessly. 'To use an old Yiddish expression, I never got to first base with Samat.'

'What was he doing here?'

'Hiding.'

'From what? From whom?'

The rabbi tried his tea again. This time he managed to sip at it. 'What am I, a reader of minds? How would I know, from what, from whom? Look, coming to live in one of these Jewish settlements in the middle of all these Arabs is a little like joining the French foreign legion: When you sign on the dotted line, nobody asks to see your curriculum vitae, we're just glad to have your warm body. What I do know is that Samat went to the Kiryat Arba security officer and asked for a weapon. He said it was to protect his wife if the Hamas terrorists ever attacked.'

'Did he get the weapon?'

The rabbi nodded. 'Anybody living in a settlement

who can see what he's shooting at can get a weapon.' Ben Zion remembered another detail. 'Samat evidently had an endless supply of money. He paid for everything he bought with cash – an upscale split-level house on the side of Kiryat Arba where you get to enjoy the sunsets, a brand new Japanese car with air conditioning. He never played pinochle with the boys, he never accompanied Ya'ara to the synagogue, even on the high holy days, though it didn't go unnoticed that she always left an envelope stuffed with cash in the charity box. Admit it, Mr American detective, I'll bet you don't know that *shamus* is a Yiddish word.'

'I thought it was Irish.'

'Irish!' The rabbi slapped a palm against one of his knees. 'The shamus was the synagogue beetle, which was the sobriquet for the member of the congregation who took care of the synagogue.' Ben Zion shook his head in puzzlement. 'How, I ask you, is it possible to detect an AWOL husband if you can't detect the origin of the word shamus?'

The sudden arrival of Ya'ara and Stella saved Martin from having to account for this lapse in his education; it also provided him with his first good look at Samat's wife. She was a short, overweight woman with a teenager's pudgy face and a matronly body endowed with an ample bosom that put a strain on the buttons of her blouse; Martin feared that one of them would pop at any moment. In the space between the buttons he caught a glimpse of the pink fabric of a heavy brassiere. She wore an ankle-length skirt popular with Lubavitch women and a round flat-brimmed felt hat that she nervously twisted on her head, as if she were trying to find the front. The little patches of skin on her body that Martin could see were chalk white from lack of being exposed to sun light. Her cheeks were streaked with traces of tears. Stella, dry eyed, wore the ghost of a smile fixed on her lips that Martin had noticed the day she turned up at his pool parlor.

The rabbi bounded to his feet when the women appeared at the door; Ya'ara stopped to kiss the mezuzah before she came in. Grabbing one of her hands in both of his, bending at the waist so that his head was level with hers, the rabbi bombarded her with a burst of Hebrew which, to the shamus's ear, sounded more Brooklyn than biblical. Martin concluded that the rabbi was offering condolences because Ya'ara started sobbing again; tears cascaded down her cheeks and soaked into the tightly buttoned collar of her blouse. Ben Zion led Ya'ara to the *yortseit* candle and, rocking back and forth on the soles of his sneakers, started praying in Hebrew. Ya'ara, blotting her tears on the back of a sleeve, joined in.

'Aren't you going to pray for your father?' Martin whispered to Stella.

'I only pray for the living,' she retorted fiercely.

When the prayer ended the rabbi excused himself to organize the Sabbath pilgrimage to the Cave of Machpela, and Martin got his first opportunity to talk to Stella's sister. 'I'm sorry about your father,' he began.

She accepted this with a shy closing of her lids. 'I was not expecting him to die, and certainly not of a heart attack. He had the heart of a lion. After all he had been through—' She shrugged weakly.

'Your sister has hired me to find Samat so that you can get a religious divorce.'

Ya'ara turned on Stella. 'What good will a divorce do me?'

'It is a matter of pride,' Stella insisted. 'You can't let him get away with this.'

Martin steered the conversation back to matters of tradecraft. 'Do you have anything of his – a book he once read, a telephone he once used, a bottle of alcohol he once poured a drink from, a toothbrush even? Anything at all?'

Ya'ara shook her head. 'There was stationery with a London letterhead but it disappeared and I don't remember the address on it. Samat filled a trunk with personal belongings and paid two boys to carry it down to the taxi when he left. He even took the photographs of our wedding. The only photograph left of him was the one Stella snapped after the ceremony and sent to our father.' At the mention of their father, tears trickled down her cheeks again. 'How could Samat do this to a wife, I ask you?'

'Stella told me he was always talking on the phone,' Martin said. 'Did he initiate the calls or did people call him?'

'Both.'

'So there must be phone records showing the numbers he dialed.'

Again she shook her head. 'The rabbi asked the security office here to try and get the phone numbers. Someone even drove to Tel Aviv to interview the phone company. He reported back that the numbers were all on a magnetic tape that had been erased by error. There was no trace of the numbers he called.'

'What language did he use when he spoke on the phone?'

'English. Russian. Armenian sometimes.'

'Did you ever ask him what he did for a living?'

'Once.'

Stella said, 'What did he say?'

'At first he didn't answer. When I pressed him, he told me he ran a business selling Western-manufactured artificial limbs to people who had lost legs to Russian land mines in Bosnia, Chechnya, Kurdistan. He said he could have made a fortune but was selling them at cost.'

'And you believed him?' Stella asked.

'I had no reason not to.' Ya'ara's eyes suddenly widened. 'Someone once called when he wasn't here and left a phone number for him to call back. I thought it might have something to do with these artificial limbs and wrote it down on the first thing that came to hand, which was the back of a recipe, and then copied it onto the pad next to the telephone. I tore off the page and gave it to Samat when he returned to the house that day and he went to the bedroom and dialed a number. I remember that the conversation was very agitated. At one point Samat was even yelling into the phone, and he kept switching from English to Russian and back to English again.'

'The recipe,' Stella said softly. 'Do you still have it?'

Both Stella and Martin could see Ya'ara hesitate. 'You would not be betraying your husband,' Martin said. 'If and when we find him, we are only going to make sure you get the famous *get* so you can go on with your life.'

'Samat owes that much to you,' Stella said.

Sighing, moving as if her limbs were weighted down by gravity, Ya'ara pushed herself to her feet and shuffled into the kitchen alcove and pulled a tin box from one of the wall cupboards. She carried it back to the living room, set it on the folding table, opened the lid and began thumbing through printed recipes that she had torn out of *Elle* magazine over the years. She pulled the one for apple strudel out of the box and turned it over. A phone number starting with the country code 44 and city code 171 was scrawled on the back in pencil. Martin produced a felt tipped pen and copied the number into a small notebook.

'Where is that?' Stella asked Martin.

'Forty-four is England, 171 is London,' he said. He turned back to Stella. 'Did Samat ever leave Kiryat Arba?' he asked.

'Once, sometimes twice a week, he drove off by

176

himself, sometimes for a few hours, sometimes for several days.'

'Do you have any idea where he went?'

'The one time I asked him he told me it was not the business of a wife to keep track of a husband.'

Stella looked brightly at Martin. 'We went with him once, Martin.' She smiled at her half sister. 'Don't you remember, Elena—'

'My name is Ya'ara now,' Stella's sister reminded her coldly.

Stella was not put off. 'It was when I came for the wedding,' she said excitedly. 'I had to be at Ben-Gurion Airport at seven in the evening for my flight back to New York. Samat was going somewhere for lunch. He said if we didn't mind killing time, he had to see someone on the coast and could drop me at the airport on the way back to Kiryat Arba.'

'I remember that,' Ya'ara said. 'We made bologna sandwiches and packed them in a paper bag and took a plastic bottle of apple juice.' She sighed again. 'That was one of the happiest days of my life,' she added.

Stella said to Martin, 'He drove north from Tel Aviv along the expressway and got off at the exit marked "Caesarea." There was a labyrinth of streets but he never hesitated, he seemed to know his way around very well. He dropped us on the edge of the sand dunes near some A-frame houses. We could see those giant chimneys down the coast that produced electricity.'

Ya'ara's face lit up for the first time in Martin's

presence; the smile almost made her look handsome. 'I wore an enormous straw hat to protect my face from the sun,' she recalled. 'We ate in the shade of a eucalyptus tree and then hunted for Roman coins in the sand.'

'And what did Samat do while you were scouring the dunes for Roman coins?' Martin asked.

The girls looked at each other. 'He never told us. He picked us up at the A-frames at five-thirty and dropped me off at the airport at six-forty.'

'Uh-huh,' Martin said, his brows knitting as he began to fit the first blurred pieces of the jigsaw puzzle into place.

Martin took a tiny address book (tradecraft ruled: Everyone in it was identified by nickname and phone numbers were masked in a simple cipher) from his pocket and used his AT&T card to call Xing's Mandarin Restaurant (listed in the address book as 'Glutamate') under the pool parlor on Albany Avenue in Crown Heights. Given the time difference, Tsou would be presiding from the high stool behind the cash register, glowering at the waitress who had replaced Minh if she failed to push the more expensive dishes on the menu. 'Peking duck hanging in window for two days,' he'd once informed Minh, his gold teeth glistening with saliva, his face a mask of earnestness (so she had gleefully recounted to Martin), 'is aphlodisiac, good for elections.'

'Xing's Mandalin,' a high pitched voice – so

distinct it could have been coming from the next room – announced when the phone on the other end was picked up. 'Filled up at lunch, same tonight. No flea table until lunch Sunday.'

'Don't hang up,' Martin cried into the phone. 'Tsou, it's me, Martin.'

'*Yin shi*, from where you calling, huh?'

Martin knew that Fred would be keeping track of his whereabouts through Asher and the Israeli Shabak, so he figured he was not giving anything away if he told the truth.

'I'm in Israel.'

'Islael the Jewish kingdom or Islael the Jewish delicatessen on Kingston Avenue?' Tsou didn't wait for an answer. 'You know about Minh, huh?'

'That's why I'm calling. Tell me what happened, Tsou.'

The story spurted out. 'She goes up to check the hives the way you asked. She does not come back. Clients begin to fidget. No food in sight. I go out back and shout up "Minh." She does not shout back. I climb file escape, find Minh laying on back, not moving, not conscious, clazy bees stinging life out of Minh's face. Disgusting. Makes me want to vomit. Call police on loft phone, Matin, hope you do not mind, let them into loft when they ling bell, they put on face masks and chase bees with can of Laid found below sink, they take Minh away in ambulance, face bloated big like basketball. She dead before ambulance leach hospital, Matin. Minh's death makes page two *Daily News*, big headline say "Deadly Bees Kill Clown Heights Woman."'

'What did the police say, Tsou?'

'Two detectives come for lunch next day, sons of bitches leave without paying check, I wave it in faces but they do not take hint. They ask about you and I tell them what I know, which is nothing. They tell me ASPCA in white clothing came to kill bees. They tell me hive exploded, which is what made bees clazy to attack Minh. Comes as news to me honey can explode.'

Through the window Martin could see the orange streaks of sunset in the sky and the rabbi assembling a group of settlers for the stroll down the road toward Hebron and the Cave of Machpela. 'It comes as news to me, too,' he said very softly.

'What you say?' Tsou shouted.

'I said, honey doesn't normally explode.'

'Huh. So. Detectives, they say Minh not even Minh's name, she illegal immigrant from Taiwan named Chun-chiao. Business picked up when *Daily News* ran name Xing's Mandolin on page two even though they spelled Xing 'Zing.' I admit it, whole thing leave bad taste in my mouth. Velly upsetting.'

Martin assumed Tsou was referring to Minh's death. 'Yeah, very,' he agreed.

Tsou, however, seemed to be more concerned with Minh's false identity than her death. 'Cannot believe anyone anymore these days, huh, *yin shi*? Minh not Minh. Maybe you not Matin.'

'Maybe the *Daily News* was right,' Martin said, 'maybe your real name is Tsou Zing with a "Z."'

'Maybe,' Tsou agreed with a sour laugh. 'Who can say?'

With Rabbi Ben Zion and Martin strolling along in the lead and the two Kastner sisters bringing up the rear, the group of thirty or so ultranationalist orthodox settlers, the men sporting tzitzit and embroidered yarmulkes, the women in ankle-length skirts and long sleeved blouses and head scarves, made their way down the road toward the Cave of Machpela to greet the Sabbath at the holy site where the Patriarch Abraham was said to be buried. Two policemen wearing blue uniforms and blue baseball caps, along with half a dozen of the younger settlers, walked on either side of the group, rifles or Uzis slung over their shoulders.

The sun had disappeared behind the hills and the darkness was starting to blot out the twilight between the buildings. Instinctively, the murky dusk left Martin feeling queasy. Agents who worked the field liked daylight because they could see danger coming, and night-time because they could hide from it; the penumbra between the two offered none of the advantages of either. The massive fortress-like structure built over the sacred cave loomed ahead like a ship adrift in a fog.

'What do the Palestinians here think of your pilgrimages to the shrine?' Martin asked the rabbi, all the while inspecting the spaces between the

181

Palestinian houses off to the right for any telltale sign of activity. Martin tensed as a shard of light ricocheted off a roof; as his eyes grew accustomed to the dimness, he realized it was nothing more than a lingering sliver of sunlight glinting off the solar heating panels atop a three-story building.

'The Palestinians,' the rabbi replied, waving toward the surrounding houses, 'say we're walking on their toes.'

'You are, aren't you?'

The rabbi shrugged. 'Look, it's not as if we're being unreasonable. Those of us who believe the Lord God gave this land to Abraham and his descendants for eternity are willing to let the Palestinians remain here as long as they accept that the land is ours.'

'What about the others?'

'They can emigrate.'

'That doesn't leave them – or you, for that matter – much room for maneuver.'

'It's easy for visitors to come here from the outside and criticize, Mr Odum, and then fly back to the safety of their country, their city, their homes . . .'

'My home,' Martin ventured, 'turns out to be less safe than I thought.' He made a mental note to get more details of the death of Stella's father. He wondered if there had been an autopsy.

'You're talking about crime in the streets. It's nothing compared to what we have to put up with here.'

182

'I was talking about exploding honey—'

'Come again – I must be missing something.'

'Private joke.'

Eyeing potential danger areas, Martin spotted a spark in an alleyway between two Palestinian homes to his right and uphill from the group of settlers walking toward the cave. Suddenly flames erupted and a blazing tire, thick black smoke billowing from it, started rolling downhill toward them. As the settlers scattered to get out of its path, the short hollow cough of a high-powered rifle resounded through the neighborhood and a spurt of dust materialized in the road immediately ahead of Martin. His old reflexes kicked in – he figured out what was going on in an instant. The tire was the diversion; the rifle shot had come from the other side of the road, probably from the top of the cement cistern a hundred and fifty yards away on a small rise. The two policemen and the settlers armed with weapons had reacted instinctively and were charging uphill in the direction of the alleyway where the tire had come from. One of the policemen was shouting into a walkie-talkie. Back at Kiryat Arba, a siren, its pitch rising as it whimpered into life, began shrieking across the countryside.

'The shot came from behind us,' Martin shouted and he lunged for cover behind a low stone wall as the second shot nicked the dirt a yard beyond the spot where he'd been standing. Crouching behind the wall, massaging the muscles in his bad leg, Martin could see Stella and her sister, with her skirt hiked, running back up the hill toward the settlement, which was ablaze with searchlights sweeping the area. Moments later two Israeli jeeps and an open truck filled with soldiers came roaring down the road from the nearby army base. Leaping from their vehicles, the soldiers, bent low and running, charged the slopes on either side of the road. From behind the cistern came the staccato sound of automatic rifles being fired in short bursts. Martin suspected that the Palestinian rifleman – assuming he was Palestinian – had melted away and the soldiers were shooting at shadows.

Dusting the dirt off of his sabbath suit, the rabbi came up to Martin. 'You okay?' he asked breathlessly.

Martin nodded.

'That was too close for comfort,' Ben Zion said, his chest heaving with excitement. 'If I didn't know better, I would have thought they were shooting at you, Mr Odum.'

'Now why would they want to do that?' Martin asked innocently. 'I'm not even Jewish. I'm just a visitor who will soon go back to the safety of his country, his city, his home.'

1997: MARTIN ODUM MEETS A BORN-AGAIN OPPORTUNIST

Benny Sapir listened intently to Martin's account of the incident in Hebron. When he finally broke his silence it was to pose questions only a professional would think to ask.

'How can you be sure it wasn't some Arab kids letting off steam? That kind of thing happens all the time around Kiryat Arba.'

'Because of the diversion. The attack was synchronized. The tire came first. Everyone looked off to the right. The two cops and the armed settlers raced uphill to the right. That's when the first shot was fired. It came from the left.'

'How many shots were there?'

'Two.'

'And both of them hit the road near you?'

'The shooter's rifle must have been pulling to the left. The first shot hit a yard or so ahead of me, which means he was firing short and left. The shooter must have cranked in a correction to the rear sight and elevated slightly. The second shot was on target – it hit beyond where I'd been standing, which means the bullet would have hit

185

my chest if I hadn't leaped for cover behind the low wall.'

'Why didn't he shoot again?'

'Fact that he didn't is what makes me think he was shooting at me. When I disappeared from view behind the low wall, there were still a dozen or so settlers crouching or lying flat on the ground. The search lights from Kiryat Arba were sweeping the area so he could easily see them. If he was shooting in order to kill Jews, he had plenty of targets available.'

'Maybe the lights and the siren scared him off.'

'Soldiers scared him off. But that happened five, maybe eight minutes later.'

'*Beseder*, okay. So why would someone want to kill you, Dante?'

'Retirement hasn't dulled your edge, Benny. You're asking the right questions in the right order. Once we figure out the "why", we move on to the "who."'

Returning to Jerusalem from Kiryat Arba (Stella had remained behind to be with her sister), Martin had braved the rank stench of a phone booth and had asked information for the phone number of a Benny Sapir. He was given five listings under that name. The second one, in a settlement community thirteen kilometers outside of Jerusalem, turned out to be the Benny Sapir who had briefed Dante Pippen in Washington before the mission to the Bekaa Valley eight years before; Benny, normally the Mossad's point man on things

Russian, had been covering for a colleague home on sick leave at the time. When he came on line now, Benny, who had retired from the Mossad the previous year, sounded winded. He recognized the voice on the other end of the phone immediately. 'The older I get, the harder it is to remember faces and names, but voices I never forget,' he said. 'Tell you the truth, Dante, never expected our paths to cross again.' Before Martin could say anything, Benny proposed to pick him up in front of the Rashamu Restaurant down from the Jewish *shouk* on Ha-Eshkol Street in half an hour.

Exactly on time, a spanking new Skoda pulled up in front of the restaurant and the driver, a muscular man with the body of a wrestler, honked twice. Benny's hair had gone gray and his once-famous smile had turned melancholy since Martin had last seen him, eight years before, standing at the foot of his hospital bed in Haifa. 'Lot of water's flowed under the bridge since we last saw each other, Dante,' Benny said as Martin slid onto the passenger seat. 'You sure it wasn't blood?' Martin shot back, and they both laughed at the absence of humor in the exchange. At the intersection ahead of them, two Israeli soldiers of Ethiopian origin were frisking an Arab boy carrying a tray filled with small porcelain cups of Turkish coffee. 'So you are going by the name of Martin Odum these days,' Benny noted, wheeling the car into traffic and heading out of Jerusalem in the direction of Tel Aviv. The one-time spymaster glanced quickly at the American. 'Sorry about that, Dante, but I was obliged to touch base with the Shabak.'

'I would have done the same thing in your shoes.'

It was obvious Benny felt bad about it. 'Question of guarding one's flanks,' he mumbled, apologizing a second time. 'The people who run the show these days are a new breed – cross them and your pension checks start arriving late.'

'I understand,' Martin said again.

'Be careful what you tell me,' Benny warned. 'They want me to file a contact report after I've seen you. They're not quite sure what you're doing here.'

'Me, also, I'm not quite sure what I'm doing here,' Martin admitted. 'Where we going, Benny?'

'Har Addar. I live there. I invite you for pot-luck supper. You can sleep over if you need a bed for the night. Does Martin Odum have a legend?'

'He's a private detective working out of the Crown Heights section of Brooklyn.'

Benny rocked his head from side to side in appreciation. 'Why not? A detective is as good a cover as any and better than most. I've used various legends in my time – my favorite, which was my cover when I was running agents in what used to be called the Soviet Union, was a defrocked English priest living in sin in Istanbul. The sin part was the fun part. To support my cover story, I had to practically memorize the Gospels. Never got over the trauma of reading John. If you're looking for the roots of Christian anti-Semitism, you don't have to go further than the Gospel According to John, which, by the way, wasn't written by the disciple named John. Whoever wrote the text commandeered his name. Now that I think of it, you could make the case that this is an example of an early Christian legend.'

Benny turned off the Jerusalem–Tel Aviv highway and was wending his way up through the hills west of Jerusalem toward Har Addar when Martin asked him if the agents he'd run in the former USSR had been Jewish.

Glancing quickly at his companion, Benny said, 'Some were, most weren't.'

'What motivated them to work for Israel?'

'Not all of them knew they were working for Israel. We used false flags when we thought it would get results. What motivated them? Money. Resentment for personal slights, real or imagined. Boredom.'

'Not ideology?'

'There must have been individuals who defected for ideological reasons but I personally never came across any. The thing they all had in common was they wanted to be treated as human beings, as opposed to cogs in a machine, and they were ready to risk their lives for the handler who understood this. The most remarkable thing about the Soviet Union was that nobody – *nobody* – believed in communism. Which meant that once you recruited a Russian, he made an outstanding spy for the simple reason that he'd been raised in a society where everyone, from the Politburo members on down to the Intourist guides, dissembled in order to survive. When a Russian agreed to spy for you, in a very real sense he'd already been trained to lead two lives.'

'You mean three lives, don't you? One where he outwardly conforms to the Soviet system. The second where he despises the system and cuts corners to get ahead within it. The third where he betrays the system and spies for you.'

'Three lives it is.' Benny became pensive. 'Which, when you think of it, may be par for the course. When you come right down to it, all men and some women live with an assortment of legends that blur at the edges where they overlap. Some of these IDs fade as we get older; others, curiously, become sharper and we spend more time in them. But that's another story.'

'Consider the possibility that it isn't another story . . . Is Benny Sapir the last of your legends or the one your parents gave you?'

Instead of answering, Benny sniffed at the air, which was growing chillier as the car climbed into the hills. Martin kicked himself for having asked. He grasped what professional interrogators took for granted: Each time you posed a question, you revealed what you didn't know. If you weren't careful, the person being interrogated could wind up knowing more about you than you did about him.

Benny delicately changed the subject. 'Does your leg give you trouble these days?'

'I got used to the pain.'

A grimace appeared on Benny's prize-fighter's lips that looked as if they had been in one fight too many. 'Yes, pain is like the buzzing in an ear – it's something you learn to live with.'

As Benny shifted into second and turned onto a narrow road that climbed steeply, the small talk gave way to a comfortable silence that exists between two veteran warriors who have nothing to prove to each other. Benny had the car radio on and tuned to a classical music station. Suddenly the program was interrupted and Benny reached to turn up the volume. The announcer delivered a bulletin of news. When the music came back on, Benny lowered the volume.

'There was another *pigu'a*,' he informed Martin. 'That's a terrorist attack. Hezbollah in the Lebanon ambushed an army patrol in the security corridor we occupy along the border. Two of our boys were killed, two wounded.' He shook his head in disgust. 'Hezbollah makes the mistake of thinking that we're all hanging out in Tel Aviv nightclubs or raking in millions in our Israeli Silicon Valley, that prosperity has drained the fight out of us, that we've grown soft and fat and are not willing to die for our country. One of these days we'll have to set them straight . . .'

The outburst took Martin by surprise. Not knowing how to respond, he said, 'Uh-huh.'

Twenty-five minutes after picking Martin up near the *shouk*, Benny drove into what looked like a rich man's housing project filled with expensive two-story homes set back from the street. 'We're a kilometer inside the West Bank here,' he noted as he eased the Skoda to the curb in front of a house with a wraparound porch. Martin followed him through the metal gate and along the porch to the back of the house, where Benny pointed out the low clouds in the distance drenched with saffron light. 'It's Jerusalem, over the horizon, that's illuminating the clouds,' he said. 'Beautiful, isn't it?'

'No,' Martin shot back; the word escaped his lips before he knew what he was going to say. When Benny looked quickly at him, Martin added, 'It makes me uneasy.'

Benny asked, 'What makes you uneasy – cities beyond the horizon? Clouds saturated with light? My living on the Palestinian side of the sixty-seven border?'

Martin said, 'All of the above.'

Benny shrugged. 'I built this house in 1986, when Har Addar was founded,' he said. 'None of us who came to live here imagined we would ever give this land back to the Palestinians.'

'Living on the wrong side of the green line must be something of an embarrassment for you.'

Benny punched a code into a tiny number pad fixed on the wall to turn off the alarm. 'If and when we agree to the creation of a Palestinian

192

state,' he said, 'we'll have to adjust the frontier to take into account Israeli communities like this one.' He unlocked the door and let himself into the house. The lights came on the instant he crossed the threshold. 'Modern gadgets,' he explained with a snigger. 'The alarm, the automated lights are Mossad perks – they supply them to all their senior people.'

Benny set out a bottle of imported whiskey and two thick kitchen glasses on a low glass table, along with a plastic bowl filled with ice cubes and another with pretzels. They both scraped over chairs and helped themselves to a stiff drink. Martin produced a Beedie from a tin box. Benny provided a light.

'To you and yours,' Martin said, exhaling smoke, reaching to clink glasses with the Israeli.

'To legends,' Benny shot back. 'To the day when they become war surplus.'

'I'll drink to that,' Martin declared.

Martin glanced around, taking in the framed Hockney prints over the sofa, the brass menorah on the sideboard, the three blown-up photographs, each bordered in black, of young men in army uniforms on the wall over the chimney. Benny noticed him noticing. 'The two on the left were childhood friends. They were both killed in action on the Golan, one in sixty-seven, the other in seventy-three. The one on the right is our son, Daniel. He was killed in an ambush in the Lebanon a year and a half ago. Roadside bomb hidden in a dead dog blew up as his jeep went past. His mother . . . my wife died of grief five months later.'

Now Martin understood the source of the pain that Benny had learned to live with, and why he had grown melancholy. 'I'm sorry,' was all he could think to say.

'Me, also, I'm sorry,' was all Benny could trust himself to answer.

They both concentrated on their drinks. Finally Benny broke the silence. 'So what brings you to the Holy Land, Dante?'

'You were the Mossad's Russian expert, Benny. Who the hell is Samat Ugor-Zhilov?'

'Why are you interested in him?'

'He ran off from Kiryat Arba without giving a divorce to his wife. She's religious. Without a divorce she can't remarry. Her sister, who lives in Brooklyn, hired me to find Samat and get him to give her the divorce.'

'To know who Samat is, you have to understand where he was coming from.' Benny treated himself to another shot of whiskey. 'How much do you know about the disintegration of the Soviet Union?'

'I know what I read in the newspapers.'

'That's a beginning. The USSR we knew and loathed imploded in 1991. In the years that followed the country became what I call a klepto-cracy. Its political and economic institutions were infiltrated by organized crime. To get a handle on

194

what happened, you need to understand that it was Russia's criminals, as opposed to its politicians, who dismantled the communist superstructure of the former Soviet Union. And make no mistake about it, the Russian criminals were Neanderthals. In the early stages of the disintegration, when almost everything was up for grabs, the Italian mafia came sniffing around to see if they could get a piece of the action. You will have a better handle on the Russian mafia when you know that the Italians took one look around and went home; the Russians were simply too ruthless for them.'

Martin whistled softly. 'Hard to believe anyone could be more ruthless than the Cosa Nostra.'

'When the Soviet Union collapsed,' Benny went on, 'thousands of gangs surfaced. In the beginning they ran the usual rackets, they offered the usual protection—'

'What the Russians call a roof.'

'I see you've done your homework. The Russian word for roof is *krysha*. When two gangs offered their clients *krysha*, instead of the clients fighting each other if they had differences, the gangs did. The warfare spilled onto the streets in the early nineties. The period is referred to as the Great Moscow Mob Wars. There were something in the neighborhood of thirty thousand murders in 1993 alone. Another thirty thousand people simply disappeared. The smarter gangsters bought into legitimate businesses; the Russian Ministry of Internal Affairs once estimated that half of all private businesses or state-owned companies, and almost all of the banks in the country, had links to organized crime. The infamous Tzvetan Ugor-Zhilov, known as the *Oligarkh* since he appeared on the cover of *Time,* began life as a small time hoodlum. When he couldn't bribe his way out of one particularly messy muddle, he wound up serving eight years in a gulag camp. When he finally returned to his native Armenia, Gorbachev was on the scene and the Soviet Union was breaking apart at the seams. Working out of a cramped communal apartment in Yerevan, the capital of Armenia, Ugor-Zhilov started offering *krysha*. Soon he was running his own small bank and his *krysha* clients were made to understand that they would be smart to use its services. At some point the *Oligarkh* branched out and bought into the used-car business in Yerevan. But being a big fish in a small pond didn't satisfy him, so he set his sights on Moscow – he moved to the capital and in a matter of months became the kingpin of the used-car business there.'

'I heard all about his cornering the used-car market in Moscow. He bought out his competitors. The ones who wouldn't be bought out wound up in the Moscow River wearing cement shoes.'

'The used-car racket was the tip of the iceberg. Look, Dante, you put your life on the line for Israel once and I'm going to return the favor. What I'm about to tell you isn't public knowledge – even the Sixth Chief Directorate of the KGB, which was supposed to be keeping tabs on the *Oligarkh*, didn't know it. For Tzvetan Ugor-Zhilov, the used-car dealerships were merely a stepping stone to bigger and better things. Russia happens to be the world's second largest producer of aluminum. When the Soviet system collapsed, Ugor-Zhilov branched out into the aluminum business. He somehow raised seed money – I'm talking billions; his used-car dealerships were bringing in cash but not that much and to this day it's a mystery where he got the money – and used it to make lucrative deals with smelters. He did all this through a holding company in which he was a silent partner. He bought three hundred railroad freight cars and built a port facility in Siberia to offload alumina, the bauxite extract that's the principal ingredient in aluminum. He imported the bauxite tax free from Australia, processed it at the smelters into aluminum and exported it, tax free, abroad. His profits soared. In the West aluminum brought five dollars a ton profit, in Russia it brought two hundred dollars a ton profit to the people who exported it. By the early nineties, as Yeltsin's privatization swept across the Soviet republics in an attempt to transform Russia into a market economy, the *Oligarkh* presided over a secret empire with the vast profits from aluminum at its base. His holding company expanded into other raw materials – steel, chrome, coal – and eventually bought into factories and businesses by the hundreds. He opened banks to service the empire

197

and launder its profits abroad. Naturally he kept the skids greased with kickbacks to people in high places. At one point there were rumors that he'd paid off Yeltsin himself, but we were never able to pin this down.'

'Did the CIA's Soviet division people know about this?'

'We were the ones with assets in Moscow. We shared enough of the take with them to convince them we were sharing all of it.'

The phone rang. Benny raised it to his ear and listened. Then: 'As a matter of fact, he is . . . He's doing what he was doing at Kiryat Arba, trying to pick up the trail of Samat Ugor-Zhilov so his wife can get a divorce . . . Actually, I do believe him, yes. Let's not forget that Dante Pippen is one of the good guys . . . *Shalom, shalom.*'

When Benny had hung up, Martin said, 'Thanks for that.'

'If I didn't believe it, you wouldn't be sitting here. Where was I? Okay. A certain number of Russian mafiosi were Jewish. When the mob wars broke out in Moscow in 1993, Israel became a safe haven for some of them. Here they were far away from the day to day mayhem. Even some of the gangsters who weren't Jewish came to Israel under our Law of Return – they concocted new identities claiming a Jewish mother or a Jewish grandmother and slipped into Israel along with the seven hundred and fifty thousand Russian Jews who came here in the nineties. As new immigrants, the gangsters were able to bring in large sums of money without anybody asking where it came from. When our Shabak people finally wised up to the danger, we tapped their phones, we infiltrated their entourages, all the time looking for evidence that the Russians were engaged in criminal activities here. But they were careful to keep a low profile. They didn't spit where they ate, as the saying goes. We used to joke that they wouldn't cross an intersection on a yellow light. Using Israeli banks as conduits, they continued their illegal activities, but always abroad. They smuggled uranium yellow cake out of Nigeria and sold it to the highest bidder. They bought into the diamond business, smuggling uncut stones out of Russia to Amsterdam. They could get you a diesel submarine in mint condition for a mere five-and-a-half million dollars, not counting a crew of Baltic sailors to run it – that was extra. They sold Soviet surplus tanks with or without ammunition, jeeps, half-tracks, portable bridges to cross rivers, anti-aircraft missiles, radars of all sizes and shapes. Payments had to be in U.S. or Swiss currency deposited in numbered accounts in Geneva, delivery guaranteed within thirty days of the payment being received. All contracts were concluded with corporate affiliates in Liechtenstein.'

'Why Liechtenstein?'

Benny bared his teeth. 'They have strict banking secrecy laws.'

'Uh-huh.'

'The *Oligarkh*'s brother was one of those who

immigrated to Israel. His name was Akim Ugor-Zhilov. One fine day in 1993 he turned up at Ben-Gurion airport with a wife and three young children in tow, claiming that he had a Jewish grandmother and had, in any case, converted to Judaism; naturally he had affidavits to prove all this. He has a livid scar over one eye. Claims he was wounded in Afghanistan, though there is no evidence he ever served in the Soviet army. He installed himself in a heavily guarded villa in Caesarea surrounded by a high electrified wall and staffed by Armenians who served in the army and knew how to use weapons. The Russian speakers in the Mossad called them *chelovek nastroeniia* – 'moody people.' One minute Akim would scream insults at the Armenians who worked for him, the next he would be purring like a cat and bragging about his business prowess. Besides the fortress in Caesarea, he has a duplex in London's Cadogan Place and a house on the Grande Corniche above Nice.'

'How did he make ends meet in Israel?'

'He brought in something like fifty million dollars over the years and invested it in government bonds, which earn six or seven percent interest, tax free. He also has a piece of a newspaper delivery service, a hotel in Eilat, half a dozen gas stations around Haifa.'

'Where does Samat fit into this picture?'

'Akim and Tzvetan Ugor-Zhilov are brothers. It turns out there was a third brother, name of Zurab. He was a medical doctor, a member of the Armenian Communist Party and married to a Jewish woman. When Tzvetan was convicted of shaking down local merchants and sent to Siberia, his brother Zurab was arrested as an enemy of the people – under the Soviet system relatives of criminals usually suffered the same fate as the criminal. Zurab wound up in a Siberian gulag and died there of scarlet fever.'

'What happened to Zurab's wife?'

'After the arrest of her husband, we lost all trace of her. She vanished from the face of the earth. The two brothers, Tzvetan and Zurab, had been very close, which explains, in part at least, why Tzvetan loathed the Soviet system: He blamed the communists for his brother's death. Zurab left behind him a son named Samat.'

'Which makes Samat the *Oligarkh*'s and Akim's nephew.'

'Samat was taken under uncle Tzvetan's wing when he returned from Siberia; the *Oligarkh*, who had no children of his own, became a surrogate father to him. In the post-Stalinist Soviet Union, and especially after Gorbachev came on the scene, the fact that Samat's father had died in Siberia counted for him instead of against him. Samat was admitted to the elite Forestry Institute, the not-so-secret home of the Soviet space program, where he studied computer science. Later he earned a doctorate from the State Planning Agency's Higher Economic School. His computer skills must have attracted the attention of the KGB because the next thing we know he was working for the Sixth Chief Directorate, where he learned all there was to know about money laundering schemes and off-shore banks. When the *Oligarkh*, offering *krysha* and starting out in the used-car business in Armenia, decided to go into the banking business to service his expanding empire, he turned to his nephew. Samat quit the KGB and opened the first bank for Tzvetan Ugor-Zhilov in Yerevan. And it was Samat, with a reputation of something of a genius when it came to juggling accounts and obscuring currency trails, who created the money laundering scheme under which dozens of millions of dollars were siphoned off abroad and then squirreled away in off-shore banks and shell holding companies. The *Oligarkh*'s holding companies are rumored to have financial interests in a Spanish insurance company, a French hotel chain, a Swiss real estate consortium, a German movie theater chain. Thanks to Samat's sleight of hand, the threads that linked these accounts were untraceable – God knows our people tried. So for that matter did your CIA. Samat's impenetrable labyrinth of banks stretches from France to Germany to Monaco to Liechtenstein to Switzerland to the Bahamas and the Cayman Islands, not to mention Vanuatu in the South Pacific, the Isle of Man, the British Virgin Islands, Panama, Prague, Western Samoa – all of them suspected of being involved in laundering the *Oligarkh*'s considerable riches. He eventually opened bank accounts in North America, where a third of his empire's aluminum was marketed. There were shells within shells within shells. Working out of the *Oligarkh*'s isolated dacha in a village half an hour from Moscow along the Moscow-Petersburg highway, Samat was constantly shifting assets from one shell to another. Wire transfers between banks, some of which consist of nothing more than a single room and a computer on some remote island, are the easiest way to move large amounts of money – one billion in one-hundred-dollar bills weighs something like eleven tons. And it was said that the *Oligarkh*'s banker never committed anything to paper; the entire structure of his uncle's off-shore holdings was in his head.'

'Which was why it became urgent to get him out of Russia when the mob war heated up,' Martin guessed.

'Precisely. We didn't figure out the connection between Samat and the second of his two uncles, Akim, until one of our teams watching Akim's villa at Caesarea caught them on film – Akim emerged from the villa and embraced Samat as he got out of his Honda, at which point we started looking into the identity of this new immigrant who had paid in cash when he bought a split-level home in Kiryat Arba.'

Benny offered Martin a refill and, when he shook his head no, he poured himself a short one and downed it in one gulp. It was almost as if the recounting of the story had sapped his energy.

Martin said, 'Samat's wife mentioned that he once dropped her on the dunes in Caeserea while he went to see someone. Now I know whom he saw.'

Benny's pot-luck supper consisted of cold dishes he'd brought back in a doggie bag from an Arab restaurant in Abu Gosh and a bottle of red wine from the Golan. Martin, who didn't eat meat, made do with the vegetable dishes. Later, Benny broke out a bottle of fifteen-year-old French cognac and carefully poured some into two snifters. 'There was an office bash when I retired last year,' he explained. 'This was one of my going away presents, along with a jockstrap medal for long and loyal service.'

'How many years?'

'Forty two.'

'Could Israel have survived without the Mossad?' Martin asked.

'Of course. We got as much wrong as we got right. We messed up badly in seventy-three – we told Golda Meir that the Egyptians wouldn't be ready to wage war for at least ten years. A few weeks later they swarmed across the Suez canal and overran our Bar Lev fortresses stretched along the Israeli side of the waterway.'

'What went wrong?' Martin asked.

'I suppose the same thing that went wrong in the middle and late eighties when your CIA failed to predict the breakup of the Soviet empire and the demise of the communist system. Looking in from the outside, which is what I do these days, I can see that intelligence services are fatally flawed. They're self-tasking – they define the threats and then try to neutralize them. Threats that don't get defined slip through the mesh and suddenly turn up as full-blown disasters, at which point those who are outside the intelligence community start yapping about how we've been asleep on the job. We haven't been asleep. We've just been defining it differently.'

'They say a camel is a horse designed by committee,' Martin said. 'For my money, the CIA is an intelligence agency designed by the same committee.'

Benny shrugged. 'For me, Dante, it all comes down to that dead dog at the side of the road in Lebanon, the one that exploded and decapitated my son. If we had been doing the job we were paid to do, we would have anticipated the dead dog filled with PETN, and identified the terrorist behind it. I have trouble . . . I have trouble getting past that reality.' Benny climbed heavily to his feet. 'I think I'll turn in now, if you don't mind. The bed's made in the room next to the downstairs bathroom. Sleep well.'

'I never sleep well,' Martin murmured; he, too, was having trouble getting past the dead dog that decapitated Benny's son. 'I wake up in the middle of the night in a cold sweat.'

An ugly grin deformed Benny's lips. 'Occupational disease, for which there is no known cure.'

The next morning Benny drove Martin into Jerusalem and let him off at the bus station. 'One departs for Tel Aviv every twenty minutes,' he said. He handed him a slip of paper. 'Phone number for Akim in Caesarea. It's unlisted. I'd appreciate it if you didn't tell him where you got it. I'll nose around about the phone company's magnetic tapes and let you know what I find out. By the way, Samat's not in Israel. Shabak says he flew to London two days before the rabbi at Kiryat Arba reported him missing.'

'Thanks, Benny.'

'You're welcome, Dante. I hope you find what you're looking for.'

'I've trimmed my sails, Benny. I am thankful for light winds.'

From the brick guard shack atop the high wall surrounding Akim Ugor-Zhilov's seaside villa in Caesarea, Martin could almost hear the his as the sun knifed into the western Mediterranean. 'Great view,' Akim said, though he was standing with his back to it, sizing up his visitor, trying to figure out of his three-piece suit was custom made or off the rack. The livid sickle-shaped scar slashing across his high forehead over his right eye and vanishing into a long sideburn appeared to shimmer. 'The Israelis think you are an Irishman named Pippen,' Akim was saying, his heavy Russian accent surfacing indolently from the depths of his throat. 'Then someone named Odum

– which was the name on the passport you used to enter the country a week ago today – calls me from a phone booth in Tel Aviv and invites himself over to my house. Needless to say, the fact that a name is on a passport does not mean nothing. So which is it, friend, Pippen or Odum?'

'The answer is complicated—'

'Simplify.'

Martin decided to stick close to the truth. 'Pippen was a pseudonym I used years ago when I worked as a freelance explosive expert. Odum is the name I've been using since.'

Akim brightened. 'Pseudonyms are something I can relate to. In Soviet Russia, everybody who was anybody used them. You have heard of Vladimir Ilyich Ulyanov? He was known as Lenin, after the River Lena in Siberia. Iosif Vissarionovich Dzhugashvili took the alias Stalin, which meant steel, which is how he wanted people to think of him. Lev Davidovich Bronstein escaped from prison with the help of a passport made out in the name of one of his jailers, a certain Trotsky. Me myself, I managed to avoid being sent with my two brothers to the gulag by adopting the identity of a sleight-of-hand magician named Melor Semyonovich Zhitkin. You are familiar with the gulag? That's where temperatures fall below minus fifty and alcohol freezes and you suck on vodka icicles carefully so they do not stick to your tongue. Using the name Melor was a stroke of genius, even if it is me who says so. Melor is a Soviet name, stands for Marx-Engels-Lenin-Organizers-of-Revolution, which made the KGB think I was a diehard communist. I was diehard all right,' he added with a sinister cackle. 'They could not kill me, which is what made me diehard.'

Without blinking one of his heavy lids or narrowing his eyes, Akim's expression turned hard. Martin wondered how he did it. Perhaps it was the shadows playing on his face, perhaps the pupils of his eyes had actually grown smaller. Whatever it was, the effect was chilling.

Akim's voice shed its laziness. 'Pippen was an agent for the American Central Intelligence Agency who infiltrated the Hezbollah in the Bekaa Valley posing as a freelance explosive expert with connections to the IRA. You and the CIA are said to have parted company, though I am embarrassed to say none of my sources knows why. You are startled to see how well informed I am, right? You see, in Israel, as in every civilized country, information can be purchased as easily as toothpaste. Now you claim to be a Brooklyn, New York, detective named Odum. There are some who think this is simply another fabricated identity. There are others who say Odum is who you were before you were Pippen.'

'I did work for the CIA once. I no longer do. Odum is as close to the real me as I can get.'

Akim accepted this with a wary nod. 'Time for my insulin shot,' he announced. He beckoned with a pinky bearing a heavy gold ring with a diamond set into it. Martin followed him down the narrow steps and across the lawn, past the swimming pool where three women in diaphanous dresses with low necklines were playing mahjongg; he suddenly longed for the days when he investigated un-complicated things like mahjongg debts and kid-napped dogs and Chechen-run crematoriums in Little Odessa. He must have been off his rocker to think he could trace a husband who had jumped ship. Finding a needle in a haystack would be child's play by comparison. Akim reached the shaded veranda behind the mansion and motioned Martin to one of the deck chairs. Two of Akim's Armenians, wearing sports jackets that didn't conceal the auto-matic pistols in their shoulder holsters, stood nearby. A male nurse dressed in a white hospital smock was squirting liquid through a needle to expel any air left in the syringe. Akim collapsed into a deck chair and tugged the tails of his shirt out of his trousers to bare a bulging stomach. He sipped fresh orange juice through a plastic straw as the male nurse jabbed the needle under his dry skin and injected the insulin.

'Thanks a lot, Earl. See you tomorrow morning.'

'My pleasure, Mr Zhitkin.'

When the male nurse was out of ear shot, Akim said, 'As you can see I still use the name Zhitkin from time to time. Funny how you become attached to an alias that saved your life.' At the pool, one of the women shrieked with pleasure. Akim burst out angrily, 'Keep it quiet, ladies. Don't you see I have a visitor?' Massaging the spot on his stomach where the insulin had been injected, he said, 'So what do you think I can do for you, Mr Pippen or Mr Odum or whatever your name is today?'

'I really am a detective,' Martin said. 'I was hired to find your nephew, Samat, who seems to have skipped out on his wife. I was hoping you would tell me where to start looking.'

'What's she want, the wife, alimony payments? A piece of his bank account, assuming he has got a bank account? What?'

'I was hired by the wife's sister and father—'

'Who is a dead man now.'

'You *are* well informed. They hired me to find Samat and get him to give her a divorce. She's religious. Without the divorce she can't marry again, can't have children with another man.'

Akim tucked the tails of his shirt back into his trousers. 'You have met the wife in question?' he asked.

'Yes.'

'You have seen how she dresses? Who would marry *her*? Who would fuck her even to have children?'

'She's young. She may even be a virgin. The rabbi who married her thinks she and Samat never slept together.'

Akim waved his hand in disgust. 'Rabbi needs to stick to the bible. I do not want to hear private things about my nephew. Who he fucks – *whether* he fucks – is not my business.'

Another Armenian shouted something in a strange language from the driveway guard house. Akim said, 'My people want to turn on the spotlights after dark, but the neighbors complain to the police. Every time we turn them on the police come around and order us to turn them off. What kind of a country is this where a man of means cannot light up the wall around his property? It is like as if they personally hold being rich against me.'

Martin said, 'Maybe what they hold against you is the way you got rich.'

'I am starting to like you,' Akim admitted. 'You talk to me the way I talked to people like me when I was your age. Fact is if I did not get rich, someone else would have got rich in my place. Making money was the only thing to do when the Soviet Union disintegrated – it was a matter of not drowning in Gorbachev's perestroika, because only the rich were able to keep their heads above water. Anyway, America brought it on, the collapse, the gangsters, the mob wars, all of it.'

'I'm not sure I understand what you're driving at,' Martin remarked.

'I am driving at history, Mr Odum. In 1985 the Saudi oil minister, who happened to be a big wheel in the OPEC oil cartel, announced to the world that Saudi Arabia would no longer limit production to support oil prices. You want to sit there and tell me the Americans had nothing to do with this? Eight months later oil prices had plummeted seventy percent. Oil and gas exports is what kept the Soviet Union afloat for years, even for decades. The fall in oil prices started the economy downhill. Gorbachev tried to save what could be saved with his half-baked reforms, but the ship sank under his feet. When things quieted down, Russia's borders had shrunk to where they were in 1613. It is people like me and my brother who started poking through the debris and picking up the pieces. If things are better today for the masses it is because money has been trickling down. Ha! It is an economic fact that in order for wealth to trickle down, you need to have rich people at the top to do the trickling.'

'If I'm reading you correctly, you are a born-again capitalist.'

'I am a born-again opportunist. I did not go to school like Samat – I learned what I learned in the gutter. I understand capitalism contains within itself the seeds of its own destruction. Do not smile, Mr Odum. The villain was your Genry Ford. By inventing the assembly line and mass producing his cars, he lowered the price to where the assembly-line workers became consumers of their own products. And with buy-now, pay-later schemes and plastic credit cards, people were able to spend money before they accumulated it. Instant gratification killed the Protestant work ethic, which glorified work and encouraged saving. Remember you heard it here first, Mr Odum: America is on a slippery slope. It will not be far behind the Soviet Union in crashing.'

'What will be left?'

'We will be left. The *Oligarkhs*.'

One of Akim's bodyguards came around the side of the house to the veranda. He caught Akim's eye and tapped a fingernail against the crystal on his Rolex. Akim swung his short legs off the deck chair and stood up. 'I am meeting a member of the knesset for supper in Peta Tikva,' he said. 'Let us stop circling each other like wrestlers, Mr Odum. Wears out shoe leather.' Waving to the women playing mahjongg, he shouted something in Armenian. Then, gesturing for Martin to accompany him, he started toward the enormous SUV parked in the driveway, exhaust streaming from its silver tail pipe. 'How much they paying you to find Samat?' he demanded.

'I'm sorry?'

Akim stopped in his tracks and eyed Martin. Once again his face turned menacing without so much as his moving a muscle. 'Are you thick in the skull or what?' he said, his voice a low, lazy growl. 'Do I have to spell this out? Okay, I am asking what the wife's sister's father, who is a dead man, offered you to find my nephew Samat. I am saying that whatever he offered is nothing alongside what I will put on the table if you can lead me to him. What would you think of one million American dollars in cash? Or the equivalent in Swiss francs or German marks.'

'I don't get it.'

Akim groaned in exasperation. 'You do not need

213

to *get* it,' he insisted. He started toward the car again. 'A hundred and thirty million U.S. dollars have disappeared from six of my holding companies around the world that Samat controlled. That mouse of a wife in Kiryat Arba is not the only one wants a divorce. Me, too, I want one. I want to divorce my nephew. I want him to become my ex-nephew. So do we have an arrangement, Mr Odum? You have my phone number. If you get your hands on Samat before I get my hands on him, pick up the phone and give me a call and you will become a rich man. Then you will be the one to trickle down to the proletariat so they can buy more of Mr Genry Ford's automobiles.'

Stella and Martin hefted their valises onto the table and opened the locks. One of the female soldiers, wearing white surgical gloves, started to rummage through the contents. The other female soldier, her eyes black with mascara, began asking questions and ticking off items on a clipboard when she heard the answers. Had anyone given them a parcel to take out of Israel? Who had packed their valises? Had the valises been left alone after they were packed? What was the purpose of their trip to Israel? Had they been to any Arab towns or villages or the Arab sections of Jerusalem? How had they come to the airport? Had the valises been in sight all the time after they got out of the taxi?

Finally the young woman looked up. 'You are traveling together?'

'Yes,' Martin replied.

'Excuse me for being personal but you do not have the same family name.'

'We're just friends,' Stella told her.

'Excuse me again but how long have you known each other?'

'Something like two weeks now,' Martin said.

'And you decided to come to Israel together after knowing each other only two weeks?'

Stella bristled. 'Is it written that people have to be lovers in order to travel together?'

'I am only asking the questions that we're instructed to put to all the passengers.' She addressed Stella. 'I see from your tickets that you both came to Israel from Athens. But your friend is flying to London and you are flying to New York. If you're traveling together, why are you no longer traveling together?'

'I'm returning to New York to bury Kastner,' Stella explained.

'Who is Kastner?'

'My father.'

'You call your father by his family name?'

'I call my father whatever I damn well decide to call him.'

The young woman said, 'So your father is dead.' She jotted something on the space reserved for comments.

'I'm not planning to bury him alive, if that's what you mean.'

The woman remained unfazed. 'You are traveling

under an American passport but you speak English with a slight East European accent.'

'It's a Russian accent, actually. I immigrated to the United States from Russia nine years ago.'

'At that period Soviet borders were not open to people who wanted to emigrate. How did you get out of the Soviet Union?'

Stella squinted at her interrogator. 'My father and my sister and I went on vacation to the Black Sea in Bulgaria. The American CIA slipped us Greek passports and we joined a tour ship returning through the Bosporus to Piraeus.'

The two female soldiers exchanged looks. 'Airport security is not a joking matter,' snapped the one searching the luggage.

'There was a time in my life when I was paid for being funny.' Stella retorted. 'This is not one of them.'

The young woman with the clipboard raised a walkie-talkie to her lips and muttered something in Hebrew. 'Wait here a moment,' she ordered. She walked over to two men in civilian clothing and, pointing with her face at Stella and Martin, said something to them. One of the men pulled a small notebook from his pocket and thumbed through it until he came to the page he was looking for. He glanced over at Martin and then handed the female soldier an envelope. The girl shrugged. Returning to the table, she passed the envelope to Martin. 'You can close your valises and check in now.'

'What was that all about?' Stella asked Martin after they had presented their passports and boarding passes and gone up the escalator to the vast waiting room.

Martin slit open the envelope with a forefinger and unfolded the sheaf of paper in it. 'Uh-huh,' he muttered.

'Uh-huh what?'

'My old Mossad friend, the one who fed me pot-luck supper, says the magnetic tapes showing incoming and outgoing calls from Kiryat Arba were erased, just as the rabbi said. But they weren't erased by error. The Mossad did it as a favor for their CIA colleagues.'

'The plot thickens!'

'We knew the CIA didn't want me to find Samat – my old boss told me as much when she invited me down to the Chinese restaurant.' Martin thought about the exploding honey that had killed Minh and the two bullets that a sniper had shot at him in Hebron. He led Stella to one of the rows of plastic seats out of earshot of other passengers. 'How did things go with your sister after I left?'

'She tried to talk me into staying in Israel. What would I do here?'

Martin said, 'Israel is also a pressure cooker – you could go around telling anti-Israeli jokes for a living.'

'Very funny. As a matter of fact I know a good one. The rabbi told it to me. Question: What is anti-Semitism? Answer: Hating Jews more than necessary.'

'That's not funny,' Martin said.

'What's funny about it,' Stella insisted angrily, 'is that it's not funny. I could kick myself for trying to make someone without a sense of humor laugh.'

'My pal Dante had a sense of humor,' Martin said, a faraway look in his eyes. 'He left it in a room over a bar in Beirut.'

Stella decided to change the subject. 'Samat's uncle sounds like a real Russian mobster.'

'I thought he could give me an idea where to start looking for Samat. He said if he knew where to look he wouldn't need me.'

'Do you think Samat really ran off with all that money? What will his uncle do if he catches up with him?'

A voice over the public address system announced that the flight to London was about to start boarding. Martin climbed to his feet. 'What will he do to him? I suppose he'll tickle him to death.'

Stella said, 'You're stepping out of character and telling a joke.' Squinting, she studied Martin's face. 'Okay, you're not telling a joke.' Around them passengers were collecting their hand luggage and starting to head toward the stairs leading to the boarding gate. 'I wish I were going with you. I'm getting used to your sense of humor.'

'I thought you said I didn't have one.'

'That's the part I'm getting used to.' She stood

and grazed his elbow with the back of her hand. 'I hope against hope you'll call me from London.'

His eyes took in the triangle of pale skin on her chest. 'I admire your ability to hope against hope.'

She toyed nervously with the first button on her shirt that was buttoned. 'Maybe I can infect you.'

'Not likely. I've been inoculated.'

'Inoculations wear off.' She stood on her toes and kissed him lightly on the lips. 'Bye for now, Martin Odum.'

'Uh-huh. Bye.'

Crystal Quest was in wrathful dudgeon. 'There's only one thing more revolting than having to target one of your own,' she declared to the wallahs scattered around her sanctum, 'and that's bungling the hit. Where do we hire marksmen these days, will somebody kindly enlighten me. Coney Island popgun concessions where you win a plastic doll if you topple the clown into the pan filled with dish water? Oh my God, it's pathetic. *Pa-the-tic.*'

'We should have given the assignment to Lincoln Dittmann,' one of the newer wallahs suggested. 'I understand he's a crackerjack shot—'

Quest, her head angled, her eyes unblinking, gazed at the speaker as if he just might have come up with the solution to their problem. 'Where did you pick up that nugget of information?' she inquired in a husky whisper, humoring the wallah before decapitating him.

The young man sensed that he had ventured

onto quicksand. 'I was reading into the Central Registry 201 files to get a handle on our assets in the field . . .' His voice faltered. He looked around for a buoy but no one seemed interested in throwing him one.

Quest's mouth sagged open as her skull bobbed up and down in wonderment. 'Lincoln Dittmann! Now there's an idea whose time has come. Ha! Will somebody put the neophyte here out of his misery.'

Quest's chief of staff, a thick skinned timeserver who had weathered his share of storms in the DDO's seventh floor bailiwick, said very evenly, 'Dittmann and Odum are one and the same individual, Frank. You would have seen that they were cross-referenced in the 201 files if you'd read the fine print on the first page.'

'That's strike one,' Quest informed Frank. 'If you read the fine print on *your* employment contract, you'll see that we operate by the *three-strikes-and-you're-out* rule in the DDO.' She swiveled three hundred and sixty degrees in her chair as if she were winding herself up. 'Okay. I'll recapitulate,' she said, stifling her irritation. 'We made an honest effort to talk Martin Odum out of walking back the cat on Samat Ugor-Zhilov. Martin's consenting adult. He's doing what he has to do. And we're going to do what we have to do to make sure he never catches up to the Samat in question. This is a priority matter, which means it gets our full and undivided attention. Where did

Martin Odum go when he left Israel? What leads is he following? Who is he planning to talk to? And what resources do we have on the ground – what resources can we throw into the theater of eventual operations – to make sure I get to wear my sackcloth and ashes before this thing blows up in our faces?'

1997: MARTIN ODUM PLAYS INNOCENT

Leaning over the dead dog, Martin slit open its stomach with a safety razor, then reached in with the gloved hand to cut out the organs and create a stomach cavity. He motioned to one of the fedayeen students, who removed the frame from the hive and gingerly set it down on the road next to the dead dog. 'Honey is very stable,' Martin said with a laugh. 'Tell him it won't blow up in his face until it's detonated.' Using a spatula, he carefully scraped the beeswax from the honeycombs until he had accumulated a quantity the size of a tennis ball, then wired it to the tiny home-made plastic radio receiver and slipped the package into the stomach cavity. Using a thick needle and a length of butcher cord, he sewed up the opening. Rising to his feet, he stepped back to survey his handiwork.

'Any questions?' he demanded.

One of the fedayeen said something in Arabic and the Russian with the heavy gold ring on his pinky translated it into English. 'He asks from how far away can we set off the charge?'

'Depends on what equipment you're using,' Martin said. 'A cordless phone or a Walkman will work up to a half a mile away. One of those automatic pagers that doctors wear on their belts can set off a charge five, six miles away. A VHF scanner or cellular mobile phone is effective for ten or twelve miles as long as the weather is good and there is no frequency jamming.'

Martin, trailed by his three students and the translator, set off up the slope and went to ground behind the rusty wreck of a U.N. jeep. They didn't have long to wait. The Israeli patrol, led by a soldier scanning the dirt road with a magnetic mine detector, appeared around the bend. The soldier searching for mines passed his metal detector over the dog and, getting no reading, continued on. The officer behind him came abreast of the dog. Something must have caught his eye – the crude stitches on the stomach, probably – because he crouched next to the animal to have a closer look. Martin nodded at the fedayeen holding the automatic pager that had been rigged to transmit a signal to the plastic receiver inside the dog's stomach. Below, a dull blast stirred up a fume of mustard-colored smoke. When it cleared, the Israeli officer was still crouching next to the dog but his head could be seen rolling slowly toward the shoulder of the road.

'Comes as news to me that honey can explode,' the Russian whispered, his thick Slavic accent surfacing indolently from the depths of his throat.

The sulfurous stench of the burnt beeswax reached Martin's nostrils and he had trouble breathing. Gasping for air, he bolted upright in bed and blotted the cold sweat from his brow with a corner of the sheet. His heart was beating furiously; a migraine was pressing against the back of his eyeballs. For a terrible moment he didn't know who he was or where he was. He solved the second problem first when he heard the hacking cough of the old man two rooms down the corridor of the boarding house and knew where he *wasn't*: southern Lebanon. When he figured out which legend he was inhabiting, his breathing gradually returned to normal.

When his plane landed at Heathrow, four days before, Martin had breezed through passport control without a hitch. 'Here on business or pleasure, is it?' the woman custom's agent in the booth had asked. 'With any luck, pleasure, in the form of licensed tabernacles and museums, and in that order,' he'd answered. The woman had flashed a jaded smile as she stamped him into the country. 'If it's pubs you're looking for, you have come to the right corner of the world. Enjoy your stay in England.'

Collecting his valise from the baggage carousel, Martin had started following the signs marked 'Underground' when a portly young man with a peaches-and-cream complexion had materialized in front of him. 'Mr Odum, is it?' he'd asked.

'How come you know my name?'

The young man, his body wrapped in a belted trench coat a size too large for him, had ignored Martin's question. 'Could I trouble you to come with me, sir,' he had said.

'Do I have a choice?'

'I'm afraid you don't.'

'What are you, five or six?'

'MI5, thank you, kindly. Six thinks you're radioactive, wouldn't touch you with a ten-foot pole.'

Martin could see three other men in trench coats closing in on him as he limped behind the young man across the arrival hall and up a flight of steps to a balcony overlooking the hall. Peaches-and-cream stopped before an opaque glass door with the word 'Perishables' stencilled on it. He rapped on the glass twice with his knuckles, opened the door and politely stepped aside. Inside, a middle-aged woman dressed in a man's pinstriped suit and tie was busy calling up file folders on a computer terminal. Without looking up, she inclined her head toward an inner door with the words 'Supervisor, Perishables' stencilled on the glass. In the inner office, Martin discovered a black man with a shaven head studying the baggage carousels below through the slats of a partly closed venetian blind. The black man swiveled around in his seat and sank back into it. 'I'll admit it, you don't look like your average serial killer to me,' he said in a soft purr.

'What does an average serial killer look like?'

'Glassy stare as he avoids your eye, bitten finger nails, mouth drooping open, saliva drooling down the stubble of his chin. Bela Lugosi sort of role.'

'Are you a cop or a movie critic?'

Snickering at Martin's question, the Supervisor, Perishables began reading from a yellowing index card. 'Last trace we had on you, you were a bloke with two incarnations. In the first, you were Pippen, Dante, an Irishman who declined to help us with our inquiries after the IRA blew open a bus in central London. In the second, you were Dittmann, Lincoln, an American arms merchant peddling his wares to the highest bidder in the Triple Border area of Latin America.'

Martin said, 'Case of mistaken identity. You're confusing me with the antiheroes of B films.'

'Don't think we are,' the Supervisor, Perishables allowed. He arched his brows and took a long look at Martin, who was shifting his weight from one foot to the other. 'If we had chairs, I'd invite you to rest your arse on one of them. Sorry 'bout that.'

'Been sitting from Tel Aviv to here,' Martin said. 'Glad to stretch my legs.'

'Yes, well, in Israel you were passing yourself off as Martin Odum, a ruck of a private detective working out of the New York borough of' – he checked his file card – 'Brooklyn. That's quite inventive, actually. Some nonsense about hunting for a missing husband so his wife could get a religious divorce. It goes without saying, knowing your track record, neither our antenna in Israel nor our Perishables division here in London swallowed the cover story. So what are you hawking this time round, Mr Dittmann? Used one-owner Kalashnikovs? That Ukrainian-manufactured passive radar system they say can detect Stealth aircraft at five hundred miles distance? Nerve gas masquerading as talcum powder? Seed stock for biological agents that cause cholera or camelpox?'

'None of the above.' Martin smiled innocently. 'Search me.'

'Don't mind if I do.' He touched a button on a console. Martin could hear a buzzer wheeze in the outer office. The young man with the peaches-and-cream complexion and the woman who had been working on the computer terminal entered the room. 'Would you be so kind as to give us the key to your valise, Mr Dittmann,' the woman asked, 'and then disrobe.' The black man came around the desk. Martin could see he was the kind who worked out at a gym often enough to hope the man who was supposed to help the police with their inquiries would resist.

Martin glanced at the woman. 'I'm the timid type,' he remarked.

'Nothing you 'ave, guv'nor, she 'asn't seen,' snapped peaches-and-cream in a mock cockney accent.

The two men concentrated on Martin, stripping him to the skin and going over every square inch of his three piece suit, underwear and socks. The Supervisor, Perishables paid particular attention to his shoes, inserting them one at a time into a contraption that projected an X-ray image of the shoe onto a glass plate. The woman emptied the contents of the valise onto the desk and began examining each item. Toothpaste was squeezed out of its tube into a plastic container that had Chinese writing on the side. Cold capsules were split open and inspected. The small container of shaving cream was emptied and then cut in half with a hacksaw. Standing in the middle of the room, stark naked, Martin tried to imagine the anti-British joke that Stella would concoct out of the episode, but he couldn't come up with a punch line. Stella was surely right when she said he didn't have a sense of humor. 'I suppose you are going to compensate me for property destroyed,' he ventured as he started to pull on his clothing.

The Supervisor, Perishables took the question seriously. 'You go ahead and replace the items in question and send us the bill,' he said. 'If you address it to Heathrow, Perishables, it should get here, shouldn't it, lads and ladies? Everyone knows who we are. Mind if I ask how long you reckon on staying in the country, Mr Dittmann?'

'No. Ask.'

Supervisor, Perishables didn't crack a smile. 'How long you reckon on staying in the country, Mr Dittmann?'

'My name is Odum. Martin Odum. I'm in Britain to tell anti-English jokes that will spread across the country like wildfire and take people's minds off the drudgery of day-to-day life. I plan to stay as long as folks keep laughing.'

'He's certainly original,' the black man told his associates.

Peaches-and-cream accompanied Martin down to the arrival hall. 'No hurt feelings, I hope, gov'nor,' he said, falling back into his phony cockney accent and trying to sound ironic.

Following the signs leading to the underground, Martin quickly spotted the two men who were following him, one about fifteen paces behind, the other ten paces behind the first. What gave them away was their habit of concentrating on the windows of the boutiques every time he turned in their direction. As Martin reached the escalator down to the train level, the first man peeled away, the second closed the gap and a third hove into view behind him. The resources they were devoting to keep track of Lincoln Dittmann made Martin feel important; it had been a long time since anyone thought he was interesting enough to lay on a staggered tail. As always in situations like this, Martin was more preoccupied with the agents he didn't see than the ones he was meant to spot. He took the Piccadilly line to Piccadilly Circus and the escalator to the street, then leaned against the side of a kiosk to give his game leg a rest. After awhile he strolled toward Tottenham Court Road, stopping at a chemist shop to buy toothpaste and shaving cream, eventually at a pub with a neon sign sizzling over the door that brought back memories of the Beirut waterfront and Dante's Alawite prostitute named Djamillah. He settled onto a stool at the dimly-lit end of the bar and sipped at his half pint of lager until half of it was down the hatch. Opening his valise, he slipped the packet of false identity papers into the white silk bandanna, then mopped his brow with it and stuffed it into the pocket of his suit jacket. Hefting his small valise onto the bar, folding his Burberry across it, he asked the bartender to keep an eye on his things while he used the loo in the back. Martin didn't even bother checking the tails, two outside in the street, one at a corner table in the front of the pub; they were all young, and young meant green, so they would fall for the oldest trick on the books: They would keep their eyes glued to the half consumed glass of lager and the valise with the raincoat on it, and wait for him to return. Depending on their relationship with the Supervisor, Perishables, they might or might not report that Martin had gone missing when he failed to come back.

Martin remembered this particular men's lavatory from a stint in London a lifetime ago. He'd been on his way to the Soviet Union and stopped off for a briefing from MI6's East European desk. What cover had he been using then? It must have been the original Martin Odum legend because Dittmann and Pippen came later, or so it seemed to him. In a remote corner of a lobe of his brain he had filed away one of those tradecraft details that field hands collected as if they were rare stamps: This particular lavatory had a fire door that was locked, but could be opened in an emergency by breaking a glass and removing the key hanging on a hook behind it. To Martin's way of thinking, this clearly qualified as an emergency. He found the glass and retrieved the key and opened the fire door. Moments later he found himself in a narrow passage that gave onto a side street and, as luck would have it, a taxi stand.

'Paddington,' he told the driver.

He changed taxis twice more and only gave his real destination to the final driver. 'Golders Green,' he said, settling into the backseat and enjoying his fleeting triumph over the warm bodies from five.

'Any particular place on Golders Green?' the driver asked over the intercom.

'You can let me off near the clock at the top. I'll walk from there.'

'Right you are, gov'nor. You American, are you?'

'What makes you think that?'

'It's the accent, gov'nor. I know American when I hear it.'

'Actually I'm Polish,' Martin had said, 'but I've lived in America and it rubbed off.'

The driver had tittered into the microphone. 'I can tell someone what's pulling me leg, gov'nor. If you're Polish, that makes me an Eskimo.'

Martin had paid off the taxi in front of the Golders

Green underground station. Standing under the word 'Courage' engraved in the stone monument at the top of Golders Green, he took his bearings, then set off down the broad avenue awash in sunlight and filled with midday pedestrians – Filipino maids pushing old ladies tucked into wheel chairs, teenage boys in embroidered skull caps careening past on mountain bikes, dozens of ultra-religious women wearing wigs and long dresses window shopping in front of stores with signs in English and Hebrew. Martin found a second-hand store run by a Jewish charity and bought himself an old valise that looked as if it had been around the world several times. He made a slit in the frayed silk lining under the lid and hid his stash of documents, then filled the valise with threadbare but serviceable clothing. He came across a second-hand Aquascutum that they were practically giving away because the belt was missing and the hem was in tatters. At a chemists, he bought more toothpaste, a disposable razor and a small tube of shaving cream. On Woodstock Avenue off Golders Green he spotted a ramshackle house next to a synagogue with a sign on the unkempt lawn advertising rooms for rent. He paid the grumpy landlady for a week in advance, stored his gear and went around the corner for a bite to eat at a kosher delicatessen across the street from a church. Midafternoon he walked up Golders Green to the Chinese Medicinal Center for a session of acupuncture on his game leg. When he complained that his leg felt sorer after the acupuncture, the old Chinese man, plucking the long needles deftly out of Martin's skin, said it was well known that things had to get worse before they could get better. Leaving a ten pound note on the counter, Martin promised he would bear that in mind. Starting back toward the rooming house, he noticed he was able to walk with less pain than before; he wondered whether it was due to the acupuncture needles or the power of suggestion. He bought a phone card at a tobacco shop and ducked into a fire-engine red booth on the corner of Woodstock and Golders Green that had a burnt phone book dangling from a chain. He rummaged in his wallet for the scrap of paper with the phone number that Elena had found on the back of the strudel recipe and, inserting his plastic card, dialed it.

Martin retrieved Dante Pippen's rusty Irish accent for the occasion. 'And who would I be speaking to, then?' he inquired when a female voice came on the line.

'Mrs Rainfield, dear.'

'Good morning to you, Mrs Rainfield. This is Patrick O'Faolain from the phone company. I'm up on a pole on Golders Green trying to sort out your lines. Could you do me the favor of pressing the number five and the number seven on your phone, in that order.'

'Five, then seven?'

'That's the ticket, Mrs Rainfield.'

'Did you hear it?'

'Loud and clear. Do it once more to be sure, will you, now?'

'Okay?'

'Beautiful. We ought to be hiring the likes of you.'

'Will you tell me what's going on?'

'Don't ask me how but your cable seems to have gotten itself twined around your neighbors' lines. One of them complained she heard cross talk when she tried to use her phone. Did you experience any static on yours, Mrs Rainfield?'

'Now that you mention it, the phone did seem fuzzier than usual this morning.'

'You ought to be hearing me clear as a bell now.'

'I am, thank you.'

'We spend most of our time climbing up phone poles to fix things that aren't broken. Now and then it's gratifying to fix something that is. You get half the credit – it was child's play once you hit the five and the seven. For my work sheet I'll be needing your full name and an address to go with your phone.'

'I'm Doris Rainfield,' the woman said, and she gave an address on North End Road, a continuation of Golders Green, behind the railroad station.

'Thanks a mill.'

'Ta.'

Martin pressed the buzzer next to the enormous steel door with 'Soft Shoulder' engraved on a brass plaque and looked up into the security camera.

234

There was a burst of static over the intercom. A woman's nasal voice surfed above the static.

'If you're delivering, you need to go round to the loading dock in back.'

'Mr Martin Odum,' Martin called, 'come to see the director of Soft Shoulder.'

'Are you the bloke what's shipping the prostheses to Bosnia?'

'Afraid not. I was sent by a friend of the director's, a Mr Samat Ugor-Zhilov.'

'Wait a min, love.'

The static gave way to an eerie quiet. A moment later the woman whom Martin took for Mrs Rainfield came back on the intercom. 'Mr Rabbani, he wants to know how you know Mr Ugor-Zhilov.'

'Tell him,' Martin said, employing the phrase Kastner had used the day they met on President Street, 'we're birds of a feather.'

'Come again?'

'Yes, well, you can tell Mr Rabbani that I know Samat from Israel.'

There was another interval of silence. Then a discreet electric current reached the lock in the door and it clicked open the width of a finger. Martin pushed it wide open and strode into the warehouse. He heard the door click closed behind him as he headed down the cement passageway lined with calendars from the 1980s, each with a photograph of a spread-eagled movie starlet flirting with nakedness. In the glass enclosed cubical at the end of the passageway, a young woman with pointed breasts and short hair the color and texture of straw sat behind a desk, painting her fingernails fuchsia. Martin poked his head through the open door. 'You will be Doris Rainfield,' he guessed.

The woman looked up, intrigued. 'Samat went and told you 'bout me, did he, dear?' She batted the fingers of her right hand in the air to dry the nail polish. 'I like Samat, I do. Oh, he's one for putting on airs, waltzing in with that topcoat of 'is flung over 'is shoulders like it was some kinda cape or other. He looked like the sheik in one of them Rudy Valentino silent period pictures, if you get my drift.'

'I do get your drift, Mrs Rainfield.'

The woman lowered her voice to share a confidence. 'Truth is I'm not Mrs Rainfield. I used to be Mrs Rainfield but I got myself legally hitched six weeks and three days back to Nigel Froth, which makes me Mrs Froth, doesn't it, dear? Do you recognize the name? My Nigel's a world class snooker player. Made the quarter finals of the UK snooker championship last year, lost to the bloke who came in second, he did, which was a feather in 'is cap, I'm referring to Nigel's cap, not the bloke who came in second's cap. I still use my first husband's name at the office because that's what Mr Rabbani calls me. All the paperwork 'ere is in the name of Rainfield and he says it'd be a bloody pain in the you know what to switch over.'

Martin leaned against the door jamb. 'Does Mrs Rainfield act any differently than Mrs Froth?'

'I s'pose she does, now that you mention it. My Mr Froth fancies me in miniskirts and tight sweaters, he does. Mr Rainfield wouldn't 'ave let me outa me house dressed like this. It's a lot like Samat's cape, isn't it, dear? What you wear is who you want to be.' Fluttering unnaturally long lashes, Mrs Rainfield pointed out the door at the bitter end of the passageway with her eyes. 'Through there, then cross the warehouse on a diagonal and you'll fall on Mr Rabbani's bailiwick. His factotum, an Egyptian named Rachid – trust me, you won't miss him – minds the door.'

'Is Rachid his real name or is it a matter of Mr Rabbani not wanting to redo the paperwork?'

Mrs Rainfield giggled appreciatively.

Martin said, 'Thank you' and started down the corridors created by stacks of cartons, all of them stencilled with the word 'Prosthesis' and 'Arm' or 'Leg' and a measurement in inches and centimeters, along with a notation in smaller print that the articles had been manufactured in the United States of America. Above Martin's head, diffused sunlight streamed through skylights stained with soot and bird droppings. A heavy-set man with unshaven jowls and untidy hair, clearly the body guard, loomed beyond the last cartons. A handwritten nametag pinned to the wide lapel of his double-breasted suit jacket identified him as Rachid.

'You carrying?' he inquired, sizing Martin up with eyes that conveyed indifference to the visitor's fate in the unlikely event he resisted inspection.

Martin played a role he wasn't accustomed to: innocent. 'Carrying what?'

Rachid snapped, 'Something the municipal police might mistake for a handgun.'

Grinning, Martin spread his legs apart and raised his arms. The bodyguard frisked him very professionally, passing his hand so high up the crotch that he grazed his penis with his knuckles, causing Martin to shudder.

'You ticklish, then?' the bodyguard remarked with a smirk. He inclined his head in the direction of a door with a neatly lettered plastic placard on it that said 'Taletbek Rabbani – Export.' Martin knocked. After a moment he knocked again and heard the scratchy voice of an old man call out weakly, 'So what are you waiting on, my son, a hand delivered invite?'

Looking like a parenthesis, Taletbek Rabbani sat on a high stool hunched over a high desk, a thick cigarette dangling from his bonedry lips, a smog of smoke hovering over his bald head like a rain cloud. An old man who must have been nudging ninety, he was not much thicker that the pencil clasped in his arthritic fingers. A tuft of coarse white hair protruded from under his lower lip and served as a receptacle for the ash that dropped off the burning end of the cigarette. A swell of warm air enveloped Martin as he stepped into the room; the old man kept his office heated to near sauna temperatures. Settling onto a tattered settee with the tag 'Imported from Sri Lanka' still attached to one spindly wooden leg, Martin could hear the water gurgling through the radiators. 'Taletbek Rabbani sounds like a Tajik name,' he remarked. 'If I had to take a wild guess, I'd say you were a Tajik from the steppes of the Panjshir Valley north of Kabul. I seem to remember there was a tribal chief named Rabbani who presided over a cluster of mountain villages near the frontier with Uzbekistan.'

Rabbani waved his skeletal fingers to dispel the cigarette smoke and get a better look at his visitor. 'You have been to Afghanistan?' he demanded.

'In a previous incarnation I hung out for the better part of a year near the Khyber Pass.'

Rabbani was still trying to get a handle on Martin's curriculum vitae. 'What were you doing, my son, buying or selling?'

'Buying. Stories. I was debriefing fighters going into and out of Afghanistan and writing them up for a wire service.'

An ephemeral smile crossed Rabbani's age-ravaged eyes. 'Wire service, my foot. Only people who hung out at the Khyber Pass were American intelligence agents. Which means you were on the same side as my older brother, the tribal chieftain Rabbani.'

Martin had guessed as much once he'd placed Rabbani's name; he hoped that this would get him off on the right track with the old codger who, he now noticed, kept his left hand out of sight below the desk. His fingers were certainly wrapped around the butt end of a pistol.

'What happened to your brother after the Russians were kicked out?'

'Along with everyone else in the valley, he got caught up in the civil war – he fought alongside Ahmed Shah Massoud against the Taliban when they abandoned their medrassahs in Pakistan and started to infiltrate into Afghanistan. One day the Taliban invited my brother to meet under a white flag in the outskirts of Kabul.' The same smile appeared in Rabbani's eyes, only this time it was tainted with bitterness. 'I advised him against going, but he was strong headed and fearless and shrugged off my counsel. And so he went. And so the Taliban cut his throat, along with those of his three bodyguards.'

'I vaguely remember the incident.'

Rabbani's left hand came into view, which told Martin that he had passed muster.

'To have been at the Khyber, to remember Rabbani,' the old man said, 'you must have worked for the CIA.' When Martin neither confirmed nor denied it, Rabbani nodded slowly. 'I understand there are things that are never spoken aloud. You must forgive an old man for his lack of discretion.'

Martin could hear trains pulling into or out of the station next to the warehouse with the rhythmic throb that was almost as satisfying as travel itself.

'If you don't mind my asking, Mr Rabbani, how did you wind up in London?'

'I was dispatched by my brother to England to purchase medical supplies for our wounded fighters. When my brother was murdered, a cousin on my mother's side profited from my absence to usurp the leadership of the tribe. My cousin and I are sworn enemies – tribal custom prevents me from exposing to you the reason for this feud while there is no representative of my cousin present to defend the other side of the matter. Suffice it to say that it became healthier for me to stay on in London.'

'And you went into the business of selling prostheses with Samat?'

'I don't know how well you know Samat,' Rabbani said, 'but he is a philanthropist at heart. He provided the start-up money to lease this warehouse and open the business.'

'The Samat I know does not have a reputation as a philanthropist,' Martin said flatly. 'He wheels and deals in many of the weapons that lead to the loss of limbs. If he is in the business of selling false limbs to war-torn countries, there must be a healthy profit in it.'

'You misread Samat, my son,' Rabbani insisted. 'And you misread me. Samat is too young to be interested only in profit, and I am too old. The cartons filled with false limbs that you saw on the way to my office are sold at cost.'

'Uh-huh.'

'You clearly do not believe me.' Rabbani slipped awkwardly off of the high stool and, retrieving two wooden canes that had been out of sight behind the desk, made his way across the room. When he stood before the settee, he hiked the trouser on his left leg, revealing a skin-colored plastic prosthesis with a Gucci loafer fitted onto the end of it.

Martin asked quietly, 'How did you lose your leg?'

'I was told it was a land mine.'

'Don't you remember?'

'Some nights fleeting images of what happened surface in my brain: a deafening explosion, the taste of dirt in my mouth, the stickiness of my stump when I reached down to touch it, the feeling I had for months that the leg was still there and I could feel pain in it. The images seem to come from the life of another, and so I have trouble reconstructing the event.'

'Psychiatrists call that a survival mechanism, I think.'

Leaning on one cane and then the other, Rabbani returned to his high chair and hefted himself into it. 'I first met Samat when I was buying Soviet surplus arms and munitions in Moscow in the early nineties so that Massoud and my brother could defend the Panjshir. The Russian army units pulling out of their bases in the former German Democratic Republic after the Berlin Wall came down were selling off everything in their arsenals – rifles, machine guns, mortars, land mines, radios, jeeps, tanks, ammunition. Samat, representing the business interests of someone very powerful, was the middleman. It was a period of my life when I felt no guilt about buying and using these arms. I did to the Taliban what they eventually did to me. That was before I myself walked on a land mine. Take it from someone who has been there, Mr Odum, it's an exhilarating experience, stepping on a mine. One instant you are attached to the ground, the next you are defying gravity, flailing away in the air. When you fall back to earth you have one limb less and nothing – not your body, not your mind – is ever the same. It was Samat who arranged for me to be flown to a Moscow hospital. It was Samat who came around with my manufactured-in-America artificial leg. It would not be an exaggeration to say that I became another person. Which is why you find me presiding over a warehouse filled with prostheses that we sell at cost.'

'And where does the name "Soft Shoulder" come from?'

'Samat and I were traveling in the U.S. once,' Rabbani explained. 'We were driving a large American automobile from Santa Fe, in New Mexico, to New York, when we stumbled across the idea of going into the business of exporting artificial limbs at prices that would make them more easily affordable to the victims of war. We had pulled up at the side of the road to urinate when we shook hands on the project. Next to the car was a sign that read "Soft Shoulder." Neither of us knew what it meant, but we decided it would make a fitting name for our company.'

The intercom buzzed. Rabbani depressed a lever with a deft jab of a cane and barked irritably, 'And what is it now, my girl?'

Mrs Rainfield's voice came over the speaker. 'Truck's here for the Bosnia shipment, Mr Rabbani. I sent them round back to the loading dock. They gave me a certified bank check for the correct amount.'

'Call the bank to confirm it issued the check. Meanwhile get Rachid to supervise the loading.' Rabbani tripped the lever closed with his cane, cutting the connection. 'Can't be too vigilant,' he moaned. 'Lot of shady dealers make a lot of money peddling prostheses – they are not happy when someone else sells them at cost.' He pried the stub of the cigarette out of his mouth and lobbed it across the room into a metal waste basket. 'When were you in Israel, Mr Odum?'

'Went there roughly ten days back.'

'You told Mrs Rainfield to tell me you knew Samat from Israel. Why did you lie?'

Martin understood that a lot depended on how he answered the question. 'In order to get past the front door,' he said. He angled his head. 'What makes you think I was lying?'

Rabbani pulled an enormous handkerchief from a pocket and wiped the perspiration under his shirt collar at the back of his neck. 'Samat left Israel before you got there, my son.'

'How do you know that?'

The old man shrugged his bony shoulders. 'I will not ask you how you know what you know. Do me the courtesy of not asking me how I know what I know. Samat fled from Israel. If you came knocking on my door today, it is because you somehow found a record of his phone conversations and traced the calls he made to this address in London, despite the fact that these phone records were supposed to have been destroyed. I will not ask you how you did that – the phone company is not permitted to reveal addresses corresponding to unlisted numbers.'

'Why did you let me in if you knew I was lying about Samat?'

'I calculated if you were clever enough to find me, you might be clever enough to lead me to Samat.'

'Join the queue, Mr Rabbani. It seems as if everyone I meet wants to find Samat.'

'They want to find Samat in order to kill him. I want to find him in order to save his life.'

'Do you know why he fled Israel?'

'Certainly I know. He fled from Israel for the same reason he fled to Israel. Chechen hit men were after him. Have been since the Great Mob Wars in Moscow. Samat works for the *Oligarkh* – you're smart, I'll give you that, but not so smart that you've heard of him.'

245

Martin couldn't resist. 'Samat's uncle, Tzvetan Ugor-Zhilov.'

The old man cackled until the laugh turned into a grating cough. Saliva trickled from a corner of his mouth. He dabbed at it with the handkerchief as he gasped for breath. 'You *are* a smart one. Do you know what happened during the Great Mob War?'

'The Slavic Alliance battled the Chechen gangs. Over territory. Over who controlled what.'

'At the height of the war the Chechens had about five hundred fighters working out of the Rossiya Hotel not far from the Kremlin. The leader of the Chechens was known by his nom de guerre, which was the Ottoman. The *Oligarkh* arranged to have him and his lady friend at the time kidnapped. Samat was sent to negotiate with the Chechens – if they wanted their leader back they would have to abandon Moscow and settle for some of the smaller cities that the *Oligarkh* was willing to cede to them. The Chechens said they needed to discuss the matter with the others. Samat decided they were playing for time – even if they agreed, there was no guarantee they would give up Moscow. He persuaded the *Oligarkh* that the Chechens needed to be taught a lesson. Next morning people going to work found the body of the Ottoman and his lady friend hanging upside down from a lamppost near the Kremlin wall – newspapers compared it to the death of Mussolini and his mistress in the closing days of the Great Patriotic War.'

'And you call Samat a philanthropist?'

'We all of us have many sides, my son. That was one side of Samat. The other was selling prostheses at cost to provide limbs to land-mine victims. I was one person before I stepped on the land mine and another after. What about you, Mr Odum? Are you one dimensional or do you have multiple personalities like the rest of us?'

Martin brought a hand up to his forehead to contain the migraine throbbing like the trains pulling into and out of the station. Across the room the old man carefully pulled another cigarette from a desk drawer and lit it with a wooden match, which he ignited with a flick of his fingernail. Once again the smog of a rain cloud rose over his head. 'Who is paying you to find Samat, Mr Odum?'

Martin explained about the wife Samat had abandoned in Israel; how she needed to find her husband so he could grant her a religious divorce in front of a rabbinical court. Puffing away on his cigarette, Rabbani thought about this. 'Not like Samat to abandon a wife like that,' he decided. 'If he ran for it, it means the Chechens tracked him to that Jew colony next to Hebron. Chechens have long knives and long memories – I've been told some of them carry photographs cut from the newspapers of the Ottoman and his lady hanging upside down from a Moscow lamppost. The Chechens must have been knocking on Samat's door, figuratively speaking, for him to cut and run.'

Rabbani hauled open another drawer and retrieved a metal box, which he opened with a key attached to the fob of the gold watch in his vest pocket. He took out a wad of English bank notes and dropped them on the edge of the desk nearest Martin. 'I would like to find Samat before the Chechens catch up with him. I would like to help him. He does not need money – he has access to all the money he could ever want. But he does need friends. I could arrange for him to disappear into a new identity; into a new life even. So will you work for me, Mr Odum? Will you find Samat and tell him that Taletbek Rabbani stands ready to come to the assistance of his friend?'

'If Samat is being hunted by the Chechens, helping him could come back to haunt you.'

Rabbani reached for one of the canes and tapped it against his false limb. 'I owe Samat my leg. And my leg has become my life. A Panjshiri never turns his back on such a debt, my son.'

Martin pushed himself to his feet and walked over to the desk and fanned the stack of bank-notes as if it were a deck of cards. Then he collected them and shoved them into a pocket. 'I hope you are going to tell me where to start to look.'

The old man picked up the pencil, scratched something on the back of an envelope and handed it to Martin. 'Samat came here after he left Israel – he wanted to touch base with the projects to which he was especially attached. He stayed two days, then took a plane to Prague. There is an affiliate in Prague – another one of Samat's pet projects – that's doing secret work for him on the side. I met one of the directors, a Czech woman, when she came here to see Samat. She gave me her card in case I ever visited Prague.'

'What kind of secret work?'

'Not sure. I overheard the woman talking with Samat – the project had something to do with trading the bones of a Lithuanian saint for sacred Jewish Torah scrolls. Don't ask what the bones of a saint have to do with Torah scrolls. I don't know. Samat was very compartmented. The Samat I knew exported prostheses at cost. There were other Samats that I only caught glimpses of – one of them was concocting a scheme at the address I gave you in Prague.'

Martin glanced at the paper, then held out a hand. Rabbani's bony fingers, soft with paraffin-colored skin, gripped his as if he didn't want him to leave. Words barely recognizable as human speech bubbled up from the old man's larynx. 'I see things from the perspective of someone who is knocking at death's door. Apocalypse is just around the corner, my son. You are looking at me as if I belong in an asylum, Mr Odum. *I am in an asylum.* So come to think of it are you. Western civilization, or what is left of it, is one big asylum. The happy few who understand this are more often than not diagnosed as crazy and hidden away in lunatic bins.' Rabbani struggled for breath. 'Find

Samat before they do,' he gasped. 'He is one of the happy few.'

'I'll do my best,' Martin promised.

Making his way back through the aisles toward the front of the warehouse, Martin passed three lean men wrestling cartons onto a dolly. Rabbani's body-guard, Rachid, stood apart, watching them with his unblinking eyes. The three men, all clean shaven, were dressed alike in orange jumpsuits with the insignia of a shipping company sewn over the zipper of the breast pocket. As Martin walked past, they raised their eyes to scrutinize him; none of them smiled. There was something about the men that troubled Martin – but he couldn't put his finger on it.

Mrs Rainfield waved from her cubical as he headed down the cement corridor toward the front door. As he reached it a discreet crackle of electric current sizzled through the lock and the door clicked open. Out in the street, Martin waved cheerfully at the security camera over his head. He was still trying to figure out what it was about the three shippers that had caught his eye as he started up the street in the direction of Golders Green and the rooming house.

The three men in orange jumpsuits piled the cartons so high on the dolly that the topmost one began to teeter. Rachid jumped forward to keep it from falling to the ground. 'Watch what you are doing—' he started to say. He turned back to find himself staring into the bore of a silencer screwed into the barrel of an Italian Beretta. It was aimed directly at his forehead.

Rachid nodded imperceptibly, a Muslim authorizing the assassin to end his life. The man in the orange jumpsuit nodded back, acknowledging that Rachid was the master of his destiny, and squeezed the trigger. There was a muted hiss from the handgun, which recoiled slightly as a neat puncture wound materialized in Rachid's forehead. The second man caught him under the armpits and lowered the body to the cement floor. The third man crossed the warehouse to Mrs Rainfield's office and rapped his knuckles on the glass door. She motioned for him to come in. 'What can I do you, dear?' she asked.

He produced a silenced pistol from the zippered pocket of his jumpsuit and shot her through the heart. 'Die,' he replied as she slumped onto the desk, her lifeless eyes frozen open in bewilderment.

Back in the warehouse, the two other men knocked on the door of Taletbek Rabbani's office and entered. One of them held out the manifest. 'Mr Rabbani, there are two cartons of size six foot-prostheses missing,' one of them said as they approached his desk.

'That is absolutely impossible,' Taletbek Rabbani said, snatching up his canes and pushing himself to his feet. 'Did you ask Rachid—' He became aware of the handgun fitted with a silencer inches from his skull. 'Who are you?' he whispered harshly. 'Who sent you?'

'We are who we are,' the man with the gun responded. He wrenched the canes out of Taletbek's hands and, grabbing him by the wrists, dragged him across the warehouse, a Gucci loafer trailing at the end of the plastic prosthesis, to a stanchion near the body of Rachid. The man who had shot Mrs Rainfield brought over a spool of thick orange packing cord and tied the old man's wrists. Then he lobbed the spool over an overhead pipe and pulled on the cord until Taletbek's arms, stretched directly above his head, were straining in their shoulder sockets and the toe of his good foot was scraping the cement. The man who appeared to be the leader of the team approached the old man.

'Where is Samat?'

Taletbek shook his head. 'How is it possible to tell you something I myself do not know?'

'You will forfeit your life if you refuse to help us find him.'

'When you arrive in hell, I will be waiting for you, my son.'

'Are you a Muslim?' the leader inquired.

Taletbek managed to nod.

'Do you believe in the Creator, the Almighty? Do you believe in Allah?'

Taletbek indicated he did.

'Have you made pilgrimage to Mecca?'

Rabbani, his face contorted with pain, nodded again.

'Say your prayers, then. You are about to meet the one true God.'

The old man shut his eyes and murmured: *'Ash'hadu an la illahu ila Allah wa'ash'hadu anna Muhammadan rasulu Allah.'*

From the inside of his boot, the leader of the team of killers drew a razor sharp dagger with a groove along its thin blade and a yellowing camel bone handle. He stepped to one side of the old man and probed the soft wrinkles of skin on his thin neck looking for a vein.

'For the last time, where is Samat?'

'Samat who?'

The leader found the vein and slowly imbedded the blade into Taletbek's neck until only the hilt remained visible. Blood spurted, staining the killer's orange jumpsuit before he could leap out of the way. The old man breathed in liquidy gasps, each shallower than the previous one, until his head plunged forward and his weight sagged under the cord, pulling his arms out of the shoulder sockets.

Martin dialed Stella's number in Crown Heights from the booth and listened to the phone ringing on the other end. It dawned on him that he was looking forward to hearing her voice – there was no denying that she had gotten under his skin. 'That really you, Martin?' she exclaimed before he could finish a sentence. 'Goddamn, I'm glad to hear from you. Missed you, believe it or not.'

'Missed you, too,' he said before he knew what he would say. In the strained silence, he imagined her tongue flicking over the chip in her front tooth.

She cleared her throat. 'What do you say we get the business part of the conversation out of the way first. Yes, there was an autopsy. For obvious reasons, it was done by a CIA doctor. The FBI man who Kastner dealt with when he needed something sent it to me, along with a covering letter. In it he said the police found no evidence of a break-in. The doctor who performed the autopsy concluded that Kastner'd died of a heart attack.'

Martin was thinking out loud. 'Maybe you should get a second opinion.'

'Too late for another autopsy.'

'What does that mean, too late?'

'When nobody claimed Kastner's body, the CIA had him cremated. All they gave me was his ashes. I walked halfway across the Brooklyn Bridge and screamed out the punch line from one of those old anti-Soviet jokes that Kastner particularly liked – "Be careful what you struggle for because you may get it" – and scattered the ashes in the river.'

'Uh-huh.'

'I hate when you say *Uh-huh* because I'm never sure what you mean by it.'

'I don't mean anything. I'm just buying time for my brain to work things out. Did you get to talk to Xing in the Chinese restaurant?'

'Yes. He was very suspicious until I convinced him I was a friend of yours. He was annoyed you hadn't come back for the funeral of the Chinese girl your bees killed.'

'What did you tell him?'

'I said you were busy detecting and he seemed to settle for that. The girl—'

'Her name was Minh.'

'Minh died in great pain, Martin. The police who investigated it decided her death was an accident.'

Martin offered up a short laugh. 'The honey exploded by accident.'

'What does that mean?'

'Nothing. Did you find out what she was wearing when the bees attacked her?'

'The *Daily News* story said she was wearing a white jumpsuit with the sleeves and legs rolled up. A pith helmet with mosquito netting attached to it was found near her body.' A police cruiser with a screaming siren tore past Martin, drowning out all conversation. When it quieted down Martin could hear Stella saying, 'Oh, I see.'

'What do you see?'

'The rolled up sleeves and legs – it was your jump suit, wasn't it? Do you think . . . could it be that someone . . . oh, dear.' Stella lowered her voice. 'I'm frightened, Martin.'

'Me, too, I'm frightened. Seems as if I'm always frightened.'

'Did your trip work out for you?'

'Don't know yet.'

'Are you coming back?'

'Not right now.'

'Want me to fly over and meet up with you? Two heads are better than one, remember. Two hearts, also.' He could almost hear the slight gasp of embarrassment. 'No strings attached, Martin, it goes without saying.'

'Why do things that go without saying get said?'

'To avoid confusion. Hey, you want to hear a good Russian joke?'

'Save it for when we meet again.'

'I'll settle for that.'

'For what?'

She said it very quietly. 'For our meeting again.'

Another police car could be heard coming down Golders Green, its siren wailing. Martin said quickly, 'Bye.'

'Yeah. Bye. Take care of yourself.'

'Uh-huh.'

The police car was almost abreast of Martin and Stella had to shout to be heard. 'There you go again.'

Martin found a pub at the top of Golders Green and slid into a booth at the back. The waitress, a skinny young thing with one ear and one nostril and one eyebrow pierced and her navel visible below her short T-shirt, came around with the menu printed in chalk on a small blackboard. Martin ordered the special of the day and a half-pint of lager. He was sipping the lager and waiting for the special when there was a commotion in the front of the pub. People abandoned the bar and their tables to gather under the television on an overhead shelf. The screen was not facing the back of the pub so Martin couldn't make out what was being said. When the waitress came around with the pot pie and chips, he asked her what was happening.

'People've been murdered in a warehouse stone's throw from 'ere. Most exciting thing that's 'appened on Golders Green in a month of Sundays, don't you know. That's what all them police sirens was about.'

Martin went around to the front of the pub and caught the end of the news item. 'A warehouse, located immediately behind the train station, was the grisly scene of the multiple murders,' the male anchor said. 'According to municipal records, the warehouse was being used as a depot for prostheses being shipped by a humanitarian group called Soft Shoulder to war ravaged countries.' The female anchor chimed in: 'We're now being told that three bodies were removed from the warehouse. They were identified as a Mr Taletbek Rabbani, aged eighty-eight, an Afghan refugee who directed the humanitarian operation and who bled to death from a knife wound to his neck while tied to an overhead pipe; his associate, an Egyptian known only as Rachid, who was killed by a single shot to the head; and a secretary, Mrs Doris Rainfield, who was also shot to death. A fourth woman is missing and police fear she may have been kidnapped by the team of hit men when they fled the scene of the crime. She was identified as Mrs Froth, and was said to be the wife of the well known snooker player Nigel Froth.'

Returning to his table, Martin found he'd lost all appetite for the pot pie. He raised a finger and caught the waitress's eye and called, 'Whiskey, neat. Make that a double.'

He was nursing the whiskey and his bruised emotions when he suddenly remembered what it was about the three men in orange jumpsuits at the warehouse that had troubled him. Of course! Why hadn't he seen it sooner? They had all been clean shaven. The upper halves of their faces had been ruddy, as if they'd spent most of their waking hours outdoors. But the lower halves had been the color of sidewalk – one of the men had razor nicks on his skin – which suggested that they had only recently shaved off thick beards in order to make it more difficult to identify them as Muslims.

Martin closed his eyes and summoned up an image of Taletbek Rabbani suspended from an over-head pipe while an assassin stabbed him in the neck. Trying to pick up Samat's trail, the Chechens, beardless in London, had come back to haunt the old one-legged Tajik warrior sooner than he'd imagined.

1994: THE ONLY FODDER WAS CANNON FODDER

'When we left off last week, Martin,' Dr Treffler was saying, 'you were commenting on the fact' – her eyes flicked down to the notes in her loose-leaf notebook – 'that you are able to do some things well the first time you try.'

The Company psychiatrist, wearing a tight skirt cut above the knee, uncrossed and recrossed her legs. As her thigh flashed into view, Martin turned his head away. He understood that everything she did had a purpose; the business with the legs was her way of harvesting information about his sex drive, assuming he had a sex drive. He wondered what another psychiatrist would make of Dr Treffler's way of taking notes, filling the loose-leaf pages from top to bottom and edge to edge with a runty scrawl, the letters all leaning into some nonexistent emotional blizzard. Solzhenitsyn had written *Ivan Denisovich* that way, but he'd been coming off eight years in Stalin's gulag. What was her excuse? What did it mean when you didn't like margins?

'Yes, I remember now,' Martin said finally. through the panes of the window and the green metal mesh (put there to keep clients from jumping?) he could make out a bit of Maryland countryside; could see the last brown leaves clinging to the branches of trees. He felt an instinctive admiration for their tenacity. 'It's always intrigued me,' he continued because she expected him to; because she sat there with her legs crossed and her thigh visible and her Mont Blanc fountain pen poised over the loose-leaf page. 'It struck me as funny how some things you do, you do them well the first time.'

'Such as?' she inquired in a voice so toneless it betrayed absolutely no curiosity about the answer.

'Such as peeling a tangerine. Such as cutting a fuse for plastic explosive long enough to give you time to get out of its killing range. Such as pulling off a brush pass with a cutout in one of Beirut's crowded souks.'

'What legend were you using in Beirut?'

'Dante Pippen.'

'Wasn't he the one' – Bernice (they'd been on a first name basis for the last several sessions) had flipped to another page in her loose-leaf notebook – 'who was supposed to have been teaching history at a junior college? The one who wrote a book on the Civil War that he printed privately when he couldn't find a publisher willing to take it on?'

'No, you're thinking of Lincoln Dittmann, with two t's and two n's. Pippen was the Irish dynamiter from Castletownbere who started out as an explosives instructor on the Farm. Later, posing as an IRA dynamiter, he infiltrated a Sicilian Mafia family, the Taliban mullahs in Peshawar, a Hezbollah unit in the Bekaa Valley of Lebanon. It was this last mission that blew his cover.'

Dr Treffler nodded as she added a note to the page. 'I have a hard time keeping track of your various identities.'

'Me, too. That's why I'm here.'

She looked up from the loose-leaf notebook. 'Are you sure you have identified all of your operational biographies?'

'I've identified the ones I remember.'

'Do you have the feeling you might be repressing any?'

'Don't know. According to your theory, there's good chance I'm repressing at least one of them.'

'The literature on the subject more or less agrees—'

'I thought you weren't convinced that I fit neatly into the literature on the subject.'

Dr Treffler flashed one of her very rare smiles, which looked like a foreign object on her normally expressionless face. 'You are *hors genre*, Martin, there's no doubt about it. Nobody in my profession has come across anyone quite like you. It will cause quite a stir when I publish my paper—'

'Changing the names to protect the innocent.'

'Changing the names to protect the guilty, too.'

'You're getting into the spirit of things, Bernice.

The people who pay you for shrinking my head will be very pleased.'

'A psychiatrist doesn't shrink the patient's head, Martin. We shrink their problems.'

'I'm relieved to hear it.'

'Tell me more about Lincoln Dittmann.'

'Such as?'

'Anything that comes to mind will do nicely.' When he still hesitated, she said, 'Listen, Martin, you can tell me anything you can tell the Director of the CIA.'

'Anything?'

'That's why you're in this room. This is a private clinic. The doctors who work here have been cleared to hear state secrets. We get to treat the people who, for one reason or another, need help before returning to civilian life.'

'If you were the Director and I was sitting like this facing you, our knees almost touching—'

Bernice nodded encouragement. 'Go on.'

'I'd tell you that a camel is a horse designed by a committee. Then I'd tell you that the CIA is an intelligence agency designed by the same committee. And then I'd remind you that in every civilization known to man, the ratio of horses asses to horses has been greater than one.'

'You're angry.' She jotted something on the loose-leaf page. 'It's perfectly all right to be angry. Don't be afraid to let it out.'

Martin shrugged. 'I thought I was just expressing some healthy cynicism.'

'Lincoln Dittmann,' she said, tugging the conversation back to her question.

'He was raised in a small town in Pennsylvania named Jonestown. His mother was a Polish immigrant who had come to America after World War Two. His father owned a chain of hardware stores, with the main depot in Fredericksburg, on the Virginia side of the Potomac. He wound up spending several months a year in Fredericksburg and took his son with him when the trips fell during school vacations. Lincoln used his free time to scour the battlefield for souvenirs – in those days you could still find rusting bayonets or cannon balls or the barrels of muzzle loading rifles in the fields after a torrential rain. By the time he reached his teens, when the other kids his age were reading Batman comics, Lincoln could recount every detail of the battle of Fredericksburg. At Lincoln's urging, his father began buying Civil War paraphernalia from the farmers during his turn around the hardware stores – he returned home with rifles and bayonets and powder horns and Federal medals on the backseat of his Studebaker—'

'Not Confederate medals?'

'The Confederates didn't give medals to their soldiers. When Lincoln went off to college, he already had quite a collection. He even owned a rare English Whitworth, the weapon of choice for Confederate sharpshooters. The paper cartridges were damned expensive but a skilled sniper could hit anything he could see.'

'Where did he go to college?'

'University of Pennsylvania. Majored in American history. Wrote his senior thesis on the battle of Fredericksburg. When he began teaching at the junior college, he turned it into a book.'

'That was the book he printed himself when he couldn't find a publisher?'

'It was a bitter disappointment to him, not finding a legitimate publisher.'

'What was it about Fredericksburg that was so special?'

Martin's hand, clammy with perspiration, came up to massage his brow. The involuntary gesture wasn't lost on Dr Treffler. 'It was early in December of 1862,' he began, staring vacantly out of the window at the horizon, watching for the flashes of the great battle being fought beyond it. 'There was a new Federal general in charge of the Army of the Potomac, his name was Burnside. Ambrose Burnside. He thought he saw a way to end the war with one swift assault across Virginia to capture the Confederate capitol, Richmond. It was a brilliant plan. President Lincoln signed off on it and Burnside force-marched his troops down the Potomac to a point across the river from Fredericksburg. If he could surprise the rebels and take the city, the road to Richmond would be open and the war would end almost before it got going. Burnside had put in an urgent order for pontoon bridges, but when he reached Fredericksburg he discovered that the War Department hadn't dispatched them. The Union army wound up bivouacking for ten days on its side of the river waiting for the Goddamn bridges, giving Robert Lee time to bring up his army and mass it on the heights above the city. When the bridges finally arrived and Burnside crossed the river, he found Bobby Lee and seventy-five thousand Confederates blocking the road to Richmond. The weather was wintry, the autumnal mud in the rutted roads had turned hard. The Federals, advancing across sloping open ground, came on all day, wave after wave of them in their spanking bright factory-made uniforms. The Rebels in homespun dyed with plant pigments, fighting from behind a low stone wall at the edge of a sunken road at the foot of Marye's Hill, beat back every attack. The sharpshooters, armed with Whitworths, picked off the Federal officers so easily that many of them began tearing off their insignias as they went into the line. Groups of Federals tried to take cover behind some brick houses on the plain but the Yankee cavalry, using the flats of sabres, forced them back to the battle. Burnside kept track of the progress of the fighting from the roof of the Chatham Mansion across the river. From a knob up on the heights, the Mansion was within eyeshot and Bobby Lee pointed it out to Stonewall Jackson – he told him that thirty years before he'd courted the lady he wound up marrying at that very house. On the ridge line, a Confederate band belted out waltzes for the southern gentlemen and ladies who had come down from Richmond to see the battle. Old Pete Longstreet, with a woman's woolen shawl draped over his shoulders, watched the fighting unfolding below him through a long glass fixed to a wooden tripod in front of the Confederate command post. It took a time to convince him that the Federal attack on the sunken road wasn't a feint – he couldn't swallow the idea that Burnside was squandering his life's blood in a frontal attack that had no chance of succeeding. At one point an Irish Brigade made it to within fifteen paces of the sunken road and even the Rebels watching from the heights cheered their courage. But the 24th Georgians behind the low stone wail, firing and loading and firing so steadily their teeth ached from biting off the paper cartridges, turned back that attack, too. Burnside launched fourteen assaults on the heights before darkness blotted out the killing fields. When the Federals finally retreated across the river the next day and counted noses, they discovered that nine thousand Union men had fallen at Fredericksburg.'

Martin sat humped over in the chair now, his lids squeezed shut, the flat of a hand pressed to his forehead damming the migraine building up behind his eyes. 'When Lincoln Dittmann went to Washington to research the book, he dis-covered Burnside's original order for the pontoon bridges in the army archives. The word "Urgent" had been inked out, probably by a Confederate sympathizer working at the War Department. You asked what was so special about Fredericksburg

– Dittmann concluded that if the pontoon bridges had been delivered on time, the war might have ended there in 1862 instead of dragging on until 1865.'

Martin, drained, went quiet. For some while the only sound in the small airless room came from the whir of the tape recorder and the nib of Dr Treffler's pen etching long lines of runty letters onto the loose-leaf page. When she finally looked up from her notebook, she asked, very softly, 'How does Martin Odum know all this? The fact that the Confederates didn't give medals, the flats of sabres driving the Federals away from the shelter of *brick* houses, the Chatham Mansion, the band playing waltzes on Marye's Hill while Longstreet, with a shawl over his shoulders, watched the Georgians in homespun dyed with plant pigments fight off fourteen attacks on the sunken road – *it's almost as if you'd been there!*'

Martin's mouth had gone dry and the words that emerged from his lips rang tinny and hollow, the second half of an echo that had lost some of its shrillness on the way back. 'Lincoln Dittmann was there,' he said. 'He told me the details.'

Dr Treffler leaned forward. 'You heard Lincoln Dittmann's voice describing the battle?'

'Uh-huh.'

'Did he tell you he'd been there *during* the battle? Did he tell you he'd seen the fighting with his own eyes?'

'Not in so many words . . .'

'But you – you being Martin Odum – you assumed he'd been an eyewitness at Fredericksburg.'

'He must have been there,' Martin insisted plaintively. 'How else could he have known all the things he knew? Lincoln told me lots more that isn't in any books.' The words spilled out of Martin now. 'The night of the battle temperatures plunged to below freezing . . . even in the cold of winter there were horseflies drawn to the blood oozing from wounds . . . the maimed Federals who were still alive dragged the dead into heaps and burrowed under the corpses to keep warm . . . riderless horses pawed at the frozen ground looking for fodder, but the only fodder at Fredericksburg on 13 December 1862 was cannon fodder.' Martin took a deep breath. 'That was the last line of Lincoln's book. The title came from the line. The book was called *Cannon Fodder.*'

Dr Treffler waited for Martin's breathing to settle down before she spoke. 'Listen to me, Martin. Lincoln Dittmann is your contemporary. He wasn't alive in 1862, which means he couldn't have been at the battle of Fredericksburg.'

Martin didn't respond. Dr Treffler caught herself staring at him and turned away quickly, then laughed out loud and looked back. 'Wow! This is stunning. You heard Lincoln Dittmann's voice at our first session – he gave you the lines of that Walt Whitman poem you recited.'

'I remember. "Silent cannons, soon to cease your silence, soon unlimber'd to begin the red business." That wasn't the first time I heard Lincoln's voice – he's been whispering in my ear for years. By the way, it's Walter Whitman, not Walt. Lincoln told me he'd come across Whitman in a Federal field hospital after Burnside retreated from Fredericksburg – the poet was worried sick about his brother who'd taken part in the battle and was looking everywhere for him. Lincoln recalled that the soldiers who knew Whitman called him Walter.'

'Lincoln told you about Whitman being in the field hospital? About the soldiers calling him Walter?'

'Uh-huh.'

'Did he recall it from having been there or from having read about it somewhere?'

Martin seemed not to want to deal with the question.

Dr Treffler decided Martin had had enough stress for one session. 'Your headache starting in again?' she asked.

'It's blinding me.'

'What do you see when your eyes are shut tight like that?'

Martin thought about that. 'A long blur of headlights, as if a camera has been set up on an overpass and the lens has been locked open to capture the streak of the cars speeding past underneath. Or the cosmos, yes, the entire cosmos in its big-bang mode, expanding, inflating like a balloon with small black spots painted on it, and each spot on the balloon receding from every other spot.'

'And how will this big bang end?'

'With me, marooned on one of the spots, alone in the universe.'

1990: LINCOLN DITTMANN TAKES ON A LIFE OF HIS OWN

To the abiding satisfaction of its eight sitting members, the Legend Committee had been upgraded from its windowless basement storage space at Langley to a fourth-floor conference room drenched in sunlight. That was the upside. The downside was that the new digs had an impregnable view of the vast outdoor parking lot used by the Company plebeians. (The patricians from the seventh floor, including Crystal Quest, the current Deputy Director of Operations and the Committee's immediate boss, all rated parking spaces in the underground garage, along with an elevator that whisked them to work without stopping at other floors along the way.) 'Can't have everything,' sighed the former station chief who chaired the Legend Committee the first time he set foot in the room the housekeepers were proposing and looked out one of the windows; he'd been hoping for Virginia countryside, not asphalt. To mask his disappointment he came up with the aphorism that had been engraved over the door to the inner sanctum when he presided over Cairo

271

Station oh so many years ago: '*Yom asal, yom basal* . . . One day honey, one day onions.'

'Where the heck are we?' he was asking Maggie Poole, who had specialized in medieval French history at Oxford and had never entirely lost her acquired British accent, an affectation particularly remarkable when she slipped French words into the conversation.

'We're on the fourth *étage*,' she replied now, purposefully misunderstanding the question to get his goat. 'Up here the water coolers are in the corridor outside the rooms, not inside.'

'Oh, for Pete's sake, that's not what I meant and you know it. You do that every occasion you can.'

'*Moi*?' Maggie Poole blurted out innocently. 'Certainly not.'

'What he's asking,' said the Yale-educated aversion therapist, 'is where are we up to with the new legend for Dante Pippen.'

Dante, sitting with his spine against a soft pillow to relieve the pressure on the shrapnel wound in his lower back, thought of these sessions as indoor sport. It was a painless way to pass an afternoon even if his game leg and the back wound ached more or less round the clock. He closed his eyes to shield them from the bright sunlight slanting through the open venetian blinds and relished the warmth on the skin of his face. 'I thought this time around,' he offered, and he could almost hear the bones creaking as the ancient mariners of the Legend

Committee craned their necks to stare at him, 'we could begin in Pennsylvania.'

'Why Pennsylvania?' demanded the lexicographer on loan from University of Chicago and happy to be; the per diem the Company deposited in his bank account somehow never got reported to the Internal Revenue Service.

The committee's doyen, a CIA veteran who began his professional career creating legends for the OSS agents during World War Two and never let anyone forget it, fitted on a pair of perfectly round wire spectacles and flipped open the original Martin Odum 201 Central Registry folder. 'Pennsylvania,' he observed, straining to make out the small type on the bio file, 'seems as good a place to start as any. Mr Pippen's predecessor, Martin Odum, spent the first eight years of his life in Pennsylvania, in a small town called Jonestown. His mother was a Polish immigrant, his father ran a small factory producing underwear for the U.S. Army.'

'Jonestown was within driving distance of several Civil War battlefields and Martin wound up going to a bunch of them while he was in grade school,' Dante said from the sideline. 'His favorite, which he must have visited two or three times, was Fredericksburg.'

'Could visiting Fredericksburg make someone a Civil War *expert*?' Maggie Poole inquired eagerly; she had caught a glimpse of where they could be heading.

'Martin was a Fredericksburg expert, for sure,' Dante said with a laugh. His eyes were still tightly closed and he was beginning, once again, to enjoy the business of legend building; it seemed to him the closest he'd ever come to novel writing. 'His stories about the battle there were so graphic, people who heard them sometimes jokingly wondered if he'd taken part in the Civil War.'

'Can you give us some examples?' the chairman asked.

'He would describe Bobby Lee, up on Marye's Hill inland from Fredericksburg, pointing out Burnside's command post in the Chatham Mansion across the Potomac to Stonewall Jackson and recalling that he'd courted his wife under that roof thirty years before. Martin would describe Old Pete Longstreet, his shoulders draped in a woman's woolen shawl, watching the battle unfolding below him through a long glass fixed to a wooden tripod and telling everyone within earshot that the Federal attack on the sunken road had to be a feint, that the main attack would come somewhere else.'

The Legend Committee chairman peered at Dante over the rim of his wire eyeglasses. 'Was Bobby Lee the General we know as Robert E. Lee?' he asked.

'One and the same,' Dante said from his place along the wall. 'The Virginians called him Bobby Lee – though never to his face.'

'Well, this does open avenues for exploration,' the chairman told the others. 'Our man may not be a Civil War expert, but with a little help from his friends he could certainly pass for one, couldn't he?'

'Which brings us to the name,' Maggie Poole said. 'And what could be more *logique* for a Civil War *expert* than calling him Lincoln?'

'I suppose you were thinking of using Abraham as a first name,' sneered the aversion therapist.

'*Va te faire cuire un oeuf*,' Maggie Poole shot back. She glared at the aversion therapist, clearly tempted to stick her tongue out at him. 'I was thinking along the lines of using Lincoln as a *prenom* because it would tend to give credibility to a Civil War legend.'

'Lincoln something or other sounds quite elegant to me,' Dante called from the wall.

'*Merci*, Mr Pippen, for being so open minded, which is more than I can say for some others in this room,' ventured Maggie Poole.

'I once knew a gun collector in Chicago whose name was Dittmann – that's with two "t"s and two "n"s,' said the lexicographer. 'There was some suggestion that Dittmann wasn't his real name but that's neither here nor there. He specialized in Civil War firearms. His pride and joy was an English sniper rifle, it was called the Whentworth or Whitworth, something like that. As I recall, the paper cartridges were exorbitant, but in the hands of a skilled sharpshooter the rifle was considered to be a lethal weapon.'

'Lincoln Dittmann is a name with . . . weight,'

the chairman decided. 'How does it strike you, Mr Pippen?'

'I could learn to live with it,' he agreed. 'And it would certainly be original to turn a field agent into a Civil War expert.'

The members of the Legend Committee knew they had hit pay dirt and the ideas started to come thick and fast.

'He could start building the legend by visiting all the battle grounds.'

'He ought to have a *collection personnelle* of Civil War firearms, I should think.'

'I like having guns around,' Pippen announced from his seat. 'Come to think of it, a personal collection of Civil War weapons would make a great cover for an arms dealer, which is where Fred Astaire is heading with this legend.'

'So we need to think in terms of a legend for an arms dealer?'

'Yes.'

'Who in God's name is Fred Astaire?'

'It's Mrs Quest's in-house nickname.'

'Oh, dear.'

'In what part of the world would Lincoln Dittmann be operating? Who would be his clients?'

Lincoln had to be careful not to give away family jewels. 'His clients would be a hodgepodge of people who are out to hurt America,' he said.

'To step into Lincoln Dittmann's shoes, you would have to do your homework.'

'Do you mind reading up on a subject, Mr Pippen?'

'Not at all. Sounds fun to me.'

'He'd need professional credentials.'

'Okay. Let's summarize. He was raised in Jonestown, Pennsylvania, and visited Fredericksburg so often as a child that he knew the battlefield backward and forward at a time when his young friends were reading Batman comics.'

'His father could have owned a chain of hardware stores with the central depot in Fredericksburg, which meant he would have had to spend a lot of time there in any given year. Nothing would have been more natural than to have taken his young son with him whenever he could . . .'

'Of course! He would have taken him along to Fredericksburg during school vacations. The young Lincoln Dittmann would have joined the boys scouring the battlefield for Civil War souvenirs that wash up to the surface after heavy rainfalls.'

'At some point Lincoln would have encouraged his father to hunt for rifles and powder horns and medals when he drove around – let's give him a Studebaker, which was a popular car after the war – checking on his hardware stores. The local farmers keep these Civil War things in their attics and Lincoln's father would have brought something back with him after each trip.'

'If I collected medals,' Pippen noted, 'they'd all have to be from the Union Army. Confederate Army didn't award medals.'

'How did they get their soldiers to soldier if they didn't award medals?'

'They were fighting for a cause they believed in,' Pippen said.

'They were defending slavery, for God's sake—'

'Most of the Confederate soldiers didn't own slaves,' Pippen said. (Things that Martin had picked up during those visits to Fredericksburg so many years earlier were coming back to him.) 'They were fighting so the North wouldn't try and tell them what they could do and what they couldn't do. Besides which, when the war started, Lincoln – I'm talking about Abraham, the president – didn't have the slightest intention of abolishing slavery and freeing the slaves. Nobody on either side of the Mason-Dixon line would have accepted this because nobody had any idea what to do with the millions of slaves in the Confederate states if they were freed. Yankees didn't want emancipated slaves trekking north and stealing their manufacturing jobs for lower salaries. Southerners didn't want them homesteading Confederate land and growing cotton that could be marketed cheaper than plantation cotton. Or even worse, voting in local elections.'

'He really *is* something of a Civil War buff already.'

'Our Lincoln Dittmann ought to have been a *professeur* at one point, don't you think?'

'He could have taught Civil War history in some college. Why not?'

'Problem: To teach in a college you need an advanced degree. Even if he reads up on the Civil

War, he might not be able to convince a real Civil War expert that he earned a Ph.D. in the subject.'

'Let him teach at a junior college, then. That way he wouldn't need an advanced degree. And what he knows about the Civil War could pass muster.'

'It would add to his credibility if he were to write a book on the subject.'

'Hang on,' Pippen said. 'I don't think I have the stamina to write a book.'

'Takes more than stamina. I know because I've written three. You need mettle if you're going to refuse to be intimidated by all the options.'

'We could farm out the book. We could get it written for you and have a small university press that owes us a favor publish it under your name. *The Battle of Fredericksburg* by Lincoln Dittmann.'

'I've got the perfect title: *Cannon Fodder*. With a subtitle: *The Battle of Fredericksburg.*'

'Let's not get bogged down with the title, for goodness sake.'

'What do you think of all this, Mr Pippen?'

'It's first rate cover. Nobody would suspect an arms dealer who had been teaching Civil War history at a junior college of being CIA.'

'There's something's missing from this legend.'

'What?'

'Yes, what?'

'Motivation is what's missing. Why has Lincoln Dittmann sunk so low. Why is he associating with the scum of the earth, people who, by definition, are not friends of *l'Amerique?*'

279

'Good point, Maggie.'

'Because he's angry at America.'

'Why? Why is he angry at America?'

'He got into a some sort of jam. He was humiliated—'

Dante piped up from the sideline. 'I don't mind being humiliated, but I'd appreciate it if sex weren't involved. You people always think of sex when you want to put something into a biography that discredits the principal. Next thing you know Lincoln Dittmann will be a closet transvestite or something like that.'

'We take your point, Mr Pippen.'

'What if the jam involved plagiarism.'

'He swiped the heart of *Cannon Fodder* from a treatise published in the twenties or thirties that he found in the stacks of a library.'

'That would simplify matters for us. We wouldn't have to pay someone to write the book on Fredericksburg; we could find a treatise – there must be thousands of them lying around on shelves gathering dust – and copy it.'

'My luck,' Dante groaned, 'I finally get to be the author of a book and it turns out I plagiarized it.'

'It's that or sexual deviation.'

'I'll take plagiarism.'

'A reviewer in an historical periodical – tipped off by an anonymous letter sent by us – could blow the whistle on Dittmann, at which point he would lose his tenure and his job.'

'His professional reputation would be ruined.'

'Nobody else in the wide world of academia would touch him with a ten-foot pole.'

'Now we're getting somewhere. The colleges put pressure on you to publish or perish and they expect you to hold down a full teaching load and do the research and writing in your free time.'

'The experience left Lincoln Dittmann a bitter cynic. He wanted to get back at the college, at the system, at the country.'

'I'd say we're halfway home, gentlemen and ladies. The only thing that remains is to try all this out on our taskmaster, the DDO, Crystal Quest herself.'

Dante Pippen reached for the cane propped against the wall and used it to push himself to his feet. Dull pain stabbed at his lower back and sore leg, but he was so elated he barely noticed it. 'I think Crystal Quest is going to be very satisfied with the Lincoln Dittmann legend,' he told the members of the Legend Committee. 'I know I am.'

1991: LINCOLN DITTMANN WORKS THE ANGLES OF THE TRIANGLE

'How did you get into the business of selling weapons?' the Egyptian wanted to know.

'Chances are you won't believe me if I tell you,' Lincoln Dittmann said.

'If he don't believe you,' said the short American with the tooled cowboy boots and tapered Levis and slicked back hair, 'you're in deep shit.' He spoke in a Texas drawl so silky that Lincoln had to strain to make out the words.

The Egyptian and the Texan, strange bedfellows in this godforsaken Paraguayan frontier town across the border from Brazil, both laughed under their breaths, though there was no trace of mirth in their voices. Lincoln, sprawled on a sofa, his bad leg stretched straight out in front of him, the cane within arm's reach, his hands clasped behind his head, laughed with them. 'I was teaching Civil War history at a junior college,' he said. 'My area of expertise – I wrote a book on the subject once – was the battle of Fredericksburg. Collecting Civil War weapons seemed like the natural thing to do. My pièce de résistance is a rare English Whitworth.'

'That there's a sniper rifle, ain't it?' said the Texan.

Lincoln looked impressed. 'Aren't many people around who can tell the difference between a Whitworth and an ordinary barnyard Enfield.'

'My daddy had one,' the Texan said proudly. 'Feds went an' impounded it along with his other guns when he was nabbed for burning a nigger church to the ground in Al'bama.' He tilted his head back and regarded Lincoln warily. The Texan, who had introduced himself as Leroy Streeter when he'd picked Lincoln up in front of the mosque with the gold-tinted roof on Palestine Street across the border in Fox do Iguaçú, said, 'Go and describe your Whitworth?'

Lincoln smiled to himself. Back at Langley, they'd learned from the FBI that Leroy Streeter's father had once owned a Civil War Whitworth; they'd reckoned the son would be familiar with the weapon. If Leroy's quiz was what passed for checking bona fides in Triple Border, it certainly was amateur hour; an undercover agent wouldn't name drop – even the name of an antique rifle – if he couldn't backstop it with details. Fact of the matter was that Lincoln did own a Whitworth – a collection of Civil War weapons went with the Dittmann legend. He'd even fabricated cartridges and gone out to a remote landfill in New Jersey to see if the rifle was as accurate as its reputation held. It was. 'Mr Whitworth's rifle,' he told Leroy now, 'came factory-equipped with a low-powered brass scope fixed atop the hexagonal barrel. Not many of the Whitworths around these days, even in museums, still have the scope. Mine also has the original brass tampon to plug the barrel against humidity and dust. The scope's fitted with little engraved wheels to sight the rifle and adjust for latitude and longitude errors.'

As he spoke, Lincoln kept his eyes on the Egyptian, who obviously ran the show here. He had not been introduced – though Lincoln had a good idea of his identity; the FBI's briefing book back in Washington had contained a blurry photo taken with a telephoto lens of an Egyptian known as Ibrahim bin Daoud talking to a man identified as a Hezbollah agent in front of the entrance to the Maksoud Plaza Hotel in São Paulo the previous year. The long delicate nose and carefully trimmed gray beard visible in the photo were conspicuous on the Egyptian sitting on the sill across from him now.

Stretched out on the unmade bed in the room above a bar in Ciudad del Este on the Paraguay side of Triple Border, the muddy heels of his boots digging into the mattress, Leroy was nodding emphatically at the Egyptian. 'He sure as hell's got hisself a Whitworth,' he confirmed.

Lincoln was hoping that gun collecting could provide a useful bond between him and the Texan. 'Crying shame about your daddy's Whitworth,' he said. 'Bet the FBI goons didn't have the wildest idea what a goddamn prize they had in their hands when they confiscated it.'

'They was too fucking dumb to tell the difference between fool's gold and actual gold,' Leroy agreed.

Lincoln looked back at the Egyptian. 'To answer your question: From the Whitworth and my other guns, it was just a matter of branching out to Kalashnikovs and TOW antitank missiles, with the grenades and ammunition thrown in for good measure. Pays a lot better than teaching Civil War history at a junior college.'

'We are not in the market for Kalashnikovs and TOWs,' the Egyptian noted coldly.

'He's not interested in Ak-47s and TOWs,' the Texan explained. 'Now that Commie Russia's got one foot in the grave, you trip over this kind of hardware out here on Triple Border. He's interested in Semtex or ammonium nitrate, something in the neighborhood of eighty thousand pounds of it, enough to fill one of those big moving vans. We pay cash on the barrelhead.'

Lincoln locked his eyes on the Egyptian. He was a skeletal man with a round pockmarked face and hunched shoulders, probably in his late fifties, though the gray beard could have been adding years to his appearance. The upper third of his face had disappeared behind dark sunglasses, which he wore despite being in a dingy room with the shades drawn. 'Semtex in small quantities is no problem. Ammonium nitrate in any quantity is also no problem,' he said. 'You probably know that ammonium nitrate is used as fertilizer – mixed with diesel or fuel oil, it is highly explosive. The trick'll be to buy a large amount without attracting attention, which is something I and my associates can organize. Where do you want to take delivery?'

Leroy smiled out of one side of his mouth. 'At a site to be specified on the New Jersey side of the Holland Tunnel.'

Lincoln heard the cry of the muezzin – it wasn't a recording but the real thing – summoning the faithful to midday prayer, which meant he'd been taken somewhere within earshot of the only mosque in Ciudad del Este after Leroy had picked him up in front of the mosque in Foz do Iguaçú. He'd been shoved into the back of a Mercedes and ordered to strap on the blackened-out ski goggles he found on the seat. 'You taking me to the Saudi?' he'd asked Leroy as the Mercedes drove in circles for three quarters of a hour to confuse him. 'I'm taking you to meet the Saudi's Egyptian,' Leroy had answered. 'If the Egyptian signs off on you, that's when you get to meet the Saudi, not before.' Lincoln had asked, 'What happens if he doesn't sign off on me?' Leroy, sitting up front alongside the driver, had snorted. 'If'n he don't sign off on you, he'll like as feed you to the pet crocodile he keeps in his swim pool.'

Now Lincoln could feel Daoud scrutinizing him

through his dark sunglasses. 'Where did you hurt your leg?' the Egyptian asked.

'Car accident in Zagreb,' Lincoln said. 'The Croats are crazy drivers.'

'Where were you treated?' Daoud was looking for details he could verify.

Lincoln named a clinic in a suburb of Trieste.

The Egyptian glanced at Leroy and shrugged. Something else occurred to him. 'What did you say the title of your book on Fredericksville was?'

Leroy corrected him. 'It's Fredericks*burg*.'

'I didn't say,' Lincoln replied. 'Title was the best part of the book. I called it, *Cannon Fodder*.'

Apparently Leroy was still fighting the War of Secession because he blurted out, 'Cannon fodder is sure as hell what they was.' His normal drawl, pitched a half octave higher, came across loud and clear. 'Federal cannon fodder, fighting to free the niggers and legitimize intermarriage and dictate the North's way of thinking on southern gents.'

The Egyptian repeated the title to make sure he'd gotten it right, then muttered something in Arabic to the fat boy piecing together the jigsaw puzzle on the linoleum-covered table in the alcove. The boy, who was wearing a shoulder holster with a plastic gun in it and chewing bubble gum that he inflated every time he fitted in a piece, sprang to his feet and rushed out of the room. The Egyptian followed him. Lincoln could hear their footfalls on the staircase of the ramshackle building as the boy headed downstairs and Daoud climbed up one flight. He let himself into the room overhead and crossed it and dragged up a chair as a telephone sounded. Lincoln guessed that the Egyptian was phoning abroad to get his people to check out details of the Dittmann legend.

The DDO's people in Langley had anticipated this and laid in the plumbing. If someone nosed around the Trieste clinic, he would come across a record of a Lincoln Dittmann being treated by a bone specialist for three days, and paying his bill in cash the morning he was discharged. As for the book, *Cannon Fodder* had a paper trail. The Egyptian's contact would discover a 1990 reference to the publication of the book in *Publishers Weekly*. If he dug deeper he would come up with two reviews, the first in a Virginia junior college student newspaper praising one of the school's own teachers for his Civil War scholarship; the second in a Richmond, Virginia, historical quarterly devoted to the War of Secession, accusing Lincoln Dittmann of having plagiarized great chunks of a privately printed 1932 doctorate treatise on the battle of Fredericksburg. There would be a small item in a Richmond newspaper repeating the plagiarism charge and reporting that a committee of the author's peers had examined the original treatise and Dittmann's *Cannon Fodder*, and discovered entire passages that matched. The article went on to say that Lincoln Dittmann had been fired from his post teaching history at a local junior college. Chain bookstores would have reported modest sales before the book was withdrawn from circulation. If anyone hunted hard enough, copies of the first and only edition (what was left of the original five-hundred-book print run) could be found in the Strand in Manhattan and several other second-hand bookstores across the country. On the inside of the back jacket there would be a photograph of Dittmann with a Schimelpenick jutting from his lips, along with a brief biography: born and raised in Pennsylvania, a Civil War buff from the time he started visiting battlefields as a youngster, an expert on the Battle of Fredericksburg, currently teaching Civil War history at a Virginia junior college.

Waiting for the Egyptian to return, Lincoln plucked a Schimelpenick from the metal tin in his jacket pocket and held the flame of a lighter to the end of it. He inhaled deeply and let the smoke gush through his nostrils. 'Mind if I smoke?' he inquired politely.

'Smoking,' Leroy remarked, 'poisons the lungs. You ought to give it up.'

'Trouble is,' Lincoln said, 'to give up smoking you need to become someone else. Tried that once. Went cold turkey for a while. But it didn't work out in the end.'

After awhile the Egyptian returned to the room and settled into the wooden chair set catty-corner to the sofa. 'Tell me more about what you did in Croatia?' he instructed Lincoln.

Croatia had been Crystal Quest's brainchild. For

all her imperiousness, she was old school: She believed a good legend needed more than a paper trail to give it authenticity. 'If he's supposed to be an arms merchant,' she'd argued when she dragged Lincoln up to the seventh floor at Langley to get the director to sign off on the operation, 'there's got to be a trail of genuine transactions that the opposition can verify.'

'You're proposing to actually set him up in the arms business?'

'Yes, sir, I am.'

'Whom would he sell to?' the director had demanded, clearly unsettled by the notion of one of the Company's agents establishing his bona fides by becoming a bona fide arms merchant.

'He'll buy from the Soviets who are running garage sales from their arsenals in East Germany, and deliver to the Bosnians. Since U.S. policy tilts toward the Bosnians, our Congressional oversight commissars won't give us a hard time if they get wind of it, which they won't if we're careful. The idea behind this is to put Lincoln in the path of one Sami Akhbar, an Azerbaijani who buys arms for an al-Qa'ida cell in Bosnia.'

'As usual you've covered all the bases, Fred,' the director had noted with a flagrant lack of enthusiasm.

'Sir, that's what you pay me for,' she'd shot back.

Lincoln had spent the next four months tooling around the Dalmatian coast in a serviceable Buick, avoiding the Serb undercover agents like the plague, using a fax to contact a shadowy Frankfurt entity and purchase truckloads of the Soviet surplus arms being sold off by Russian soldiers soon to be recalled to the USSR from East Germany, meeting the drivers at night on remote back roads as they came across Slovenia, then arranging for delivery at crossing points on the Dalmatian coast between Croatia and Bosnia. It was at one of these pre-dawn meetings that Lincoln first felt the fish nibbling at the bait. 'Could you get your hands on explosives?' a Muslim dealer who went by the name Sami Akhbar had casually asked as he took possession of a two-truck convoy loaded with TOW antitank missiles and mortars and handed Lincoln a satchel filled with crisp $100 bills bound in wrappers from a Swiss bank.

Lincoln had dealt with Sami five times in the past four months. 'What do you have in mind?' he had inquired.

'I have a Saudi friend who is shopping around for Semtex or ammonium nitrate.'

'In what quantities?'

'Very large quantities.'

'Your friend looking to celebrate the end of Ramadan with a big bang?'

'Something like that.'

'Russians aren't peddling Semtex or ammonium nitrate. It would have to come from the States.'

'Are you saying it is within the realm of possibility?'

'Everything is within the realm of possibility, Sami, but it will cost a pretty penny.'

'Money is not a problem for my Saudi friend. Thanks to Allah and his late father, he is very rich.'

The Muslim had produced a scrap of paper from a shirt pocket and, pressing it to the fender of the truck, had printed out with the stub of a pencil the name of a town and the street address of a mosque, along with a date and an hour. Lincoln had crouched in front of the Buick parking lights to read it. 'Where in hell is Foz do Iguaçú?' he'd asked, though he knew the answer.

'It is in Brazil right across the frontier from Paraguay at a place called Triple Border, where Brazil and Paraguay and Argentina meet.'

'Why can't we get together somewhere in Europe?'

'If you are not interested, only say so. I will find someone else who is.'

'Hey, don't get me wrong, Sami. I'm interested. I'm just worried that it's a long way to go for nothing.'

Sami had coughed up a laugh. 'You guys who deal arms tickle me. I do not call two hundred and fifty thousand U.S. nothing.'

Lincoln had glanced again at the scrap of paper. 'Are you sure your rich Saudi friend will contact me if I am standing outside the mosque on Palestine Street at ten in the morning ten days from today?'

Sami had nodded into the darkness. 'A person will contact you and take you to him.'

In the small room over the bar, the Egyptian

listened in silence to Lincoln's account of his dealings in Croatia. In the alcove, the boy, working again at his jigsaw puzzle, blew bubbles with the gum until they burst against his fleshy lips. Leroy cleaned the fingernails of his left hand with a fingernail of his right hand. When Lincoln reached the end of the story, the Egyptian, lips pursed, sat without moving a muscle, weighing his next move. Finally he announced, 'Leroy will take you back to your hotel in Foz do Iguaçú. Wait there until you hear from me.'

'How long will that take?' Lincoln asked. 'Every day I'm away from the Balkans costs me money.'

The Egyptian shrugged. 'If you become bored, you are free to yawn.'

'How did it go?' Lincoln asked Leroy when the two were alone in the car and heading toward the bridge and Foz do Iguaçú.

'The fact that you're still alive can only mean it went well.'

Lincoln glanced at the Texan, whose face flashed in and out of the light as cars passed in the opposite direction. 'You're serious, aren't you?'

'Fucking A, I'm serious. Get it into your skull,' he said, drumming a forefinger against his own. 'You're associating with tough customers down here.'

Lincoln had to swallow a smile. Felix Kiick had used much the same words as he wound up the briefing back in Washington. 'Holy mackerel, watch your ass when you get to Triple Border,' he'd said. 'You'll be rubbing shoulders with mighty ornery folks.'

The briefing in Washington had taken place on neutral turf, a nondescript Foggy Bottom conference room that had been swept by Company housekeepers and then staked out until the principals showed up at the crack of noon. From word one, the tension had been as thick as the fog Lincoln had braved driving to work that morning from the safe house in Virginia. It wasn't so much the FBI briefer, a short, stumpy veteran counter-terrorism maven named Felix Kiick with the low center of gravity of a NFL linesman; the CIA had dealt with him on any number of occasions (most especially when he directed the FBI's counter-terrorism team at the American embassy in Moscow) and considered him to be a straight shooter. The tension could be traced to the clash of cultures; to the mistrust J. Edgar Hoover (who had run the FBI with an iron hand until his death in 1972) had sewn into the agency's bureaucratic fabric during his forty-eight years at the helm. The fact that the FBI, acting in obedience to a formal presidential 'finding,' was being obliged to pass on to its arch competitor at Langley an operation and the assets that went with it, or what was left of them, only made matters worse. Kiick put the best possible face on the situation in his opening remarks. 'Triple Border,' he told Lincoln as Crystal Quest and several of her wallahs looked on, 'which

294

is the nickname for the zone where Brazil, Paraguay and Argentina meet up, is a cesspool filled with scum from Hamas, Hezbollah, Egypt's Islamic Brotherhood, the Irish Republican Army, the Basque separatist group ETA, Colombia's FARC, all of them operating under false identities or false flags. The FBI's interest in Triple Border goes back roughly ten years when a large expatriate population fleeing the civil war in Lebanon gravitated into the area. The local authorities, some of them bribed, some of them intimidated, turned their backs on the sharp rise in crime in their backyard. You could buy and sell almost anything down there – passports for two-thousand dollars a clip, including the mug shot and the official government stamp; stolen cars; cheap electronics; along with the staples on any lawless frontier these days, drugs and arms. Several terrorist organizations set up guerilla training camps in the *mato graso* – the outback – to teach recruits how to rig car bombs or shoot the Soviet hardware that anyone could purchase in the back alleys of the border towns using money conveniently laundered by the banks at Triple Border.'

'Sounds like your people have a handle on the problems,' Lincoln said. 'Why are you backing off?'

'They're backing off,' Crystal Quest said, 'because the director has convinced the White House that American interests would be better served if the CIA held the Triple Border action.'

Quest fingered some crushed ice out of a bowl and began munching on it. 'Drugs, contraband cars, a black market in computer software or pirated Hollywood films are small potatoes. We have reason to believe that Triple Border has become a staging area for Muslim fundamentalist groups working in the western hemisphere; at Triple Border they can purchase all the arms their hearts desire and launder the money to pay for it. And their fedayeen can get some R and R at the local bars, out of sight of the mullahs who expect them to remain chaste and pray five times a day. The mosques in Foz de Iguaçú on the Brazilian side and Ciudad del Este on the Paraguayan side are filled with Sunnis and Shiites who in other parts of the Muslim world don't give each other the time of day. In Triple Border we suspect that they're plotting to attack the United States and kill Americans.'

Kiick spoke up. 'Despite what the CIA thinks of our collective abilities, the FBI did manage to run a handful of assets in Triple Border. With some persistence one of them struck pay dirt, pay dirt being the Egyptian named Ibrahim bin Daoud who runs the fundamentalist training camp called Boa Vista. Daoud, whose real name is Khalil al-Jabarin, has a record – al-Jabarin was convicted of being a spiritual leader of the Muslim Brotherhood and served serious time in a Cairo military prison. He has the physical and mental scars to show for it; electrodes attached to testicles are said to be the torture of choice of Egyptian jailers. No doubt

about it, Daoud himself is a cold-blooded killer –
whether it's the result of his suffering or his genes
we don't know. What we do know is that last month
he snuck a crocodile into a swimming pool in São
Paolo and then pushed in a man accused of being
a police informer while some local hookers holding
paper plates filled with defrosted hors d'oeuvres
looked on. Money was spread around and the
murder was hushed up. We know the story's not
apocryphal because one of the hookers was a collat-
eral asset. The dead informer was our principal
asset in Triple Border.'

'So the FBI has gone blind out there?' Lincoln
asked.

'For all intents and purposes, yes.'

'The principal asset who got close to Daoud
didn't have an understudy?'

'We didn't get around to it in time,' Kiick
admitted.

'What else can I expect to find at Triple Border
besides ravenous crocodiles?'

Kiick – Lincoln had a nodding acquaintance
with him from having sat in on several of the rare
joint CIA-FBI coordinating sessions – slid an FBI
briefing book across the conference table. 'What
we've picked up is all in here,' he said. 'You're
likely to come across a Texan who goes by the
name Leroy Streeter. He's what we call a crossover
– in his case, an Aryan nationalist nut who is
making common cause with the Muslim funda-
mentalists. Mind you, the mix is potentially lethal.

If and when Muslim terrorists do attack the United States, the white supremacists could provide infrastructure support and eventually hit men, since it's easier for an American to gain entrance to public places than an Arab from the Middle East. Leroy Streeter may or may not be the Texan's real name, by the way. The guy you'll meet – he's five foot two, a hundred and thirty pounds, speaks with a Texas drawl – travels under a passport made out to a Leroy Streeter Jr Leroy Streeter Sr was the führer of a Texas-based white supremacist splinter group called the Nationalist Congress; he died of cancer in Huntsville while he was serving time for blowing up a black church in Birmingham. State Department consulate in Mexico City issued a passport to a Leroy Streeter Jr four years ago, but Argentina's Secretariat for State Intelligence thinks that he drowned on a Rio beach two years back; as far as we know, no body was recovered. Which means that Leroy Streeter Jr has risen from the dead or someone is using his passport. Either way, he's high on the FBI's most wanted list.'

'Don't let yourself get sidetracked,' Crystal Quest told Lincoln. 'Leroy Streeter is not the target of this operation. The person we're after down there is the Saudi.'

'Does the Saudi have a name?' Lincoln inquired.

'Everyone has a name,' Quest snapped. 'FBI just doesn't know it.'

'From what our principal asset was able to tell

us before his untimely death,' continued Kiick, unfazed by Quest's dig at the Bureau, 'we understand the Saudi is the kingpin of a fundamentalist group that recently surfaced as a blip on our radar screen. It's been operating out of Afghanistan since the Russians were evicted from the country two years ago and calls itself al-Qa'ida, which means "The Base." The Saudi appears to be organizing al-Qa'ida cells across Europe and Asia and running them from the Sudanese capital of Khartoum.'

'How do I get to this Saudi?'

'With any luck, he gets to you,' Quest said. 'He's in the market for explosives, lots of it. The FBI asset picked up rumors that the Saudi is shopping around for a truckload and is offering a small fortune if it can be delivered to an address in the United States. The explosives may be the tip of the iceberg – the Saudi may have his heart set on acquiring something that will render the explosives more lethal.'

'You're talking about a dirty bomb,' Lincoln guessed.

'He's talking about gift wrapping the explosives with plutonium or enriched-uranium radioactive waste,' Quest said, 'which would result in the contamination of a wide area when the charge is detonated. Hundreds of thousands could be effected. It's because of this threat that the president decided to bring the CIA into the picture.'

Kiick said, 'Mind you, Lincoln – I understand that that's the name you're using now – the business about a dirty bomb is a worstcase scenario, and pure speculation.'

Quest ignored the FBI representative. 'We're going to come at the Saudi obliquely,' she told Lincoln. 'We know of an al-Qa'ida cell in the Balkans that's been running guns and ammunition to the Muslims in Sarajevo in the belief that war between the Serbs and Bosnians is inevitable. Guy who directs it is an Azerbaijani who uses the name Sami Akhbar. Our plan is to hang you out to dry on the Dalmatian coast, which is Sami's stamping ground, and let him stumble across you. Once you've established your bona fides and whet his appetite, you reach the Saudi by working your way up the chain of command. In Triple Border, he's said to use Daoud as a doorkeeper; nobody gets to the Saudi without getting past the Egyptian.'

Crystal Quest, dressed in one of her signature pantsuits with wide lapels and a dress shirt with frills down the chest, scraped back her chair and stood up. Taking their cue from her, the wallahs from the DDO jumped to their feet. 'Get it into your head that Triple Border isn't the Club Med,' Quest reminded Lincoln. 'The group we know least about – the group which interests us the most – is this al-Qa'ida entity. Bring home the bacon on the Saudi and al-Qa'ida, Lincoln, and I'll personally see to it you get one of the Company's jockstrap medals.' She added with a leer: 'Pin it on you myself.' The DDO contingent all laughed. As Quest headed for the door, Kiick offered his hand across the table and Lincoln, half rising from his chair, shook it. 'Our cutout will make herself known to you by saying something about Giovanni da Varrazano and the bridge named after him.' Kiick added, 'Holy mackerel, watch your ass when you get to Triple Border. You'll be rubbing shoulders with mighty ornery folks.'

Crystal Quest's voice, suffused with satisfaction at her own morbid sense of humor, came drifting back over her shoulder: 'Whatever you do, Lincoln, stay away from swimming pools.'

Hanging out with Leroy Streeter in a booth at the rear of the Kit Kat Klub on the main drag of Foz do Iguaçú for the second night running, polishing off the last of the sirloin steak and French fries, washing it down with cheap Scotch in a shot glass and lukewarm beer chasers drunk straight from the bottle, Lincoln watched the hookers slotting coins into the jukebox and swaying in each other's arms to the strains of 'Don't Worry, Be Happy,' which, judging from the fact that it was played over and over, night after night, was either number one on the Brazilian hit parade or the only 45-rpm record in the machine still functioning. Leroy had just come down the narrow stairs leading to a dark hallway with two bedrooms off of it, having gotten his ashes hauled (as he put it) for the second time that night. The skinny teenage girl with the red-dyed hair worked into a chignon on the top of her head to add height and age came down behind him, ironing the folds of a thin shift with her palms as she tottered back to the bar on spiked high heels. 'I prefer jailbait,' Leroy informed his new found friend as he signalled for another bottle of beer. 'They got theirselves tight snatches and do whichever you tell 'em to without raising a fuss or renegotiating the price. Can't figure what you got 'gainst getting laid, Lincoln. Like I told you, the girls here is all clean as whistles.'

'They're only clean as the last whistle they blew,' Lincoln said. 'Last thing I need to come down with is gonorrhea. Wind up costing me two hundred fifty grand to get screwed.'

'I see what you're saying,' Leroy said. He looked over at the dancers padding around on the broad pine planks of the floor in front of the jukebox; one young man, whom Leroy had identified as a Pakistani he'd seen at Daoud's boondock training camp, was hugging Leroy's skinny friend with the red-dyed hair and dancing in place, shifting his weight from foot to foot in time to the music. 'I don't hold with females dancing with females,' the Texan told Lincoln, aiming his chin in the direction of the hookers who hung limply in each other's arms, their backs slightly arched, their painted lids closed, their heads falling off to one side as if their necks weren't strong enough to support the weight of their elaborate hairdos. 'It ain't normal, is my view, in the sense that lesbian love ain't normal. If God meant women to fuck women he would have given some of them dicks. The hell kind of music is that anyway? Don't worry, be happy is how I aim to pass the rest of my days on earth once all this is over with.'

Lincoln decided the moment had come to see whether his efforts at bonding with the Texan had paid off. Bending over the table, lowering his voice so the two Brazilians in the next booth couldn't make out what he was saying, he asked, 'Once all *what* is over with? It's got to do with the ammonium nitrate, right? Tell me something, Leroy – what the fuck would anyone do with a moving van stuffed with ammonium nitrate?' He managed to ask the question very casually, as if he were only trying to hold up his end of the conversation; as if he couldn't care less about the answer.

Leroy, a little man who wanted people to think of him as big, couldn't resist bragging. 'Between you and me and the fly on the wall over there, I'm gonna go and personally drive it through the Holland Tunnel,' he replied, leaning forward until their foreheads were almost touching. 'Gonna set the fuse and blow it up in downtown Manhattan and flatten a square mile of Wall Street real estate, is what I'm gonna do with it.'

Sinking back, Lincoln whistled through his teeth. 'You guys aren't fucking around – you're going straight for the jugular.'

'Fucking A we're not fucking around,' Leroy said, squirming gleefully on his banquette.

Lincoln raised the bottle to his lips and swallowed

a mouthful of warm beer. 'What you got against Wall Street, Leroy? Did you lose money on the stock market?'

Leroy sniffed at the air in the Kit Kat Klub, which reeked of beer and marijuana and perspiration. 'I hate the Federal gov'ment,' he confided, 'and that there Wall Street is a branch of the Federal gov'ment. Wall Street is where them Jews hang out, running the country from behind their polished mahogany desks, plotting to take over the whole entire world. Whether you admit it or not, you know I'm right or you wouldn't be doing what you're doing. You're a foot soldier like me in the war of liberation. Hell, we may have to destroy America to liberate her, but one way or another we are gonna go and set the clock back to where right thinking folks can get on with their lives without being dictated to by some pompous asshole in Washington. It's the Civil War all over again, Lincoln. The Federal gov'ment's trying to tell us what we can do and what we can't do. Things keep up the way they been going, hell, they're gonna throw away the Constitution and decide you need to get yourself a license before you can own a handgun.' Leroy kept his voice pitched low but he was starting to rant now. 'A license to buy a handgun! Over my dead body! Listen up, Lincoln, you got yourself book learning so you know the country is going to the dogs. Give the kikes an' niggers an inch, they'll come right back at you for a country mile. If we don't draw the limit line in the dirt, if we don't make our stand now, why, one day soon they're gonna bus the niggers to every goddamn school in the country until there won't be such a thing as a white man's school left between the Pacific and the Atlantic.'

Leroy seemed to run out of steam just as the mulatto girl working the bar turned up with his beer. She deftly flicked off the cap with a church key hanging between her breasts at the end of a long gold necklace. 'Ready for a refill?' she asked Lincoln.

The bottle of beer on the table in front of him was still half full. 'I'm okay,' he said.

'He is definitely okay,' Leroy agreed impatiently.

The waitress told Leroy, 'My girlfriend Paura, she's the dark haired one in toreador pants dancing all by herself over there, has taken a shine to your friend here.'

'You don't say,' Leroy said. He smirked across the table at Lincoln. 'Why don't you invite Paura over for a beer, Lincoln. If'n you don't fancy her I'll take her on.'

'I told you—' Lincoln started to say, but Leroy had already grabbed the waitress's wrist. 'Go and tell this Paura chic to get her ass over here.'

The waitress could be seen laughing and saying something to her friend as she headed back to the bar. Paura, holding an enormous joint between two fingers of her left hand, slowly turned her head and sized up the two men in the booth, then went on with her dancing though each shuffling step brought her closer to the rear of the bar. She kept dancing even after the record stopped and wound up swaying like a leaf in a faint breeze next to the booth as 'Don't Worry, Be Happy' started in again. She took a drag on her joint and swallowed the smoke and said, 'I bet she told you my name's Paura.'

'She did,' Leroy affirmed.

'She never gets it right.' The girl spoke English with what Lincoln took to be an Italian accent. 'I'm Paura some days. On others I'm Lucia. Today is a Lucia day.'

Lincoln, an aficionado of legends as well as firearms, asked, 'Are these different names for the same person or two distinct people?'

Lucia scrutinized Lincoln to see if he was mocking her. When she saw he was serious, she answered his question seriously. 'They're as distinct as night and day. Lucia is day. Her name in Italian means light. Sunshine and daylight fill her heart, she is grateful to be alive and lives from day to day, she doesn't see past tomorrow. She goes down on anyone who pays without haggling, she considers it a matter of principle to give a client his money's worth. She passes on half of what she earns to her pimp and does not hold back his share if a client should happen to leave a tip.'

'And Paura? What's she like?'

'Paura is night. Her name means fear in Italian.

Everything about her can be traced to fear – she is afraid of her shadow during the day, afraid of the darkness when the last light has been drained from the day, afraid of the customers who remove their belts before they take off their trousers. She's afraid of swimming pools. She is afraid life on earth will end before dawn tomorrow, afraid it will go on forever.' She regarded Lincoln with her frightened eyes. 'Would you like me to read your palm? I can tell you on what day of the week your life will come to an end.'

Lincoln politely declined. 'I have no visible lifeline,' he said.

The girl tried another tack. 'What sign were you born under?'

Lincoln shook his head. 'I'm a Zodiac atheist. Don't know my sign, don't want to know.'

'That more or less narrows our relationship down to dancing,' Lucia said, her body starting to sway to the music again. Shrugging the filmy blouse so far off one shoulder that the aureole on a breast came into view, she held out a hand.

'She's a nut case,' Leroy muttered. 'But she sure has got the hots for you.'

'I have a bad leg,' Lincoln informed the girl.

'Go 'head and put her out of her misery,' Leroy urged. 'Jesus Christ, you can't catch nothing jus' dancing with her.' When Lincoln still hung back, Leroy nudged his ankle under the table. 'You ain't being a gentleman, Lincoln, that's for goddamned sure.'

Lincoln pulled a face and shrugged and slid off the banquette to his feet. The Italian girl gripped one of his large hands in hers and pulled him limping into the middle of the room, then turned and, stomping out her joint on the floor boards, melted against him, both of her bare arms flung around his neck, her teeth nibbling on the lobe of his ear.

In the booth, Leroy slapped the table in delight.

Lincoln was a good dancer. Favoring his game leg, and with the girl glued to his lanky frame, he launched into an awkward little three step that set the other girls around the bar to watching in admiration.

After a bit Lucia whispered in Lincoln's ear. 'You don't need to tell me your names if you don't want to. Wouldn't change anything if you did – around here nobody uses real names.'

'Name's Lincoln.'

'That a first name or family name?'

'First.'

'That your name during daylight or at night?'

Lincoln had to smile. 'Both.'

Without missing a beat, Lucia said, 'Giovanni da Varrazano, who gave his daylight name to the bridge that connects Brooklyn to an island named Staten, was killed by Indians during an expedition to Brazil in 1528. A little bird whispering in my ear told me you would be thrilled to know that.'

Lincoln stopped in his tracks and pushed her off

to arm's length. The smile sat like a mask on his face. 'As a matter of fact, I am.'

Lucia, quite pleased with herself, tucked her breast into her blouse with a dip and toss of her shoulder and sank back into his arms, and they started dancing again. Lincoln, suddenly edgy, pressed his mouth to her ear. 'So it's you, the cutout,' he said. He thought of Djamillah in the room over the bar in Beirut, with the faded night moth tattooed under her right breast; he remembered telling her *I am addicted to fear – I require a daily fix.* You had to be addicted to fear to get into the business of spying; this is the thing he had in common with the Italian girl Paura – she had surely been the cutout who had seen the FBI asset thrown to the crocodile. Lincoln identified the source of his edginess: He hoped against hope she wouldn't suffer the same fate. 'Do you have a good memory?' he asked her now. Without waiting for a reply, he said, 'Here goes nothing: I was picked up by the Texan sitting at the table with me, I believe his name really is Leroy Streeter because he mentioned that his father had burned down a Negro church in Alabama. He took me to a room over a bar in Ciudad del Este. The Egyptian named Daoud was there.'

'It's no skin off my nose if you don't want sex,' Lucia said. 'I've had enough sex for one day. My pussy and my mouth are both sore.'

'Daoud checked out my bona fides – I heard him go upstairs and make a phone call – my guess is he was getting his people to confirm that I'd been treated in a Trieste clinic, that I'd written the book I said I wrote. I must have passed the initial muster because he sent me back here and told me to hang out with Leroy until I was contacted again, which is what I'm doing now.'

'The reason we play the same record all the time,' Lucia whispered, her tongue flicking inside his ear, 'is because "Don't Worry, Be Happy' is the opposite of our lives down here. Except for Lucia, all we do is worry about not being happy.'

'With any luck, the next step is for me to be taken to meet the Saudi.'

'The girls who work here,' Lucia said, 'use abortions as birth control. If you ever come back again, it will be appreciated if you would bring us a carton of condoms.'

'Leroy told me why they're shopping around for ammonium nitrate,' Lincoln went on. 'I don't know if he's bragging or inventing, but he says he plans to fill a moving van with explosives and blow it up in the middle of Wall Street.' He let one of his palms slip down to her tight toreador pants and the swell of a buttock. 'What will you do when all this is over?'

Lucia dropped one of her hands to reach under the back of Lincoln's shirt. 'All this will never be over,' she breathed.

Her answer startled Lincoln; that was what the Alawite prostitute Djamillah had told Dante Pippen as he was leaving the room over the bar in Beirut a legend ago. 'It will end one day,' Lincoln promised her. 'Where will you go? What will you do?'

'I would go back to Tuscany,' she said, clinging to him, burrowing into his neck so that her words were muffled. 'I would buy a small farm and breed baby polyesters and shear them twice a year and sell the hair to make silk-soft cloth.'

'Polyester is a synthetic fabric,' Lincoln said.

Lucia's hand came in contact with the leather of the holster nestling in the cavity in Lincoln's lower back. She caressed the cold metal on the butt of the small-caliber automatic in the holster. 'I will raise baby acrylics, then,' she said, annoyed at his nitpicking. Her fingers worked their way under the holster; when they reached the smooth scar of the healed wound she stopped dancing abruptly. 'What gave you that?' she asked.

But Lincoln only murmured her night name, Paura, and she didn't repeat the question.

Hanging out at the Kit Kat Klub the following night, Lincoln made a point of dancing with two other girls and taking the second one up to a room so that suspicion wouldn't fall on Paura if he was compromised. Once in the room, the girl, a bleached blonde who called herself Monroe Marilyn, named her price. Lincoln counted out the bills and set them on the table. Monroe washed in a chipped bidet and insisted he wash too, and watched him to make sure he did. She took off the rest of her clothing except for a black lace brassiere, which she claimed to have bought in Paris, and stretched out on the mattress covered with a stained sheet, her legs apart, her eyes fixed on the filaments in the electric bulb dangling from the ceiling. In the bar below 'Don't Worry, Be Happy' started to play again on the jukebox. Lincoln shut his eyes and imagined he was making love to Paura. Under him, Marilyn moaned and cried out with pleasure; to Lincoln her sensual clatter came across as a recorded announcement, played over and over like the 45-rpm disk on the juke-box downstairs. He finished before 'Don't Worry, Be Happy' did.

'So you got your ashes hauled after all,' Leroy said when Lincoln came limping back to the booth and slid onto the banquette across from him. 'You must of broken some kind of speed record. You need to get laid at least once a day not to be sex starved. The trick is to make it last as long as you can. That way you get more fuck for your buck.'

'You ought to write a lonely hearts column for the newspapers,' Lincoln said. 'You could advise men how to solve their sexual problems.'

'I just may do that when I'm too old to take on the Federal gov'ment in Washington.'

'How old will you be when you're too old for the good fight?'

'Thirty, maybe. Maybe thirty.'

Around eleven, an old man wearing a long shabby overcoat and a threadbare scarf wound loosely around his thin neck came into the bar to sell lottery tickets. He had turned up the same hour every night since Lincoln had been hanging out at the Kit Kat. As he stepped through the door, the hookers dropped what they were doing to crowd around him, hunting for lucky numbers on the lottery slips attached to his clipboard. When they'd each bought a ticket that suited them, the girls drifted back to the tables or took up where they'd left off on the dance floor. The lottery vendor shuffled across the floor to a vacant booth not far from where Lincoln and Leroy were sitting. The mulatto waitress filled a tall glass with tap water and set it down in front of him. The old man half bowed to her from a sitting position – the gesture seemed to come from another world and another century. A new girl Lincoln had not seen before came down the steps behind a corpulent Lebanese client and, noticing the old man with the clipboard in the booth, hurried over to buy a ticket. When the music went silent, Lincoln could hear their voices – he could even make out what they were saying. The girl was asking when the drawing would be held and how she would know if she'd won anything. The old man told her that he kept the stubs attached to his clipboard for months. Each morning he tore the list of winning numbers from the newspaper, he said, and made it his business to personally seek out winners who had bought a ticket from him.

The idea of a hooker hoping to strike it rich

from a lottery ticket intrigued Lincoln. He wondered if her pimp would take half the proceeds if she did win.

Leroy was listening to them also. He reached across the table and tapped Lincoln on the wrist. 'The hell language they talking?' he wanted to know.

Lincoln hadn't realized they were talking a foreign language until Leroy called his attention to it. 'Not sure,' he replied, although, to his astonishment, he found that he knew very well. The old lottery vendor and the hooker were talking in Polish, which was the language Martin Odum's mother had used when she told him bedtime stories in Jonestown, Pennsylvania, a lifetime ago.

At the booth, the girl could be heard asking, *'Ile kosztóje bilet?'* When the old man told her how much a ticket cost, she carefully counted out coins from a small purse and tore one from the clipboard.

'Sounds foreign to me,' Leroy was saying. 'Don't like foreigners, don't like the languages they talk. Don't know why foreigners don't learn American. Make the world simpler if everyone talked American, is how I see it.'

Lincoln couldn't resist baiting Leroy. 'You want them to talk American with a Texas drawl like you or a clipped Boston accent like John Kennedy?'

Leroy took the question seriously. 'Don't matter none to me. Any American beats out a foreign language, hands down.'

Near midnight, as the girls began to drift over to the bar to settle up what they owed for the rooms they'd used, the fat Arab boy who'd been doing the jigsaw puzzle in Ciudad del Este burst into the bar. He was still wearing the shoulder holster with the plastic grip of a toy gun jutting from it. Spotting the two Americans in the rear booth, he padded over on his Reeboks and thrust out a folded note. Leroy read it and raised his eyes and cried out excitedly, 'Bingo, Lincoln. Daoud is waiting for us behind the bar.'

Daoud's coal black Mercedes was idling in the shadows at the street end of the alley when the two Yankees, the one with the cane limping along behind the short American in cowboy boots, came around the side of the Kit Kat and settled into the backseat. The fat Arab boy slid in next to Daoud in front. 'Where are you taking us?' Lincoln asked, but Daoud didn't bother to reply. He gestured to the driver and the car lurched past the halal butcher shop on the corner into the poorly lit main drag and headed in the direction of the Little Dipper and Polaris, hanging in the night sky over the rooftops. Twenty minutes out of Foz do Iguaçú the paved road abruptly gave way to a rutted dirt track and the driver had to slow down to keep the passengers from hitting their heads against the roof of the car. In the headlights, Indians leading donkeys piled high with burlap sacks could be seen stumbling through the pitch darkness. 'In the outback,' Leroy told

Lincoln, 'lot of smuggling goes on during the night.' After one particularly rough bump Daoud flung an arm over the shoulder of the fat teenager and said something to him in Arabic. The boy said, '*Inch'Allah.*'

Lincoln leaned forward to ask the Egyptian if the boy were his son. Daoud turned his head only slightly and said, 'He is the son of my son.'

'And where is his father?'

'His father, my son, was killed in the attack on the American Marines at Beirut Airport in 1983.'

Lincoln reminded himself he was living deep in a legend; that he ought to be commiserating with the Egyptian. 'It must be a source of great sadness to have lost your son—'

'It is a source of great pride to have given a son to the jihad. Along with my son, two hundred and forty one American marines and sailors lost their lives in the Beirut attack, after which your President Reagan lost his nerve and disengaged from Lebanon. Every father should have such a son.'

An hour and twenty minutes out of Foz de Iguaçú, the headlights of the Mercedes picked up the first of two road blocks. Soon after the second one, located beyond a sharp curve in the track, the car slowed to give three armed men with red-and-white checkered kaffiyehs over their faces time to drag open a chain-link gate. One of the guards said something into a walkie-talkie as he waved the Mercedes through. The driver headed downhill toward a group of wooden army barracks set in what looked like a dry river bed and pulled up before a structure that was lower and wider than the other buildings. On a flat rise behind the barracks, in a dirt field illuminated by floodlights powered by a gasoline-driven motor whose put-put was audible in the still night air, a dozen men in khaki fatigues were practicing penalty shots against a goalie outfitted in a yellow Hertz jump-suit. When one of them scored, Lincoln could make out the other players taunting the guardian.

Daoud's grandson darted from the Mercedes to pull open a narrow door in the side of the building. The young Pakistani whom Lincoln had seen dancing at the Kit Kat with Leroy's jailbait hooker stood in the corridor inside the door, an Israeli Uzi with spare clips taped to the folding metal stock tucked under an arm, his finger on the trigger. He tensed when he saw the two Americans and muttered something to Daoud, who translated. 'He wants to know if you are armed.' Lincoln, laughing, reached under his shirt behind his back and pulled the small-caliber automatic from the holster worn high on his belt so that it would disappear into the shrapnel wound. The Pakistani took the automatic and waved the party through.

The corridor gave onto a square room with a low ceiling. It took a moment for Lincoln's eyes to become accustomed to the dimness. About thirty or so men sat around the room on straw matting, their backs against thin cushions attached to the walls. Daoud motioned Lincoln and Leroy to a spot along the near wall, then crossed the room and took a free place against the opposite wall near the figure who was clearly presiding. Lincoln set his cane on the cement floor and settled down, his bad leg stretched out in front of him, the other ankle tucked under his thigh. Next to him, Leroy sank into an awkward cross-legged position. Lincoln reached for his tin of Schimelpenicks, but a lean young Arab posed a hand gently but firmly on his wrist. Lincoln noticed that nobody in the room was smoking. He nodded and grinned at the young Arab, who turned away, expressionless.

Lincoln tried to distinguish the features of the figure across from him. The man, who looked to be in mid-thirties, was ruggedly handsome, with a stringy ash-colored beard and dark thoughtful eyes exuding an inner calm that could have easily been taken for arrogance. He was extremely tall and dressed in a collarless coarse off-white ankle-length robe with what Lincoln took to be a thick Afghan goat-hair vest over it. Bareheaded, with socks and heavy walking sandals on his feet, he sat crosslegged on the mat with a supple elegance, his back off the wall and hunched slightly forward as he read something from a sheet of paper to those within earshot, occasionally tapping the long forefinger of his right hand on a word to empha-size its importance. All Lincoln could make out

318

was the honeyed undertone of someone who didn't need to raise his voice to be heard.

There appeared to be some sort of queue because the two men sitting between Daoud and the figure Lincoln identified as the Saudi spoke next, raising problems that needed to be solved or providing information that needed to be weighed against what was already known. Finally Daoud's turn came. Leaning forward, talking quietly, he spoke to the Saudi for several minutes. Once he tossed his head to indicate the two Americans sitting across the room. Only then did the Saudi's gaze settle on the visitors. He scratched at his chest with several fingers and uttered a single word. Daoud looked over and motioned for Lincoln to approach. Leroy assumed the gesture included him and started to get up, but Daoud wagged a finger and he collapsed back into his cramped position. Leaning on his cane, Lincoln pushed himself to his feet and walked over to the Saudi and sank onto his haunches facing him. The Saudi saluted him with a palm to his heart and Lincoln mimicked the gesture. A thin man with greasy hair parted down the middle and thick spectacles slipping along his nose was sitting next to the Saudi with a lined notebook open on his lap; Lincoln took him for a secretary. The Saudi murmured something and the secretary repeated it in a loud voice. Instantly all the men sitting around the walls sprang to their feet and headed for the door. Across the room, only Leroy remained, squirming uncomfortably in a position he would never grow accustomed to. Lincoln looked from Daoud to his host and back as Daoud delivered a short speech in Arabic. The Saudi listened intently, nodding from time to time in apparent agreement, his eyes darting occasionally to Lincoln and, once, to Leroy across the room. Finally the Saudi, scratching again at his chest, started to put questions. The secretary with the greasy hair translated them into English.

'He welcomes you to Boa Vista. He asks how you arrived to here from Croatia.'

'I flew Lufthansa from Zagreb to Munich to Paris, then Air France to New York, then PanAm to São Paolo. I chartered a small plane that flew me into Foz do Iguaçú.'

When the secretary had translated this, the Saudi, never lifting his eyes from Lincoln, put another question. The secretary said, 'He asks how the struggle is going in Bosnia? He asks whether the Bosnians, in the event of war, will be able to defend Sarajevo if the Serbs capture the hills overlooking the city.'

'The Serb military is by all accounts a great deal stronger than anything the Bosnians can field,' Lincoln said. 'What will strengthen the Bosnians in the event of war is that they have no place to go; their backs are against Croatia, and the Croats hate them as much as the Serbs.'

'He agrees with your analysis. He tells the story of the Greek general who warned his officers not to attack a weaker force trapped in a canyon without a line of retreat available, because the weaker force would then conquer the stronger force.'

The Saudi spoke again; again the secretary translated. 'He asks how you plan to accumulate large quantities of ammonium nitrate without attracting the attention of the police.'

Almost against his will Lincoln felt himself falling under the spell of the Saudi. He saw, now that he was close to him, that the skin on the Saudi's face and neck appeared yellowish, but he assumed it was due to the low wattage of the bulbs burning in the room. He couldn't help but like his style – no wonder young men were flocking to join his al-Qa'ida cells in Afghanistan and Yemen. Watching his unflinching eyes, Lincoln could feel the magnetic pull of his personality; the Saudi spoke softly but he carried a big stick. Seeing how uncomfortable his visitor was, the Saudi reached out to offer him a cushion. Lincoln sat on it, his game leg thrust forward, and provided an explanation that had been prepared back at Langley: His several associates would spread out across America and, pretending to represent farmers' cooperatives in various southern and eastern states, would buy up whatever ammonium nitrate was available and truck it to New Jersey, where it would all be loaded onto a moving van. At a site to be designated, Leroy Streeter would take possession of the ammonium nitrate and pay the fee in cash.

'He asks if you are curious to know what Mr Streeter plans to do with the ammonium nitrate.'

'I suppose he plans to explode it someplace. Tell you the truth, I couldn't care less.'

'He asks why you could not care less.'

'I believe America has grown too rich and too fat and too insolent and needs to be taken down a peg or two.' It was clear from the secretary's expression that he didn't understand the expression 'a peg or two.' Lincoln repeated the thought another way. 'America needs to be taught a lesson in humility.'

'He asks what kinds of arms you sold in the Balkans.'

'All kinds. My clients would give me a wish list and I did my best to fill it.'

'What is it, a wish list?'

'A list of the arms and munitions that they wished to have.'

'He asks if you have limited your operations to conventional weapons.'

'My operations have been limited to selling what the Soviet military has in its stocks. Up to now I have procured almost all of the weapons and munitions from Soviet army units in East Germany. Many of the Russians I dealt with have returned to the Soviet Union and would be able to supply me with other articles from the Soviet arsenal. Do you have something particular in mind?'

'He asks whether you could supply spent plutonium or enriched uranium.'

Lincoln thought about that for a moment. 'Spent

plutonium or enriched-uranium waste could be obtained from nuclear power plants like the one in Chernobyl, north of Kiev in the Ukraine—'

The Saudi interrupted Lincoln and the secretary translated what he said. 'He is curious why you mention Chernobyl, since its reactor exploded five years ago and the radioactive waste has been sealed under an enormous concrete sheath.'

'It was the plant's number four reactor that exploded. Two other reactors remain in use. The radioactive waste is trucked to various nuclear disposal sites in the Soviet Union. There is another source of spent plutonium – the Soviet nuclear submarine fleet based in Archangel and Murmansk is known to be decommissioning vessels because of budgetary shortfalls. Plutonium pits are removed from the decommissioned subs and trucked to the same nuclear disposal sites. The bottom line is that there is no shortage of weapons-grade plutonium or uranium for anyone willing to run the risks involved in negotiating the acquisition. It goes without saying, very large sums of money would be required to conclude such a deal.'

The Saudi accepted the translation with a preoccupied nod. He muttered something to the secretary, who said: 'He asks how large?'

'How much radioactive waste would be required?'

'He says to you a tenth of a short ton to start with.'

'Where would he want it delivered?'

'At a site to be specified in Afghanistan.'

'I would need to consult my associates before setting a price. Off the top of my head, I should think we are talking about something in the neighborhood of a million dollars U.S., a down payment in cash when I have located the spent pits, the rest to be paid into a numbered account in an offshore bank.'

'He asks is it so that nuclear bombs can be fitted into something the size of a common valise.'

'He's referring to what the Americans have designated the MK-47. The Soviets are said to have constructed several hundred of these devices. Imagine something shaped like an army canteen, only larger, roughly the size of a bulging valise, with an automobile gas cap on the top and two metal handles on either side. Because of its size and mobility, the nuclear device can be easily smuggled into a target city and exploded by a crude timing mechanism. The MK-47s contain twenty-two pounds of uranium which, when exploded, is equivalent to one thousand tons of conventional TNT, one twentieth the size of the first Hiroshima atomic bomb.'

'He asks about the shelf life of these valise-bombs.'

'The Russians have been miniaturizing their nuclear payloads since the mid 1980s. Whatever they have in their stockpiles could be expected to function for ten to fifteen years.'

'He wants to know if such a valise-bomb can be acquired?'

'For obvious reasons, the Russian military keep these devices under lock and key, with a high degree of command and control accountability. But if someone were to offer an enormous sum of money, plus safe passage out of Russia for the seller, it is conceivable that something might be worked out.'

'He asks how much money is an enormous sum.'

'Again, off the top of my head, I would say something in the neighborhood of three to five million U.S for each valise-bomb.'

The Saudi sank back into the cushion fastened to the wall behind him and scratched absently at his upper arm and his ribs. Lincoln noticed that the Saudi was sweating despite the chill in the room; that the sweat on his brow seemed to crystalize into a fine white powder.

'He says to you that for the time being we will concentrate on the spent plutonium or uranium pits. He says that nobody can say what the future holds. Perhaps one day he will raise the subject of the valisebomb again with you.'

Lincoln smiled and nodded. 'It's your call.'

There was a large glass bowl filled with fruit, and another overflowing with nuts, near the Saudi. He pointed first to one and then the other with a hand turned palm up, offering something to eat to his guest. Lincoln reached out to help himself to some nuts.

'He notes that it turns cold at night out here,' the secretary translated. 'He asks if you and your friend would like some herbal tea.'

Lincoln looked at Leroy over his shoulder and said, 'He is offering us hot herbal tea.'

'Ask 'em if they got anythin' slightly more alcoholic,' Leroy said.

'Leroy, these people don't drink alcohol. It's against their religion.'

'Goddamn. How can they expect folks to convert to a dry religion?'

The Saudi apparently caught the gist of Leroy's remark because he replied in Arabic without waiting for the secretary to translate. The secretary said: 'He tells the story of the czar who converted Russia to Christianity – it was near the end of the first millennium. Vladimir I of Kiev was tempted by Islam but decided against it because he did not think Russians could get through their cruel winters without something the Arab chemists who developed the technique of distillation called *al-kuhl*. History might have turned out differently if the Prophet had not abstained from alcohol – the long cold war would have been between Christianity and Islam.'

Lincoln said, 'With the collapse of the Soviet Union, perhaps there will be another cold war – a new struggle for Jerusalem between the spiritual descendants of Richard the Lionheart and the heirs of the Sultan Saladin.'

Listening to the translation, the Saudi reached for a glass filled with water and, popping two large oval pills into his mouth, washed them down with a long swig. Lincoln watched his Adam's apple bob in his long neck. Wiping his lips with the fabric on the back of a wrist, the Saudi said, in labored English, 'A new struggle is surely a possibility.'

'You speak English?' Lincoln asked him directly.

The Saudi responded in Arabic and the secretary translated. 'He says to you he speaks English as well as you speak Arabic.'

Lincoln grinned. 'I understand four words of Arabic: *Allah Akbar* and *Inch'Allah.*'

'He compliments you. He says to you the person who understands only these four words grasps the heart of the holy Koran. He says to you there are pious men, descendants of the Prophet, who can recite all one hundred and fourteen suras from memory but do not hold in their hearts the significance of these four words.'

Lincoln looked at the Saudi. 'Are you pious? Do you practice your religion?'

'He says to you he practices as much of it as needs to be practiced to be a faithful Muslim. He says to you that he resides in what Muslim's call *dar al-harb*, the home of war; above all other things he practices *jihad*. He would have you know that waging war on behalf of Islam and Allah against the infidel is a Koranic obligation.'

Lincoln nodded at the Saudi, who inclined his head in a sign of esteem for the foreigner who appeared to respect him.

'What happened then?' Crystal Quest demanded when Lincoln, back in Washington, described the meeting at the training camp in the Brazilian *mato graso*.

'He threw questions at me for another twenty minutes and I fielded them. It was all very low keyed. At one point he got into a long discussion with the Egyptian, Daoud; for five or so minutes it was almost as if I didn't exist. Then, without saying another word to me, the Saudi climbed to his feet and departed. I heard the motors of three or four cars kick into life behind the building and saw their headlights sweep into and out of the room as they headed deeper into the *mato graso*. Daoud signaled that the meeting had come to an end and ushered Leroy and me back to his Mercedes and we started back toward Foz do Iguaçú. The Egyptian told me I had made a good impression on the Saudi. He said I was to return to the United States and organize the purchase and delivery of the ammonium nitrate at mid month to an abandoned hangar off the Pulaski Skyway in New Jersey.' Lincoln produced a page that had been torn out of a lined notebook. 'The address is written here.'

Quest snatched the scrap of paper. 'What about the Saudi and his radioactive waste?' she asked.

'Daoud invited me to return to Boa Vista on the night of the new moon to meet the Saudi and organize with him the delivery of the two hundred pounds of spent plutonium.'

'Describe the Saudi again, Lincoln.'

'It's all in my mission report. His name was never

328

mentioned, either by Daoud or by the secretary translating for him at the meeting in Boa Vista. I would estimate he was roughly six foot five and in his middle thirties—'

Quest cut in. 'Guessing someone's age has never been your strong suit. How old do you think the cutout was?'

'The hooker in the Kit Kat? I'd say she was in her late thirties or early forties.'

'Proves my point,' Quest told the wallahs who had crowded into her office to attend Lincoln's debriefing. 'The girl, the youngest daughter of an old Roman family, is twenty-seven. Her real name is Fiamma Segre. She's been doing hard drugs for years – that's why she looks old before her time. Go on with your description of the Saudi.'

Lincoln, resting his elbows on the cane stretched like a span between the two arms of the chair, closed his eyes and tried to summon an image of the Saudi. 'He's charismatic—'

'That's a load of crap, Lincoln. What do we put on the advisory we send out to our stations? "Wanted, dead or alive, one charismatic Saudi."'

Lincoln's patience was wearing thin. He was bone tired – the car ride back to São Paolo and the flight back to the States had worn him out. The grilling by Fred and her wallahs was shaping up as the straw that would break the camel's back. 'I'm doing the best I can—'

'Your best needs to be better.'

'Maybe if he were to get some shuteye,' ventured one of the bolder wallahs.

Quest didn't like to be second guessed. 'Maybe if you were to get yourself a posting to another division,' she shot back. 'How about it, Lincoln. Give us something concrete to go on. Rack your memory. I'm looking for what you didn't put into your report.'

From a remote corner of his subconscious, Lincoln dredged up several details he had over-looked when he drafted his report. 'Something's very wrong with the Saudi—'

'Mentally or medically?'

'Medically. He kept scratching at different parts of his body – his upper arm, his chest, his ribs. He seemed to itch all over. His skin was sallow – at first I thought it was because of the dim lighting, but when he stood up to go he passed under a bulb and I saw that he really was yellowish. Another thing: He was sweating even though it wasn't warm in the room. The perspiration on his forehead appeared to crystalize into a fine white powder.'

Crystal Quest sat back in her chair and exchanged looks with the M.D. on her staff who directed the section that provided psychological and medical profiles of world leaders. 'What do you make of that, Archie?'

'There are several possibilities. The start of chronic kidney failure has to be one of them. It's a condition that could go on for five, ten years without becoming life threatening.'

'He took pills,' Lincoln remembered.

'Small? Big? Did you notice the color or the shape?'

'Oval. Very big, the kind I'd have trouble swallowing. It was dark so I'm not sure of the color. Yellow, maybe. Yellow or orange.'

'Hmmm. If it is chronic kidney failure, a bunch of early treatments come to mind. Could be calcium carbonate and calcium acetate – both are big yellowish pills, oval shaped, taken several times a day to lower the phosphorus level of the blood when the kidney isn't filtering properly. Diet would be critical – dairy products, liver, vegetables, nuts are high in phosphorus and would need to be avoided.'

Lincoln remembered another detail. 'There was a bowl of nuts on the floor between us – he offered them to me but he never helped himself to any.'

For once Quest looked pleased. 'That should give us something to go on. A Saudi operating out of Khartoum who may be suffering from chronic kidney failure – if he's taking pills it would mean he's been diagnosed by a doctor somewhere, or even undergone clinical tests in a hospital. When you've gotten forty winks, Lincoln, I want you to work with one of the artists on the third floor and see if you can't come up with a portrait. Meanwhile we'll get our people to collect enough ammonium nitrate to fill a moving van so you can make that rendezvous in New Jersey with the would-be Wall Street bomber, Leroy Streeter.'

'Do I go back to Boa Vista the night of the new moon to sell radioactive waste to the Saudi?' Lincoln asked.

'I don't think that'll be necessary,' Quest said. 'We have a good working relationship with SIDE. We'll send in a para team to back up the Argentine State Intelligence people. They can encircle Boa Vista the night of the new moon—'

'That's the fourth of next month,' one of the wallahs noted.

'We'll let SIDE pick up the Saudi and work him over.' She added with a harsh laugh, 'Their methods of interrogation are less sophisticated than ours, but more cost efficient. When they're finished interrogating him they can feed him to one of Daoud's alligators and America will have one less enemy to worry about.'

'I want to make sure we get the Italian girl out before all hell breaks look at Triple Border,' Lincoln said. He fingered his cane and rested the tip of it on Crystal Quest's desk. 'I don't want her to end up like Djamillah in Beirut.'

'You're a vulgar romantic,' Quest complained. 'We'll sneak her out of there the afternoon of the day we close in on the Saudi.'

'I want you to give me your word.'

The sudden silence in the room roared in Lincoln's ear. The wallahs had never heard anyone talk to the DDO quite like that. They kept their eyes fixed on their boss so as not to miss the eruption; it would be another tantrum to add to the

332

Crystal Quest saga when the subject came up, as it invariably did, at happy hour. The color drained from her rouged cheeks, her eyes bulged and she looked as if she were about to choke to death on a fish bone stuck in her gullet. Then an unearthly bleat seeped from between her resplendently crimson lips. It took a moment for the people in the room to realize she was laughing. 'We'll get the girl out, Lincoln,' she said as she gasped for breath. 'You have my word.'

They met an hour shy of first light in an enormous abandoned hangar under a curve of the Pulaski Skyway, twenty minutes from the mouth of the Holland Tunnel leading to Manhattan. At the rear of the hangar sheets of corrugated roofing had sagged to the ground, creating a makeshift wall that blocked the gusts sweeping in from the coast. Beyond the hangar, in a hard dirt field strewn with thousands of empty plastic bottles, a small campfire burned; twenty or so homeless migrants who picked up work as longshoremen on the Hoboken docks were sitting with their backs against the dilapidated panel truck they used as a mobile bunkroom, drinking coffee brewed over the open fire. Carried on the gusts of damp air, the tinny syncopated clatter of a Mexican mambo band reached the hangar from the panel truck's radio. Inside, Ibrahim bin Daoud scrambled up the narrow metal ladder into the back of the moving van and began inspecting the large burlap sacks, all of them stencilled in black letters 'AMMONIUM NITRATE.' Daoud had turned up with a sample of ammonium nitrate in a small jar and started comparing the contents of the sacks against his sample.

Leroy, watching from the ground, called impatiently, 'Well?'

'It is ammonium nitrate, all right,' the Egyptian confirmed.

Smiling out one side of his mouth, Leroy hefted a large valise out of the trunk compartment of Daoud's rented Toyota, set it on the car's hood and snapped open the lid. Lincoln, leaning on his cane, could see a transparent plastic sack filled with $100 bills bound in yellow wrappers. A six-volt car battery, a coil of electric wire, a small satchel filled with tools and several army surplus percussion caps were also in the valise. Lincoln pointed at the money with his cane. 'Count it,' he told the wiry man who had driven the moving van from Pennsauken outside of Camden, the assembly point for the pick-up trucks bringing ammonium nitrate from various parts of the East Coast. Lincoln leaned back against a rusting stanchion to watch; he could feel the holster and small-caliber automatic rubbing against the skin in the cavity at his lower back. Up in the van, Daoud opened each of the burlap sacks in the first two rows to inspect the contents. He played a flashlight into the depths of the van, counting the sacks out loud in Arabic.

Satisfied, he backed down the metal ladder and walked over to Lincoln.

'You are clearly someone we can do business with,' he said.

The man counting the wads of bills, wearing a corduroy sports jacket with the butt of a pistol visible in a shoulder holster, looked up from the ground. 'If there are a hundred bills in each packet like they say,' he told Lincoln, 'the count is right.'

'The last thing we would do is cheat you,' Daoud said. 'We still have unfinished business in Boa Vista on the night of the new moon. Have you made progress with the problem of radioactive waste?'

'I have located twenty-three-thousand spent plutonium pits stored in two sheds at a secret military site. Security is insignificant – it consists of barbed-wire around the sheds and padlocks on the doors.'

Daoud was someone who didn't display emotions easily. Now, unable to contain his excitement, he danced a little jig on the cement floor of the hangar. 'My Saudi friend will be extremely pleased. In what area of Russia are these sheds?'

Lincoln only smiled.

Daoud said quickly, 'It was not my intention to be indiscreet. I am trying to calculate how difficult it will be to retrieve a quantity of these pits and transport them across the various frontiers into Afghanistan.'

'It can be accomplished. I shall require a down payment of two hundred and fifty thousand dollars

335

U.S., in used one-hundred-dollar bills, payable when I meet the Saudi in Boa Vista on the night of four February.'

Daoud started to say that the down payment would be waiting at Boa Vista when everyone was distracted by a commotion at the rear of the hangar. Daoud's fat grandson could be seen squirming through a gap in the corrugated roofing. Crying out in Arabic, he came padding toward his grandfather. Daoud plunged a hand into the deep pocket of his raincoat; it emerged clutching a pistol fitted with a silencer. 'My grandson tells that the men around the camp fire in the field are armed with automatic rifles – he crept close and saw people distributing them from the back of the panel truck. It appears we have walked into a trap—'

The headlights of a dozen automobiles, glimmering in the predawn mist that clung to the ground, materialized on the ramp coming off the Pulaski Skyway half a mile away. The cars formed up in a line abreast and headed in the direction of the hangar.

Leroy cried, 'Give me the detonator – I'll set off the sacks and blow 'em all to hell,' but before he could do anything the wiry man who was counting the money scooped up the valise and darted out the side of the hangar, disappearing into the darkness. Daoud pulled his grandson under the moving van. Leroy grabbed Lincoln's arm and drew him toward the fallen squares of corrugated roof as the headlights began to play across the interior of the hangar. 'Goddamn,' Leroy muttered, hauling a shiny wooden-handled Webley and Scott from his belt and spinning the chambers angrily. 'You was followed here, Lincoln,' he said in a harsh whisper.

'You or Daoud were the ones who were followed,' Lincoln retorted.

Behind them they could make out the distant shouts of men coming across the field from the direction of the campfire.

Leroy crouched behind a sheet of tin. 'My daddy died in one of their jails,' he said. 'Listen up, Lincoln – it's still night out. All we got to do is shoot down one or two of 'em – when the others panic an' go to ground, we can squirm off into the field and make a run for it.'

The automobiles, with their headlights flickering over the moving van, pulled up around the hangar. Silhouettes could be seen running in front of the headlights as men took up positions on the hangar's perimeter. Some of them were armed with rifles, others carried plastic shields. A voice Lincoln thought he recognized came echoing over a bull-horn. 'This is the FBI. We know you're in there. You are completely surrounded. You have two minutes to come out with your hands raised over your heads.'

In the middle of the hangar Daoud rolled clear of the moving van and rose to his feet. He raised one hand to shield his eyes from the headlights and started to walk in the direction of the bullhorn.

When he was halfway there the hand holding the pistol emerged from behind his back. Lincoln could hear the hiss of two silenced shots before several rifles firing on automatic cut him down. The Egyptian, propelled backward by the bullets slamming into his chest, crumpled to the cement. Sobbing like a baby, the fat Egyptian boy crawled from under the van to his grandfather's body and flung his arms around him. Then the boy stumbled to his feet and, peering through his tears into the headlights, tugged the pistol from his shoulder holster. Before he could get it clear, high powered bullets burrowed into his chest.

Sweeping the ground before them with blinding hand-held klieg lights, a line of armed men wearing black windbreakers started advancing through the hangar. When one of them turned to shout an order, Lincoln noticed the large white letters 'FBI' on the back of his jacket. 'Wait till we can see the whites of their eyes,' Leroy whispered to Lincoln, who was hiding behind a stanchion next to the crouching Texan. 'I'll plug the one who's leading the pack.'

The FBI agents drifted past the van, the beams of their klieg lights spearing the darkness ahead of them as they closed in on the sheets of corrugated roofing at the rear of the hangar. Lincoln thought he recognized the stumpy figure of Felix Kiick in the lead, hunched low with a bullhorn in one hand, a pistol in the other. When Kiick was fifteen yards away he brought the bullhorn to his lips. 'This is your last chance – Leroy Streeter, Lincoln Dittmann, you can't escape. Come out with your hands over your heads.'

Kiick took several more steps as he spoke. Leroy, steadying his shooting arm with his left hand, his left elbow locked into his gut, raised the Webley and Scott and took careful aim at Kiick's head. Lincoln had hoped they would be captured without a fight, but the timing of the raid on the hangar had gone wildly wrong. The op order had called for the agents at the campfire in the field to arrive at the back of the hangar as the head-lights coming off the Pulaski ramp became visible. Leroy and Daoud, distracted by the approaching automobiles, would be easily overpowered before they could put up a fight. Now there was nothing for Lincoln to do but save Kiick from the bullet. In one flowing gesture he raised his cane and brought it crashing down on Leroy's arm, shat-tering his wrist. Kiick jumped when he heard the bone splinter. Leroy gazed up with more pure hate in his eyes than Lincoln had ever seen in a human being. His lips moved but no words emerged until he managed to croak, 'You're one of them!'

'Felix, we're over here,' Lincoln called, stepping around the corrugated sheeting into view.

Kiick came over and played his light on Leroy, who was gaping in astonishment at his right hand hanging limply from the wrist. The wooden-handled Webley and Scott lay on the cement. Two FBI agents gripped Leroy under his armpits and dragged him toward the automobiles. Using a handkerchief, Kiick retrieved Leroy's weapon and held it by the barrel. 'Something tells me I owe you one,' he said.

Lincoln and Kiick walked over to where Daoud and his grandson lay. Medics were kneeling next to both of them, listening with stethoscopes for any signs of life. The medics looked up at the same moment and shook their heads. Someone illuminated the corpses with a klieg light and started taking photographs from different angles. Other agents covered the corpses with lengths of silver plastic. An agent wearing elastic surgeon's gloves brought over the handgun that had been retrieved from under the corpse of the fat Egyptian boy. He held it out, grip first, so Kiick could get a better look at it.

'Holy mackerel,' Kiick said. He shook his head in disgust. 'It sure looked like the real McCoy to me.'

Presiding over the formal postmorten in the DDO's seventh floor bailiwick at Langley, Crystal Quest made no effort to tame the shrew in her. Everything that could go wrong had gone wrong, she seethed. The adults pretending to be FBI agents in the field behind the hangar had been spotted by a child – *by a child!* – before the raid was even underway. Daoud had walked into a hail of bullets so as not to be taken alive. Lincoln Dittmann's legend was blown when he saved Kiick's life. As an added extra bonus, the FBI clowns under Felix Kiick's command had gunned down a juvenile armed with a plastic pistol. Holy Christ, it hadn't even been loaded with water. Leroy Streeter Jr., who would get a life sentence for attempting to blow up a square mile of Wall Street, knew precious little about the al-Qa'ida cells and less about the Saudi who was organizing them; Streeter's expertise was limited to a small group of nutty white suprem-acists in Texas that had already been infiltrated by so many state and Federal agents half the group's dues came from the government. To add humilia-tion to embarrassment, any hope of nabbing the Saudi had evaporated the night before when the cretins from the Argentine State Intelligence had bungled the raid on Boa Vista. Talk about stealth, they had headed into the Brazilian *mato graso* in half a dozen giant army helicopters flying at treetop level *with their running lights on*, for God's sake, and kicked up such a storm of sand when they touched down at the training camp that half the fedayeen managed to slip away in the confusion. Naturally the Saudi who had been presiding over the meeting in the low-roofed building was nowhere to be found when the SIDE agents, backed up by a handful of the Company's paramilitary people who were currently hunting for new jobs, burst through the door. So what did the raid net? I'll tell you what it netted. Are you ready for this, gentlemen and ladies? It netted two jokers from Hamas, two more from Hezbollah, seven from Egypt's Islamic

Brotherhood, a drunk Irishman from the IRA and two young females from the Basque ETA who listed *fashion model* under profession when they were interrogated. Fashion models my ass! One of them was so flat chested she put padding in her brassiere to break even, for Christ's sake. No shit, we could have snared twice as many terrorists using fly paper tacked to the rafters of any bar on the main drag of Foz do Iguaçú.

Quest appeared to come up for air. In the several seconds of silence, Lincoln was able to get a word in. Well, he said, we did pin down the identity of the Saudi.

The speculation about the chronic kidney failure had been the starting point. On the theory that Leroy Streeter's offhand remark about the Saudi's wealth ('Thanks to Allah and his late father, he is very rich') would suggest he'd been diagnosed and treated by an expensive private physician, Riyadh intelligence authorities had combed the clinics frequented by the royal family and affluent members of the business community. If they came up with anything, they kept it to themselves. Confronted with the Saudi foot dragging, the American secretary of state had been persuaded to take the matter up with his Saudi counterpart. Within days the intelligence authorities in Riyadh had pouched a thick dossier to Langley filled with hundreds of photographs and associated biographical information. Lincoln had sorted through the photos in the conference room next to the

DDO's office, with Quest peering anxiously over his shoulder. He came across several that gave him pause. *No, no, that's not him,* he would finally say, *our* Saudi had incredibly intense eyes that seemed to look into you rather than at you. Going through the pouch a second time, Lincoln had used a magnifying glass to study the group photographs. Suddenly he had leaned over the table to get a closer look at one man.

I think maybe—

You think maybe what, for Christsake?

Maybe this is our Saudi. Yes, there's no doubt about it. Look at those goddamn eyes.

The group photograph had been taken years before at the wedding of a seventeen-year-old Saudi to a Syrian girl who was a distant relative of his. The bridegroom's name, according to the caption provided by the Riyadh intelligence people, was Osama bin Laden. He turned out to have a Central Registry file dating back to when he became involved in the anti-Soviet jihad in Afghanistan. The son of the Yemeni-born construction tycoon Muhammad Awad bin Laden, who had made a fortune in Saudi Arabia, Osama, according to Riyadh, was considered to be the black sheep of the fifty-three siblings in the extremely wealthy bin Laden family, in part because of his disdain for the ruling Saudi royal family and their ties to the United States, in part because of his recent obsession with Islamic fundamentalism.

Okay, we have his name and a mug shot to go

with it, Quest was conceding, the shrew in her only partly assuged. A goddamn pity we don't have his warm body also.

What we need to do, one of the staffers ventured from the side-line, is put pressure on the Sudanese to hand him over to us, or at least expel him from Sudan.

I've promoted bin Laden to the top of our wish list, Quest announced. We wish he were dead. Something tells me we had better get our paws on this Osama character before he gets his paws on radioactive waste and builds himself a dirty bomb.

Amen, said Lincoln.

Six weeks later Lincoln, in Rome for two weeks of R and R, hired a taxi to drive him out to Hadrian's sprawling villa near Tivoli and spent the afternoon limping around the site in a light spring rain, trying to distinguish myth from reality. Which was the flesh and blood Publius Aelius Hadrianus, which the legend he had consigned to history? Was he the emperor who ruthlessly suppressed the Jewish revolt of 132 and paraded the survivors through Rome in chains? Or the patron of the arts who presided over the construction of the vast country villa outside of Rome, and most especially its entrancing circular library where he spent afternoons studying the manuscripts he accumulated? Or, as seemed likely, was there something of the real Hadrian present in both incarnations?

Didn't truth provide the spinal column in every legend?

In early evening Lincoln had the driver drop him off across the Tiber on the Janicular. He checked the address scrawled on the slip of paper in his wallet and headed up hill, walking at a leisurely pace so as not to tire his leg, until he came to the luxurious four-story apartment house near the fountain where Romans lingered to inhale the negative ions from the cascading water. He settled onto the stone railing near the fountain, with Rome stretched out behind him, and breathed in some of the negative ions himself. It surely wouldn't hurt him, he thought. These days he was walking without the aid of a cane, but his leg tired easily; the doctors at the Company clinic in Maryland had warned him the pain would never completely go away. He would learn to live with it, they promised; that's what everyone did with pain.

The bells on a church uphill from the fountain tolled the hour and Lincoln checked his wristwatch. Either it or the bells were four minutes off, but what did it matter? In the end time was something you killed. Across the street a doorman in a long blue overcoat with gold piping removed his cap to salute the very elegantly dressed woman emerging from the building. She held the leash of a small dog in one gloved hand, in the other she clasped the small hand of a little boy dressed in short pants and a knee-length overcoat buttoned up to the neck. With the dog leading the way, the woman and the boy crossed the street to pass the fountain on their way downhill to the music school. Lincoln slipped off the stone rail as they came abreast of him.

'Hello,' he said.

The woman stopped. 'Do I know you?'

'Don't you remember me?'

The woman, who spoke English with what Lincoln took to be an Italian accent, looked puzzled. 'I'm sorry, no. Should I?'

Lincoln noticed a small silver crucifix hanging from the delicate silver chain around her neck. 'My name's Dittmann. Lincoln Dittmann. We met in Brazil, in a border town called Foz do Iguaçú. Your name – your daytime name was Lucia.'

'Mama, que dice?'

A nervous smile tugged at the corners of the woman's mouth. 'My daytime name happens to be the same as my nighttime name. It is Fiamma. Fiamma Segre.'

Lincoln found himself speaking with some urgency, as if a great deal depended on convincing her that daytime names were never the same as nighttime names. 'I told you it would end. You said you would breed baby polyesters on a farm in Tuscany. I am elated to see you've found something more interesting to do with your life.'

The nervous smile worked its way up to the woman's frightened eyes. 'Polyester is a synthetic fabric,' she said softly. She pulled gently at the

346

boy's hand. 'I am afraid we must be on our way. It was a pleasure talking to you, Lincoln Dittmann. Good-bye.'

'Good-bye,' Lincoln said. Although his heart wasn't in it he forced himself to smile back at her.

1997: MARTIN ODUM IS MESMERIZED TO TEARS

The jetliner elbowed through the towering clouds and emerged into an airspace as cheerless as sky gets without sun. Dark pitted fields ribbed with irrigation gutters unfurled under the belly of the plane. From his window seat, Martin Odum watched Prague tilt up in its oval frame as if it were perched on the high end of a teeterboard. In his mind's eye he imagined the buildings yielding to gravity and sliding downslope into the Vltava, the broad mud-colored river meandering through the center of the city that looked, to Martin's jaundiced eye, like a beautiful woman who had been tempted by a face lift too many. The plane's wing dipped and Prague leveled out and the hills rimming the bowl of the city swam into view on the horizon, with the prefabricated Communist-era high rise apartment boxes spilling over the crests into the bleak countryside. A moment later the tarmac rushed up to graze the wheels of the plane. 'Welcome to Prague,' announced a recorded voice over the public-address system. 'We hope your flight has

348

been enjoyable. The captain and his crew thank you for flying Czech Airlines.'

'You're definitely welcome,' Martin heard himself respond. The buxom English woman in the next seat must have heard him too, because she favored him with a look reserved for passengers having conversations with recorded announcements. Martin felt obliged to decipher his remark. 'Any airline that gets me where I'm going in one piece has my unstinting gratitude,' he informed her.

'If you are frightened of flying,' she retorted, 'you should entertain the idea of traveling by train.'

'Frightened of trains, too,' Martin said gloomily. He thought of the Italian girl Paura that Lincoln Dittmann had come across in Foz do Iguaçú, the one who was afraid of her shadow. He wondered what had become of her. To this day he wasn't one-hundred percent sure the woman Lincoln had accosted on the Janicular and the call girl in Brazil were one and the same person. There had been a physical resemblance, so Lincoln had claimed, but the two women had been a world apart in mood and manner. 'Frightened of arriving at places I haven't been to before,' Martin told his neighbor now. 'Frightened of motion *and* movement, frightened of the going *and* the getting there.'

The English woman was eager to put an end to the exchange and formulated a cutting remark that would accomplish it. But she decided she might be dealing with an authentic maniac after all and kept her mouth shut.

Making his way through the crowded terminal following the overhead signs with images of busses on them, a thin Beedie glued to his lower lip, Martin found his path blocked by a slight young man with an ironic grimace pasted on his fleshy lips. He was dressed in khaki jodhpurs that buttoned at the ankles and a green Tyrolean jacket with tarnished brass buttons. For an instant Martin thought he had been spotted by the local constabulary, but the young man quickly made it clear he was freelancing. 'Mister, no difference if you are come to Praha for business or pleasure, in both conditions you will be requiring a fixer whose honorarium will be conspicuously less than what you would find yourself expending on hotels and transportation and meals if you do not accept to employ my services.' The young man, anxious to please, doffed his deerstalker and, pinching one of the two visors between a thumb and two fingers, held it over his solar plexus. 'Radek at your beck and call for an insignificant thirty crowns an hour, which translates into one lousy U.S. dollar.'

Martin was tempted. 'What made you pick me?' he wanted to know.

'You look reasonably U.S. and I need to varnish my English for the year-end examinations that must be passed with floating colors to arrive into medical school.'

'Flying colors, not floating colors.'

The young man beamed. '*Flying colors* it will be from this second in time until Alzheimer's sets in.'

Martin knew himself to be a poor judge of age, but Radek looked a little old to be thinking of going to medical school, and he said so.

'I am a late blossomer,' the young man said with a disarming grin.

Martin wasn't so much interested in saving money as time. His instinct told him that he had to get into and out of Prague before Crystal Quest, whose operatives would not be far behind, informed the local security people of his presence; before the Chechens who murdered Taletbek Rabbani caught up with him. He produced a ten dollar bill from his shirt pocket. 'Fair enough, Radek – here are ten hours in advance. I want to take a bus into the city. I want to rent a room in a cheap hotel in the Vyšehrad quarter that has a fire staircase leading to an employees' entrance. Then I want to make a phone call from the central post office, after which I would like to eat a copious vegetarian meal in a cheap restaurant—'

'I know definitely the cheap hotel. It is former secret police dormitory turned into a student bed and breakfast when communism demised. When you are checkered in, I will pilot you to a mom and pop's Yugoslav eatery, not much grander than a crackle in the wall, all vegetarian except for the meat.'

Martin had to laugh. 'Sounds like just the ticket.'

Radek tried the phrase on his tongue. '*Just the*

ticket. I see the meaning. And for after the meal, what about girls? I know a bar where university students in miniskirts wait on tables to supplement their stipends. Some of them are not against supplementing the supplements.'

'We'll save the girls for my next trip to Prague, Radek.' Martin took a last drag on the Beedie and embedded the burning end in the sand of an ashtray. 'After the mom and pop's crackle in the wall, I want to go to' – he hauled out the envelope that Taletbek Rabbani had given him in London and looked at what the old man had written on the back of it – 'to the Vysěhrad Train Station on Svobodova street.'

'The Vysěhrad Station was shut closed by the communists. Trains pass there but do not stop. For a while it was an abandoned building where you could buy drugs. I am hearing it was hired to Czech people who buy and sell.'

'Buy and sell what?'

Radek shrugged. 'Only God knows and He has so far not shared the information with me.'

'I want to know, too. I want to find out what they buy and sell.'

Radek fitted his deerstalker back onto his head at a rakish angle. 'Then please to follow me, Mister.'

The hotel in the Vysěhrad quarter turned out to be spotlessly clean and inexpensive if you didn't formally register and paid two nights in advance with American dollars, which Martin immediately agreed to do. And the narrow fire staircase led, four floors down, to the kitchen and a back door giving onto a courtyard that gave onto a side street. The central post office, reached after a short ride on a red-and-cream double trolley, had a window for international calls. Martin jotted the Crown Heights phone number on a pad and waited his turn and squeezed into the empty booth that smelled of stale cologne when his ticket was called.

'Hello,' he cried into the phone when he heard Stella's voice breasting the static on the other end.

'Why are you shouting?' she demanded.

He lowered his voice. 'Because I'm farther away than the last time I called.'

'Don't tell me where you are – there's been a bizarre echo on my line the last few days.'

'Doesn't matter,' Martin said. 'They'll take two or three minutes to figure out it's an international call. Then they'll need two or three days to find out which city it came from. And another week to get the local spooks to determine I'm calling from the central post office in Prague.'

'Now you've gone and told them.'

'They won't believe me. They'll think I'm planting phony clues to throw them off. What did you do with yourself today?'

'Just came back from the dentist – he's making me a new front tooth.'

'Money down the drain. I liked the chipped tooth. Made you look . . .'

'Finish what you started to say, for God's sake.

353

Every time you get personal you let go of the end of the sentence and it drifts off like a hot air balloon.'

'Breakable. That's the word that was on the tip of my tongue.'

'I'm not sure how to take that. What's so great about looking breakable.'

'For starters, means you're not already broken. People who are broken have several selves. Estelle is your real name, isn't it?'

'The family name, Kastner, was assigned to us when we came to America. They wanted to change my first name, too, but I wouldn't let them. Estelle is me.' When he didn't respond, she said, 'You still there?'

'I'm thinking about what you said. I know I must have met people who aren't living in legends, I just don't remember when.'

'Legends, as in having different names?'

'It's much more than different names; it has to do with having several biographies, several attitudes, several ways of looking at the world, several ways of giving and taking pleasure. It has to do with being so broken that the king's horses and the king's men would have a hard time putting you together again.'

'Listen up, Martin—'

'Terrific! Now they'll know it's me calling.'

'How can they be sure I'm not using a phony name to throw them off?'

'There's something in what you say.'

'I lied to you the last time we spoke. I said if I joined you in Europe there wouldn't be strings attached. If you let me come, there will be. Strings attached.'

Martin didn't know what to say. He stifled the *uh-huh* and let the silence stand.

'You don't know what to say,' Stella guessed.

'Strings are attached to puppets,' Martin finally said. 'It's not an image of you that I put much store in.'

'The strings wouldn't be attached to me or you, they'd be attached to my coming over. Remember when we were going into Israel and I told that policeman you were my lover?'

Martin smiled to himself. 'And I told him you had a tattoo of a Siberian night moth under your right breast.'

'Got one,' Stella announced.

He didn't understand. 'Got what?'

'Tattoo of a Siberian night moth under my right breast. A Jamaican tattoo artist on Empire Boulevard did it. That's the string that's attached when we next meet. I'm going to have to show it to you to prove it's there, since it's not your style to take my word for something as important as that. Then we'll see if one thing leads to another.'

Martin thought of the whore Dante had come across in Beirut. 'I heard of a girl who actually had a moth tattooed under her breast. Her name was Djamillah. Did you really get one?'

He could hear the laughter in her voice. 'Uh-huh.'

'Stealing my *uh-huhs*,' Martin said.

'Plan to steal more than that,' she shot back.

He changed the subject. 'I was scared today.'

'Of what?'

'Where I'm at I've never been to before. That frightens me.'

'Okay, here's the deal. You better get used to being where you've never been to before. I'll hold your hand. Okay?'

'I suppose so.'

'If this is you enthusiastic, I'd hate to see you reluctant.'

'Fact is, I'm not sure.'

'Ever hear the story of the Russian peasant who was asked if he knew how to play the violin? *I'm not sure*, he replied. *Never tried.*' She snickered at her own joke. 'You need to try, Martin, to know if you can or you can't.'

'I can see you're right. I just don't *feel* you're right.'

She digested that. 'Why did you call me?'

'Wanted to hear your voice. Wanted to make sure you're still you.'

'Well, you've heard it and I've heard yours. Where does that leave us, Martin?'

'I'm not sure.' They both laughed at the *I'm not sure*. 'I mean, I still have to find the person who went AWOL from his marriage.'

'Let it go. Forget Samat. Come home, Martin.'

'If I let it go, the person who came home wouldn't be me. Aside from that, lot of questions are out trawling for answers.'

'When the answers are elusive you have to learn to live with the questions.'

'I need to go. Stella?'

'Okay, okay, go. I'll replay the conversation in my head after you hang up. I'll sift through it looking for meanings I missed.'

'Don't worry, be happy.'

'Don't worry, be happy? What's that supposed to mean?'

'It's a song from the top ten in the late eighties. Thought of it today – they were playing it over and over on a jukebox in Paraguay when a guy I know was there.'

'Was the *they* a girl?'

'A bunch of girls. Prostitutes working a bar who bought lottery tickets from an old Polish gentleman.'

'You depress me, Martin. There's so much about you I don't know.'

'I depress me, too. For the same reason.'

The *plat du jour* at the mom and pop's turned out to be spicy Yugoslav meatballs served in soup dishes with vegetables that had been overcooked and were difficult to identify. Martin exchanged his meatballs for Radek's vegetables and helped himself to half the boiled potatoes. The wine was a kissing cousin to Greek ouzo, flavored with anise and easy to drink once the first few mouthfuls numbed your throat. Radek sat across the small table from Martin, mopping up the sauces in his soup dish with pieces of stale bread and washing them down with gulps of wine. 'My dream is to go to U.S. the beautiful before Alzheimer's sets in,' he confided, sucking on a tooth to free the food caught in his gums. 'Is it so that they pave the streets with Sony Walkmans when the cobblestones wear out?'

Martin leaned back and treated himself to an after-dinner Beedie. 'Where did you pick up that juicy detail?'

'It was written in a university satirical magazine.'

'Don't believe everything you read in university satirical magazines. Can you ask for the bill.'

Radek studied the bill when it came, then got into an argument with the owner, who wound up crossing out two items and reducing the price of the wine. 'I saved you sixty crowns, which is two lousy U.S. dollars,' Radek noted. 'That adds up to two hours of my honorarium, Mister. So where to now?'

'A trolley to Svobodova Street.'

'How is it a rich U.S. like you does not hire taxi cabs?'

'I have a theory that you don't really know a city until you've ridden its public transportation.'

Radek rolled his head from side to side in dismay. 'Here all the people who take public transportation dream to take private transportation. You want to go to the Vyšehrad Station?'

'I would like to get off a hundred meters before it and walk the rest of the way to work off the meal.'

Radek laid a forefinger along a nostril. 'You want to case the joint first.'

'Where did you pick up *case the joint*?'

'So I am crazy about old U.S. movies.' He transformed a thumb and an index finger into a pistol and jammed it into the pocket of his Tyrolean jacket. '*I have a gub in my pocket, Mister.*'

'What movie is that from?'

'Woody Allen. *Take the Money and Run.*'

'Uh-huh. Let's go.'

Sitting in the back of the trolley, listening to the sparks crackling off the overhead electric cable, Martin studied the faces around him looking for the one that was conspicuously uninterested in him. Normally he prided himself on being able to blend into a crowd even when there wasn't one. Now, however, he was in too much of a hurry to take the usual precautions. His American clothes, especially his shoes, made him stand out in any Czech crowd and people, naturally curious, would inspect him, some openly, some furtively. Martin figured if someone were following him he would be careful not to look at him at all. In the long ride from the mom and pop's eatery to Mala Strana, then queuing to wait for a trolley on another line, Martin, still an artisan of tradecraft, didn't have the feeling he was being tailed. Which, he knew from experience, could mean that the people following him were very good at it. Radek noticed him noticing the passengers around him. 'If you are not wanting girls, what are you wanting?' he asked. He leaned closer so the haggard woman on the aisle seat brazenly scrutinizing the American couldn't overhear him. 'Cannabis, ganja, hemp, hashish, bhang, sinsemilla, cocaine, crack, angel dust, horse, methadone, LSD, PCP, uppers, downers. Only identify it, Radek will find it for less lousy U.S. dollars than you pay me a day.'

'I've never even heard of half these things,' Martin said. 'What I'm wanting is to stretch my legs when we're within walking distance of the Vyšehrad Station.'

'Next stop,' Radek said, obviously disappointed that his procurement talents were not being put to the test. He plucked at the cord running the length of the trolley above the windows as if it were a guitar string. Up front a bell sounded. As the trolley ground to a halt, the doors scraped open. Once on the sidewalk, Radek pointed with his nose. In the distance, on the other side of the wide street, Martin could make out a shabby communist gothic structure trapping the last quarter hour of sunlight slanting in over the Vltava on its dilapidated roof, which was crawling with pigeons. He turned to Radek and offered his hand. 'I won't be needing your services anymore,' he announced.

Radek looked dejected. 'You paid for ten hours, Mister. I still owe you seven and a half.'

'Consider the unused hours a gratuity.' When Radek still didn't shake hands, Martin brought his own up to his eye and snapped off a friendly salute. 'Good luck to you in medical school, Radek. I hope you find a cure for Alzheimer's before Alzheimer's sets in.'

'I kick myself for asking someone like you only thirty lousy crowns an hour,' Radek muttered as he turned and headed in the opposite direction.

Sucking on a Beedie, Martin strolled down Svobodova Street in the direction of the river. He passed a row of apartment buildings, one with the date '1902' etched over the door and a 'Flat for Sale' sign in English on the inside of a ground floor window. Across the street loomed the Vysěhrad Station in all its communist-era decadence. The station consisted of a central carcass and two broken wings. Dirty white stucco peeled away from the facade like sunburnt skin, exposing the dirty red bricks beneath. The windows on the Svobodova side were boarded over, though there were hints of fluorescent light seeping between the cracks in several of the second-floor windows that weren't well jointed. The pigeons, in twos and threes, were fluttering away from the roof in search of the last rays of sun as Martin made his way back up Svobodova, this time on the station side of the street. Trolleys clattered by, causing the ground to tremble underfoot. Behind the station a commuter train sped past in the direction of *Centrum*. Dog-eared posters advertising Hungarian vaccum cleaners and reconditioned East German Trabants were thumb tacked to the boards covering the ground floor windows. Near the gate leading to a path around the side of the left wing of the station, someone had chalked graffiti on the wall: *The Oklahoma City bomb was the first shot of World War III.* Martin eased open the gate on its rusty hinges, climbed the brick steps and walked around to the back of the station. The passage was obviously in daily use because the weeds and vines on either side had been cut away from the brick footpath. Making his way along what used to be the platform when the station had been in use, Martin glanced into one of the wings through a sooty window shielded by rusting metal bars. Inside, two young men whom he took to be gypsies, wearing vests and corduroy trousers tucked into the tops of leather boots, were emptying large cartons and setting out what looked like packets of medicines on a long trestle table. Two young women dressed in long colorful skirts were repacking the items into smaller boxes and sealing them with masking tape. One of the young men caught sight of Martin and gestured with his thumb toward the main station doors further down the platform. Martin nodded and, a moment later, pushed through the double door into the station's once-ornate central hall, fallen into dilapidation and smelling of wet plaster, evidence that someone had tried to patch over the worst of the building's wounds. A broken sign over the door read '*Vychod – Exit.*' The tiles on the floor, many of them cracked, shifted under his feet. A wide stairway curled up toward the second floor. Painted on the wall above the stairway were the words 'Soft' and 'Shoulder.' A squat dog with a blunt nose stood on the top landing, yelping in a hoarse voice at the intruder. A handsome, elegantly dressed woman in her fifties peered down from the railing. 'If you are looking for Soft Shoulder, do come up,' she called. 'Don't mind the dog. His bite is worse than his bark, but I will lock him up.' Reaching for the dog's leash, the woman pulled him, still yelping, into a room and shut the door. With the dog barking behind the door she turned back toward Martin, who was leaning on the banister to take the weight off his game leg as he climbed toward her. A half dozen thin Indian bracelets jangled on her thin wrist as she held out a slender hand. 'My name is Zuzana Slánská,' she said as Martin took her hand.

He noticed that her fingers were weedy, her nails bitten to the quick, her eyes rheumy. He suspected that the wrinkled smile on her gaunt lips had been worn too many times without laundering. 'Mine's Odum,' he said. 'Martin Odum.'

'What African country are you buying for?'

Figuring he had nothing to lose, Martin said the first thing that came into his head. 'The Ivory Coast.'

'We don't often deal with clients in person, Mr Odum. Most of our business is mail order. As a matter of record, who sent you to us?'

'An associate of Samat's named Taletbek Rabbani.'

He produced the back of the envelope with Rabbani's barely legible scrawl on it and showed it to the woman.

A shadow passed over her face. 'News of Mr Rabbani's death reached us earlier this week. When and where did you meet him?'

'The same place you met him – at his warehouse behind the train station in the Golders Green section of London. I was probably the last person to see him alive – not counting the Chechens who murdered him.'

'The small item in the British newspaper made no mention of Chechens.'

'It may be that Scotland Yard doesn't know this detail. It may be they know it but do not want to tip their hand.'

Smiling nervously, the woman led Martin into a large oval room lit by several naked neon fixtures suspended from the ceiling. The three windows in the office were covered with planking, reminding Martin of the time Dante Pippen had followed Djamillah into the mercantile office above the bar in Beirut – the windows there had been boarded over, too. He looked around, taking in the room. Large cartons with 'This Side Up' stenciled on them were stacked against one wall. A young woman in a loose fitting sweater and faded blue jeans sat at a desk, typing with two fingers on a vintage table-model Underwood. At the edge of the desk, a scroll of facsimile paper spilled from a fax machine into a carton on the floor. A loose-lead book lay open on a low glass table filled with coffee stains and overflowing ashtrays. The woman motioned Martin to a seat on the automobile banquette against the wall and settled onto a low three-legged stool facing him, her crossed ankles visible through the thick glass of the table. 'I assume Mr Rabbani explained how we operate here. In order to keep our prices as low as possible, we do business out of this defunct station to reduce the overhead and we only sell our generic medicines in bulk. Is there anything in particular you are looking for, Mr Odum? Our best sellers are the Tylenol generic, acetaminophen, the Valium generic, diazepam, the Sudafed generic, pseudoephedrine, the Kenacort generic, triamcinolone. Please feel free to thumb through the loose-leaf catalogue. The labels of our genetic medicines are pasted onto the pages. I am not aware of any particular epidemic threatening the Ivory Coast aside from the HIV virus – we unfortunately do not yet have access to generic drugs for AIDS, but hope governments will put pressure on the drug conglomerates . . .' She gazed at her visitor, a sudden question visible in her eyes. 'You didn't mention your medical credentials, Mr Odum. Are you a trained doctor or a public health specialist?'

Another commuter train roared by behind the station. When it had passed, Martin said, 'Neither.'

Zuzana Slánská's fingers came up to touch the small Star of David attached to the chain around her neck. 'I am not sure I comprehend you.'

Martin leaned forward. 'I have a confession to make. I am not here to buy generic medicines.' He looked directly into her rheumy eyes. 'I have come to find out more about Samat's project concerning the exchange of the bones of the Lithuanian saint for the Jewish Torah scrolls.'

'Oh!' The woman glanced at the secretary typing up order forms across the room. 'It's a long story,' she said softly, 'and I shall badly need a brandy and several cigarettes to get me through it.'

Zuzana Slánská leaned toward Martin so that he could light her cigarette with a match from the book advertising Prague crystal. 'I have never smoked a Beedie before,' she noted, sinking back, savoring the taste of the Indian cigarette. She pulled it from her mouth and carefully examined it. 'Is there marijuana mixed with the tobacco?' she asked.

Martin shook his head. 'You're smelling the eucalyptus leaves.'

She took another drag on the Beedie. 'I am wary of the experts who argue so passionately that smoking is dangerous for your health,' she remarked, the words emerging from her mouth along with the smoke. As she turned away to glance at the two fat men sucking on thick cigars at a nearby table, it struck Martin that she had the profile of a woman who must have been a stunner in her youth. 'There are a great many things dangerous for your health,' she added, turning back. 'Don't you agree?'

Concentrating on his own cigarette, Martin said, 'For instance?'

'For instance, living under high tension wires. For instance, eating fast food with artificial flavoring. For instance, being right when your government is wrong.' She favored the old waiter with a worn smile as he carefully set out two snifters half-filled with three-star Jerez brandy, along with a shallow Dresden bowl brimming with peanuts. 'I am speaking from bitter experience,' she added, 'but you surely will have grasped that from the tone of my voice.'

She had led him on foot across the river to the *salon du thé* on the top floor of a gaudy hotel that had only recently opened for business. From the window next to the table at the back of the enromous room, Martin could see what he'd spotted from the plane: the hills rimming Prague and the communist-era apartment buildings spilling over them. 'My husband,' the woman was saying, caught up in her own story, 'was a medical doctor practicing in Vinohrady, which is a district of Prague behind the museum. I worked as his nurse. The two of us joined a literary circle that met once a week to discuss books. Oh, I can tell you, it was an exhilarating time for us. My husband was fearless – he used to all the time joke that old age was not for the weak of heart.' She gulped down some of the brandy and puffed furiously on her Beedie, as if time were running out; as if she had to relate her life's story before her life ended. 'Tell me if all this bores you to tears, Mr Odum.'

'The opposite is true,' Martin assured her. 'It mesmerizes me to tears.'

Zuzana Slánská hiked one slim shoulder inside her tailored Parisian jacket. 'We were ardent Marxists, my husband and I. We were convinced it was the great Russian bear that had suffocated communism and not the other way around. Our Czech hero, Alexander Dubcek, was still a loyal party-line apparatchik when we began signing petitions demanding reforms. The Soviet-appointed proconsuls who reigned over us could not distinguish between dissidents who were anticommunist and those, like us, who were pro-communist but argued that it had gone wrong; that it needed to be set right in order for Marxism to survive. Or if they did distinguish between us, they calculated that our form of dissidence was the more threatening of the two. And so we suffered the same fate as the others.'

Martin could see the muscles on her face contorting with heartache remembered so vividly that she seemed to be experiencing it now. 'You must know the story,' she rushed on, barely bothering to breathe. 'The one about the NKVD commissar admitting to Yosif Vissarionovich Stalin that a particular prisoner had refused to confess. Stalin considered the problem, then asked the commissar how much the state weighed, the state with all its buildings and factories and machines, the army with all its tanks and trucks, the navy with all its ships, the air force with all its planes. And then Stalin said, dear God, he said, *Do you really think this prisoner can withstand the weight of the state?'*

'Did you feel the weight of the state? Were you and your husband jailed?'

Zuzana Slánská had become so agitated that she began swallowing smoke and brandy in the same gulp. 'Certainly we felt the weight of the state. Certainly we were jailed, some months at the same time and once even in the same prison, some months at different times so that we passed each other like ships in the night. I discovered that when you left prison you took the stench of it with you in your nostrils; it took months, years to get rid of it. Oh, once my husband returned from prison so beat up that I didn't recognize him through the spy hole in the door and called the police to save me from a lunatic, and they came and looked at his identity card and told me it was safe to let him in, the lunatic in question was my husband. Does it happen in America, Mr Odum, that the police must assure you it is safe to let your husband pass the door of your apartment? And then one day my husband was arrested for treating the broken ankle of a youth who turned out to be an anti-communist dissident hiding from the police. The journalists from America covering the trial pointed out in their stories that the same thing had happened to the American doctor who treated the broken ankle of A. Lincoln's assassin.'

From some murky past – from some murky legend? – the story of the Prague trial surfaced in Martin's memory. 'You're the wife of Pavel Slánský!'

'You recognize the name! You remember the trial!'

'Everyone who followed events in Eastern Europe was familiar with the name Pavel Slánský,' Martin said. 'The Jewish doctor who was arrested for setting the broken ankle of a dissident; who at his trial pleaded innocent to that particular charge, but used the occasion to plead guilty to wanting to reform communism, explaining in excruciating detail why it needed reforming to survive. He was the forerunner of the reformers who came after him: Dubcek in Czechoslovakia, eventually Gorbachev in the Soviet Union.'

An uncontaminated smile, as fresh as laundered linen on a clothesline, materialized on Zuzana Slánská's face. 'Yes, he was ahead of his time, which in some countries is counted as a capital crime. The American authorities showed little sympathy for him – one suspects they did not want to see anyone attempt to reform communism, lest they succeed. My husband was declared to be an enemy of the state and condemned to ten years in prison for anticommunist activities. And I became like the poet Akhmatova, queuing at the prison guardhouse through the winters and springs and summers and falls to deliver packages of socks and soap and cigarettes addressed to prisoner 277103. The number is seared into my memory. The wardens took the packages and signed receipts promising they would be delivered. And then one day one of my packages was returned to me in the mail bearing the stamp *Deceased*. This tendency of bureaucracies in killer states to adhere to normal procedures and regulations has yet to be explained, at least to my satisfaction. In any case, that was how I discovered that my husband, the prisoner Slánský, was no longer among the living.' Zuzana Slánská raised a cold palm to swat away the cigar smoke drifting toward her from the nearby table. 'May I have another of your amusing cigarettes? I need the eucalyptus to overpower the stench of their cigars. Oh, Mr Odum, if one was able to put up with the inconveniences, I must tell you that dissidence was exhilarating.'

'Aside from prison, what were the inconveniences?'

'You lost your job, you were required to crowd into a fifty-square-meter apartment with the two couples already living in it, you were sent off to a psychiatric clinic to work out to the satisfaction of the state what made a dissident criticize something that was, by definition, perfect. When we would gather at an apartment late at night to discuss, oh, say, Solzhenitsyn's *Ivan Denisovich*, our small group considered all the angles, all the scenarios except the possibility that the gangsters who presided over the Soviet Union would become freelance gangsters presiding over the territory they had staked out when communism collapsed. Looking back, I can see now that we were incredibly naive. We were blinded by the exhilaration – each time we made love we thought it might be the last time and this turned us into ardent lovers, until the day came when we had no one to make love to. And so we stopped, most of us, being lovers and became haters.'

'And the generic drugs – how did you get into that?'

'I was a trained nurse but, after the trial of my husband, no doctor dared employ me. For years I worked at menial tasks – cleaning medical offices after they shut for the day, removing garbage cans from the courtyards of apartment houses to the street before dawn so the trucks could empty them. Finally, when our own communists were expelled from power in 1989, I decided to do what my husband always dreamed of doing – sell generic medicines to the third world at the lowest possible prices. I met Samat during one of his first trips to Prague and told him about my idea. He accepted at once to fund it as a branch of an existing humanitarian enterprise called Soft Shoulder – it was with his money that we rented the Vysĕhrad Station and bought the first stocks of generic medicines. Now I eke out enough profit to employ four gypsies and a part-time secretary. I once attempted to reimburse Samat but he refused to accept money. It must be said, he is something of a saint.'

'I suppose it would take a saint to get involved in repatriating the bones of a saint,' Martin remarked.

'I can say that I was the one who first told Samat about the Jewish Torah scrolls in the Lithuanian church.' Her hand drifted up to her neck to finger the Star of David. 'My older sister was deported during the war to a concentration camp in Lithuania. She managed to escape into the steppe and joined the communist partisans harassing the German rear. It was my sister – her partisan name was Rosa, after the German communist Rosa Luxemburg; her real name was Melka – who attempted to warn the Jews in the shtetls not yet overrun by the Germans and the *einsatzsgruppen* murderers who followed behind them. Few believed her – they simply did not imagine that the descendants of Goethe and Beethoven and Brahms were capable of the mass murder of an entire people. But in several of the shtetls the rabbis hedged their bets – they collected the sacred Torah scrolls and princeless commentaries, some of them many hundreds of years old, and gave them to a Lithuanian Orthodox bishop to hide in a remote church. After the war my sister passed on to me the name of this church – *Spaso-Preobrazhenski Sabor*, which means Church of the Transfiguration, in the town of Zuzovka, on the Neman River just inside Lithuania near the frontier with Belarus. When I told the story to Samat, he dropped what he was doing – Samat, who was not as far as I know Jewish, went directly to the church to recover the Torah scrolls and bring them to Israel. The Metropolitan of the diocese refused to give them back; refused even to sell them back when Samat offered him a large sum of money. The Metropolitan was willing, however, to trade the Torah scrolls for the relics of Saint Gedymin, who established the Lithuanian capital in Vilnius in thirteen hundred something. Saint Gedymin's bones had been stolen from the church by German troops during the war. After years of inquiry, Samat was finally able to trace the bones of the saint to Argentina. They had been smuggled there by Nazis fleeing Europe at the end of the war and deposited in a small Orthodox church near the city of Córdoba. When the church refused to part with the bones of Saint Gedymin, Samat went to see a person he knew in the Argentine government; in the Defense Ministry, actually. Samat told me he had persuaded the Defense Ministry to repatriate the saintly relics to Lithuania—'

'In return for what?'

'I'm afraid I don't know. Samat mentioned that he'd been to see the people at the Argentine Defense Ministry. But he never told me what they wanted in exchange for the relics of Saint Gedymin.'

'When did he tell you about the Defense Ministry?'

'The last time he passed through Prague.'

'Yes, and when was that?'

'After he left Israel he went to London to see

Taletbek Rabbani. From London he flew here to see me on his way to—'

Martin became aware that Zuzana Slánská's rheumy eyes had focused on something over his shoulder. He noticed her fingers slipping the Star of David out of sight under the collar of her blouse as he twisted in his seat to see what she was looking at. Radek, holding his deerstalker over his solar plexus, his other hand buried in the pocket of the Tyrolean jacket, stood at the doors of the *salon du thé* surveying the clients. He spotted Zuzana Slánská and Martin across the room and pointed them out with one of the brims of his deerstalker as he started threading his way through the tables toward them. A dozen men in civilian suits fanned out behind him.

A gasp of pure dread escaped from Zuzana Slánská's throat as she rose to her feet. She uttered the words, 'Old age is not for the weak of heart,' then, her eyes fixed on Radek, her lips barely moving, she said: 'There is an island in the Aral Sea twenty kilometers off the mainland called Vozrozhdeniye. During the Soviet era it was used as a bioweapons testing range. On the island is the town of Kantubek. Samat's contact in Kantubek is a Georgian named Hamlet Achba. Can you remember all that?'

'Vozrozhdeniye. Kantubek. Hamlet Achba.'

'Warn Samat . . .' Radek was almost upon them. 'Oh, it's for sure I will not survive the stench of another prison,' she murmured to herself.

Around them the waiters and the clients had frozen in place, mesmerized by the progress of Radek and his companions toward the two customers at the small table in the back of the room. Radek, a faint smile of satisfaction disfiguring his lips, reached the table. 'I have a gub in my pocket,' he informed Martin. 'It is a German Walther P1. You are arrested, Mister. You, also, Misses, are arrested.'

Martin could feel the gentle rise and fall of the deck under his shoes (the laces, along with his belt, had been confiscated) as he waited for the interrogation to begin again. They had come for him at odd hours for the last several days, a technique designed to deprive him of sleep more than elicit information. As there was no porthole in his small cell immediately over the bilges of the houseboat or in the compartment above it, where the interrogations took place, he soon lost track of whether it was night or day. The only sound that reached his ears from outside were the foghorns of passing river ferries and the doppler-distorted shriek of sirens as police cruisers raced through the streets of Prague. From somewhere in the bowels of the houseboat came the dull throb of a generator; from time to time the bulb hanging out of reach over his head dimmed or brightened. Soon after Radek hustled him from the police van to the houseboat, which was tied to bollards on a cement quay down river from the Charles Bridge, he thought he caught the muted cry of a woman coming from another deck. When he re-created the sound in his head he decided it could have been the caterwaul of a cat prowling through the garbage bins on the quay. The grilling sessions in the airless compartment didn't appear to fatigue the interrogator, a stooped, gaunt bureaucrat with an unshaven face and a shaven skull and an aquiline nose that looked as if it had been broken and badly set at some point in his life. Holding court from behind a small desk bolted to the planks of the deck, he fired off questions in a dispassionate monotone, only occasionally lifting his eyes from his notes. Radek, dressed now in a neat three-piece brown suit with narrow Austrian lapels, leaned against a bulkhead next to one of the two guards who escorted Martin to and from his cell. Martin sat facing the inquisitor on a chair whose front legs had been shortened so that the prisoner would feel as if he were constantly sliding off of it. Bright spotlights positioned on either side of the desk burned into his retinas, causing his eyes to tear and his vision to blur.

'Do you have a name?' Martin had asked the gaunt man behind the desk at the very first session.

The question appeared to have dismayed the interrogator. 'What would it serve, your knowing my name?'

'It would permit me to identify you when I file a complaint with the American embassy.'

The interrogator had glanced at Radek, then

looked back at Martin. 'If you lodge a complaint, say that you were arrested by a secret unit attached to a secret ministry.'

From his place along the wall, Radek had choked off a guttural laugh.

Now the interrogator slid a small Pyrex percolator toward Martin. 'Help yourself,' he said, gesturing toward the pot of coffee.

'You've spiked it with caffeine to keep me awake,' Martin said tiredly, but he poured some into a plastic cup and sipped it anyway; they had fed him salted rice and not provided drinking water since his arrival on the houseboat. 'Your techniques of interrogation are right out of those old American movies that Radek here is so crazy about.'

'I do not deny it,' the interrogator said. 'One must not be a snob when it comes to picking up tricks of the trade. In any case, it has been my experience that these techniques work in the end – I say this as someone who has been on both sides of the interrogation table. When I was arrested for anti-communist activities by the communists, in four days they were able to convince me to admit to crimes I had not committed using these very same techniques. And what has been your experience, Mr Odum?'

'I have no experience with interrogations,' Martin said.

The interrogator sniggered skeptically. 'That is not the impression your Central Intelligence Agency gave us. Their chief of station in Prague confides to us that you were once one of their paramount field operatives, someone so skilled at tradecraft it was said of your that you could blend into a crowd even in the absence of one.'

'If I were half that good, how come I fell for Radek's pitch at the airport?'

The interrogator shrugged his stooped shoulders, which raised them for an instant to where they normally should have been. 'Perhaps you are past your prime. Perhaps you were preoccupied with other thoughts at that particular moment. In any case, if you had not hired Radek—'

'For the equivalent of one lousy U.S. dollar an hour,' Radek groaned from the wall.

'If you had not hired him, you would surely have wound up in one of the three taxis we had positioned outside. The drivers, all of whom call themselves Radek, work for us.'

Martin identified a piece of the puzzle that was missing: How could Radek's service have known he would turn up in Prague? Obviously the CIA chief of station had been talking to his Czech counterpart about Martin. And the chief of station reported to the Deputy Director of Operations, Crystal Quest. Which brought Martin back to what he'd told the late Oscar Alexandrovich Kastner in the windowless walk-in closet on President Street a lifetime ago: *I'd like to know why the CIA doesn't want this particular missing husband found.*

'Your station chief,' the interrogator was saying, 'claims you are no longer employed by the CIA. He says you are a freelance detective. It could be true, what he says; it could also be that they are simply denying any connection to you because you have been caught in the act. So tell me, Mr Odum. What weapon systems were you contracting to buy at the Vyšehrad Station. More importantly, who were you buying them for?'

'Zuzana Slánská sells generic medicines.'

'The woman you call Zuzana Slánská was never legally married to the doctor Pavel Slánský, who, as you surely know, was convicted as an enemy of the state during the communist period. Her real name is Zuzana Dzurova. She assumed the name Slánská when she learned of Pavel's death in prison. As for the generic medicines, we have reason to believe they are a front for one of the most prolific weapons operations in Europe.' The interrogator pulled a report from one of the cardboard file boxes on the desk, pried a staple loose with his thumbnail and extracted the third page. He fitted on a pair of rimless reading glasses and began to quote from the text. '. . . operating in conjunction with Mr Taletbek Rabbani in London, who claims to be selling prostheses at cost to third world countries . . .' The interrogator looked up from the paper. 'It is surely not lost on you that both Mr Rabbani's prosthesis operation in London and Zuzana Slánská's generic medicine operation here in Prague were funded by the same individual, a

Mr Samat Ugor-Zhilov, who until recently was living in a Jewish settlement on the West Bank of the Jordan River in order to shelter himself from the gang wars raging in Moscow.'

Martin's muscles ached from the effort of keeping his body from sliding off the chair. He strained to bring the interrogator into focus. 'Both Mr Rabbani and Zuzana Slánská described Samat Ugor-Zhilov as a philanthropist—'

Radek emitted a single hiccup. 'Some philanthropist!' he cried from the wall.

The interrogator threw Radek a dark look, as if to remind him that there was a pecking order; that birds on the junior end of it should be seen but not heard. Then, angling the sheet of paper toward the light, he began reading phrases from it. 'Both Mr Rabbani and Zuzana Slánská are marketing a French device that corrects the error the U.S. Pentagon builds into the satellite GPS system to thwart rogue missile launchings . . . Soviet-surplus radar units from the Ukraine . . . ah, yes, armored personnel carriers from a Bulgarian state-run company, Terem, sold to Syria for eventual delivery to Iraq . . . engines and spare parts for the T-55 and T-72 Soviet tanks from assorted Bulgarian armaments factories . . . ammunition, explosives, rockets, training manuals in missile technology from Serbia . . . spare jet-fighter parts and rocket propellants from an aviation factory in eastern Bosnia. And listen to this: The London prosthesis warehouse and the Prague generic medicine operation are used as clearing houses for orders for an ammunition factory in the town of Vitez and missile guidance systems fabricated in a research center in the city of Banja Luka . . . payments for items on the inventory were made in cash or in diamonds.' The interrogator flicked the nail of his middle finger against the sheet of paper. 'I could continue but there is no point.'

In one of his legends – Martin couldn't recall which – he remembered taking a course at the Farm designed to prepare agents in the field for hostile interrogation. The various techniques of interrogation discussed included one where the interrogator would invent flagrant lies to disorient the person being questioned. Agents who found themselves in this predicament were advised to hang on to the facts they knew to be true and let the fictions of the interrogator pass without comment.

Martin, his head swimming with fatigue, heard himself say, 'I know absolutely nothing about the sale of weapons.'

The interrogator removed his eyeglasses and massaged the bridge of his nose with the thumb and third finger of his left hand. 'That being the case, what brought you to Mr Taletbek Rabbani's warehouse in London and the Vyšehrad Station in Prague?'

Martin longed to stretch out on the metal army cot in his cell. 'I am trying to trace Samat Ugor-Zhilov,' he said.

'Why?'

In disjointed sentences, Martin admitted that he had once been employed by the CIA; that it was perfectly true that he had set up shop as a private detective in Brooklyn, New York, after he left the service. He explained about Samat walking out on his wife in Israel, leaving her in a religious limbo; how the wife's sister and father had hired him to track down Samat and convince him to give her a religious divorce so that she could get on with her life. 'I have no interest in purchasing false limbs or generic drugs. I am simply following a trail that I hope leads to Samat.'

Smiling thinly, the interrogator humored Martin. 'And what will you do once you find him?'

'I will take Samat to the nearest town that has a synagogue and oblige him to grant his wife a divorce in front of a rabbi. Then I will return to Brooklyn and spend the rest of my life boring myself to death.'

The interrogator turned Martin's story over in his mind. 'I am familiar with the school of intelligence activities that holds that a good cover story must be made to seem preposterous if it is to be believed. But you are pushing this thesis to its limits.' He rifled through the papers on the desk and came up with another report. 'We have been observing people entering or leaving the Vysĕhrad Station for weeks now,' he continued. 'We even managed to plant a listening device in the upstairs office. Here is a transcript of a very recent conversation. Perhaps it will seem familiar to you. A man was heard to say: *I have a confession to make. I am not here to buy generic medicines. I have come to find out more about Samat's project concerning the exchange of the bones of the Lithuanian saint for Jewish Torah scrolls.*' The interrogator raised his eyes from the paper to look directly at his prisoner. 'Curious that you make no mention of divorce before a rabbi. Bones of the Lithuanian saint, Jewish Torah scrolls – I take that to be coded references to weapons systems originating in Lithuania and Israel. I can tell you that, aside from the illegality of selling weapons and weapon systems, what intrigues us most about Mrs Slánská is her motive. She was not doing it for money, Mr Odum. She is an idealist.'

'Last time I checked, being an idealist was not a crime, even in the Czech Republic.'

'The American writer Mencken once defined an idealist as someone who, on observing that a rose smelled better than a cabbage, concluded that it would also make better soup. Yes, well, like Mencken's idealist, Mrs Slánská's idealism is very particular – she remains a diehard Marxist, plotting the comeback of the communists. She desires to set the clock back and is thought to be using the considerable profits from the sale of weapons to finance a splinter group hoping to do here in the Czech Republic what the former communists have done in Poland and Rumania and Bulgaria: win elections and return to power.'

It occurred to Martin there might be a way to beat the fatigue that made it appear as if everything around him was happening in slow motion. He closed one eye, thinking that one lobe of his brain could actually sleep while the other eye and the other lobe remained awake. After a moment, hoping the interrogator wouldn't catch on to his clever scheme, he switched eyes and lobes. He could hear the interrogator's voice droning on; could make out, through his open eye, the blurred figure getting up and coming around to half sit on the desk in front of him.

'You arrived here from London, Mr Odum. The British MI5 established that you lived for several days in a rooming house next to a synagogue off Golders Green. The warehouse where Mr Taletbek Rabbani was murdered the day before you departed from London was within walking distance of your rooming house.'

'If everyone living within walking distance of the warehouse is a suspect,' the half of Martin's brain still functioning managed to say, 'MI5 is going to have its hands full.'

'We have not excluded the possibility of concluding a deal with you, Mr Odum. Our principal objective is to discredit Mrs Slánská; to show that she and Mr Rabbani were in league with Mr Samat Ugor-Zhilov's weapons operation; that both the warehouse in London and the defunct train station in Prague were funded by the same Samat Ugor-Zhilov, a notable Moscow gangster

385

who is associated with the Ugor-Zhilov known as the *Oligarkh*. The object for us is to tie the communist splinter group to Zuzana Slánská's illegal weapons operation and discredit them once and for all . . . Mr Odum, are you hearing me? Mr Odum? Mr Odum, wake up!'

But both lobes of Martin's brain had yielded to exhaustion.

'Take him back to his cell.'

Once, several incarnations back, Dante Pippen had barely survived an interminable bus trip that took him from a CIA safe house in a middle class neighborhood of Islamabad (furnished, for once, not in ancient Danish modern but in modern Pakistani kitsch) to Peshawar and the tribal badlands of the Khyber Pass, where he spent the better part of a year debriefing fighters infiltrating into and out of Afghanistan. The bus trip (Crystal Quest's notion of how an Irish reporter working for a wire service – Dante's cover at the time – would travel) had turned out to be a nightmare. Squeezed onto the wooden bench at the back of the bus between a mullah from Kandahar wearing a filthy *shalwar kameez* and a bearded Kashmiri fighter in a reeking djellaba, Dante had been eternally grateful when the bus pulled up, sometimes smack in the middle of nowhere, other times on the sewage-saturated streets of what passed for a village, to let the passengers stretch their legs, reckon the direction of Mecca and murmur the verses of the Koran a Muslim is required to recite five times a day. Now, slouching on the plush banquette in the back of the air-conditioned double-deck tourist bus, surrounded by well-dressed and, more importantly, well-scrubbed Germans on their way home from the spa at Karlovy Vary, Martin Odum suddenly thought of Dante's Khyber trip and the memory brought a smile to his lips. As always, remembering a detail from Dante's past reminded Martin that he, too, must have had a past, and this gave him a measure of hope that he could one day retrieve it. He patted the Canadian passport in the inside breast pocket of his jacket in anticipation of arriving at the Czech-German frontier. This particular passport, one of several he'd swiped from a safe when he was clearing out his office after being dismissed from the CIA, had been issued to a resident of British Columbia named Jozef Kafkor, a name Martin didn't recognize but found easy to remember because it reminded him of Franz Kafka and his stories of anguished individuals struggling to survive in a nightmarish world, which was more or less how Martin saw himself. Lulled by the motion of the bus and the ticking of its diesel engine, Martin closed his eyes and dozed, reliving the events of the last twelve hours.

He could hear Radek's voice whispering in his ear. *Please, Mr Odum, you must wake up.*

Martin had drifted up toward the mirrored

surface of consciousness in carefully calibrated increments, a deep sea diver rising languidly to avoid the bends. When he finally located the appropriate muscles and worked his lids open, he had discovered Radek, dressed again in jodhpurs and the Tyrolean jacket, crouching next to the metal army cot in his cell. 'For the love of God, wake up, Mr Odum.'

'How long have I been asleep?'

'Four, four and a half hours.'

Martin had struggled stiffly into a sitting position on the cot, with his back against the wooden bulkhead. 'What time is it?'

'Twenty to six.'

'Antemeridian or postmeridian?'

'Before dawn. Are you able to focus on what I say? The guards on the quay, the staff on the houseboat have been sent home. People in high places want you to vanish into thin air.' He handed Martin his shoes, both of which had laces, along with his belt. 'Put these on. Follow me.'

Radek led Martin up the metal staircase to the weather deck. In a tiny room next to the midships passageway, he returned his Aquascutum and valise, which he had retrieved from the bed and breakfast. Martin snapped open the valise and touched the white silk scarf folded on top of the clothes. He ran his fingers across the underside of the lid.

'Your false papers, as well as your dollars and English pounds, are where you hid them, Mr Odum.'

Martin regarded Radek warily. 'You provide a great deal for thirty lousy crowns an hour.'

There was a flicker of pain in Radek's eyes. 'I am not the man I appear to be,' he whispered. 'I am not the person my superiors take me for. I did not rebel in my youth against the communists to serve so-called state capitalists who use the same methods. I refuse to be complicit with criminals.' He pulled the German Walther P1 with a clip inserted in it from a pocket of his Tyrollean jacket and offered it to Martin, butt first. 'At least you are forewarned.'

Thoroughly confused, Martin took the weapon. 'Forewarned and forearmed.'

'I was instructed to release you at fifteen minutes to seven. I surmise that your body would have been found floating in the Vltava. Your valise, filled with American dollars and British pounds and false identity papers, would have been recovered from the quay. The authorities would have speculated that a suspicious American, involved in the illegal sale of weapons and weapons systems, had been murdered by international gangsters. A small item to that effect would have appeared in the local newspapers. The American embassy would give the matter superficial attention – your CIA station chief might even hint that the national interest would be better served if they did not dig too deeply into the affair. With the ink still wet on the various reports, the case would be closed.'

'A quarter to seven – that gives me less than an hour,' Martin noted.

'My automobile, a gray Skoda, is parked fifty meters down the quay. The gas tank is full, the keys are in the ignition. Drive along the quay until you come to the first ramp leading to the street, then cross the river at the first bridge you come to and head due south, following the signposts to Ceské Budějovice and beyond that, Austria. If they stop you at the frontier, use one of your false passports. The whole trip should take you about two hours if you do not meet too much traffic.'

'If I'm running, I want to take Zuzana Slánská with me.'

'Her life is not in danger. Yours is. She faces a prison sentence if the evidence is sufficient to convict her.'

Martin was worried about Radek. 'How will you explain that your handgun is missing?'

'I would take it as a service if you would strike my head above the ear hard enough to break the skin and draw blood. They will find me only just beginning to regain consciousness. I will claim that you overpowered me. They will have their doubts – I will certainly be demoted, I may even lose my employment. So what. I resist, therefore I am.'

The two men shook hands. 'I hope our paths cross again,' Martin said.

Radek flashed a sheepish grin. 'Be warned, Mister – next time I will not be such a fool as to settle for one lousy U.S. dollar an hour.'

Gritting his teeth, Radek shut his eyes and angled his head. Martin didn't stint – he knew Radek stood a better chance of talking his way out of trouble if the head wound were real. Gripping the handgun by the barrel, wincing in empathy, he forced himself to swipe the butt sharply across the young man's scalp, drawing blood, stunning Radek, who slumped onto his knees.

'Thank you for that,' he groaned.

'It was not my pleasure,' Martin observed.

He collected his belongings and made his way across the gangplank to the quay, which appeared deserted. Radek's Skoda was parked in the shadows to his left. He went to the car and opened the door and threw his belongings onto the passenger seat. When he turned the key in the ignition, the motor started instantly. He checked the gas gauge – it was full, just as Radek had said. He threw the car into gear and started down the quay. He'd gone about half a kilometer when his headlights fell on the ramp leading to the street. Suddenly Martin's foot went to the brake. Killing the headlights, he pulled the car into the shadows at the side of the quay. He sat there for a moment, shaken by the pulse pounding in his ear. An old instinct had triggered an alarm in the lobe of his brain that specialized in tradecraft. He retrieved the German handgun from the pocket of his jacket, removed the clip, flicked the first of the icy 9-millimeter Parabellum bullets into the palm of his hand and hefted it.

He caught his breath. The bullet looked real enough. But it was too light!

Contrary to what the interrogator had said, Martin was not past his prime!

Checking out the bullets in a handgun was a piece of tradecraft Dante Pippen had picked up during a brief stint with a Sicilian Mafia family. When you gave someone a handgun, or left one where it was sure to be found, there was always the danger that it could be turned against you. In Sicily it was indoor sport to plant handguns loaded with dummy bullets that looked and (if you pulled the trigger) sounded like real bullets. But dummy bullets didn't have the same weight as real bullets – someone familiar with handguns could sense the difference.

Radek had set him up for a fall.

Martin remembered the pained look in the young man's eyes; he could hear his voice, oozing sincerity, delivering his manifesto: *I am not the man I appear to be.*

Who amongst us is the man he appears to be?

Martin thought about going back to liberate Zuzana Slánská. But he quickly abandoned the idea – if he returned to the houseboat for her now, they would know that he'd figured out the scheme. And they would fall back on Plan B, which was bound to be less subtle but more immediate.

Martin could imagine the scenario of Plan A: The prisoner, carrying multiple false identity papers and arrested in the company of an arms dealer, overpowers his guard, swipes his handgun and escapes from the safe house where he is being questioned, heading for Austria. Somewhere along the route, or perhaps at the border crossing itself, he is stopped for a routine passport control. In front of witnesses he produces the gun and tries to shoot his way out of a tight spot, at which point he is gunned down by uniformed police. Open and shut case of self defense. Happens all the time in the former Soviet wastelands of Europe these days.

Knowing that Radek had been setting him up for a hit, Martin certainly didn't want to use the Skoda, though if he parked it on a side street, where it could go unnoticed for hours or even for days, the authorities might spend precious time looking for Radek's car on the highways leading south. Once he ditched the Skoda (he would throw the handgun in the river but leave the bullets on the driver's seat to taunt Radek), the quickest way out of the country was the best: There were trains departing all through the day for Karlovy Vary, the spa in the northwestern corner of the country a long stone's throw from the German frontier. And there were double-decker tourist busses heading back to Germany from Karlovy Vary by the dozens every afternoon; even under the communist regime it had been possible to bribe one of the bus drivers to take you across the border. If the frontier guards verified identities, he could use the Canadian passport that he'd stashed in the tattered lining of his Aquascutum.

Checking the lining again, he felt there was a good possibility that Radek had not discovered that one.

The driver's tinny voice, coming from small speakers in the roof of the tourist bus, stirred Martin from his reverie. *'Bereitet Eure Pässe, wir werden an der Grenze sein.'* Up ahead he could make out the low flat-roofed wooden buildings that housed the money changers and the toilets, and beyond that the border guards in brown uniforms and berets. There was one tourist bus ahead of theirs and three behind, which Martin knew was a stroke of luck; the guards tended toward cursory inspections at rush hours. When it was the turn of his bus, a young officer with a harassed expression on his face climbed onto the bus and walked down the aisle, glancing at faces more than the open passports, looking for Arabs or Afghans surely. Sitting on the banquette, Martin opened the passport to the page with his photo and, smiling pleasantly, held it out, but the young officer barely gave it, or him, a second glance. When the bus started up again and eased across the red stripe painted across the highway, the German passengers, relieved to be back in civilization, broke into a raucous cheer.

Martin didn't join in the celebration. He was having second thoughts about leaving Zuzana Slánská in the clutches of the devious Radek. In his mind's eye he could visualize the weight of the state crushing the breath out of her brittle body.

★   ★   ★

Standing on the fo'c'sle, Radek had watched the red taillights grow dimmer as the Skoda made its way along the quay toward the ramp. When the lights brightened and the car braked to a stop, the interrogator, standing next to him and peering through binoculars, grunted in irritation. Moments later, when the taillights finally started up the ramp and disappeared on the street above the quay, the two men clasped hands to salute a scheme well hatched. The interrogator flicked back the sleeve of his leather jacket to look at the luminous dial of his wristwatch. 'I will alert our people that the American is on his way south,' he said. 'The *Oligarkh* has wired instructions to our ministry – he wants the trail to Samat to end at the Slánská woman.'

Radek, pressing a handkerchief to his head wound to stop the bleeding, took out a small flashlight and signalled with it in the direction of the green garbage bin down the quay from the houseboat. Moments later the two heavies who had escorted Martin to and from his cell appeared on the gang-plank. Radek motioned for them to follow him as he headed for the small cell two decks under the bow. They found Zuzana Slánská sitting on her metal cot, her eyes swollen with fear, her legs tucked under her body, her arms hugging the blanket over her shoulders despite the absence of a breath of air in the room. 'Is it time for another interrogation already?' she asked, her fingers toying with the Star of David at her neck as she unwound from the

395

sitting position on the cot and stood up. Instead of waving her through the door, the two guards positioned themselves on either side of the woman and gripped her arms above the elbows. Zuzana's eyes widened as Radek stepped forward and wrenched her blouse out of the waistband, baring her stomach. When she caught sight of the small syringe in his hand, she struggled to break free, but the two men only tightened their holds on her arms. Thoroughly terrified, Zuzana began to sob silently as Radek jabbed the needle into the soft flesh of her navel and depressed the plunger. The drug took effect rapidly – within seconds Zuzana's eyelids drooped, then her chin fell forward onto her chest. While the two heavies held her up, Radek produced a small pocket knife and began cutting strips from the blanket on the cot. He twisted the strips into cords and tied two of them end to end. Then he dragged the metal cot into the center of the cell under the light bulb and, climbing up on the bed, attached one end of the makeshift cord to the electric wire above the bulb. He pulled on it to make sure it would hold. The heavies hauled Zuzana's limp body onto the cot under the bulb and held her up while Radek fashioned a noose and tightened it around the woman's neck. Then he jumped free of the cot and kicked it onto its side and the three men stepped back and watched Zuzana's body twisting slowly at the end of the cord. Radek grew impatient and motioned with a finger – one of the heavies grabbed her around the hips and added his weight to hers to speed up the execution. Clucking his tongue, Radek rolled his head from side to side in mock grief. 'It is clearly not the state's responsibility if you turned out to be suicidal,' he informed the woman strangling to death in the middle of the room.

Crystal Quest's features clouded over as she fitted on narrow spectacles and read the deciphered 'Eyes Only' action report from Prague Station that her chief of staff had deposited on the blotter. The two wallahs who had been briefing her on the mass graves recently uncovered in Bosnia exchanged looks; they had lived through enough of the DDO's mood swings to recognize storm warnings when they saw them. Quest slowly looked up from the report. For once she seemed tongue-tied.

'When did this come in?' she finally asked.

'Ten minutes ago,' the chief of staff replied. 'Knowing your interest, I thought I'd walk it through instead of rout it.'

'Where did they find the Skoda?'

'On one of those narrow cobblestoned streets on the Hradcany Castle side of the river.'

'When?'

'Twelve hours ago, which was a day and a half after the Czechs watched him drive off down the quay.'

The wallahs slumped back in their chairs and gripped the arm rests to better breast the storm.

To their utter surprise, a cranky grin crept over Quest's crimson lips.

'I love that son of a bitch,' she whispered harshly. 'Where did they find the bullets?'

The chief of staff couldn't help smiling, too. 'On the front seat of the car,' he said. 'Six 9-millimeter Parabellums set out in a neat row. They never found the handgun.'

Quest slapped at the action report with the palm of her hand. To the attending wallahs it came across as applause. 'Naturally they never found the handgun. He would have deep-sixed it in the Vltava. Oh, he's good, he is.'

'He ought to be,' agreed the chief of staff. 'You trained him.'

Quest was rolling her head from side to side in satisfaction. 'I did, didn't I. I trained him and ran him and repaired him when he broke and ran him again. Some legends back, when we were playing Martin as Dante Pippen, I remember him coming in from a stint with that Sicilian Mafia family that was offering to sell Sidewinders to the Sinn Féin diehards in Ireland. He had us all in stitches telling us about how the Sicilians left pistols lying around where anybody could pick them up and shoot them. The catch was they were loaded with dummy bullets, which weighed less than real bullets if you took the trouble to heft them in your palm. Dante' – Quest started giggling and had to catch her breath – 'Dante wanted us to leave pistols loaded with dummy bullets lying around

Langley. He was only half kidding. He said it would be a quick way to separate the street-smart agents from the street-dumb ones.'

'They may still find him if he went to ground in Prague,' observed the chief of staff.

'Dante isn't in the Czech Republic,' Quest said flatly. 'He would have found half a dozen ways of getting across their silly little border.'

'We'll catch up with him,' the chief of staff promised.

But Quest, her head still bobbing with pleasure, was following her own thoughts. 'I love the guy. I really do. What a goddamned shame we have to kill him.'

'I need to get this off my chest,' Stella said, cutting short the small talk. 'I've never had an erotic phone relationship before.'

'I didn't realize our conversations were erotic.'

'Well, they are. The fact that you call is erotic. The sound of your voice coming from God knows where is erotic. The silences where neither of us knows quite what to say, yet nobody wants to end the conversation, is endlessly erotic.'

They both listened to the hollow silence. 'It is not written that we will ever become lovers,' Martin said finally. 'But if we do, we must make love as if each time could be the last.'

His remark took her breath away. After a moment she said, 'If we were to make love, I have the feeling time would stop in its tracks, death would cease to exist, God would become superfluous.' She waited for Martin to say something. When he didn't she plunged on: 'It exasperates me that we only just met – I lost so much time.'

'Uh-huh.'

'Translate that, please.'

'Time is something you can't lose,' Martin said. 'Memory is another story.'

He listened to her breathing on the other end of the phone four thousand miles away. 'Consider the possibility,' he said, 'that we can talk intimately because of the distance between us – because the phone provides a measure of safety. Consider the possibility that the intimacy will evaporate when we come face to face.'

'No. No. I don't think it will; I'm sure it won't. Listen, before Kastner and I came to America I was in love with a Russian boy, or thought I was. I look back on it now as something that was pleasantly physical, as first loves tend to be, but not erotic. The two are a universe apart. My Russian boy friend and I talked constantly when we weren't groping each other on some narrow bed in some narrow room. Thinking about it now, I remember endless strings of words that had no spaces between them. I remember conversations that were without silences. You know how you can split an atom and get energy. Well, you can do the same with words. Words contain energy. You can split them and harness the released energy for your love life. Are you still there, Martin? How do you interpret my love affair with the Russian boy?'

'It means you weren't ready. It means you are now.'

'Ready for what?'

'Ready for naked truths, as opposed to crumbs of truth.'

'Funny you should say that. Do you know Vassily Grossman's *Life and Fate*? It's a great Russian novel, one of the greatest, right up there with *War and Peace*. Somewhere in it Grossman talks about how you can't live with scraps of truth – he says a scrap of truth is no truth at all.'

Martin said, 'I've had to make do with scraps – maybe that's what's pushing me to find Samat. Maybe somewhere in the Samat story there's a naked truth.'

'What makes you say that?'

'Not sure.' He laughed under his breath. 'Intuition. Instinct. Hope against hope that the king's horses and the king's men can somehow put the pieces together again.'

1997: MARTIN ODUM IS ACCUSED OF HIGH *AND* LOW TREASON

'Look, if you please, directly ahead of us – there are the hulls,' Almagul shouted over the din of the ancient Soviet outboard that was powering her eight-meter skiff across the Aral Sea toward Vozrozhdeniye Island. 'Ten years ago there was a bay here with the port for Kantubek at the top of it. The ships you see became stranded when the rivers feeding the Aral Sea were diverted and the sea level sank.'

Martin shielded his eyes with a hand and squinted into the dazzling sunlight. He could make out the hulls of a tanker, a tug boat, a Soviet-era torpedo boat, eight ships in all, half sunken into the sand and the salt residue in what had once been a bay. 'I see them,' he called to the girl.

'You must wear gloves now,' she shouted, and she raised a hand from the outboard tiller to show that she had already fitted hers on over the sleeves of the frayed fisherman's sweater that buttoned across one shoulder. Martin pulled the yellow latex kitchen gloves over the cuffs of his shirt sleeves and attached thick rubber bands at the wrists of each of them. He knotted Dante's white silk scarf around his neck for good luck and tucked his pants legs into the knee-length soccer stockings the girl had given him when they left the Amu Darya – one of the two rivers trickling into the Aral Sea – the night before. As the skiff drew closer to the salt beach a flock of white flamingoes, frightened by the clatter of the motor, beat into the air. Martin spotted the first buildings of Kantubek, now a deserted shell of a town except for the scavengers who came from the mainland to plunder what was left of the once grandiose Soviet bioweapon testing site. Almagul, something of a tomboy who claimed to be sixteen, though she easily might have been a year or two younger, had been coming here regularly with her father and her twin sister before they both died two years before – of a mysterious illness that had left them feverish, with swollen lymph glands and mucus running from their nostrils. (Before her sister's death, Almagul had been known as Irina but, following local tradition, had taken the name of her twin sister, Almagul, to perpetuate her memory.) On the island, the father and his daughters would collect lead and aluminum and zinc-covered steel water pipes and copper wiring, as well as stoves and sinks and faucets and, when nothing else could be found, wooden planking pried up from the floors of buildings, and sell everything on the mainland to men who loaded the loot onto flatbed trucks and headed over the dusty plains toward Nukus or up to the city of

Aral on the Kirgiz Steppe. Almagul hadn't been back to Vozrozhdeniye since the death of her father and her sister but Martin, arriving on a Yak-40 milk from Tash Kent, learned that she was the only person in Nukus with a skiff and a working outboard who had been to the island. He tracked her down to a one-room shack at the edge of the river and made her an offer she couldn't refuse – and then doubled it when he discovered she was studying English in the *gymnasium* and could translate for him as well. They had started down the Amu Darya loaded with spare jerry cans of gasoline and a straw hamper filled with camel-milk yogurt, goat cheese and watermelon.

'Over there is Kantubek,' the girl was shouting now as she veered toward a dune at the foot of the town and idled the motor to let the skiff glide onto the sandy shore. Martin scrambled onto the bow and jumped the last half-meter to shore and turned to haul the skiff higher onto the beach. Clearly emotional at this first trip back to the island since the death of her father, Almagul joined him and stood with her gloved hands on her hips, looking around anxiously. Her Soviet manufactured *djeans*, tied with a rope through the loops at the waist, were tucked into fisherman's rubber boots secured at the tops with lengths of elastic. She kicked at broken test tubes and petri dishes half buried in the sand, and waved toward the piles of debris littering the path that curved up the dunes toward dozens of wooden buildings in various stages of dilapidation. Martin could see mountains of rusting animal cages of all shapes and sizes, rotting timber, scores of broken crates. He glanced at the sky, measuring the height of the sun. 'I'll explore the town,' he told the girl. 'If all goes well, I'll be back here by mid afternoon.'

'I am not able to remain past the setting of the sun,' Almagul informed him. 'My father had an iron rule never to spend the night on the island. In the light of day is possible to see rodents, maybe even fleas. After it turns dark . . .'

Heading down the Amu Darya at half throttle the night before so as not to anger the men fishing from its banks with spotlights and grenades, Almagul had explained about the dangers awaiting visitors to Vozrozhdeniye. Fearing that American inspection teams monitoring the 1972 treaty banning biological weapons would turn up on the island, the Soviets, in 1988, had hidden tens of tons of bacterial agents in hastily dug pits. They had also buried in shallow ditches thousands of cadavers of monkeys, horses, guinea pigs, rabbits, rats and mice that had been used to test the lethality of the bacterial agents. When the Soviet Union collapsed in the early '90s, Uzbekistan and Kazakhstan took custody of the island, but never bothered to dig up the buried spores or the cadavers, which had infected the island's rodent population. The rodents tended to survive the anthrax, glanders, tularemia, brucellosis, plague, typhus, Q fever, smallpox, botulinum toxin or Venezuelan equine encephalitis, but

405

eventually transmitted the sicknesses to fleas which, in turn, transmitted them to other rodents. Which meant that a simple flea bite on the island could be fatal to a human. The risks were very real. In the two years since the death of her father, Almagul knew of fourteen men from Nukus who had disappeared while scavenging on Vozrozhdeniye Island; local authorities around the rim of the receding Aral Sea presumed the missing men had been bitten by fleas and had died of plague or another sickness on the island's dunes, and their bones picked clean by the flamingoes.

Almagul had dropped hints that bio agents or viruses spread by fleas weren't the only things to be found in the ghost town on the island. When Martin drew her out, she said that a handful of scavengers, commanded by a warlord, had installed themselves in the ruins of Kantubek. *Did the warlord have a name?* Martin asked. *My father, who read the bible each night before going to sleep, called the warlord Azazel after the evil spirit in the wilderness to whom a scapegoat is sent on the day of Atonement,* the girl replied. *Others in Nukus say he is a Danish prince with the name of Hamlet Achba. This Hamlet and his gang demand twenty-five percent of the value of what anyone carries off from the island.* Almagul was betting that the warlord wouldn't bother a visiting journalist who wanted to write about the once secret Soviet bioweapons testing range for a Canadian magazine, or the girl who took him there and back to earn enough to see her through the winter.

Favoring his game leg, Martin started up the track that snaked through the dunes. At the top he turned to wave at Almagul, but she had hiked herself onto a crate to watch the flamingoes, with their distinctive bent bills, returning to the beach and didn't notice him. Topping a rise, he headed toward the ghost town along the main road, which consisted of slabs of concrete set end to end. In a field at the edge of town he spotted a basketball court that had been converted into a helicopter landing pad – a great white circle had been white-washed onto the cement and its surface blackened by engine exhaust. Farther down the street he passed a vast hangar that had once housed Kantubek's motor pool. Most of the sections of corrugated roofing had been carted off but the vehicles, buried in drifts of sand, remained – gutted green trucks, two treadless T-52 tanks, two armored personnel carriers sitting on their axles, a faded orange bus that had been driven up onto a cement ramp to be serviced and never driven off, a once-red fire engine with the hood open and the entire motor missing, the rusting hulks of half a dozen ancient tractors with faded Soviet slogans painted on their sides. Continuing on into the town, Martin came upon an enormous building with a ragged Soviet hammer and sickle flag still flapping from the pole jutting over the tarnished double doors that led to an ornate lobby. A giant mosaic depicting the weight of the state, in the form of formations of tanks and squadrons of planes and fleets of ships, filled the entire window-less wall at the side of the lobby. Signs with the Cyrillic lettering bleached out by the sun hung off lampposts. Dust and sand stirred by gusts of wind swirled around Martin's feet at the intersections.

And then his street sense kicked in – he felt the eyes burning into the back of his neck before he caught sight of the scavengers edging into view from behind buildings around the intersection. There were five of them, all wearing canvas laced leggings and canvas gloves that stretched to the elbows and glass face masks that Uzbek cotton farmers used when their crops were being dusted. Each of the men wore a curved Cossack saber from his belt and cradled a vintage bolt-action rifle in the crook of an arm, with a condom over the muzzle to protect the barrel from sand and mois-ture. Martin's fingers instinctively slipped behind his back to where his automatic would have been if he'd been armed with one.

One of the scavengers motioned for Martin to raise his hands over his head. Another came over and frisked him for weapons. Martin's hands were secured in front of him at the wrists with a dog's leash and he was pulled around a corner and down a side street. When he stumbled, a rifle butt jabbed him sharply between the shoulder blades. Two blocks farther along a door was pushed open and Martin was prodded into a building and across a lobby with only a handful of its white marble tiles still in place. He and the others splashed across a shallow trough filled with a liquid that smelled of disinfectant, then walked under a shower head that sprayed him and the guards with a fine mist of disinfectant. He could hear the voices of other scavengers, speaking in a strange language he couldn't identify, exchanging remarks with the five who had brought him in. Double doors were jerked open and Martin found himself in an auditorium with most of the folding seats unbolted and stacked against one wall. Eight men wearing white laboratory coats and latex gloves were sitting on the few seats still intact. Slouched in a high-backed throne-like wooden chair set in the middle of the stage, with a painted backdrop from an old socialist realist operetta behind him, the warlord presided over the assemblage. He was a dwarf of a man, so short that his feet didn't reach the ground, and dressed in a rough gray sleeveless scapular that plunged to the tops of spit-shined paratrooper boots resting on an upturned ammunition box. His bare arms were as muscular as a weight lifter's. He wore a shoulder holster over the scapular, with the steel grip of a large navy revolver jutting from it. The old-fashioned motorcycle goggles covering his eyes gave him the appearance of an insect. A stiff czarist-era admiral's hat sat atop his oversized head. He talked for several minutes in a low growl with one of the men in jumpsuits standing behind him before raising his head to look directly at Martin. Lifting one stubby arm, he gestured for him to approach and, his voice pitched girlishly high, barked something in the strange language of the scavengers.

At a loss for a response, Martin mumbled 'Uh-huh.'

From the back of the auditorium, a girl's voice translated. 'He insists to know for what reason you come to Kantubek.'

Martin stole a glance behind him. Almagul was standing inside the auditorium door, an armed scavenger on either side of her. She smiled nervously at him as he turned back to the warlord and saluted him. 'Explain to him,' he called over his shoulder, 'that I am a journalist from Canada.' He produced a laminated ID card identifying him as a wire service reporter and waved it in the air. 'I am writing an article on the philanthropist Samat Ugor-Zhilov, who is said to have come to Vozrozhdeniye Island when he left Prague.'

When Almagul translated Martin's reply, the warlord bared his teeth in disbelief. He snarled something in a high-pitched voice to the men standing behind the throne, causing them to titter. The warlord kicked over the ammunition box so that his feet danced in the air as he raged at the girl standing in the back of the auditorium. When he ran out of breath he slouched back into the throne. Almagul came up behind Martin. 'He tells you,' she said in a low, frightened voice, 'that Samat Ugor-Zhilov is the governor of this island and the director of Kantubek's experimental weapons programs.'

★   ★   ★

410

The muffled voices talking to each other in an unintelligible language had worked their way into the texture of Martin's dream; he decided he was Lincoln Dittmann at Triple Border, listening to the Saudi he'd later identified as Osama bin Laden conferring with the Egyptian Daoud. When he finally realized that the men weren't speaking in Arabic, he forced himself through the membrane that separated sleep from wakefulness and sat up. It took a moment for his eyes to become accustomed to the dim light cast by feeble bulbs burning in sockets on the stone walls of the vaulted basement. He reached out and touched the cold bars and remembered that the guards had forced him into a low cage, the kind used to house monkeys in laboratories. He could make out Almagul curled up on a pile of rags in the cage next to his. Beyond her cage were other cages – more than he could count. Eight of them contained prisoners sleeping on the floor or sitting with their backs to the bars, dozing with their bearded chins on their chests.

Near the stone staircase, three men in white lab coats stood around a high stainless-steel table talking among themselves. Martin could hear their voices. Gradually a migraine mushroomed behind his eyes and he felt himself being sucked into another identity – one in which the language the men were speaking seemed vaguely familiar; to his astonishment he discovered that he understood fragments.

. . . very stable, even in sunlight.

. . . the advantage of anthrax over plague. Sunlight renders plague stock harmless.

. . . should concentrate on anthrax.

. . . I agree . . . especially pulmonary anthrax, which is extremely lethal.

. . . Q fever persists for months in sand.

. . . What are you suggesting? . . . bombard New York with sand and then attack America with Q fever?

. . . still think we are making a mistake focusing on bacterial agents, which are, in general, difficult to stabilize, difficult to weaponize.

Of course! The men were speaking Russian, a language Martin had studied in college in what seemed like a previous incarnation. He remembered the shrink at the Company clinic telling him of a case where one alter personality was able to speak a language that the other personalities didn't understand. It was a perfect example, she'd said, of how compartmented legends can be in the brain.

. . . not going to make the case for nerve agents over bacterial agents again, are you? Samat himself decided the question months ago.

. . . Samat said we could revisit the issue at any point in our program. Nerve agents – VX in particular, but Soman and Sarin also – can be deadly.

. . . they have serious manufacturing problems.

. . . I want to remind you that tabun is relatively easy to manufacture.

. . . Tabun is only moderately stable.

. . . we are turning in circles . . . try one of the hemorrhagic fevers – the Ebola, for instance – on one of our clients.

. . . Ebola is taking us down a dead-end street. I grant you it is lethal, but it is also relatively unstable, which makes an ebola program problematic.

. . . still, we have the spores Konstantin developed in his laboratory, so we might as well test them on one of the guinea pigs.

. . . only eight guinea pigs left.

. . . not to worry . . . two new ones.

The three scientists, if that's what they were, fitted on Russian army gas masks equipped with enormous charcoal filters. One of them selected a test tube from a cluster in a refrigerator and, removing the wax seal with a pocket knife, carefully poured a single drop of yellowish liquid onto a wad of cotton in a petri dish and quickly covered it with a glass lid. The scientists pulled a low table up to the cage at the far end of the basement and positioned a small ventilator so that it would blow over the petri dish into the cage. The bearded giant of a man sitting with his back to the bars in the cage rocked forward onto his knees and began to shout at the men in the language of the scavengers. His ranting woke the other prisoners. Almagul climbed onto her knees and, grasping the bars, yelled at the men in lab coats in Uzbek. The prisoner in the cage next to hers began raging at them, too. Almagul looked at Martin, her face contorted with terror. 'They are experimenting on one of the scavengers,' she cried, pointing toward the men in white lab coats.

In the last cage, the bearded man sank back onto his haunches and, covering his mouth with the tail of his shirt, breathed through the fabric. One of the scientists brought over a Sony camera attached to a tripod and began filming the prisoner. Another scientist checked the time on his wristwatch, noted it on his clipboard, then removed the cover on the petri dish and stepped away from the cage.

Martin's thoughts went back to the trial that had landed him and the girl in the monkey cages. The court martial – the warlord's term for the proceedings – had started after the lunch break and lasted twenty minutes. Presiding from the makeshift throne on the stage of the auditorium, Hamlet had acted as prosecutor and judge. Martin, his wrists secured with the dog's leash, had been charged with both high and low treason. Almagul, accused of aiding and abetting, had stood behind Martin, nervously whispering translations in his ear. Hamlet had opened the proceedings by announcing that he was absolutely convinced of the guilt of the accused; that the sole purpose of the court martial was to determine the degree of guilt and, eventually, the appropriate punishment.

'Guilty of what?' Martin had asked after pleading innocent to the formal charge of high and low treason.

'Guilty of working for a foreign intelligence

agency,' Hamlet had shot back. 'Guilty of trying to steal Russia's biowarfare secrets.'

'My only interest,' Martin had had Almagul say, 'is to interview Samat Ugor-Zhilov.' And he had explained about Samat's humanitarian quest – repatriating to a village in Lithuania the bones of Saint Gedymin in order to obtain the sacred Torah scrolls and bring them to Israel.

'And where,' Hamlet inquired, leaning forward, cocking his big head so as to better catch Martin's response, 'would Samat find the bones of Saint Gedymin?'

'I was told he'd traced them to a small Orthodox church near the city of Córdoba in Argentina.'

'And what,' the warlord continued, his short feet dancing on the ammunition box, 'would Samat offer the Argentines in return for the bones of the saint?'

Martin realized he'd reached the mine field. 'I have no idea,' he replied. 'That's one of the questions I wanted to ask Samat.'

At which point Hamlet launched into a tirade so fierce that Almagul had all she could do to keep up with him. 'He says you know very well what Samat would trade, otherwise you would not have come to this island. He says the Russian nuclear arsenal will become obsolete in ten years time and the Americans will rule Russia unless Samat is able to perfect bioweapons to counter the American threat. He says bioweapons are the only cost efficient answer to Russia's problem. He says it costs

$2 million to kill half the population of one square kilometer with missiles loaded with conventional warheads, $80,000 with a nuclear weapon, $600 with a chemical weapon and $1 with a bioweapon. Vozrozhdeniye Island, he reminds you, was once the center of bioweapon research for the Soviet Union: Under Samat's direction, and with Samat's financial backing, Vozrozhdeniye is once again developing a bioarsenal that will save Russia from American domination.'

Hamlet collapsed back into the throne. One of the white coated scientists brought over a porcelain basin filled with water smelling of disinfectant and the warlord rang out the sponge in it and mopped his feverish brow.

Martin said, very quietly, 'Are you suggesting that Samat gave bioweapon seed stock to the Argentineans in exchange for the bones of the saint?'

'That is not what I am suggesting,' the warlord groaned when he heard Alamgul's translation. 'Is that what I am suggesting?' he asked the scientists in lab coats.

'*Nyet, nyet*,' they responded in a discordant chorus.

'There is the proof,' Hamlet cried, waving toward the scientists as if they were his star witnesses.

'Then what are you suggesting?' Martin had Almagul ask.

'Who is on trial here, you or me?' the warlord

retorted furiously. 'I am not suggesting Samat provided the Argentinean military with bioweapons. I am also not suggesting that he provided them with the orbits of American spy satellites. That rumor is without substance. It is a fact of life, as any idiot knows, that to get high-quality photographs, the spy satellites are obliged to orbit earth at low altitudes, circling the planet in a polar orbit every ninety minutes. It is a fact of life that they are over any one point on the earth's surface for only a few minutes. If you know when one of the satellites is due overhead, you can suspend operations you do not want the Americans to photograph. India and Pakistan have been doing this for years. So has Iraq. From whence comes the rumor that it is from Saddam Hussein in Iraq that Samat obtained the American satellite orbits that he traded to the Argentines for the bones of the saint.'

It dawned on Martin that Hamlet and the people around him were stark raving mad; characters that Alice might have come across when she fell down the rabbit hole. He decided it was in his interest to humor the mad warlord. 'And what in the world could Samat have given to Saddam Hussein in return for the orbits?'

Almagul whispered, 'It is perilous to know the answer,' but Martin, drunk on state secrets, ordered her to translate the question.

Hamlet drew his navy revolver from its holster and spun the chamber, sending the ticking sound reverberating through the auditorium. Then he raised the revolver and sighted on Martin's head and said 'Bang, bang, you are extinguished.' He laughed at his little joke and the others in the auditorium laughed with him, albeit somewhat anxiously, so it seemed to Martin. After a moment Hamlet said, 'If Samat had wanted to go down that path, he could have traded to Saddam Hussein anthrax spores and hemorrhagic seed viruses that were harvested here on the island in exchange for the orbits.' The warlord lifted the goggles off of his eyes and scratched thoughtfully at the side of his bulbous nose with the barrel of the revolver. A stunted grin materialized on his thick lips. 'He could have traded the orbits for the bones of the saint. And the bones of the saint for the Torah scrolls. But it goes without saying, none of this actually happened.'

Hamlet, tiring of the game, gaveled the butt of his revolver down on the arm of the throne. 'You and the girl are guilty as charged and sentenced to the monkey cages, to be used as guinea pigs in our experiments. Case closed. Trial over. Court adjourned.'

The groaning of the giant scavenger in the last cage shook Martin out of his reverie. Almagul, sitting on the icy floor with her back to the bars in the cage next to Martin, buried her head between her knees. Her body shook with silent sobs. Martin reached through the bars to touch her shoulder. 'I recognize the men in the cages,' the girl whispered hoarsely. 'They are the ones missing from Nukus. We are all surely going to die like my father and my sister,' she added. 'They have already killed six scavengers from Nukus and thrown their bones to the flamingoes. The worst part is that I have no sister to take my name.'

In the last cage the giant scavenger pitched forward onto his knees, with his head touching the ground, and then rolled onto his side. The scientist filming the test called to the two others in Russian to come over and look. The man with the clipboard produced a large skeleton key and opened the padlock on the monkey cage and the three Russians in lab coats, still wearing their gas masks, ducked inside and crouched around the body. One of them raised the scavenger's limp wrist and let it flop back again. 'Konstantin will be extremely pleased with his ebola—' he started to say when the giant scavenger, bellowing with a primitive furor, sprang to life and began shattering the gas masks and the facial bones of the scientists with his fists. With blood seeping from under their gas masks, two of the scientists crawled on all fours toward the low door of the cage, but the giant caught them by their ankles and hauled them back and, climbing over their bodies, pounded their faces into the cement floor. In the other cages the prisoners called to the giant scavenger to free them, but he kept lifting the heads by the hair and smashing them into the cement. It was Almagul's voice that finally penetrated to the wild man's brain. Gasping for air, a maniacal gleam in

419

his bulging eyes, the scavenger released his grip on the bloody heads and looked up.

Almagul called his name and spoke soothingly to him in the strange language of the scavengers. The giant, his arms and shirt drenched in blood, crawled through the door of his cage and staggered to his feet. The other prisoners were all talking to him at once. Almagul spoke quietly to the giant. Martin noticed that mucus was seeping from his nostrils as he lurched across the basement to the stainless steel table, snapped off one of the legs and came back to the cages. One by one he slipped the narrow end of the steel leg through the padlocks and, using the bars for leverage, snapped open the locks. Martin was the last to emerge from the cages. The giant collapsed at his feet – Martin, reaching to help him, found he was burning with fever. 'There is nothing we can do for him,' Almagul said. The other scavengers backed away from the fallen man until Almagul snapped angrily at them. One of them came forward and brought the stainless steel table leg down on the giant's head to put him out of his misery. Then, armed with steel legs from the table and the wooden legs broken off chairs, the scavengers made their way up the stone steps. Almagul, leading the way, carefully opened the steel door leading to the biowarfare laboratory and stepped aside to let the others through. Two Russian scientists napping on cots were strangled to death by the desperate prisoners. Three other scientists were working with frozen anthrax spores in a walk-in refrigerator. Martin thrust one of the stainless steel legs through the door handles, locking the Russians inside, and then turned up the thermostat. The three scientists, realizing they were trapped, began pounding on the thick glass window in the door. One of the prisoners found a plastic jerry can in a closet filled with kerosene for the heating unit. He splashed kerosene over the shelves filled with petri dishes and filing cabinets. Almagul struck a match and tossed it into the spilled kerosene. A bluish fire skidded across the floor. In a moment the laboratory was awash in flames.

The escaping scavengers stumbled across two guards playing backgammon in an ante chamber with razor-stropped one-edged Cossack sabers stacked in four old umbrella stands. Both of the guards lunged for their rifles but were clubbed to death before they could reach them. Snatching the two rifles, stuffing their pockets with bullets, Martin and Almagul led the scavengers, armed now with sabers, up a back staircase that led to the lobby. The single guard on duty there backed against a wall and raised his hands in surrender when he saw the scavengers; one of them walked up to him and split his skull open with a single stroke of his sword. On a gesture from Martin, the men spread out and burst through the several double doors into the auditorium. The fight was short and lethal. Furiously working the bolt of his rifle, hardly bothering to take aim, Martin – a pulse pounding in his temple, his trigger finger trembling – provided covering fire from the back of the auditorium as the escaping prisoners, brandishing the sabers over their heads and screaming savagely, charged down the aisles. The warlord, who had been holding court from the throne, cowered behind it as his guards, caught by surprise, desperately tried to fight off the attackers. Two of the prisoners were killed before they reached the stage; a third was shot in the face as he climbed onto it. When Martin's bolt-action rifle jammed, he caught Lincoln's voice roaring in his ear: *Grab it by the barrel, for Christsake, use it as a club*. Gripping the hot barrel with both hands, Martin joined the battle on the stage, clubbing wildly at the guards as they tried to fend off the blows with their rifles or their arms. When one of the guards stumbled, Martin pounced on him and pinned him down while a prisoner hacked off the guard's hand holding the rifle. Breathing heavily, Martin stood up as another prisoner planted one foot on the neck of the fallen man and slit open his back, exposing his spine down to the coccyx. Gradually the prisoners, pushed by a ferocity that came from having nothing to lose and their lives to win, overpowered the guards who were still alive. The wounded guards, with blood gushing from ugly gashes, and the three who surrendered were hauled into the orchestra pit and decapitated with saber strokes to the napes of their necks. One headless man took several short steps before collapsing to the floor. Martin, sick to his stomach, watched the scavengers circle around the throne almost as if they were playing a harmless child's game. Hamlet had pulled the square of thick theater curtain that had been used as a carpet over his head. The scavengers tore it away from his clutching hands and prodded the warlord to his feet with the points of their sabers. Wiping snot from his nose, Hamlet begged for mercy as the prisoners stripped away his canvas leggings and boots and gloves and goggles and marched him through the auditorium and lobby and out into the street.

Picking his way barefoot through the gutter to avoid the fleas, Hamlet kept babbling in the strange language of the scavengers, but nobody paid the slightest attention to what he was saying. As the sun edged above the horizon, the group retraced the route Martin had taken into Kantubek, passing the ornate building with the mosaic in the lobby depicting the weight of the state. When they reached the motor pool hangar, aswirl in sand and dust, the scavengers found a roll of electric wire and lashed the warlord of Vozrozhdeniye Island to one of the gutted green trucks, his wrists bound over his head to the rusted frame of a window, his bare feet just reaching the drift of sand when he stood on his toes. The warlord whimpered something and Almagul, watching from the street, called out a translation for Martin.

'He pleads with them not to leave him here where the rodents and fleas can get to him. He appeals to be shot.'

'Ask him where Samat went when he left here,' Martin shouted.

'I do not understand his answer,' Almagul called back. 'He says something about the bones of a saint being returned to a church in Lithuania.'

'Ask him if the church is in the village of Zuzovka near the frontier with Belarus.'

'I think he has become mad. He tells only that Samat is a saint – he says this over and over.'

Hamlet Achba could be heard ranting incoherently as the four surviving prisoners and Martin and Almagul made their way along the track that ran through the dunes to the beached boat. At one point Martin stopped to look back at Hamlet. He was about to start up the dunes toward the warlord when he heard Dante's wild Irish cackle in his ear. *Don't you know the bible instructs victims how to survive emotionally? An eye for an eye, a tooth for a tooth, a burning for a burning, laddie.* When Martin hesitated, Dante sighed in despair. *Aye, you're a weak-kneed excuse for a man.* Martin had to agree. Nodding grimly, he turned and stumbled down the hill to join the others on the beach. The men rinsed the blood off their bodies in the sea and tugged the boat off the sand and climbed aboard. Almagul started the outboard, sending the white flamingoes scattering into the air. She backed the boat until the water was deep enough to swing it around and head at full throttle toward the mainland. While Almagul distributed water-melon and goat cheese from the hamper, Martin gazed back at the ghost town of Kantubek, growing smaller and smaller until it finally vanished into the tulle-like haze that thickened as the sun stepped higher in the east.

The solemn timeserver behind the counter at the central post office in Nukus had never before placed a call out of the country and needed to read the appropriate chapter in a manual before she could figure out the various codes and how to charge for the communication. On the third attempt she finally got through to a place she had never heard of – the borough of Brooklyn – and punched the chess timer that she used to measure the duration of calls.

'Stella, that you?' Martin called into the phone in the open booth while the half dozen people queuing for pension checks looked on in wonderment at someone dispatching his voice across Europe and the Atlantic Ocean to the United States of America and receiving an answer within a fraction of a second.

'Did you catch up with Samat?'

'I missed him but it couldn't have been by much. The basketball court was blackened by exhaust.'

'You okay, Martin?'

'I am now. It was touch and go for a while.'

'What does a basketball court have to do with Samat?'

'It had a white circle painted on it, which means

it'd been turned into a helicopter pad. Unlike me, Samat travels first class. I come chugging after him in open boats with outboard motors. How you making out with your new front tooth?'

'I decided you were right about the old chipped tooth – it had a certain charm even if it did make me look breakable. I don't recognize the person looking back at me in the mirror.'

'You can always chip the new tooth.'

'Very funny. Martin, don't get angry but you are tracking down Samat, aren't you?'

'What kind of a question is that?'

'I've been doing a lot of thinking lately. The fact is I hardly know you – I don't think you're a serial killer or anything like that, but you could be a serial liar. You could be phoning me from Hoboken and making the rest up.'

'I'm phoning you from a post office in Uzbekistan. The woman who put the call through had never called out of the country before.'

'I want to believe you. I really do. But the people you used to work for – you know whom I mean – sent a lady psychiatrist around yesterday. Her name was Bernice Treffler. She said she'd treated you after you were laid off.'

'What else did she say?'

'She said – oh, Martin . . .'

'Spit it out.'

'She said you were off your rocker. Are you? Off your rocker, Martin?'

'Yes and no.'

Stella exploded. 'What kind of an answer is that, for God's sake? Either you are or you aren't. There's no middle ground.'

'It's more complicated than you think. There is a middle ground. I'm not insane, but there are things I can't remember.'

'What kind of things?'

The timeserver watching the chess clock muttered something to Almagul, who came over to tug at Martin's sleeve. 'She says this is going to cost you the wages of a year.'

Martin waved the girl away. 'Somewhere along the way,' he told Stella, 'I lost track of which of the several skins I lived in was the real me.'

He could hear Stella groan into the phone. 'Oh, God, I should have known it was too good to be true.'

'Stella, listen. What I have wrong with me isn't fatal, either for me or for us.'

'Us?'

'*Us* is what we're both worried about, isn't it?'

'Wow! I admit there are moments when you sound as if you could be off your rocker. Then there are other moments when you sound perfectly sane to me.'

'I am *imperfectly* sane.'

Stella started laughing. 'I can live with imperfection—'

Suddenly the line went dead in Martin's ear. 'Stella? Stella, are you still there?' He called to Almagul, 'Tell her the line's been cut.'

When Almagul translated, the time server reached out and punched the chess clock with her fist and began calculating the cost of the call on an abacus. When she had figured out the sum, she wrote it on a scrap of paper and held it up so everyone in the post office could tell their children about the deranged foreigner who had spent a fortune to dispatch his voice to a place on the far side of the Atlantic Ocean with the unlikely name of Brooklyn.

1997: MARTIN ODUM REACHES NO-WOMAN'S LAND

Martin Odum pulled the Lada he'd rented in Hrodna, the last big burg in Belarus before the Lithuanian border, off the two-lane highway that had been repaved so many times, each layer piled on top of the previous one, it probably ranked, rising above the wetlands as it did, as an elevated highway. He killed the motor and strolled over to a mossy embankment above the Neman River, and urinated against a scorched oak that looked as if it had been struck by lightening. Martin had crossed the frontier at a dusty village, half of it in Belarus, the other half in Lithuania, with a tongue twister of a name. The young border guards, sunning themselves in deck chairs beside a low prefabricated building on the village's dusty main street, had waved him past without so much as a glance at the Canadian passport made out in the name of one Jozef Kafkor. At regular intervals the route had been blocked by sheep and he'd had to honk his way through them. The last sign post he'd seen before he stopped to relieve his bladder had put his destination, the river town of Zuzovka, at eighteen kilometers; keeping track of the distance on the odometer, Martin reckoned it would be around the next bend in the Neman. Overhead, a high-flying jetliner, its two white contrails drifting apart and thickening behind it, vanished into a fleecy mare's-tail of a cloud. Moments later the distant drone of the motors reached Martin's ears, leaving him with the impression that the noise was racing to catch up with the engines producing it.

How he ached to be on that plane, gazing down at the Baltic flatlands as he headed toward home, toward Stella. How he ached to stop looking over his shoulder every time he stepped into a street; to put the quest for Samat behind him and go back to boring himself to death, a pastime his sometime Chinese girlfriend, Minh, had once described as suicide in slow motion.

Once he'd crossed the border into Lithuania, Martin noticed that the elevated highway had gradually filled with traffic heading in the direction of Zuzovka – there were open farm trucks and dilapidated school busses crammed with peasants, and scores of men in loose shirts and baggy trousers trudging along on foot. Curiously, all of them carried pitchforks or what Dante Pippen would have called *shillelaghs* – sturdy cudgels with knobs on one end, fashioned from the thick branches of oaks. As Martin started back to his car now, two shaggy horses that looked as if they might have been on their way to the abattoir clopped past, hauling a wooden cart loaded with bricks. The old peasant perched high up in the driver's seat gripped the reins casually in one hand and with the other touched two fingers to the visor of his cap in salute when Martin called out a greeting in broken Russian. The old man clucked his tongue at the horses, which didn't need much coaxing to pull up.

Martin waved to the knots of men filling the road on their way toward Zuzovka and raised his hands, as if to ask: *Where is everyone going?*

The old man leaned over and spit eucalyptus juice onto the highway. Then, scrutinizing the foreigner through eyes with a suggestion of Mongolia in them, he allowed as how 'Saint Gedymin has come back to Zuzovka.'

'Gedymin died six hundred years ago,' Martin remarked to himself.

The peasant, speaking slowly and articulating carefully as if he were instructing a child, said, 'Gedymin's bones, which the German invaders stole from our church, have by miracle been returned.'

From some remote corner of his brain Martin assembled Russian words into a sentence. 'And how did the bones of the saint find their way back to Zuzovka?'

A cagey grin appeared on the old man's weathered face. 'How else would a saint travel except by private helicopter.'

'And how long ago did the helicopter bringing the bones of the saint arrive in Zuzovka?'

The peasant pointed his chin at the sky and shut his eyes as he ticked off the days on the fingers of a hand. 'One day before today, the widow Potesta's cow drowned in the Neman. Two days before today, Eidintas wound the cord attached to his bull around the palm of his right hand and then lost all of his fingers except for the thumb when the bull charged laundry hanging on a line. Three days before today, the wife of the drunken shepherd walked all the way to Zuzovka's pharmacy to treat a broken nose, though she refused to identify the owner of the fist that had broken it.' Looking down at Martin, the peasant grinned. 'Three days before today the helicopter brought the bones of the saint to Zuzovka.'

'And why are all the men heading toward town armed?'

'To join the Metropolitan Alfonsas and defend Gedymin from the Romish.'

The old man laughed at Martin's ignorance as he clucked at the horses and snapped at them with the reins. Martin slipped behind the wheel of the Lada, started the motor and honked twice at the peasant as he pulled into the left lane and passed him. The old man, still laughing, again touched the visor of his cap with two fingers in salute, though this time there was more derision than politeness in the gesture.

Zuzovka, a sprawling market town with a tractor repair station next to the brightly painted wooden arch that marked the beginning of its long and wide and dusty main street, materialized around the next bend. The town's two-story brick school sat on a patch of sandy land across from the tractor station; the school's soccer pitch, like the basketball court on Vozrozhdeniye Island in the Aral Sea, had been converted into a helicopter landing pad, with a great circle of white-washed stones set out in the middle of the field blackened by engine exhaust. Martin had to slow to a crawl behind the line of open trucks and men afoot, all heading in the direction of the Orthodox Church situated on a dirt lane that angled off from the main street and ran across the wetlands to the muddy bank of the Neman.

Parking his car in front of a bakery with a sign on the door announcing that, due to Catholic threats to 'liberate' Saint Gedymin, it would not open for business today, Martin melted into the throngs. He grabbed a teenage boy by the arm. '*Gdye zhenshchini*?' he asked. 'Where are the women?'

'Zuzovka is a no-woman's land,' the boy, grinning from ear to ear, shot back as he hurried after the others.

The peasants, joking among themselves about the Catholic skulls they would split open and the Catholic blood that would irrigate Orthodox soil, barely noticed the stranger among them. Dozens of rowboats were tied up at the rickety wooden docks along the river bank, and groups of armed men could be seen climbing the slope toward the church. A fire brigade band – the men dressed in knee-high boots and red parkas – was trumpeting martial aires from the iron gazebo in a fenced park across the lane. Drawing nearer to the church, Martin produced the laminated card that identified him as a wire service reporter and, brandishing it over his head, called out that he was a Canadian journalist. The crowd parted when several of the local *notables* – distinguishable from the farmers because they wore double-breasted suit jackets with their shirts buttoned up to the neck – instructed the peasants to let the foreign journalist through.

Hobbling along on his game leg, which had been acting up since he quit the Aral area, Martin shouldered through the several hundred ripe-smelling peasants toward the three onion domes, each topped with a rusted Orthodox cross. Two young Orthodox priests, dressed in sandals and black habits, waved him up the steps and into the church, and bolted its metal-studded wooden door behind him with a thick wooden crossbar thrust through iron staples and then embeded in niches chiseled into the stone walls on either side. The church reeked of incense and the smoke of beeswax candles and the dust and dankness of centuries and it took a moment for Martin's eyes to make anything out in the misty dimness. The silver and gold in the icons on the sweating walls glinted as a tall bearded man dressed in a black habit, with chiseled features and a squared black miter atop his long black hair, approached. With each step he pounded the floor with the silver tip of a thick staff.

'Do you speak Canadian?' the priest demanded in English, planting himself in front of the visitor.

Martin nodded.

'I am the Metropolitan Alfonsas,' the priest thundered, 'come from the district capital at Alytus to receive the bones of Saint Gedymin and defend the Church of the Transfiguration from the papists who connive to steal the holy relics from their rightful owners.'

'Uh-huh.'

Before he could say more, floodlight blinded Martin. Squinting, he made out the figure of a television cameraman advancing across the floor of the church. The light fixed to the heavy camera on his shoulder bored into the feretory set in a wall to one side of the pulpit. One of the young priests undid a padlock and swung open a thick glass door as the cameraman zoomed in on the velvet cushion with what looked like a bleached pelvis bone and femur nestled in it. Martin noticed a splinter of weathered wood, roughly the thickness and length of a forearm, set into a niche lined with gold cloth inside the feretory.

'And what is that morsel of wood?' he whispered to the metropolitan.

Alfonsas's eyes turned hollow with wrath. 'That is not wood,' he cried. 'It is a fragment of the True Cross.' Overcome with emotion, the metropolitan turned away and, murmuring verses in Church Slavonic, prostrated himself on the great stones of the floor, under which corpses of metropolitans and monks were interred. Guided by a producer, the cameraman panned with his floodlight and lens onto Alfonsas and held it there while a very chic young woman spoke into a microphone in what Martin took to be BBC Lithuanian.

She broke off the interview abruptly when a roar from outside the church penetrated the thick walls. One of the priests, scampering up a ladder and peering through a slit high in a bartizan, called out, 'Holy father, the battle has begun.' The metropolitan sprang to his feet and motioned for the glass door of the feretory to be shut and locked. Gripping his staff by the silver tip and resting the heavy jewel-encrusted handle on a shoulder, he planted himself in front of the holy relics of Saint Gedymin. 'Over my dead body,' he cried. He fixed Martin with his dark beady eyes. 'Bear witness,' he instructed him, 'to the perversity of the papists who falsely claim the relics of our saint.'

The cameraman cut the floodlight and the television reporters darted toward the narrow door in the back of the church. The metropolitan cried out when he saw them tugging free the crossbar – too late. The door burst open on its hinges and a mob of shrieking peasants stormed into the church. Flailing away with his heavy staff, the metropolitan defended the feretory until someone stabbed his thigh with the prongs of a pitchfork and the peasants wrestled his staff away. Martin backed up against a wall and raised his hands over his head but some deranged peasants with wild beards and wild eyes closed in on him and began punching him in the rib cage until he doubled over and sank onto the floor. Through the sea of peasants milling around, he could make out one of them raising a heavy candlestick and shattering the glass window of the feretory. The pillow with the bones of the saint was removed and the peasant army, throwing open the great front door, spilled out of the church. A howl of triumph rose from the throats of the Catholics outside. Faint from the pain in his chest, Martin saw the metropolitan, on his knees in front of the feretory, sobbing like a baby.

Lithuanian police and an army unit, pouring into Zuzovka from the north aboard camouflage-painted armored busses, eventually succeeded in separating the warring communities, but not before two of the attacking Catholics and one of the young Orthodox priests had been clubbed to death and dozens on both sides injured. Their sirens jingling, ambulances arrived behind the police. Doctors and nurses scrambled across the battleground in front of the Orthodox church, treating broken bones and broken heads and hauling the more seriously hurt off on stretchers to the district hospital in Alytus. Martin's rib cage was taped up by a male nurse, after which he was escorted by armed soldiers to the command post, set up in the gazebo, to be quizzed by an army colonel with waxed whiskers who seemed more interested in the impression he would make on television than the confrontation between the town's Orthodox and Catholic communities. Looking appropriately grave, he finished giving an interview to the woman reporter from Vilnius and asked her when it would be broadcast, and then instructed an aide to phone his wife in Kaunas to make sure she caught him on TV. With the television crew off filming the wounded in the field, the officer turned to Martin and checked his identity papers. To be sure that the story the journalist named Kafkor filed (to the news service named on the laminated ID card) would take into consideration the Catholic side of the story – like the vast majority of Lithuanians the colonel was Catholic – he insisted on personally taking Martin in his jeep to talk with the bishop of the archdiocese, come all the way from Vilnius to support the local Catholic priests and the members of the diocese.

The bishop turned out to be a cheery little man with wide hips and narrow shoulders, giving him the appearance, in his crimson ankle-length robe and embroidered stole, of a church bell. The meeting took place in the vegetable garden behind the church. Two white storks peered down at the scene from the large nest on top of the bell tower. 'Dates,' the bishop said, launching into a lecture he had obviously given before, 'are handy pegs on which to hang history. Do you not agree with this observation, Mr Kafkor?'

Martin, wincing from the pain in his ribs, used the tips of the white silk scarf silk tied around his neck to blot the perspiration on his forehead. 'Uh-huh.'

The army officer thrust a pad and ball point pen into Martin's hands. 'You must take notes,' he whispered.

As Martin scribbled, the bishop paced between the furrows, the hem of his robe growing dirtier with each step, as he explained the history of Saint Gedymin. 'It was Gedymin, as every schoolchild in Lithuania knows, who created Greater Lithuania, a vast duchy that stretched from the Black Sea to Moscow to the Baltic. He ruled over the empire from the capital he founded in Vilnius in the year of our Lord Jesus 1321. Sixty-five years later, in the year of our Lord 1386, Lithuanians, by the grace of God, adopted Catholicism as the state religion and, on the order of the grand duke, the entire population was baptized on the banks of the Neman. At which time it can be said that the last Lithuanian pagans vanished into the dustbin of history.'

'Did you get all that?' the army officer demanded.

'The first Catholic church,' the bishop plunged breathlessly on, 'was built on this very site ten years after the mass baptism, and expanded' – he pointed to the bell tower and the jesse window and the two vaulted wings – 'in the centuries that followed. The bones of Saint Gedymin, or what was left of him after the original crypt in Vilnius was desecrated by Tartar bandits, were consigned to the Catholic church at Zuzovka and remained here from early in the fourteenth century until Lithuania came under Russian domination in 1795. The Russians, being Eastern Orthodox, purloined the bones of the saint from the Catholic church and gave them to the Orthodox metropolitan, who had the Church of the Transfiguration built to house them. Despite our repeated petitions over the years, the bones remained in the possession of the Orthodox until a German army officer, retreating before a Russian offensive in 1944, stole the relics as he passed through Zuzovka.'

Hoping to cut short the story, Martin said, 'It was Samat Ugor-Zhilov who discovered the Orthodox church possessed a collection of priceless Torah scrolls and commentaries, and offered to trade the bones of Saint Gedymin, which he had traced to an Orthodox church in Argentina, for the Jewish documents.'

The bishop danced a jig at the mention of Samat's name. 'But that is not it at all! That's the fabricated story that this satanic Samat Ugor-Zhilov and the metropolitan would have the world believe. The truth is quite different.'

'Mark the truth in your notebook,' the army officer instructed Martin.

The bishop noticed the dirt that had accumulated on the hem of his robe and reached down to brush it off. 'The television tells us that Samat Ugor-Zhilov, who is identified as a Russian philanthropist, returned the bones of Saint Gedymin in exchange for the Jewish Torah scrolls and commentaries held for safekeeping in the Orthodox church since the Great Patriotic War. The television goes on to say that all he asked for himself was a minuscule crucifix, fashioned from the wood of the so-called True Cross in the possession of the Orthodox church. The TV even showed a picture of the metropolitan handing to the so-called philanthropist the crucifix, which was the size of a pinky finger on a child. Samat thanked the metropolitan and said he would donate the crucifix, fashioned from the True Cross, to the Orthodox church in the village near Moscow where his mother still lived.'

Martin looked up from his note taking, his eyes burning with excitement. 'Did he give the name of this village?'

The bishop shook his heavy head; his jowls continued to roll from side to side after his head had returned to an even keel. 'No. What does it matter?' Without waiting for a response, he continued: 'The real reason this Samat Ugor-Zhilov gave the saint's bones to the Orthodox and not to its original Catholic custodians is opium.'

Martin, unnerved, looked up again. 'Opium?'

'Opium,' the army officer repeated, tapping a forefinger on Martin's pad. 'Write the word, if you please.'

441

'Opium,' the bishop said, 'is the key to understanding what has transpired. The opium poppy is grown in what is called the Golden Triangle – Burma, Thailand, Laos. Vietnamese drug traders transport the raw opium to the Russian naval base at Cam Ranh Bay in Vietnam, and from there it is shipped to the Russian port of Nakhodka on the Sea of Japan. The Russian drug cartel, which was run by the one known as the *Oligarkh*, Tzvetan Ugor-Zhilov, until he went into hiding several years ago, processes the opium in Nakhodka and then smuggles it across Russia for distribution to markets in Europe and America. Since the late 1980s Zuzovka has served as a hub for shipping opium to northern Europe and Scandinavia. Landing strips were bulldozed onto the flatlands bordering the Neman and small planes flying at night ferried their illicit cargoes into this corner of Lithuania. To move the large quantities of opium westward, Samat Ugor-Zhilov employed runners disguised as Orthodox priests, since they are able to pass frontiers easily. When the metropolitan threatened to put a stop to this, Samat bought him off by tracking down and returning Gedymin's bones' – the bishop's eyes blinked mischievously – 'assuming that what he brought to the church were really the bones of the sainted saint.'

'What about the Torah scrolls?'

'The metropolitan did not want to be seen having commercial dealings with sacred texts so he consigned them to Samat, who sold them to an Israeli museum and donated the proceeds, less a hefty commission, to the Orthodox church.'

'And how did you come across all this information?'

The bishop glanced up at the storks in the nest atop the bell tower. 'A very large bird told me.'

Martin closed his pad and dropped it into a pocket. 'It seems as if every riddle is part of another greater riddle.'

'It is like an onion,' the bishop said consolingly. 'Under each layer is . . . another layer.'

'One last question: If you're not sure the bones Samat brought with him are those of the sainted saint, why were the Catholics battling to bring them back to the Catholic church?'

The bishop held up one of his small pristine hands as if he were directing traffic. 'Whether the bones of the sainted saint are genuine is of little consequence. The only thing that matters is that the faithful believe they are.'

That night the colonel personally drove Martin back to his Lada, still parked in front of the bakery.

'How are your ribs, Mr Kafkor?'

'They only hurt when I laugh and there's not much chance I'll be laughing a lot.'

'Well, good-bye and God speed, Mr Kafkor. I have ordered the soldiers in the jeep to escort you to the Belarus frontier.' When Martin started to protest that it wouldn't be necessary, the colonel cut him off. 'Our police discovered two bloated bodies floating in the Neman this afternoon. At first they assumed the murdered men were Catholics killed by the Orthodox, or Orthodox killed by Catholics. A specialist from Vilnius identified the long knife found on one of the corpses as a weapon popular in Chechnya, which suggests that the two dead men were Chechens.'

'Maybe they were involved in Samat's opium cartel,' Martin ventured.

The colonel shrugged. 'There may be a connection between the dead Chechens and Samat, though I doubt it had anything to do with the opium operation. Islam is not welcomed in this frontier region of Lithuania, either by the Catholics or the Orthodox. No, the only thing that could have brought Chechens here is a mission – though with them being drowned, it is impossible to speculate what it could have been. You would not have an idea?'

Martin shook his head. 'It's as much a mystery to me as it is to you.'

The following morning Martin treated himself to a good breakfast in Hrodna's only hotel and then strolled carefully (his cracked ribs hurt if he walked too fast) along the main street, past the bulletin board posted with the regional newspaper open to photographs of the riot at Zuzovka, to the town's central post office. He queued at the window with the emblem of a telephone over it, and wrote the number on the ledger when the clerk didn't understand his rudimentary Russian.

'What country uses code nine seven two?' she asked.

'Israel.'

'And what city in Israel uses the area code two?'

'Jerusalem.'

The clerk noted 'Jerusalem, Israel' on her work sheet and dialed the number. She motioned for Martin to pick up the telephone in the nearest booth. He heard a man's voice on the line protesting, 'This must be a mistake – I don't know anyone in Belarus.'

'Benny, it's me, Martin.'

'What the Christ are you doing in Belarus?'

'It's a long story.'

'Give me the short version.'

'Even the short version's too long to tell you on the phone. Listen, Benny, that night I spent at your house you told me about the *Oligarkh* living in an isolated dacha in a village a half hour from Moscow along the Moscow-Petersburg highway. You wouldn't by any chance remember the name of the village?'

'You want to hold on, I'll check my computer.'

Martin watched the people lining up at the other windows, some for stamps, some to pay electric or water bills, some to cash pension checks. None of them looked out of place, which didn't mean much; anyone who wanted to keep tabs on him would use local help.

Benny came back on line. 'The name of the village is Prigorodnaia.'

'Maybe you ought to spell that.'

Benny did, phonetically.

'Prigorodnaia. Thanks, Benny.'

'I guess you're welcome. Though come to think of it, I'm not positive.'

1994: LINCOLN DITTMANN SETS THE RECORD STRAIGHT

Bernice Treffler knew something was out of joint the moment Martin Odum strolled into the room – a grin meant to be both sardonic and seductive played on his lips, as if a session with a Company shrink came under the heading of indoor sport and she was fair game. He appeared taller, more assured, less agitated, completely in control of emotions that he could identify. His body language was new to her – his head was angled suggestively, his shoulders relaxed, one hand jingled the loose change in a trouser pocket. He walked with only the faintest trace of a limp. She could have sworn that his hair was combed differently, though she would have had to pull a photograph of Martin from the file folder to be sure, which is something she didn't want to do in front of him. Instead of sitting across the desk from her, as he usually did, he flopped gracefully into a chair next to the low table near the window, his legs extended and crossed casually at the ankles, and nodded at another chair, inviting her to join him, sure she would.

When she did, she noticed him undressing her with his eyes as she came across the carpet; she saw him inspecting her thigh when she crossed her legs. She set the small tape recorder down and edged the microphone closer to Martin. He fixed his gaze on her eyes and she found herself toying with the joint on the fourth finger of her left hand where the gold ring used to be before the divorce.

'You're wearing perfume,' he noted. 'What is it?'

When she didn't respond, he tried another tack. 'Is Treffler your married name?'

'No. I work under my maiden name.'

'You don't wear a wedding band but I could tell you're married.'

Her gaze fell away from his. 'What gave me away?'

'You sure you want to know?' he asked, clearly taunting her.

Why was Martin Odum coming on to her? she wondered. What had changed since the session the previous month? Leaning forward, aware that in this new incarnation he wouldn't miss the slight swell of her breasts above the scalloped blouse, she flipped a switch on the tape recorder. 'Mind if I check your voice level again?'

'Be my guest.' He clasped his hands behind his head and leaned back into them, thoroughly enjoying how uncomfortable he had managed to make her. 'A woman, a dog, a walnut tree,' he recited, pronouncing 'dog' *dawg*, 'the more you beat 'em, the better they be.'

'That another line from Walt . . . from *Walter* Whitman?'

He laughed softly. 'It's a ditty the boys used to sing around the campfire while they were waiting to cross the Rapahannock.'

Suddenly it hit her. 'You're not Martin Odum!'

'And you're not as thick as Martin says.'

'You're the one who claims to have been at the battle of Fredericksburg,' she breathed. 'You're Lincoln Dittmann.'

He only smiled.

'But why? What are you doing here?'

'Martin told you about my being at Fredericksburg but you didn't believe him. You thought he was making the whole thing up.' Lincoln leaned forward, the humor gone from his eyes. 'You went and hurt his feelings, Dr Treffler. Shrinks are supposed to heal feelings, not hurt them. Martin sent me round to set the record straight.'

Dr Treffler understood that she was setting out into uncharted territory. 'Okay, convince me Lincoln Dittmann was at the battle of Fredericksburg. What else did the boys talk about while they were waiting to cross the river?'

Lincoln stared out the window, his eyes wide, unblinking, unfocused. 'They talked about home remedies for diarrhea, which many considered the arch enemy, more dangerous than Johnny Reb. They traded recipes for moonshine. I recall one lieutenant from the 70th Ohio concocted something he labeled "Knock 'em stiff" – it consisted of bark juice, tar water, turpentine, brown sugar, lamp oil and alcohol. They argued whether, when they crossed the river and marched on Richmond and won the war, the slaves ought to be freed; so many were against, the few who were for were careful to keep their own counsel. They griped about having to pay $1.80 for a plug of tobacco. They griped about the Yankees who'd gone west to avoid the draft and claim free land while they were stuck on the Rapahannock fighting the Goddamn war. The griped about the factory-made shoddy—'

'Shoddy?'

'What we called *shoddy* was woolen yarn made from old clothing and then turned into material for uniforms that disintegrated under your fingers in a matter of weeks.'

'What was your rank?'

Lincoln turned back to focus on Dr Treffler. 'I wasn't in the army.'

'If you weren't in the army, what were you doing at Fredericksburg?'

'Fact is, I'd been working for Alan Pinkerton in Chicago. You ever heared of Pinkerton's detective agency?' When Dr Treffler nodded, he said, 'Thought you might have. Alan was employed by his friend Colonel McClellan to eliminate banditry from the railroads out west. When old Abe appointed the colonel to head the Army of the Potomac, McClellan brought along his friend Alan Pinkerton, who was using the pseudonym E.J. Allen at the time, if I remember right. And Alan brought along some of his operatives, me among them, to organize an intelligence service. Then came what the Federals called the battle of Antietam, after the stream, and the Confederates called the battle of Sharpsville, after the village. With the help of General Joe Hooker – who tore himself away from his camp followers, what we jokingly called *Hooker's girls* or just plain *hookers*, long enough to lead the attack on the right – McClellan won the day and Bobby Lee was obliged to pull his force, what was left of it, back into Virginia. Antietam was the first time I saw the elephant—'

'Saw the elephant?'

'That's how we described experiencing combat – you say you saw the elephant. After the battle, Alan sent several of us riding south to discern the Confederate order of battle, but that old snake in the grass Lee bamboozled us – he must have figured we could estimate his troop strength by counting the rations he issued, 'cause he doubled the rations and we doubled the size of his army and McClellan got cold feet and stayed put, which is when old Abe decided McClellan had got the slows and sent him packing back to Chicago. Alan Pinkerton went along with him but I stayed on to work for Lafayette Baker, who was setting up a Federal intelligence service in Washington. Which brings me to McClellan's successor, Ambrose Burnside, and Fredericksburg.' Leaning forward, Lincoln picked up the small microphone and spoke into it. 'A woman, a dog, a walnut tree, the more you beat 'em, the better they be. Hey, doc, what about you and me having dinner together when we're finished here?'

Bernice Treffler kept her face a blank and her voice neutral. 'You'll understand that this is simply not possible. A psychiatrist cannot have a relationship with a client outside of working hours and still hope to maintain the distance she needs to evaluate the client.'

'Where is it written there has to be a distance between you and the client? Some psychiatrists sleep with their patients in order to bridge this distance.'

'That's not the way I function, Lincoln.' She tried to make a joke out of it. 'Maybe you need another psychiatrist—'

'You'll do fine.'

'Why don't you go on with your story.'

'*My story*! You think it's a story!' He set the microphone back on the table. 'You still don't see that what I'm telling you really happened. To me. At Fredericksburg.'

'Lincoln Dittmann taught history at a junior college,' Dr Treffler said patiently. 'He turned his college thesis on the battle of Fredericksburg into a book and printed it himself, under the title *Cannon Fodder*, when he couldn't find an editor willing to publish the manuscript.'

'There are things that happened at Fredericksburg you can't find in any history book, or *Cannon Fodder*, for that matter.'

'Such as?'

Lincoln was angry now. 'Alright. Burnside force-marched the Union Army down the Rapahannock, but wound up bivouacking across the river from Fredericksburg for ten long days waiting for the damn pontoon bridges to catch up with him. Lafayette Baker'd posted me to Burnside's staff – I was supposed to figure out the Confederate order of battle so Burnside could reckon on what was waiting for him once he got across the river. Armed with an English spyglass, I spent the better part of the first nine days aloft freezing my ass off in a hot-air balloon, but the mustard-thick haze hanging over the river never burned off and I couldn't make heads or tails of what was going on up on the ridgeline behind Fredericksburg. Which is why I decided to infiltrate the Confederate lines. I found a sunken fisherman's dingy and raised it with the help of some skirmishers and greased the oar-locks and set off before sunrise to cross the river, which was in flood, creating a margin of shallow marshes on either side. When my dingy couldn't make it as far as the shore, I pulled off my boots and socks and rolled up my trousers and climbed out and waded through the slime until I reached solid ground. I found myself on the slope below the lunatic asylum. The doctors and nurses had fled inland when Burnside's army appeared on the other side of the river, leaving the demented women to fend for themselves. They were leaning out of windows, some of them clothed, some buff naked, mesmerized by the sight of the Federal soldiers urinating into the river, also by the occasional mortar shot Yankee gunners lobbed across the Rapahannock and the ensuing explosions on the heights behind Fredericksburg; the demented women were sure something dreadful was about to happen, sure, too, that they were meant to witness it and spread the story, so one young lady with tufts of matted hair hanging over her bare breasts screeched to me from a window when I made my way up the hill past the asylum.'

The memory of the poor lunatics trapped between the lines in their asylum set Lincoln to breathing hard through his nostrils. Dr Treffler said, very quietly, 'Want to take a break, Lincoln?'

He shook his head roughly. 'I purloined an orderly's smock from the laundry shed behind the asylum and put it on and walked through Fredericksburg in the direction of Marye's Hill. The city was deserted except for sentinels who, seeing the white smock, took me for someone employed at the asylum. I made a mental note of everything I saw. Fredericksburg itself was obviously not going to be defended, despite the occasional Mississippi sharpshooter firing across the river from buildings along the waterfront. I made my way out of the city, past buildings with greased paper serving as windows, past an emporium with boards nailed over the doors and windows (as if this would stop looters), and headed across the plain. I could see that no effort had been made to dig trenches or pits, and I began to wonder if there was to be a battle after all. Then I came to the sunken road under Marye's Hill, with a stone wall running the length of it, and I knew there would be a battle and that it would go against the Federals, for the sunken road was acrawl with Confederates – there were sharpshooters polishing the brass scopes of their Whitworths and setting out the paper cartridges on top of the stone wall; there were short-muzzled cannon with grape charges piled next to their wheels; there were officers afoot with swords and long-muzzled pistols directing newly arrived troops into the line; there were Confederate flags and unit flags furled and leaning against trees so the Federals, when they finally appeared, would not know what they were up against until it was too late to turn back. The single unfurled flag visible to the naked eye belonged to the 24th Georgians, known to be hard customers and surpassing marksmen when sober. No way around the sunken road and its stone wall presented itself – to the right it was too swampy for a flanking movement, to the left the road and wall went on forever. I was challenged by pickets several times but, making laughing reference to the lunatics, talked my way past and continued up the hill. And back from the crest, out of sight of Pinkerton men peering through spyglasses from balloons, was the largest army I ever set eyes on. There were more cannon than a body could count. Soldiers were watering down the road to suppress the dust as teams of horses positioned the cannon behind freshly dug earthenworks. A Confederate band belted out waltzes for the southern gentlemen and ladies who had come down from Richmond to see the battle. My footpath took me past a large gray tent set next to a copse of stunted apple trees and I saw three generals poring over maps stretched open on a trestle table. One, in a white uniform, I took for Bobby Lee himself; the second, in homespun gray with plumes fluttering from his hat, I took for George Pickett (which meant that Pickett's division had come up earlier than anticipated and was taking its place in the line); the third, with a woman's woolen shawl draped over his shoulders, I took to be Old Pete Longstreet. I was sorely tempted to try for a closer look at the generals and acted upon this desire, which proved to be my undoing. A young officer wearing a brand new uniform with a sash to hold his sword accosted me. My story about being the last orderly to abandon the lunatics to their asylum did not appear to persuade him and he set me to walking toward the divisional tent on the far side of Marye's Hill, him following close on my heels. As much as I ached to, I could not run for it – all he had to do was raise the alarum and a thousand rebels would have been upon me. Could I trouble you for a glass of water?'

'No problem.' Dr Treffler walked over to a sideboard and filled a glass from a plastic bottle and carried it back, aware that Lincoln's eyes never left her. Was he thinking of the young lunatic, leaning out the window with the matted hair covering her breasts? Was he regretting he didn't have a shrink who slept with her patients?

Lincoln drank off the glass of water in one long swallow and then ran his finger around the rim as he picked up the thread of his tale. 'I was closely questioned by a stubby, hunch-shouldered officer with a shock of hair turned silver from age and battle fatigue, so I supposed because he walked with the aid of two wooden crutches. And when he didn't esteem my answers – I admitted to having been born and raised in Pennsylvania but claimed I'd gone south to defend state's rights and slavery, for who in his right mind wanted millions of freed slaves invading the north to take away our jobs – he had me stripped to the skin and began examining each item of clothing. Which is how he came across the watch fob decorated with the symbol of Alan Pinkerton's detective agency – an unblinking eye – that Alan himself had given me back in the days when we were chasing train robbers and cattle thieves. The old officer recognized it immediately and my efforts to make out that I had got it off one of the crazed women in the asylum fell short of convincing him. *You are a Federal spy*, he said, *caught behind our lines. Make your peace with your Maker for you will be executed at dawn.'*

Lincoln, reliving the episode, wiped perspiration from his forehead with the back of a wrist. 'I was allowed to dress, after which they tied my ankles loosely so I could walk but not run and took me to a circle of hospital wagons and sat me down at a wooden crate inside one of them to write my last testament and any letters that I deemed necessary to deliver to friends or family. Night fell quickly at this time of the year. The aurora borealis, a rare sight in these latitudes, flickered like soundless cannon fire in the north; it didn't take much imagination to suppose a great war was being fought beyond the horizon. I was brought an oil lamp and a tin plate of hard crackers and water, but try as I might I was unable to swallow even the spittle in my mouth, the lump in my throat, which I identified as fear, being too big. I attempted to write my mother and father, and a girl I had been sweet on back in Pennsylvania, I wanted to tell them what had befallen me and so began: *I take the present opportunity of penning you a few lines, my health is good but it will not be so for long.* I was obliged to discontinue the letter because my brain, befuddled with chemicals released by fear, could not locate the words to describe my condition. I became convinced that it was all a terrible dream, that any moment I would become too frightened to continue dreaming; that I would force myself through the membrane that separated sleep from wakefulness and wipe the sweat from my brow and, still under the spell of the nightmare, have trouble falling back to sleep. But the wooden crate felt damp and cold under my palm and a whiff of sulfurous air – in the next wagon the surgeons, amputating the leg of a boy who had been pinned under an overturned cannon, were dousing the stump with sulfur – stung my lungs and the pain brought home to me that what had happened, and what was about to happen, were no dream.'

Dr Treffler, caught in the web of Lincoln's tale, leaned toward him when he stopped talking. 'Admit it,' he said with a sneer, 'it's beginning to dawn on you that I am recounting the truth.' When she nodded carefully, he went on. 'I was expecting execution by hanging but the old officer with the silver hair and crutches had something more dreadful in store. At first light my wrists and elbows were bound behind my back with a length of telegraph wire. I was taken from the hospital wagon by two men wearing the striped shirts of penitentiary guards and paraded to the other side of Marye's Hill and the turnpike known as Plank Road, called so because the craters gouged by several dozen exploding Federal mortar rounds had been too deep to fill with earth and had been covered over with planking to make the road pass-able. Standing at the lip of one such crater, which was roughly the size of a large wagon wheel, with the planks intended to patch it stacked at the side of the turnpike, it struck me what my interrogator intended when he spoke of execution. One of the penitentiary guards produced a square of straw-board with the words 'The spy Dittmann' lettered on it in India ink and attached the sign with cotter pins to the back of my shoddy jacket. I divined who the author of my unusual execution was when I caught sight of Stonewall Jackson, known to be a religious fanatic, sitting his horse on a rise above me, a look of unadulterated malevolence on his face. He removed the cigar from his mouth and studied me for a long while, as if he were committing me and the moment to memory. He angrily flicked cigar ashes as he issued instructions to an aide. I was too far away to make out more than a few words. *Buried, that's what I want, but alive . . .* Hundreds of Confederates on the side of the hill had stopped what they were doing to watch the execution. My interrogator plucked a cigarette from the mouth of one of the penitentiary guards and, making his way to me on his crutches, wedged it between my parched lips. *It is a matter of tradition*, he said. *A man condemned to death is entitled to a last cigarette.* Trembling, I puffed on the cigarette. The act of smoking, and the smoke cauterizing my throat, distracted me. My interrogator stared at the ash, waiting for it to buckle under its own weight and fall so they could get on with the execution. Sucking on the cigarette, I became aware of the ash, too. Life itself seemed to ride on it. Defying gravity, defying sense, it grew longer than the unsmoked part of the cigarette.'

'And then?'

'And then a whisper of wind coming off the river brought with it the distant sound of a brass band playing Yankee Doodle. Under cover of darkness

460

the Federals had finally thrown their pontoon bridges across the river and were starting to come over in force. There were scattered shots from Fredericksburg as the Confederate rear guard pretended to put up a fight to suck the Federals into the trap that awaited them once they captured Fredericksburg and started across the plain Richmond-bound. The notes of Yankee Doodle and the hollow reports of muskets set everyone to peering toward the river. Bobby Lee reined up next to Jackson, who touched his hat in salute. They talked for a moment, Lee pointing out the Chatham Mansion, which served as Burnside's command post, within eyeshot on the other side of the river. And then Lee happened to glance in my direction. His eyes fixed on me and he called, *What the blazes is going on down there?* My interrogator called up that I was a Federal spy caught behind the Confederate lines the previous evening; that they were about to bury me alive as a warning to others. Lee remarked something to Jackson, then stood in his stirrups and, removing his white hat, shouted down, *There will be enough killing on these fields today to last a man a lifetime. Tie him to a tree and let him watch the battle, and set him free when it is over.* Which is how I came to see the elephant again – to witness the carnage that unfolded below Marye's Hill that terrible December day. Burnside's army burst out of Fredericksburg onto the plain and formed up. The 114th Pennsylvania Zouaves with their white head-bands were the first to charge the stone wall along the sunken road – they came on with pennants flying while a drummer boy set the cadence for the attack until his head was severed from his body by a cannon ball. It was a massacre from start to finish. Through the afternoon wave upon wave of Federals charged the sunken road, only to be cut down by a hail of minié balls. I counted fourteen assaults in all, but not a one of them made it as far as the wall. The cause was so hapless, the Confederates looking down from the hill took to cheering the courage of the Federals. I could see the Rebel sharpshooters dipping their hands in buckets of water so they could load their Whitworths, scalding hot from being shot so much, without blistering their skin. At one point in the afternoon I could make out groups of Federals trying to take cover behind some brick houses on the plain but the Yankee cavalry, using the flats of sabres, forced them back to the battle. It was a Godawful thing to behold – there have been days since when I wished they'd gone ahead and buried me alive so that the sight and sound of battle would not be graven on my brain.'

'And they let you cross the battlefield to your lines when it was over?'

'As for the field of battle, the less said about it the better. The temperature that night dipped below freezing and my breath came out from between my chattering teeth in great white plumes as I negotiated its pitfalls. I ripped the square of strawboard off my back and started toward the flames I could see burning in Fredericksburg, tripping over the bloated bodies of horses and men, stumbling onto limbless corpses entangled at the bottom of shell craters. Even in the cold of winter there were horseflies drawn to the blood oozing from wounds. The maimed Federals who were still alive dragged the dead into heaps and burrowed under the corpses to keep warm. To my everlasting regret I could do nothing for them. I stopped to cradle a dying soldier who had a slip of paper with his name and address pinned to the back of his blouse. He shivered and murmured *Sarah, dearest* and expired in my arms. I took the paper, meaning to send it to his next of kin but somehow lost it in the confusion of the night. Riderless horses pawed at the frozen ground looking for fodder, but the only fodder at Fredericksburg on 13 December 1862 was cannon fodder.'

'You reached the town—'

'Fredericksburg resembled Sodom. Buildings had been set ablaze by the retreating Federals, the emporium lay gutted, its furniture and wares littering the planks of the sidewalk and the dirt in the street. What was left of silken gowns that had been cut up for handkerchiefs and towels hung limply from placards projecting over the entrances to stores. Mad women from the asylum, in sooty shifts and bare footed, picked through the debris, collecting pocket mirrors and colored ribbons and fine ladies hats imported from Paris France, which they pulled over their matted hair. Two of them were struggling to carry off a Regulator clock. I was surely one of the last to cross the bridge because the engineers began to unfasten the pontoons behind me. On the other side I wandered from campfire to campfire, past dispirited troops dozing on the ground, past pickets sleeping on their feet. I must have become feverish because much of what happened to me subsequent to the retreat across the pontoon bridge is disjointed and fuzzy in my head. I seem to remember great lines of woebegone soldiers trudging back toward Washington, the wounded piled three and four deep in open carts drawn by mules, the dead buried in shallow graves where they succumbed. When I came awake, I don't know how many days later, I found myself on a cot stained with dried blood in a field hospital. Doctors decided I was suffering from hypochondria, what your fancy doctors call depression nowadays. A gentleman with a kindly face and a soiled white shirt open at the throat was sponging my chest and neck with vinegar to bring down the fever. We got to talking. He told me his name was Walter. Only later did I discover him to be the celebrated Brooklyn poet Whitman, scouring the field hospitals for his brother George, who'd been listed as wounded in the battle. Luck would have it, he'd found him in the same tent as me. One morning, when I felt stronger, Walter put his arm around my waist and helped me out of the tent into the sunlight. We sat, only the two of us, with our backs to a stack of fresh pine coffins. I remember Walter staring at the heap of amputated limbs behind the tent and opining, *Fredericksburg is the most complete piece of mismanagement perhaps ever yet known in the earth's wars.* After some while orderlies appeared from the tent carrying three stretchers with corpses on them and set them on the ground to attend burial. The dead men were covered with blankets, with the toes of their stockings sticking out and pinned together. Pushing himself to his feet, Walter walked over to the bodies and, squatting, lifted aside the blanket from one and looked for a long, long time at the boy's dead face. When he sat back down next to me, he pulled a notebook from a pocket inside his jacket and, licking the stub of a pencil, began to write in it. When he finished I asked him what he'd written and he read it off and the words stuck with me all these years.' Lincoln shut his eyes – to keep back tears (so it seemed to Dr Treffler) – as he dredged up Walter Whitman's lines. *Sight at daybreak, – in camp in front of the hospital tent on a stretcher (three dead men lying,) each with a blanket spread over him – I lift up one and look at the young man's face, calm and yellow, – 'tis strange! (Young man: I think this face of yours the face of my dead Christ!).*

Lincoln, drained of arrogance, looked at Dr Treffler as he recited in a sing-song whisper, 'A woman, a dog, a walnut tree, the more you beat 'em – I can't recall the rest.'

'I believe you, Lincoln. I can see that you really were at Fredericksburg.' When he just sat there, his chin on his chest, breathing unevenly, she said, 'Shalimar.'

'What?'

'That's the name of the perfume I'm wearing. Shalimar.'

1994: BERNIGE TREFFLER LOSES
A PATIENT

D r Treffler turned around the statue of Nathan Hale outside the Central Intelligence Agency's headquarters at Langley, Virginia, studying the expression on the face of the young colonial spy from various angles, trying to imagine what might have been going through his mind as he was being led to execution. It occurred to her that nothing had been going through his mind; perhaps he had been too distracted by the lump in his throat, which is called fear, to think clearly. She couldn't remember if Nathan had seen the elephant (though the term probably didn't come into use until the Civil War) before he set off on his mission behind British lines in Manhattan Island. She wondered if the British executioners wore striped shirts; wondered, too, if they had wedged a cigarette between his lips before they hanged him on the Post Road, what today is Third Avenue in Manhattan. *It is a matter of tradition*, Lincoln Dittmann had remembered the executioner saying. *A man condemned to death is entitled to a last cigarette.*

A whey-faced young man with a laminated card pinned to the breast pocket of his three-piece suit approached. 'He was the first in a long line of Americans who died spying for our country,' he noted, looking up at Nathan's wrists bound behind his back. 'You must be Bernice Treffler.' When she said *In the flesh* he asked to see her hospital identity card and driver's license and carefully matched the photos against her face. She peeled off her sunglasses to make it easier for him. Apparently satisfied, he returned the cards. 'I'm Karl Tripp, Mrs Quest's executive assistant, which is a fancy name for her cat's-paw. I'm sorry if we've kept you waiting. If you'll come with me . . .'

'No problem,' said Dr Treffler, falling in alongside her escort. She was mesmerized by the laminated card on the suit jacket with his photo and name and ID number on it. If lightning struck him right now, right here, would she have the good sense to tear it off and send it to his next of kin?

'First visit to Langley?' he asked as he showed his ID to the uniformed guard at the turnstile, along with the signed authorization to bring in a woman named Bernice Treffler.

'I'm afraid it is,' she said.

The guard issued a visitor's pass that expired in one hour, and noted Dr Treffler's name and the number of the pass in a log book. Karl Tripp pinned the pass to the lapel of her jacket and the two of them pushed through the turnstile and made their way down a long corridor to a bank of elevators.

She started to walk into the first one that turned up but Tripp tugged on her sleeve, holding her back. 'We're taking the express to the seventh floor,' he whispered.

Several young men relegated to the plebeian elevators eyed the well dressed woman waiting for the patrician elevator, wondering who she might be, for the seventh floor was, in naval terminology, admiral's country and outsiders went there (the elevator didn't stop at other floors) by invitation only. When the door finally opened on the seventh floor, Tripp had to walk Dr Treffler through another security check. He led her down a battleship-gray corridor to a door marked 'Authorized DDO staff only,' unlocked it with a key at the end of a chain attached to his belt and motioned her to a seat at a crescent-shaped desk. 'Coffee? Tea? Diet Coke?'

'I'm fine. Thanks.'

Tripp disappeared, closing the door behind him. Treffler looked around, wondering if this tiny windowless cubbyhole could really be the office of someone as important as Crystal Quest, whom she had spoken to several times on the phone since she first began treating Martin Odum. A moment later a narrow door hidden in the paneling behind the desk opened and Mrs Quest appeared from a larger, airier office. She was obviously a good deal older than she sounded on the phone, and wearing a pantsuit with wide lapels that did nothing to emphasize her femininity. Her hair, cropped short, looked like rusting gunmetal. 'I'm Crystal Quest,' she announced matter of factly, leaning over the desk to swipe at Dr Treffler's palm with her own, then sinking back into the wicker swivel chair. She reached into the bottom drawer of the desk and pulled out a thermos. 'Frozen daiquiris,' she explained, producing two ordinary kitchen tumblers but filling only one of them when her visitor waved her off. 'So you're Bernice Treffler,' she said. 'You sound older on the phone.'

'And you sound younger – Sorry, I didn't mean . . .' She laughed nervously. 'Heck of a way to start a conversation.'

'No offense taken.'

'None intended, obviously.'

'Which brings us to Martin Odum.'

'I sent you an interim report—'

'Prefer to hear it from the horse's mouth.' Quest flashed a twisted smile. 'No offense intended.'

'Martin Odum is suffering from what we call Multiple Personality Disorder.' Dr Treffler could hear Crystal Quest grinding slivers of ice between her molars. 'At the origin of this condition is a trauma,' the psychiatrist continued, 'more often than not a childhood trauma involving sexual abuse. The trauma short-circuits the patient's narrative memory and leads to the development of multiple personalities, each with its own memories and skills and emotions and even language abilities. Often a patient suffering from MPD switches from one personality to another when he or she comes under stress.'

Crystal Quest fingered a chunk of ice out of the

kitchen tumbler and popped it into her mouth. 'Has he been able to identify the trauma?'

Dr Treffler cleared her throat. 'The original trauma, the root cause of these multiple personalities, remains shrouded in mystery, I'm sorry to report.' She could have sworn Crystal Quest looked relieved. 'Which is not to say that with more treatment it won't surface. I would very much like to get to the trauma, not only for the sake of the patient's mental health but because of the medical paper I plan to write—'

'There won't be any medical paper, Dr Treffler. Not now, not ever. Nor will there be additional treatment. How many of these multiple personalities have you detected?'

Dr Treffler made no effort to hide her disappointment. 'In Martin Odum's case,' she replied stiffly, 'I've been able to identify three distinct alter personalities, which the patient refers to as legends, a term you will surely be familiar with. There's Martin Odum, for starters. Then there is an Irishman named Dante Pippen. And finally there's a Civil War historian who goes by the name of Lincoln Dittmann.'

'Any hint of a fourth legend?'

'No. Is there a fourth legend, Mrs Quest?'

Quest ignored the question. 'How many of these legends have you personally encountered?'

'There is Martin Odum, of course. And at the most recent session, which took place last week, I came face to face with Lincoln Dittmann.'

'How could you be sure it was Lincoln?'

'The person who came into my office was quite different from the Martin Odum I know. When I realized I was confronting Lincoln Dittmann and said so, he came clean.'

'Cut to the chase. Is Martin Odum off his rocker? Should we commit him to an institution?'

'You can have it either way, Mrs Quest. Lincoln Dittmann is certainly off his rocker, as you put it. He's convinced he was present at the battle of Fredericksburg during the Civil War. Say the word and I can get a dozen doctors to certify he's clinically insane. If you wanted to, you could have Lincoln Dittmann – or his alter ego, the Irishman Dante Pippen – committed indefinitely.'

'What about Martin Odum?'

'Martin is distressed by his inability to figure out which of the three working identities is the real him. But he functions reasonably well, he is quite capable of making a living, of fending for himself, perhaps even of having a relationship with a woman as long as she is able to live with the ambiguity at the heart of his persona.'

'In short, nobody who meets Martin in a bar or at a dinner party would think he was mentally deranged?'

Dr Treffler nodded carefully. 'As long as he is unable to dredge up the details of the original childhood trauma, he will remain in this state of suspended animation – functional enough to muddle through, vaguely anguished.'

'Okay. I want you to drop this case. I'll send my man Tripp around to your clinic to collect any and all notes you might have made during the sessions. I don't need to remind you that the whole affair is classified top secret and not to be discussed with a living soul.'

Dr Treffler remembered something she'd told Martin at one of their early sessions. 'Even if I change the names to protect the guilty?'

'This is not a laughing matter, Dr Treffler.' Crystal Quest stabbed at a button on the console. 'Tripp will see you to the lobby. Appreciate your coming by.'

'That's it?'

Mrs Quest heaved herself out of the wicker chair. 'That's definitely it,' she agreed.

Dr Treffler rose to her feet and stood facing her, her eyes bright with discovery. 'You never wanted me to identify the trauma. You don't want Martin to get well.'

Quest sniffed at the scent of perfume in the windowless cubbyhole; it startled her to realize that Bernice Treffler's professional psyche reeked of femaleness, which was more than she could say for herself. 'You're in over your head,' the Deputy Director of Operations testily informed her visitor. 'In Martin's case, getting well could turn out to be fatal.'

1997: MARTIN ODUM DISCOVERS THE KATOVSKY GAMBIT

S tepping off the curb in front of the crowded airport terminal, Martin raised an index finger belt high to flag down one of the free-lancers cruising the area in search of customers who didn't want to deal with the doctored meters on the licensed cabs. Within seconds an antique Zil pulled to a stop in front of him and the passenger window wound down.

'*Kuda*,' demanded the driver, an elderly gentleman wearing a thin tie and a checkered jacket with wide lapels, along with a pair of rimmed eyeglasses that were the height of fashion during the Soviet era.

'Do you speak English?' Martin asked.

'*Nyet, nyet, nye govoryu po-Angliiski*,' the driver insisted, and then began to speak pidgin English with obvious relish. 'Which whereabouts are you coming to, comrade visitor?' he asked.

'A village not far from Moscow named Prigorodnaia. Ever hear of it?'

The driver rocked his head from side to side. 'Everyone over fifty knows where is Prigorodnaia,' he announced. 'You have been there before?'

'No. Never.'

'Well, it's not stubborn to find. Direction Petersburg, off the Moscow-Petersburg highway. Big shots once owned dachas there but they are all late and lamented. Only little shots still live in Prigorodnaia.'

'That's me,' Martin said with a tired grin. 'A little shot. How much?'

'Around trip, one hundred dollars U.S., half now, half when you resume to Moscow.'

Martin settled onto the seat next to the driver and produced two twenties and a ten – which was what Dante Pippen had paid the Alawite prostitute Djamillah in Beirut several legends back. Then, popping another aspirin from the jar he'd bought at the airport pharmacy to dull the pain from the cracked rib, he watched as the driver piloted the Zil through rush-hour traffic toward Moscow.

After a time Martin said, 'You look a little old to be freelancing as a taxi.'

'I am one miserable pensioner,' the driver explained. 'The automobile belongs to my first wife's youngest son, who was my stepson before I divorced his mother. He was one of those smart capitalists who bought up industry privatization coupons distributed to the proletarian public, and then turned around and sold them for an overweight profit to the new Russian mafioso. Which is how he became owner of an old but lovingly restored Zil automobile. He borrows it to me when the ridiculous rent on my privatized apartment needs to get paid at the start of the month.'

'What did you do before you retired?'

The driver looked quickly at his passenger out of the corner of an eye. 'Believe it or not, no skin off my elbow if you don't, I was a famous, even infamous, chess grandmaster – ranked twenty-third in Soviet Union in 1954 when I was a nineteen-year-old Komsomol champion.'

'Why infamous?'

'It was said of me that chess drove me mad as a hatter. The critics who said it did not compre-hend that, as a chess-playing psychologist once pointed out, chess cannot drive people mad; chess is what keeps mad people sane. You don't by any chance play chess?'

'As a matter of fact, I used to. I don't get much of a chance anymore.'

'You have heard maybe of the Katovsky gambit?'

'Actually, that rings a bell.'

'It's me, the bell that's ringing,' the driver said excitedly. 'Hippolyte Katovsky in the flesh and blood. My gambit was the talk of tournaments when I played abroad – Belgrade, Paris, London, Milan, once even Miami in the state of Caroline the North, another time Peking when the Chinese Peoples Republic was still a socialist ally and Mao Tse-tung a comrade in arms.'

Martin noticed the old man's eyes brimming with nostalgia. 'What exactly was the Katovsky gambit?' he inquired.

Katovsky leaned angrily on the horn when a taxi edged in ahead of him. 'Under Soviets, drivers like that would have been sent to harvest cotton in Central Asia. Russia is not the same since our communists lost power. Ha! We gained the freedom to die of hunger. The Katovsky gambit involved offering a poisoned pawn and positioning both bishops on the queen's side to control the diagonals while knights penetrate on the king's side. Swept opponents away for two years until R. Fischer beat me in Reykjavik by ignoring the poisoned pawn and castling on the queen's side after I positioned my bishops.'

His lips moving as he played out a gambit in his head, Katovsky fell silent and Martin didn't interrupt the game. The Zil passed an enormous billboard advertising Marlboro cigarettes and metro stations disgorging swarms of workers. Fatigue overcame Martin (he'd been traveling for two days and two nights to get from Hrodna to Moscow) and he closed his eyes for a moment that stretched into twenty minutes. When he opened them again the Zil was on the ring road. Giant cranes filled what Martin could see of the skyline. New buildings with glass facades that reflected the structures across the street were shooting up on both sides of the wide artery. In one of them he could make out automobiles barreling by, but there were so many of them on the road he couldn't be sure which one was his. Traffic slowed to a crawl where men in yellow hard hats were digging up a section of the roadway with jackhammers, then sped up again as the Zil spilled through the funnel. Up ahead an overhead sign indicated the junction for the Petersburg highway.

'Turnoff for Prigorodnaia very shortly now,' Katovsky said. 'I was one of Boris Spassky's advisors when he lost to Fischer in 1972. If only he would have followed my advice he could have vacuumed the carpet with Fischer, who made blunder after blunder. Ha! They say the winner in any game of chess is the one who makes the next to last blunder. Here – here is the Prigorodnaia turnoff. Oh, how time seeps through your fingers when you are not closing your hand into a fist – I remember this road before it was paved. In 1952 and part of 1953, I was driven by a chauffeur to Lavrenti Pavlovich Beria's dacha in Prigorodnaia every Sunday to teach chess to his wife. The lessons came to an end when Comrade Stalin died and Beria, who behind Stalin's back created the gulags and purged the most loyal comrades, became executed.'

As Katovsky headed down the spur, past a sign that read 'Prigorodnaia 7 kilometers,' the cracked rib in Martin's chest began to ache again. Curiously, the pain seemed . . . *familiar*.

But how in the name of God could pain be familiar?

A pulse, the harbinger of a splitting headache, began to beat in Martin's temples and he brought his fingers up to knead his brow. He found himself slipping into and out of roles. He could hear Lincoln Dittmann lazily murmuring a verse of poetry.

. . . the silent cannons bright as gold rumble
lightly over the stones. Silent cannons, soon
to cease your silence, soon unlimber'd to begin
the red business.

And the voice of the poet wearing the soiled white shirt open at the throat.

Sight at daybreak, – in camp in front of the
hospital tent on a stretcher (three dead men lying,)
each with a blanket spread over him

Other voices, barely audible, played in the lobe of his brain where memory resided. Gradually he began to distinguish fragments of dialogue.

Gentlemen and ladies . . . overlooked Martin Odum's
original biography.

His mother was—

. . . was Polish . . . Immigrated . . . after the Sec-
ond . . .

Maggie's on to . . .

. . . staring us in the face . . .

The driver of the Zil glanced at his passenger. 'Look at those chimneys spewing filthy white smoke,' he said.

'Uh-huh.'

'That's a paper factory – built after Beria's time, unnecessary to say – he never would have permitted it. Now you are knowing why only little shots live here nowadays – the stench of sulfur fills the air every hour of every day of every year. The local peasants swear you get used to it – that in time you only feel discomfortable when you breathe air that is not putrid.'

Even the reek of sulfur stinging Martin's nostrils seemed familiar.

'Comrade Beria played chess,' the driver remembered. 'Badly. So badly that it required all my cleverness to lose to him.'

. . . Lincoln Dittmann was in Triple . . . overheard an old lottery vender talking Polish to a hooker . . . catch the drift . . .

. . . his mother used to read him bedtime stories in Polish . . .

Martin found himself breathing with difficulty – he felt as if he were gagging on memories that needed to be disgorged before he could get on with his life.

Ahead, an abandoned custom's station with a faded red star painted above the door loomed at the side of the road. Across from it and down a shallow slope, a river rippled through its bed. It must have been in flood because there appeared to be a margin of shallow marshes on either side; grass could be seen undulating in the current.

Martin heard a voice he recognized as his own say aloud, 'The river is called the *Lesnia*, which is the name of the woods it meanders through as it skirts Prigorodnaia.'

Katovsky slowed the Zil. 'I thought you said me you never been to Prigorodnaia.'

'Never. No.'

'Explain, then, how you come to know the name of the river?'

Martin, concentrating on the voices in his head, didn't reply.

He aced Russian at college . . . speaking it with a Polish accent.

. . . bringing his Polish up to snuff, they could also work on his Russian.

'Pull over,' Martin ordered.

Katovsky braked the car to a stop, two wheels on the tarmac, two wheels on the soft shoulder. Martin jumped from the car and started walking down the middle of the paved road toward Prigorodnaia. Off to his left, high on the slope near a copse of stunted apple trees, he could see a line of whitewashed beehives. His game leg and broken ribs ached, the migraine lurking behind his brow throbbed as he made his way across a landscape that seemed painfully familiar even though he had never set eyes on it.

. . . Jozef as a first name?

Half of Poland is named Jozef.

. . . precisely the point . . .

I happen to be rereading Kafka . . .

. . . suggest a Polish-sounding variation. Kafkor.

Martin detected an unevenness in the tarmac under his feet and, looking down, saw that a section of roadway, roughly the size of a large tractor tire, had been crudely repaved. It had been smoothed over, but the surface was lumpy and the seam was clearly visible. Gaping at the round section of road, he suddenly felt dizzy – he sank onto his knees and looked over his shoulder at the Zil drawing closer to him. His eyes widened in terror as he felt himself being transported back in time through a mustard-thick haze of memory. He saw things he recognized but his brain, befuddled with chemicals released by fear, could no longer locate the words to describe them: the twin stacks spewing plumes of dirty white smoke, the abandoned custom's station with a faded red star painted above the door, the line of white-washed bee-hives on a slope near a copse of stunted apple trees. And then, vanquishing terror only to confront a new enemy, madness, he could have sworn he saw an elephant striding over the brow of the hill.

The old man driving the Zil was standing alongside the car, one hand on the open door, calling plaintively to his passenger. 'I could have crushed Beria every time,' he explained, 'but I thought I would live longer if I came in second.'

The voices in Martin's skull grew louder.

. . . *studied Kafka at the Janiellonian University in Kraków.*

. . . *worked summers as a guide at Auschwitz.*

. . . *job in the Polish tourist bureau in Moscow . . . contact with the DDO target without too much difficulty.*

Question of knowing where this Samat character hangs out . . .

Martin, his facial muscles contorting, heard himself whisper, *'Poshol ty na khuy.'* He articulated each of the O's in *'Poshol.'* *'Go impale yourself on a prick.'*

Pushing himself to his feet, feeling as if he were trapped in a terrible dream, Martin stumbled down the paved spur toward Prigorodnaia. Could he have met Samat before? He had a vision of himself leaning on the bar of a posh watering hole on Bolshaya Kommunisticheskaya called the Commercial Club. In his mind's eye he could make out the thin figure of a man settling onto the stool next to him. Of medium height with a pinched, mournful face, he wore suspenders that kept his trousers hiked high on his waist, and a midnight blue Italian suit jacket draped cape-like over a starched white shirt, which was tieless and buttoned up to a very prominent Adam's apple. The initials 'S' and 'U-Z' were embroidered on the pocket of the shirt. Martin saw himself placing on the burnished mahogany of the bar a Bolshoi ticket that had been torn in half. From a jacket pocket the thin man produced another torn ticket. The two halves matched perfectly.

Moving his lips like a ventriloquist, Samat could be heard mumbling, *What took you so long? I was told to expect the cutout to make contact with me here last week.*

It takes time to establish a cover, to rent an apartment, to make it seem as if we are meeting by chance.

483

My uncle Tzvetan wants to see you as soon as possible. He has urgent messages he must send to Langley. He wants assurances he will be exfiltrated if things turn bad. He wants to be sure the people you work for lay in the plumbing for the exfiltration before it is needed.

How do I meet him?

He lives in a village not far from Moscow. It's called Prigorodnaia. I invite you to his dacha for the weekend. We will tell everyone we were roommates at the Forestry Institute. We studied computer science together, in case anyone should ask.

I don't know anything about computers.

Except for me, neither does anyone else at Prigorodnaia.

Martin caught sight of the low wooden houses on the edge of the village ahead, each with its small fenced vegetable garden, several with a cow or a pig tethered to a tree. A burly peasant splitting logs on a stump looked up and appeared to freeze. The large axe slipped from his fingers as he gaped at the visitor. He backed away from Martin, as he would from a ghost, then turned and scampered along the path that ended at the small church with paint peeling from its onion domes. Nearing the church, Martin noticed a patch of terrain behind the cemetery that had been leveled and cemented over – a great circle had been whitewashed onto the surface blackened by engine exhaust. An Orthodox priest wearing a washed-out black robe so short it left his bare matchstick-thin ankles and Nike running shoes exposed stood before the doors of the church. He held a minuscule wooden cross high over his head as men and women, alerted by the log splitter, drifted through the village lanes toward the church.

'Is it really you, Jozef?' the priest demanded.

As Martin drew nearer many of the women, whispering to each other, crossed themselves feverishly.

Martin approached the priest. 'Has Samat come back to Prigorodnaia?' he asked.

'Come and departed in his helicopter. Donated this cross, fabricated from the wood of the True Cross of Zuzovka, to our church here in Prigorodnaia, where his sainted mother prays daily for his soul. For yours, too.'

'Is he in danger?'

'No more, no less than we were after it was discovered that the planks over the crater in the spur had been removed and the man buried alive had gone missing.'

Martin understood that he was supposed to know what the priest was talking about. 'Who protected Samat?' he asked.

'His uncle, Tzvetan Ugor-Zhilov, the one we call the *Oligarkh*, protected Samat.'

'And who protected his uncle?'

The priest shook his head. 'Organizations too powerful to have their names spoken aloud.'

'And who protected you when you removed the planks over the crater and freed the man buried alive?'

'Almighty God protected us,' said the priest, and he crossed himself in the Orthodox style with his free hand.

Martin looked up at the onion domes, then back at the priest. 'I want to talk to Samat's mother,' he announced, thinking she might be among the women watching from the path.

'She lives alone in the *Oligarkh*'s dacha,' the priest said.

'Kristyna is a <u>raving</u> lunatic,' said the peasant who had been splitting logs. Crossing themselves again, the other peasants nodded in agreement.

'And where is the *Oligarkh*, then?' Martin thought to ask.

'Why, none of us can say where the *Oligarkh* went to when he quit Prigorodnaia.'

'And when did the *Oligarkh* leave Prigorodnaia?'

'No one knows for sure. One day he was here, struggling down the path near the river on aluminum crutches, his bodyguards following behind, his Borzois dancing ahead, the next the dacha was stripped of its furnishings and echoed with emptiness, and only a single candle burned in a downstairs window during the long winter night.'

Martin started toward the sprawling dacha with the wooden crow's-nest rising above the white birches that surrounded the house. The peasants blocking the path gave way to let him through; several reached out to touch an arm and a toothless old woman cackled, 'Back from the dead and

486

the buried, then.' Gaunt chickens and a rooster with resplendent plumes scrambled out from under Martin's feet, stirring up fine dust from the path. Drawn by curiosity, the villagers and the priest, still holding aloft the sliver of a cross, trailed after him, careful to keep a respectful distance.

When Martin reached the wooden fence surrounding the *Oligarkh's* dacha, he thought he could make out a woman singing to herself. Unlatching the gate and circling around toward the back of the dacha, he stepped carefully through a neatly tended garden, with alternating furrows of vegetables and sunflowers, until he spotted the source of the singing. An old and frail crone, wearing a threadbare shift and walking barefoot, was filling a plastic can with rainwater from a barrel set under a gutter of the dacha. Long scraggly white hair plunged across her pale skin, which was stretched tightly over her facial bones, and she had to stab it away from her eyes when she caught sight of Martin to get a better look at him. 'Tzvetan, as always, was correct,' she said. 'You will have been better able to survive the winter once the hole was covered with snow, though I was dead set against their burying you before you had eaten your lunch.'

'You know who I am?' Martin asked.

'You didn't used to ask me silly questions, Jozef. I know you as well as I know my own son, Samat; as well as I knew his father, who hibernated to Siberia during the time of Stalin and never returned. Curious, isn't it, how our lives were utterly and eternally defined by Stalin's whimsical brutality. I knew you would come back, dear Jozef. But what on earth took you so long? I expected you would surely return to Prigorodnaia after the first thaw of the first winter.' The old woman set down her watering can and, taking Martin's hand in hers, led him across the garden to the back door of the dacha. 'You always liked your tea and jam at this hour. You will need a steaming cup to see you through the morning.'

Kristyna pushed through a screen door hanging half off of its hinges and, slipping her soiled feet into a pair of felt slippers, shuffled through a series of deserted rooms to the kitchen, all the while glancing over her shoulder to be sure Martin was still behind her. Using both thin arms, she worked the hand pump until water gushed from the spigot. She filled a blackened kettle and put it to boil on one of the rusting electric plaques set on the gas stove that no longer functioned. 'I will fetch your favorite jam from the preserves in the larder of the cellar,' she announced. 'Dearest Jozef, don't disappear again. Promise me?' Almost as if she couldn't bear to hear him refuse, she pulled up a trap door and, securing it with a dog's leash, disappeared down a flight of steps.

Martin wandered through the ground floor of the dacha, his footfalls echoing from the bare walls of the empty rooms. Through the sulfur-stained panes of the windows he could make out the priest and his flock of faithful gathered at the fence, talking earnestly among themselves. The double living room with an enormous stone chimney on either end gave onto a study filled with wall-to-wall shelves devoid of books, and beyond that a small room with a low metal field-hospital cot set next to a small chimney filled with scraps of paper and dried twigs waiting to be burned. Half a dozen empty perfume bottles were set out on the mantle. A small pile of women's clothing was folded neatly on an upside down wooden crate with the words 'Ugor-Zhilov' and 'Prigorodnaia' stenciled on several of its sides. A dozen or so picture post-cards were tacked to the door that led to a toilet. Martin drew closer to the door and examined them. They'd been sent from all over the world. One showed the duty-free shop at Charles de Gaulle airport in Paris, another the Wailing Wall in Jerusalem, a third a bridge spanning the Vltava River in Prague, still another Buckingham Palace in London. The topmost postcard on the door was a photograph of a family walking down a paved country road past two identical clapboard farm houses built very close to each other. Across the road, a weathered barn stood on a small rise, an American eagle crafted out of metal sitting atop the ornate weather vane jutting from the mansard roof. The people pictured on the postcard were dressed in clothing farmers might have worn going to church two hundred years before – the men and boys were attired in black trousers and black suit jackets and straw hats, the women and girls were wearing ankle length gingham dresses and laced-up high shoes and bonnets tied under the chin.

Martin pried out the tack with his fingernails and turned over the postcard. There was no date on it; the printed caption identifying the picture on the postcard had been scuffed off with a knife blade, the post office cancellation across the stamp read 'fast New York.' 'Mama dearest,' someone had written in Russian, 'I am alive and well in America the Beautiful do not worry your head for me only keep singing when you weed the vegetable garden which is how I see you in my mind's eye.' It was signed, 'Your devoted S.'

The old woman could be heard calling from the kitchen. 'Jozef, my child, where have you gone off to? Come take tea.'

Pocketing the postcard, Martin retraced his steps. In the kitchen the old woman, using a torn apron as a potholder, was filling two cups with an infusion that turned out to have been brewed from carrot peelings because, for her, tea had become too expensive. She settled onto a three-legged milking stool, leaving the only chair in the room for her visitor. Martin pulled it up to the table covered with formica and sat across from her. The woman kept both of her hands clasped around the cracked mug as she summoned memories and gently rocked her head from side to side at the thought of them. Her lidded eyes flitted from one object to another, like a butterfly looking for a leaf on which to settle. 'I recall the day Samat brought you back from Moscow, Jozef. It was a Tuesday. Ah, you are surprised. The reason I remember it was a Tuesday is because that was the day the woman from the village came to do laundry – she was too terrified to use the electric washing machine Samat brought from GUM and scrubbed everything in a shallow reach of the river. You and Samat had been roommates in a school some-where, so he said when he introduced you to his uncle's entourage. Later, Tzvetan took you aside and asked you question after question about things I did not comprehend – what in the world is an exfiltration? You do remember the *Oligarkh*, Jozef? He was a very angry man.'

Martin thought he could hear the angry voice of an older man raging against the regime as he lurched back and forth on aluminum crutches before people too cowed to interrupt. *My grand-father was executed during the 1929 collectivization, my father was shot to death in a field gone to weed in 1933, both were found guilty by itinerant tribunals of being kulaks. Do you know who kulaks were, Jozef? For the Soviet scum, they were the so-called rich peasants who wanted to sabotage Stalin's program to collectivize agriculture and drive the peasants onto state farms. Rich my ass. Kulaks were farmers who owned a single pair of leather shoes, which would last a lifetime because they were only worn inside church. My grandfather, my*

491

father would walk to and from church wearing peasant shoes made of woven reeds, what we called lapti, *and put on their leather shoes when they crossed the threshold. Because they owned a pair of leather shoes, my grandfather and my father were branded enemies of the people and shot. Perhaps now you understand why I wage one-man war against Mother Russia. I will never forgive the Soviets or their heirs . . .*

Martin looked across the table at the old woman sipping her infusion. 'I remember him saying something about leather shoes,' he said.

The woman brightened. 'He told the story to every newcomer to the dacha – how his grandfather and father had been executed by the Soviets because they owned leather shoes. It could have been true, mind you. Then, again, it could have been imagined. Those who lived through the Stalinist era can never get out of it. Those who were born afterward can never get in. You are too young to know the Soviet state's greatest secret – why everyone spent their waking hours applauding Stalin. I shall educate you: It is because the walls in the new apartment buildings were insulated with felt, which left the rooms well heated but infested with clothes moths. Our indoor sport was to clap our hands and kill them in mid flight. We kept score – on any given evening the one with the most cadavers was declared to be the winner. Ah,' the woman added with a drawn out sigh, 'all that is spilt milk. Samat and Tzvetan, they are both of them gone from here now.'

'And where have they gone to?' Martin asked softly.

The old woman smiled sadly. 'They have gone to earth – they have hibernated into holes in the frozen ground.'

'And in what country are these holes in the ground?'

She gazed out a window. 'I was studying piano at the conservatory when my husband, Samat's father, was falsely accused of being an enemy of the people and sent to Siberia.' She held her fingers up and examined them; Martin could see that the palms of her hands were cracking from dryness and her nails were broken and filthy. 'My husband – for the moment his name slips my mind; it will surely come back to me – my husband was a medical doctor, you see. He never returned from Siberia, though Tzvetan, who made inquiries after the death of Koba, whom you know as Stalin, heard tales from returning prisoners about his brother running a clinic in a camp for hardened criminals, who paid him with crusts of stale bread.'

'Did you and Samat suffer when your husband was arrested?'

'I was expelled from the Party. Then they cancelled my stipend and expelled me from the conservatory, though it was not because my husband had been arrested – he and Tzvetan were Armenians, you know, and Armenians wore their arrests the way others wear medals on their chests.'

'Why were you expelled, then?'

'Dear boy, because they discovered I was an Israelite, of course. My parents had given me a Christian name, Kristyna, precisely so that the Party would not suspect I had Jewish roots, but in the end the ruse did not work.'

'Did you know that Samat went to live in Israel?'

'It was my idea – he needed to emigrate because of the gang wars raging in the streets of Moscow. I was the one who suggested Israel might accept him if he could prove his mother was Jewish.'

'How did you make ends meet when you lost your conservatory stipend?'

'While he was in the gulag, Tzvetan arranged for us to be taken care of by his business associates. When he returned he personally took us both under his wing. He convinced Samat to enroll in the Forestry Institute, though why my son would want to learn forestry was beyond me. And then he sent him to the State Planning Agency's Higher Economic School. What Samat did after that he never told me, though it was clearly impor- tant because he came and went in a very shiny limousine driven by a chauffeur. Who would have imagined it – my son, driven by chauffeur?'

On a hunch, Martin said, 'You don't seem mad.'

Kristyna looked surprised. 'And who told you I was?'

'I heard one of the peasants from the village say you were a raving lunatic.'

Kristyna frowned. 'I am a raving lunatic when I need to be,' she murmured. 'It is a formula for protecting yourself from life and from fate. I wrap myself in lunacy the way a peasant pulls a sheep-skin coat over his shoulders in winter. When people take you for a raving lunatic, you can say anything and nobody, not even the Party, holds it against you.'

'You are not what you seem.'

'And you, my dear, dear Jozef, are you what you seem?'

'I'm not sure what you mean by that . . .'

'Samat brought you here – he said you were friends from school. I accepted you in place of the son I had lost at childbirth. The *Oligarkh* received you as a member of his entourage and, after several months, as a member of his family. And you betrayed us all. You betrayed Samat, you betrayed me, you betrayed Tzvetan. Why?'

'I don't . . . remember any of this.'

Kristyna looked at Martin intently. 'Does your amnesia protect you from life and from fate, Jozef?'

'If only it could . . . I run as fast as I can, but life and fate are endlessly and always right behind and gaining on me.'

Tears seeped from under Kristyna's tightly shut lids. 'Dear Jozef, that has been my experience also.'

Taking leave of Kristyna, Martin headed back toward Prigorodnaia's church. The crowd of peasants had long since followed the priest back to the church to offer up special prayers for the soul of Jozef Kafkor. Martin was unlatching the garden gate when he heard Samat's mother calling from a window.

'It was Zurab,' she shouted.

Martin turned back. 'What about Zurab?' he called.

'Zurab was the given name of Samat's father, my husband. Zurab Ugor-Zhilov.'

Martin smiled and nodded. Kristyna smiled back and waved good-bye.

When he reached the paved spur, Martin found the Zil parked off the roadway in the shade of a grove of birches leaning away from the prevailing winds. Katovsky, his shoes off and trousers rolled up, was down slope from the car soaking his feet in the cool currents of the Lesnia. 'You wouldn't by any chance be familiar with the fourth game A. Alekhine versus J. Capablanca 1927?' the driver called as he scrambled uphill toward Martin. 'I was just now playing it in my head – there was a queen sacrifice more dazzling than the thirteen-year-old R. Fischer's celebrated queen sacrifice on the seventeenth move of his Grünfeld Defense against the grandmaster Byrne, which stunned the chess world.'

'No,' Martin said as Katovsky sat on the ground to pull on his shoes. 'Never played that game.'

'On second thought you ought to avoid it, comrade visitor. Queen sacrifices are not for the weak of heart. I tried it once in my life. I was fifteen at the time and I was playing the State Grandmaster Oumansky. When he made his sixteenth move, I studied the board for twenty minutes and then resigned. There was nothing I could do to avoid defeat. The Grandmaster Oumansky accepted the victory gracefully. I later discovered he spent months replaying the game. He couldn't figure out what I'd seen to make me surrender. To me, it was as conspicuous as the nose on your face. I would have been a pawn down in four moves. My bishop would have been pinned after seven and the rook file would have been open after nine, with his queen and two rooks lined up on it. What I saw was I could not beat the State. If I had it to do over again,' the driver added with a sigh, 'I would not play the State.'

A hundred meters in from where the Prigorodnaia spur joined the four-lane Moscow-Petersburg highway, interior ministry troops in camouflage khakis had blocked off circulation, obliging the occasional automobile to slow to a crawl and slalom between strips of leather fitted with razor-sharp spikes. When Katovsky's Zil came abreast of the parked delivery truck with the DHL logo on its side, baby-faced soldiers armed with submachine guns motioned for the driver to pull off the road. A brawny civilian in a rumpled suit yanked open the passenger door and, grabbing Martin's wrist, dragged him from the car so roughly his cracked ribs sent an electric current through his chest. A second civilian wagged a finger at the driver, who was cowering behind the wheel. 'You know the rules, Lifshitz – you could get six months for operating a taxi without a license. I might forget to arrest you if you can convince me you didn't take a passenger to Prigorodnaia today.'

'How could I take a passenger to Prigorodnaia? I don't even know where it is.'

Martin, looking back over his shoulder, asked, 'Why are you calling him Lifshitz?'

Gripping the nape of Martin's neck in one huge hand and his elbow in the other, the brawny civilian steered the prisoner toward the back of the DHL truck. 'We call him Lifshitz because that's his name.'

'He told me it was Katovsky.'

The civilian snorted. 'Katovsky, the chess grand-master! He died a decade ago. Lifshitz the un-licensed taxi driver was a finalist in the Moscow district Chinese checkers tournament five, six years ago. Chess grandmaster – that's a new one in Lifshitz's repertoire.'

Moments later Martin found himself sitting on the dirty floor in the back of the DHL truck, his legs stretched in front of him, his wrists manacled behind his back. The two civilians sat on a makeshift bench across from him, sucking on Camels as they gazed impassively at their prisoner through the smoke. 'Where are you taking me?' Martin demanded, but neither of his captors showed the slightest inclination to respond.

At some point the truck must have turned off the ring road onto a main artery because Martin could sense that it was caught in bumper to bumper traffic. Horns shrieked around them.

When the truck swerved sharply, Martin could hear the screech of brakes and drivers shouting curses. The two jailers, their eyes fixed on the prisoner, seemed unfazed. After twenty or so minutes the truck descended a ramp – Martin could tell by the way the motor sounded that they were indoors – and then backed up before coming to a stop. The civilians threw open the rear doors and, gripping Martin under his armpits, hauled him onto a loading ramp and through swinging doors down a long corridor to a waiting freight elevator. The two grilled gates slid closed and the elevator started grinding noisily upward. The doors on the first five floors were sealed shut with metal bars welded across them. On the sixth floor the elevator jerked to a halt. Other civilians waiting outside tugged open the double gates and Martin, surrounded now by six men in civilian suits, was escorted to a holding room painted glossy white and saturated in bright light. The handcuffs were removed from his wrists, after which he was stripped to the skin and his clothing and his body were meticulously inspected by two male nurses wearing white overalls and latex gloves. An overripe doctor in a stained white smock with a cigarette bobbing on her lower lip and a stethoscope dangling from her neck came in to examine Martin's eyes and ears and throat, then listened to his heart and took his blood pressure and probed his cracked ribs with the tips of her fingers, causing him to wince. As she went through the motions of checking his health, Martin was more distressed by his nakedness than his plight. He concentrated on her fingernails, which were painted a garish phosphorescent green. He caught the gist of a question she posed in Polish; she wanted to know if he had ever been hospitalized. Once, he replied in English, for a shrapnel wound in my lower back and a pinched nerve in my left leg, which still aches when I spend too much time on my feet. The doctor must have understood his response because she ran her fingers down the length of the back wound, then asked if he took any medication. From time to time an aspirin, he said. What do you do between aspirins? she asked. I live with the pain, he said. Nodding, the doctor noted his response and checked off items on a clipboard and signed and dated the form before handing it to one of the civilians. As she turned to leave, Martin asked if she was a generalist or a specialist. The woman smiled slightly. When I am not free-lancing for the Service, I am a gynecologist, she said.

Martin was ordered to dress. One of the civilians led the prisoner to a door at the far end of the room and, opening it, stood aside. Martin shuffled into a larger room (once again the laces had been removed from his shoes, making it difficult to walk normally) filled with sturdy furniture, hand-me-downs, so he surmised, from the days when Stalin's KGB ruled the roost in what was then called the Soviet Union. A short, husky middle-aged man wearing tinted eyeglasses presided from behind a monster of a desk. The man nodded toward the wooden chair facing the desk.

Martin gingerly lowered himself onto the seat. 'Thirsty,' he said in Russian.

The interrogator snapped his fingers. A moment later a glass of water was set on the desk within reach of the prisoner. Holding it in both hands, he drank it off in several long gulps.

'I am a Canadian citizen,' Martin announced in English. 'I insist on seeing someone from the Canadian embassy.'

Behind the desk, the civilian angled a very bright light into Martin's eyes, forcing him to squint. A husky voice that was perfectly harmonious with the huskiness of the civilian drifted out of the blinding light. 'You are voyaging under a passport that identifies you as Kafkor, Jozef,' the interrogator said in excellent English. 'The passport purports to be Canadian, though it is, as you are no doubt aware, a forgery. The name on it is Polish. The Russian Federal Security Service has been eager to get its hands on you since your name first came to our attention. You are the Kafkor, Jozef, who was associated with Samat Ugor-Zhilov and his uncle, Tzvetan Ugor-Zhilov, better known as the *Oligarkh*.'

'Is that a question?' Martin asked.

'It is a statement of fact,' the interrogator replied evenly. 'According to our register, you met Samat Ugor-Zhilov shortly after arriving in Moscow to work for the Polish tourist bureau. You were taken by this same Samat Ugor-Zhilov to meet his uncle, who was living in the former Beria dacha in Prigorodnaia. In the four months that followed your initial visit to Prigorodnaia, you spent a great deal of time as a guest at the dacha, sometimes remaining there the entire week, other times going out for four-day weekends. The ostensible reason for the visits was that you were going to teach conversational Polish to Samat's mother, who lived in the dacha. Your superiors at the Polish tourist bureau did not complain about your prolonged absences, which led us to conclude that the tourist bureau was a cover. You were obviously a Polish national, though we suspected you had spent part of your life abroad because our Polish speakers who listened to tapes of you talking with your coworkers in Moscow identified occasional lapses in grammar and antiquated vocabulary. You spoke Russian – I assume you still do – with a pronounced Polish accent, which suggested you had studied the Russian language from Polish teachers in Poland or abroad. So, *gospodin* Kafkor, were you working for Polish intelligence or were you employed, with or without the collaboration of the Poles, by a Western intelligence service?'

Martin said, 'You are mistaking me for someone else. I swear to you I don't remember any of the details you describe.'

The interrogator opened a dossier with a diagonal red stripe across the cover and began leafing through a thick stack of papers. After a moment he raised his eyes. 'At some point your relationship with Samat and his uncle deteriorated. You disappeared from view for a period of six weeks. When you reappeared, you were unrecognizable. You had obviously been tortured and starved. Early one morning, while road workers were paving the seven kilometer spur that led from the main Moscow-Petersburg highway to the village of Prigorodnaia, two of the *Oligarkh*'s bodyguards escorted you across the Lesnia in a rowboat and prodded you up the incline to a crater that had been gouged in the spur by a steam shovel the previous day. You were stark naked. A large safety pin attached to a fragment of cardboard bearing the words *The spy Kafkor* had been passed through the flesh between your shoulder blades. And then, before the eyes of forty or so workers, you were buried alive in the crater – you were forced to lie in fetal position in the hole, which was roughly the size of a large tractor tire. Thick planks were wedged into place above you, after which the road workers were obliged to pave over the spot.'

Martin had the unnerving sensation that a motion picture he had seen and forgotten was being described to him. 'More water,' he murmured.

Another glass of water was placed within reach and he drank it off. In a hoarse whisper Martin asked, 'How can you know these things?'

The interrogator twisted the arm of the lamp so that the light played on the top of the desk. As the interrogator set out five blown-up photographs, Martin caught a glimpse of Kafkor's Canadian passport, a wad of American dollars and British pounds, the picture postcard that he'd swiped from the door of the dacha in Prigorodnaia, along with his shoelaces. He scraped his chair closer to the desk and leaned over the photographs. They were all taken from a distance and enlarged, rendering them grainy and slightly out of focus. In the first photograph, an emaciated man, completely naked, with a matted beard and what looked like a crown of thorns on his head, could be seen stepping gingerly through the shallow slime onto dry land. Two guards in striped shirts followed behind him. In the next photograph, the naked man could be seen kneeling at the edge of a crater, looking over his shoulder, his eyes hollow with terror. The third photograph in the series showed a thin figure of a man with a long pinched face, a suit jacket draped cape-like over his shoulders, offering a cigarette to the condemned man. The fourth photograph caught a heavy set man with a shock of silver hair and dark glasses in the back of a limousine, staring over the tinted window open the width of a fist. In the last photograph, a steam-roller was backing across the glistening tarmac, raising a soft fume. Workers leaning on rakes or shovels could be seen staring in horror at the scene of the execution.

'One of the workman on the road crew, the ironmonger in point of fact, was employed by our security services,' the interrogator said. 'He had a camera hidden in the thermos in his lunch box. Do you recognize yourself in these photographs, *gospodin* Kafkor?'

A single word worked its way up from Martin's parched throat. '*Nyet.*'

The interrogator switched off the light. Martin felt the world spinning giddily under his feet. His lids drifted closed over his eyes as his forehead sank onto one of the photos. The interrogator didn't break the silence until the prisoner sat up again.

Martin heard himself ask, 'When did all this happen?'

'A long time ago.'

Martin sagged back into his seat. 'For me,' he remarked tiredly, 'yesterday is a long time ago, the day before yesterday is a previous incarnation.'

'The photographs were taken in 1994,' the interrogator said.

Martin breathed the words 'Three years ago!' Kneading his forehead, he tried to work the pieces of this strange puzzle into place, but no matter which way he turned and twisted them, no coherent picture emerged. 'What happened after this individual was buried alive?' he asked.

'When the photographs were developed and circulated, we decided to mount an operation to free him – to free *you* – in the hope that you were still alive. When we reached the site of the execution, in the dead of night, we discovered the peasants, led by the village priest, had already scraped away the tarmac and pried up the planks and rescued the man buried in the crater. Before first light, our people helped the peasants replace the planks and tar over the spot.'

'And what happened to . . . this person?'

'The village's tractor repairman drove *you* to Moscow in Prigorodnaia's tow truck. His intention was to take you to a hospital. At a red light on the ring road, not far from the American Embassy, you leaped from the cab of the truck and disappeared in the darkness. Neither the municipal police nor our service was able to find any trace of you after that. As far as we were concerned, you disappeared from the surface of the earth – until today, until a custom's officer at the airport signaled the arrival of a Canadian bearing a passport issued to Kafkor, Jozef. We assumed you would be returning to Prigorodnaia, which is the reason the interior ministry troops closed the road – we knew we could pick you up on the way out.'

A secretary appeared behind the desk and, bending close, whispered in the interrogator's ear. Clearly annoyed, the interrogator demanded, 'How long ago?' Then: 'How in the world did he find out?' Shaking his head in disgust, the interrogator turned back to Martin. 'The CIA station chief in Moscow has learned that you are in our hands. He is sending a formal request through channels asking us to turn you over to his agency for interrogation when we've finished with you.'

'Why would the CIA want to question Jozef Kafkor?'

'They will want to discover if you were able to tell us what we want to know.'

'And what is it that you want to know?'

'Whose side were they on – Samat Ugor-Zhilov and the *Oligarkh*, Tzvetan Ugor-Zhilov? And where are they now?'

'Samat took refuge in a West Bank Jewish settlement in Israel.'

The interrogator carefully unhooked his eyeglasses from one ear and then the other and began to clean the lenses with the tip of his silk tie. 'Bring tea,' he instructed the secretary. 'Also those brioche cakes stuffed with fig confiture.' He fitted the glasses back on and, collecting the five photographs, slipped them back into the folder. '*Gospodin* Kafkor, the Russian Federal Security Service is underfunded and understaffed and underappreciated, but we are not dimwits. That Samat took refuge in Israel we have known for a long time. We were negotiating with the Israeli Mossad to have access to him when word reached him that Chechen hit men had tracked him to Israel, causing him to flee the country. But where did he go when he disappeared from Israel?'

The interrogator leafed through more reports. 'He was sighted in the Golders Green section of London. He was seen again in the vicinity of the Vyšehrad Train Station in Prague. He was said to have visited the town of Kantubek on the island of Vozrozhdeniye in the Aral Sea. There were reports, too, that he may have gone to the Lithuanian town of Zuzovka not far from the frontier with Belarus. There is even a rumor that he was the mysterious person who turned up in the helicopter that touched down for half an hour behind the cemetery in Prigorodnaia.'

The secretary turned up at the door carrying a tray. The interrogator motioned for him to set it on the small round table between two high-backed chairs and leave. When he was alone with the prisoner, he waved him over to one of the chairs. Settling into the other chair, he filled two mugs with steaming tea. 'You must try one of the cakes,' he advised, sliding the straw basket toward Martin. 'They are so delicious it must surely count as a sin to eat them. So, *gospodin* Kafkor, let us sin together,' he added, biting into one of the cakes, cupping a hand under it to catch the crumbs.

'My name is Cheklachvili,' the interrogator said, speaking as he took another bite out of his cake. 'Arkhip Cheklachvili.'

'That's a Georgian name,' Martin noted.

'My roots are Georgian, though I have long since offered my allegiance to Mother Russia. It was me,' he added with a distinct twinkle in his eyes, 'the ironmonger on the slope who was employed by our security services. It was me who took the photographs of you with a camera hidden in my lunch box.'

'You've come up in the world,' Martin commented.

'Photographing your execution was my first great triumph. It caught the attention of my superiors and started me up the career ladder. After you jumped from the tow truck and disappeared in Moscow, we heard rumors that you had found your way to the American Embassy on the ring road. The CIA station chief himself was said to have taken you in charge. There was a flurry of coded radio traffic for forty-eight hours, after which you were spirited out of Moscow in an embassy car heading for Finland. There were five men in the car – all of them had diplomatic passports and were able to pass the frontier without scrutiny. What happened to you after that we simply do not know. To tell you the truth, I suspect you don't know either.'

Martin stared at his interrogator. 'What makes you suppose that?'

The interrogator collected his thoughts. 'My father was arrested by the KGB in 1953. He was accused of being an American agent and sentenced by a summary tribunal to be shot. The guards took him from his cell in the vast Lubyanka headquarters of the KGB one night in March and brought him to the elevator that carried prisoners down to the vaulted basements for execution. When they discovered that the elevator was not working, they returned him to his cell. Technicians worked through the night to repair the elevator. In the morning the guards came for my father again. They were waiting for the elevator to climb to their floor when word reached them that Stalin was dead. All executions were cancelled. Several months later the new leadership killed Beria and issued a general amnesty, and my father was set free.'

'What does his story have to do with me?'

'I remember my father returning to our communal apartment – I was six years old at the time. It had been raining and he was drenched to the skin. My mother asked him where he had been. He shook his head in confusion. There was a vacant look in his eyes, as if he had glimpsed some horrible thing, some monster or some ghost. He didn't remember his arrest, he didn't remember the summary tribunal, he didn't remember the guards leading him to the elevator for execution. It was all erased from his consciousness. When I went to work for the security apparatus, I looked up his dossier and found out what had happened to him. By then my father had been put out to pasture. One day, years later, I worked up the nerve to tell him what I had discovered. He listened the way one does to the story of someone else's life, and smiled politely as if the life I had dredged up had nothing to do with him, and went on with the life he remembered. Which was the life he lived until the day he died.'

Drinking off the last of his tea, the interrogator produced a small key from the pocket of his vest and offered it to Martin. 'If you go through that door, you will find a narrow staircase spiraling down six floors to the street level. The key opens the door at the bottom of the staircase leading to a side street. When you are outside, lock the door behind you and throw the key down a sewer.'

'Why are you doing this?'

'I believe you when you say you don't remember being brought across the river and buried alive. I believe you when you say you don't know Samat Ugor-Zhilov or his uncle, the *Oligarkh*. I have concluded that you are unable to help us with our inquiries. If you are intelligent, you will quit Russia as rapidly as you can. Whatever you do, don't go to the American Embassy – the CIA station chief has been making discreet inquiries for the past several weeks about someone named Martin Odum. From his description, we suspect that Martin Odum and Jozef Kafkor are the same person.'

Martin started to mutter his thanks but the interrogator cut him off. 'The skeletal man in the third photograph, the one offering the condemned man a last cigarette, is Samat Ugor-Zhilov. The man with silver hair watching the execution from the partly open window of the automobile is the *Oligarkh*, Tzvetan Ugor-Zhilov. Keep in mind that they attempted to execute you once. They would surely try again if they discover your whereabouts. Ah, I must not forget to return to you your belongings.' He retrieved the Canadian passport, the wad of bills, the picture postcard showing a family strolling down a country road somewhere in north America and the shoelaces, and handed everything to the prisoner.

The interrogator watched as the prisoner threaded the laces through his shoes. When Martin looked up, the interrogator shrugged his heavy shoulders, a gesture that conveyed his presumption there was nothing more to say.

Martin nodded in agreement. 'How can I repay you?' he asked.

'You cannot.' The lines around the interrogator's eyes stretched into a controlled smile. 'By the way, Arkhip Cheklachvili is a legend. I assume that Jozef Kafkor and Martin Odum are also legends. The cold war is over, still we live our legends. You may well be its last victim, lost in a labyrinth of legends. Perhaps with the aid of the postcard, you will be able to find a way out.'

1992: HOW LINCOLN DITTMANN CAME TO GO TO LANGUAGE SCHOOL

'Gentlemen and ladies,' declared the former station chief who chaired the Legend Committee, rapping his knuckles on the oval table to encourage his charges to simmer down, 'I invite your attention to a remarkable detail that we seem to have overlooked in Martin Odum's biography.'

'Are you thinking what I'm thinking?' asked the Yale-educated aversion therapist. 'His mother was—'

'She was Polish, for heaven's sake,' snapped Maggie Poole, speaking, as always, with more than a trace of the British accent that had rubbed off on her at Oxford. She added brightly, 'His mother immigrated to *les Etats Unis* after the Second World War.'

'We are on to something,' said the only other woman on the committee, a lexicographer on permanent loan from the University of Chicago. 'I simply can't believe we missed this.'

'The detail has been staring us in the face every

time we worked up a cover story for him,' agreed the committee's doyen, a grizzly CIA fossil who had begun his long and illustrious career devising false identities for OSS agents during World War Two. He looked at the chairman and asked, 'What started you thinking along these lines?'

'When Lincoln Dittmann returned home from Triple Border,' the chairman said, 'the subsequent action report mentioned that he'd overheard an old lottery vender talking Polish to a hooker in a bar and discovered he could catch the drift of what they were saying.'

'That's because his mother used to read him bedtime stories in Polish when they were living in that Pennsylvania backwater called Jonestown,' the aversion therapist explained impatiently.

'*Mon Dieu*, six months of intensive tutoring and he'll talk Polish like a native,' said Maggie Poole.

'Which is not how you talk American English,' quipped the aversion therapist.

'You can't resist, can you, Troy?'

'Oh, dear, resist what?' he asked, looking around innocently.

The chairman rapped his knuckles on the table again. 'Given what the Deputy Director of Operations has in mind for Lincoln,' he said, 'he really ought to speak Russian, too.'

'Martin Odum studied Russian at college,' the lexicographer noted. 'Not surprisingly, he wound up speaking it with a Polish accent.'

'While the tutors are bringing his Polish up to

snuff,' Maggie Poole suggested, 'they could also work on his Russian.'

'Okay, let's summarize,' said the chairman. 'What we have is a Polish national who, like most Poles, speaks fluent Russian. What we need now is a name.'

'Let's be simple for once.'

'Easier said than done. *Le simple n'est pas le facile.*'

'What about using Franz-Jozef as a first name?'

'Are we being inspired by the Emperor of Austria or Haydn?'

'Either, or.'

'What about just plain Jozef,' offered Maggie Poole.

'Half of Poland is named Jozef.'

'That's precisely the point, it seems to me,' she retorted.

'That's not what you argued when we settled on the name Dante Pippen. You said nobody thumbing down a list of names would suspect Dante Pippen of being a *pseudonyme* precisely because it was so unusual.'

Maggie Poole would not be put off. 'Consistency,' she said huffily, 'is the last refuge of the un-imaginative. That's Oscar Wilde, in case you're wondering.'

'I happen to be rereading Kafka's *Amerika.*'

'For God's sake, you're not going to suggest Kafka as a family name.'

'I was going to suggest a Polish-sounding variation. Kafkor.'

'Kafkor, Jozef. Not half bad. It's short and sweet,

an easy handle to slip into, I should think. What do you think, Lincoln?'

Lincoln Dittmann, gazing out the window of the fourth floor conference room at the hundreds of cars in the Langley parking lot, turned back toward the members of the Legend Committee. 'A variation on the name of Kafka – Kafkor – seems appropriate enough.'

'What on earth do you mean by appropriate?'

'Kafka wrote stories about anguished individuals struggling to survive a nightmarish world, which was more or less how the principal of this new legend would see himself.'

'You've obviously read Kafka,' Maggie Poole said.

'He could have read *into* Kafka at the Jagiellonian University in Kraków,' someone noted.

'He could have worked summers as a guide at Auschwitz.'

'Through our contacts in Warsaw, we could land him a job in the Polish tourist bureau in Moscow. From there he ought to be able to make contact with the DDO target without attracting too much attention to himself.'

'Question of knowing where this Samat character hangs out when he's in Moscow.'

'That's Crystal Quest's bailiwick,' Lincoln remarked.

1997: MARTIN ODUM GETS TO INSPECT THE SIBERIAN NIGHT MOTH

T he phone on the other end of the line had rung so many times, Martin had given up counting. He decided to let it ring all evening, all night, all the next day if necessary. She had to return home sometime. A woman carrying a sleeping baby on her hip rapped a coin against the glass door of the booth and angrily held up her wrist so that Martin could see the watch on it. Muttering 'Find another booth – I bought this one,' he turned his back on her. Shaking her head at how insufferable certain inhabitants of the borough had become, the woman stalked off. In Martin's ear the phone continued to ring with such regularity that he ceased to be conscious of the sound. His thoughts wandered – he played back what he could remember of the previous phone calls. To his surprise, he was able to recreate her voice in his brain as if he were a skillful ventriloquist. He could hear her saying, *When the answers are elusive you have to learn to live with the questions.*

It dawned on him that the phone was no longer

ringing on the other end of the line. Another human being was breathing hard into the mouthpiece.

'Stella?'

'Martin, is that you?' a voice remarkably like Stella's demanded.

Martin was surprised when he realized how eager he was to hear that voice; to talk to the one person on earth who was not put off because he wasn't sure who he was, who seemed ready to live with whatever version of himself he offered up. Suddenly he felt the dead bird stirring in him: He ached to see the night moth tattooed under her breast.

'It's me, Stella. It's Martin.'

'Jesus, Martin. Wow. I can't believe it.'

'I've been ringing for hours. Where were you?'

'I met some Russians in Throckmorton's Minimarket on Kingston Avenue. They were new immigrants, practically off the boat. I was entertaining them with jokes I used to tell in Moscow when I worked for subsection Marx. You want to hear a great one I just remembered?'

'Uh-huh.' Anything to keep her talking.

She giggled at the punch line before she told the joke. 'Okay,' she said, collecting herself. 'Three men find themselves in a cell in the Lubyanka prison. After awhile the first prisoner asks the second, "What are you here for?" And the second prisoner says, "I was against Popov. What about you?" And the first prisoner says, "I was for Popov." The two turn to the third prisoner and ask, "Why were you arrested?" And he answers, "I'm Popov." '

She became exasperated when Martin didn't laugh. 'When I delivered the punch line at the Moscow Writers Union, people would roll on the floor. Someone in subsection Marx tracked the joke – it spread across Moscow in three days and reached Vladivostok in a week and a half. The Russians in Throckmorton's Minimarket actually applauded. And you don't get it?'

'I get it, Stella. It's not funny. It's pathetic. When your joke spread across Russia, people weren't laughing. They were crying.'

Stella thought about that. 'There may be something to what you say. Hey, where are you calling from this time? Murmansk on the Barents Sea? Irkutsk on Lake Baikal?'

'Listen up, Stella. Do you remember the first time I ever phoned you?'

'How could I forget. You called to tell me you didn't have a change of mind, you had a change of heart. You were phoning from—'

He cut her off. 'I was calling from a booth that reeked of turpentine.'

He could hear her catch her breath. 'On the corner of—'

He interrupted her again. 'Could you find the booth if your life depended on it?'

She said, very calmly, 'My life *does* depend on it.'

'Do me a favor and bring the autopsy report on your father that the FBI guy sent you.'

'Anything else?'

'Uh-huh. That time when I met your father, he removed a pearl-handled souvenir from the pocket of his robe and put it on a shelf where I could see it. I'd like to get my hands on that object, if it's possible.'

'Anything else?'

'As a matter of fact, yes. I'd like to inspect the night moth.'

'No problem,' she said. 'It goes where I go.'

They were nursing mugs of lukewarm coffee in a booth at the back of the twenty-four-hour diner on Kingston Avenue, two stores down from Throckmorton's Minimarket. Stella kept looking up at Martin; phrases formed in her mind only to become stuck on the tip of her tongue. When she had turned up at the phone booth on the corner of Lincoln and Schenectady, they had hugged awkwardly for a moment. The faint aroma of rose petals seeped from under the collar on the back of her neck. Stella had said something about how they really ought to kiss, and they did, but the kiss was self-conscious and quick, and a disappointment to both of them. At a loss for words, he'd remarked that he'd never seen her in anything but pants. She said she'd worn the tight knee-length black skirt to disguise herself as a woman. He'd actually managed a smile and said that the deception could have fooled him. He asked her if she had taken precautions to make sure she wasn't being followed. She explained how she had strolled over to an ice cream parlor on Rogers Avenue crammed with teenagers playing electronic pinball machines, then ducked out a back door into an alleyway and made her way through empty side streets to Schenectady and the phone booth. Nodding, he had taken her by the arm and steered her wordlessly in the direction of the all-night diner on Kingston. Sitting across from her now, he noticed the new front tooth; it was whiter than the rest of her teeth and hard to miss. Her hair was pulled back and twined into a braid that plunged out of sight behind her shoulder blades. He recognized the small wrinkles fanning out from the corners of her eyes, which were fixed in a faint squint, as if she were trying to peer into him. The three top buttons of her man's shirt were open, the triangle of pale skin shimmering on her chest.

Martin cleared his throat. 'You threatened to show me the tattoo the next time we met.'

'Here? Now?'

'Why not?'

Stella looked around. There were four Chinese women in a booth across the diner playing mahjongg, and a young man and a girl two booths away staring so intently into each other's eyes Stella doubted they would be distracted by anything less than an earthquake. She took a deep breath to work up her nerve and undid three more buttons on her shirt and pulled the fabric away from her right breast. Visions invaded Martin's brain: a neon light sizzling over a bar on the Beirut waterfront, a room upstairs with the torn painting depicting Napoleon's defeat at Acre, the night moth tattooed under the right breast of the Alawite prostitute who went by the name of Djamillah. 'You want the God honest truth?' he whispered. 'Your Siberian night moth takes my breath away.'

The ghost of a smile materialized on Stella's lips. 'That's what it's supposed to do. The Jamaican tattoo artist on Empire Boulevard said I could have my money back if it didn't bowl you over. Maybe now one thing will lead to another.'

He reached for her hand and she folded her other hand on top of his, and they both leaned across the table and kissed.

Settling back, Martin said, 'Business first.'

'I like your formula,' Stella said, rebuttoning her shirt.

He looked surprised. 'Why?'

'Reading between the lines, it puts pleasure on the agenda.'

A smile touched his eyes. 'Did you bring the autopsy report?'

She pulled the report and the letter that had come with it from her leather satchel and unfolded them on the table. Martin skimmed the autopsy report first: . . . *myocardial infarction . . . clot superimposed on plaque in coronary artery already constricted by cholesterol buildup . . . abrupt and severe drop in blood flow . . . irreparable trauma to a portion of the heart muscle . . . death would have been almost instantaneous.*

'Uh-huh.'

'Uh-huh what?'

'The CIA doctor seems to be saying your father died a natural death.'

'As opposed to an unnatural death? As opposed to murder?'

Martin started reading the covering letter the FBI had sent with the autopsy report. *No trace of forced entry . . . even if there had been, Mr Kastner had a charged Tula-Tokarev within arm's reach . . . no evidence of a struggle . . . unfortunately not unusual for people confined, like Mr Kastner was, to a wheelchair to experience blood clots originating in a leg that work their way up to the coronary arteries . . . minuscule break in the skin near a shoulder blade compatible with an insect bite . . . Feel free to call me on my unlisted number if you have any questions.* Martin looked up. 'Did you father go out often?'

'Kastner never left the house. He didn't even go into the garden behind the house. He spent his time cleaning and oiling his collection of guns.'

'If he didn't go out, how did he get bitten by an insect?'

'You aren't convinced by the autopsy report?'

Martin glanced at the signature at the bottom of the letter, then stiffened.

Stella asked, 'What's not right?'

'I used to know a Felix Kiick who worked for the FBI.'

'There was another agent in charge of the Witness Protection Program when Kastner and I and Elena came over in 1988. We met him several times when we were living at the CIA safehouse in Tyson's Corner outside of Washington. The agent retired in 1995 – he came to President Street to introduce the person who was taking his place. That's how we met Mr Kiick.'

'Short? Stumpy? With a low center of gravity that makes him look like an NFL linesman? Nice, open face?'

'That's the one. Do you know him?'

'Our paths crossed several times when I worked for the CIA. I knew him as a counterterrorism specialist, but they probably booted him upstairs at the end of his career. The Witness Protection people are usually running in place, waiting for retirement to catch up with them.' Martin thought of something. 'When I met your father, he mentioned that he'd gotten my name from someone in Washington. Was that someone Felix Kiick?'

Stella could see that the question was bothering Martin. She considered carefully before answering. 'Kastner called the unlisted number in Washington we'd been given in case we needed anything. Now that you mention it, it was Mr Kiick who said there was a good detective living not far from us. He recommended you, but he told Kastner not to tell you where he'd gotten your name.'

Martin seemed to be focusing on horizons that

Stella couldn't see. 'So it was no accident that I wound up walking back the cat on Samat Ugor-Zhilov.'

Stella said, 'I brought the souvenir with the pearl handle.' She opened the satchel and tilted it so Martin could see her father's Tula-Tokarev. 'It's an antique, but it still shoots. It was Kastner's favorite handgun. From time to time he went down to the basement and fired it into a carton filled with roof insulation, then he'd recover the bullet and examine it under a low-powered microscope. I brought bullets for it, too.'

Stella touched her lips to the coffee but found it had grown cold. Martin signaled for refills. The waiter, a teenage boy with long side-burns and a silver stud in the side of a nostril, brought two steaming mugs of coffee and took away the old ones. Stella said, 'What about Samat?'

'I think I know how to locate him.'

'Quit.'

'I'm sorry?'

'Quit. Forget Samat. Concentrate on locating me.'

'What about your father?'

'What's Kastner have to do with your deciding to quit?'

'He hired me. He's dead, which means he can't unhire me.' Martin reached again for her wrist but she snatched it back. 'I haven't come all this way to quit now,' he insisted.

'You're crazy.' She noticed the expression on his

face. 'I didn't mean that the way it sounded. You're not *crazy* crazy. You are *im*perfectly sane. Admit it, your behavior is sometimes borderline. In your shoes anyone else would shrug and get on with his life.'

'You mean his *lives*.'

Martin reached again for her wrist. This time she didn't pull away. He fingered her watch and began absently winding the stem. 'Samat's in America,' he said.

'How do you know that?'

He produced the picture postcard and told her how he had tracked Samat from Israel to London to Prague to Vozrozhdeniye Island in the Aral Sea to the Lithuanian village of Zuzovka, and finally to the village of Prigorodnaia not far from Moscow where Samat's mother, Kristyna, lived in the empty dacha once owned by the most hated man in Russia, Lavrenti Beria. 'She told me she was a raving lunatic when she needed to be,' Martin said. 'She told me she wrapped herself in lunacy the way a peasant pulls a sheepskin coat over his shoulders in winter.'

'Sounds to me like a survival strategy.' Stella examined the photograph on the postcard – the men and boys attired in black trousers and black suit jackets and straw hats, the women and girls wearing ankle-length gingham dresses and laced-up high shoes and bonnets tied under the chin. She turned it over and translated the message. 'Mama dearest, I am alive and well in America the

Beautiful . . . Your devoted S.' She noticed the printed caption had been scraped off. 'Where on God's green earth is *fast New York*?' she demanded, squinting at the post office cancellation mark across the stamp.

'I've done my homework. The people in the photograph are Amish. Belfast, New York is the rough center of the Amish community that lives upstate New York, and the only town upstate that ends in *fast*. It makes tradecraft sense. All the men have long beards. Instead of shaving off his beard, which is what the Russian revolutionaries used to do when they wanted to disappear, Samat would keep his and dress like the Amish and melt into the madding crowd.'

'Who's he hiding from?'

'For starters, Chechen gangsters bent on revenge for the killing of one of their leaders known as the Ottoman. Then there's your sister, also his uncle Akim, who claims Samat siphoned off a hundred and thirty million dollars from holding companies he controlled. For some reason I can't figure out, the CIA seems to be very interested in him, too.'

'Where do I come in?'

'When you described Samat to me in the pool parlor—'

'That seems so long ago it must have been during a previous incarnation.'

'You're talking to a world-class expert on previous incarnations. When you described him, you said his eyes were seaweed-green and utterly devoid of emotion. You told me if you could see his eyes, you would be able to pick him out of a crowd.' Martin lowered his voice. 'I don't mean to push you past where you're ready to go – how come you know his eyes so well?'

Stella turned away. After a moment she said, 'You wouldn't ask the question if you didn't imagine the answer.'

'You saw his seaweed-green eyes up close when you slept with him.'

Stella groaned. 'The night of the wedding, he came to my room in the early hours of the morning. He slipped under the covers. He was naked. He warned me not to make a commotion – he said it would only hurt my sister when he told her I'd . . . I'd invited him.' Stella looked into Martin's eyes. 'I'd know his eyes anywhere because I memorized them when he fucked me in the room next to my sister's bedroom on the night of her marriage to this monster of a man. I was originally planning to stay in Kiryat Arba for three weeks, but I left after ten days. He came into my bed every night I was there . . .'

'And when you returned two years later?'

'I took him aside the first day and told him I'd kill him if he came into my bed again.'

'How did he react?'

'He only laughed. At night he would turn the doorknob to torture me, but he didn't come into

the room. Martin, you've got to tell me the truth
– does this change anything between us?'

He shook his head no.

Stella permitted the ghost of a smile to settle
softly onto her lips again.

1997: MARTIN ODUM GETS THE *GET*

Driving in the vintage Packard he had borrowed from his friend and landlord, Tsou Xing, the owner of the Mandarin restaurant below the pool parlor on Albany Avenue, Martin and Stella reached Belfast after dark. The pimply boy working the pump at the gas station on the edge of town ticked off on grimy fingers the choices available to them: a bunch of descent hotels in town, some pricier than others; an assortment of motels along Route 19 either side of town, some seedier than others; several bed and breakfasts, best one by a country mile was old Mrs Sayles place on a groundswell overseeing the Genesee, the advantage being the riot of river water which lulled some folks to sleep, the disadvantage being the riot of river water which kept some folks up until all hours.

They found their way to the house on the river with 'B & B' and 'Lelia Sayles' etched on a shingle hanging from a branch of an ancient oak, and reached through the tear in the screen to work the knocker on the front door. As they didn't have luggage, Martin was obliged to cough up $30 in advance for a room with a matrimonial bed, bathroom down the hall, kindly go barefoot if you use the facilities during the night so as not to wake the ghosts sleeping in the attic. They went out to get a bite to eat at a diner across from the public library on South Main and lingered over the decaf, both of them trying to put off the moment when there would be no turning back. Parking on the gravel in Mrs Sayles's driveway afterward, Martin decided the Packard's engine oil level needed checking. 'I'm every bit as agitated as you,' Stella murmured, reading his mind as he propped up the hood. She started toward the house, then wheeled back when she reached the porch, her left palm drifting up to the triangle of pale skin visible on her chest. 'Look at it this way, Martin,' she called. 'If the sex doesn't work out to everyone's expectations, we can always fall back on the erotic phone relationship.'

'I want sex *and* the erotic phone relationship,' he replied.

Stella angled her head to one side. 'Well, then,' she said, laughter replacing the nervousness in her eyes, 'maybe you ought to stop monkeying with the damn motor. I mean, it's not as if either of us were virgins.'

'How'd it go?' Mrs Sayles asked the next morning as she set out dishes of homemade confitures on the kitchen table.

Martin, irritated, demanded, 'How'd what go?'

'*It*,' Mrs Sayles insisted. 'Heavens to Betsy, the carnal knowledge part. I may be pushing eighty from the far side, but I'm sure as hell not brain dead.'

'It went very nicely, thank you,' Stella said evenly.

'Loosen up, young fellow,' Mrs Sayles advised when she noticed Martin buttering a piece of toast for the second time. 'You'll be a better bed partner for it.'

Hoping to change the subject, Martin produced the picture postcard.

'My great-great-great-grandfather, name of Dave Sanford, built the first sawmill on the banks of the Genesee River,' Mrs Sayles explained, all the while rummaging through a knitted tote bag for her reading glasses. 'That was long about 1809. This house was built in 1829 with lumber from that mill. Belfast was a one-horse town in those days. Nothing but forests far as the eye could see, so they say, so they say. When the lumber boom wore out the forests, most folks turned to raising cattle. The White Creek Cheese Factory, which is famous 'round here, was founded long about 1872 by my great-grandfather—'

Stella tried to steer the conversation back to the Amish. 'What about the picture on the postcard?'

'It's going to stay a blur until I come up with my reading spectacles, dear child. Could have sworn I put them in here. Never could figure out how a body can find her reading spectacles if she's not wearing them. Well, I'll be, here they are, all the while.' Mrs Sayles fitted them on and, accepting the postcard from Stella, held it up to the sunlight streaming through a bay window. 'Like I was saying, I know the Amish crowd up on White Creek Road pretty good because of my family's connection with the White Creek Cheese Factory. Hmmmm.' Mrs Sayles pursed her lips. 'Truth to tell, I don't reckon I recognize any of the Amish on this here picture postcard.'

'How about the houses and the barn?' Martin said, coming up behind her, pointing to the two clapboard houses built very close to each other, to the barn with a mansard roof on a rise across from them.

'Houses, barn neither. Mind you, there are an abundance of Amish living on the small roads sloping off White Creek. Picture could have been taken on any one of them.' Mrs Sayles had an inspiration. 'There's a fellow, name of Elkanah Macy, works as a janitor over at the Valleyview Amish school on Ramsey Road. He moonlights as a handy-man for the Amish out in the White Creek area. If anybody can help you, he can. Be sure to tell Elkanah it was me sent you around.'

Elkanah Macy turned out to be a retired navy petty officer who, judging from the framed photographs lining one wall, had served on half the warships in the U.S. Navy during his twenty years in the service. He had converted the atelier in the Amish school basement into a replica of a ship's machine shop, replete with calendar pinups of naked females. 'Lelia sent you around, you say?' Macy remarked, sucking on a soggy hand-rolled cigarette as he sized up his visitors through hooded eyes. 'Bet she went an' told you the goddamn whopper 'bout Dave Sanford being her great-great-great-granddaddy. Hell, she tells that to anyone stands still long enough to hear her out. Listen to her tell it, anybody who did anything in Belfast was her kin – Sanford's sawmill on the Genesee, the old cheese factory out on White Creek Road. Bet she went an' told you 'bout the goddamn ghosts in the attic. Ha! Take it from somebody that knows, lady's got herself a springhtly imagination. Fact is, the first Sayles in Allegheny County were loansharks that went and bought up farmhouses cheap during the forties and sold them for a hand-some profit to the GIs coming back from the war. What is it you want with the Amish over at White Creek?'

Martin showed Mr Macy the picture postcard. 'You wouldn't by any chance know where we could find these houses, would you?'

'Might. Might not. Depends.'

'On what?' Stella asked.

'On how much you be willing to pay for the information.'

'You don't beat around the bush,' Stella observed.

'Heck, not beating around the damn bush saves time and shoe leather.'

Martin peeled off a fifty from a wad of bills. 'What would half a hundred buy us?'

534

Macy snatched the bill out of Martin's fingers. 'The two farm houses with the barn directly across from them are about three, three and a half miles out on McGuffin Ridge Road. Head out of Belfast on South Main and you'll wind up on 19. Look for the Virgin Mary billboard with her one-eight-hundred number. Right after, you'll cross 305 going west, bout a half mile farther on you'll hit White Creek Road going south toward Friendship. For some of the way White Creek Road runs parallel to the factual creek. Long 'bout halfway to Friendship, McGuffin Ridge Road runs off of White Creek. You got to be stone blind to miss it.'

Martin held up another fifty dollar bill. 'We're actually looking for an old pal of mine who we think moved into one of the farm houses in that area.'

'Your old pal Amish?'

'No.'

'Not complicated.' Macy snatched the second bill. 'All them Amish get me over to unplug the damn electric meters and fuse boxes when they move in. Amish don't take to electricity or the things that work off it – ice boxes, TVs, Singers, irons, you name it. You can tell an Amish lives in a house if the electric counter is hanging off the side of it, unplugged. You can tell someone who ain't Amish lives there if'n the goddamn counter's still attached.'

'Are there a lot of non Amish living out on McGuffin Ridge Road?' asked Martin.

When the janitor scratched at his unshaven chin in puzzlement, Martin came up with still another fifty dollar bill.

'A-mazing how a picture of U.S. Grant can stir up recollections,' Macy said, folding the fifty and adding it to the other two in his shirt pocket. 'Except for one house, McGuffin Ridge is all Amish. The one house is the second one on your picture postcard.'

Stella turned to Martin. 'Which explains why Samat sent this particular postcard to his mother.'

'It does,' Martin agreed. He nodded at Macy. 'That's quite a fleet,' he remarked, glancing at the framed photographs on the wall. 'You served on all those warships?'

'Never been to actual sea in my life,' Macy said with a giggle. 'Only served on them while they was in drydock, reason being I get seasick the minute a ship puts to sea.'

'You certainly picked the wrong service,' Stella said.

Macy shook his head emphatically. 'Loved the goddamn navy,' he said. 'Loved the ships. Didn't much like what they was floating on, which was the sea. Hell, I'd re-up if they'd take me. Yes, I would.'

Martin pulled the Packard into the gas station at the edge of town and bought a bottle of spring water and an Allegheny County map while Stella used the restroom. Heading out of town on 19, he felt her hand come to rest on his thigh. His body tensed – real intimacy, the kind that comes *after* sex, was a strange bedfellow to Martin Odum. In his mind's eye, he thought of himself as being somewhere between Dante Pippen, who made love and war with the same frenetic energy, and Lincoln Dittmann, who had once gone off to Rome to try and find a whore he'd come across in Triple Border. Stella sensed the tenseness under her fingers. 'I wasn't lying to Mrs Sayles,' she remarked. 'It did go very nicely, thank you. All things considered, last night was a great start to our sex life.'

Martin cleared his throat. 'I am not comfortable talking about things like our sex life.'

'Not asking you to talk about it,' Stella shot back, laughter in her voice. 'Expecting you to listen to me talk about it. Expecting you to mumble *uh-huh* once in a while in quiet encouragement.'

Martin glanced at her and said, 'Uh-huh.'

The Packard sped past the billboard advertising the one-eight-hundred number of the Virgin Mary. Half a mile beyond 305 they reached the junction with the signpost reading 'White Creek Road' and 'Friendship.' Martin turned onto White Creek and slowed down. When the highway dipped, he lost sight of the creek off to the right, only to spot it again when they topped a rise. In places the rippling water of White Creek reminded him of the Lesnia, which ran parallel to the spur that connected Prigorodnaia to the Moscow-Petersburg highway. The farmhouses along White Creek were set on the edge of the road to make it easier to get firewood and fodder in during the winter months when the ground was knee-deep in snow. The houses, spaced a quarter or a half mile apart, some of them with carpentry or broadloom work-shops behind them and samples of what was being produced set out on raised platforms or porches, all had the electric meters and fuse boxes dangling off the clapboard walls. Amish going-to-market buggies could be seen in the garages, with cart mares grazing in adjoining fields. Occasionally chil-dren, dressed like little adults in their black suits or ankle-length dresses and bonnets and lace-up high shoes, would scamper out to the side of the road to stare shyly at the passing automobile.

The McGuffin Ridge turnoff loomed ahead and Martin swung off White Creek. McGuffin was a mirror image of White Creek – the road crossed rolling farm country, with farm houses built close to the road, all of them with electric meters and lengths of black cable hanging off the walls. Three and a half miles into McGuffin Ridge, Stella tightened her grip on Martin's thigh.

'I see them,' he told her.

The Packard, moving even more slowly, came abreast of the two identical clapboard farm houses built very close to each other. Across the road, a weathered barn stood atop a small rise. A crude American eagle crafted out of metal jutted from the ornate weather vane atop the mansard roof. Two Amish men in bibbed dungarees were sawing planks behind the first of the two houses. An Amish woman sat on a rocker on the porch crocheting a patch quilt that spilled off near her feet. As the Packard passed the second house, Stella looked back and caught her breath.

'The electric meter is still attached to the house,' she said.

'It's a perfect setup for somebody who wants to melt into the landscape,' Martin said. 'He can get the Amish women next door to cook for him. If anybody comes nosing around when he's out, the Amish men will tell him. You didn't notice an automobile anywhere around the house?'

'No. Maybe he goes to town by buggy, like the Amish.'

'Not likely. No car, no Samat.'

'What do we do now?' Stella asked as Martin drove on down the road.

'We wait until Samat comes back. Then we'll dust off your father's antique Tula-Tokarev and go calling on him.'

Martin pulled the Packard off the road beyond the next rise and he and Stella walked back to a stand of maple on a butt of land. On the far side of the stand, it was possible to see the two houses and the barn across the road from them. Sitting on the ground facing each other with their backs against trees, they settled down to wait. Martin pulled Dante's lucky white silk scarf from a pocket and knotted it around his neck.

'Where'd you get that?' Stella asked.

'Girl gave it to someone I know in Beirut. She said it would save his life if he wore it.'

'Did it?'

'Yes.'

'What happened to the girl?'

'She lost her life.'

Stella let that sink in. After awhile she said out of the blue, 'Kastner was murdered, wasn't he?'

Martin avoided her eye. 'What makes you think that?'

'The FBI man, Felix Kiick, told me.'

'In so many words? He said your father didn't die of a heart attack?'

'This Felix Kiick was a straight guy. Kastner trusted him. Me, too, I trusted him.'

'So did I,' Martin agreed.

'I thought about it a thousand times. I came at it from every possible direction.'

'Came at what?'

'His letter. The actual autopsy doesn't mention the minuscule break in the skin near the shoulder blade. Mr Kiick's letter does.'

'He said it was compatible with an insect bite.'

'He was waving a red flag in front of my face, Martin. He was drawing my attention to something that was compatible with a lethal injection using a very thin needle. Kastner used to tell me about things like that – he said lethal injections were the KGB's favorite method of assassination. In his day the KGB's hit men favored a tasteless rat poison that thinned out the blood so much your pulse

540

disappeared and you eventually stopped breathing. Kastner had heard they were working on more sophisticated substances that couldn't be easily traced – he told me they had developed a clotting agent that could block a coronary artery and trigger myocardial infarction. Don't pretend you didn't notice Kiick's reference to the insect bite.'

'I noticed.'

'And?'

'Kiick's the guy who suggested your father hire me to find Samat. Kiick spent the better part of his FBI career in counterterrorism. He crossed paths with the Company's Deputy Director of Operations, Crystal Quest—'

'The one you called Fred when you first spoke to Kastner.'

'You have a good memory for things beside KGB jokes. Kiick must have known Fred didn't want Samat found. And now Kiick's waving the insect bite in front of our faces.'

Stella seemed relieved. 'So you don't think I'm raving mad?'

'You're a lot of things. Raving mad is not one of them.'

'If I didn't know better, I might take that for a compliment.'

'Someone else was killed around the time your father was being stung by an insect. Her name was Minh.'

Stella remembered the Israeli Shabak officer telling Martin about the Chinese girl who'd been stung to death by his bees on the roof over the pool parlor. 'What does one death have to do with the other?' she asked.

'If your father was murdered, it means someone was trying to close down the search for Samat. Minh was killed tending my hives, which means she was wearing my white overalls and the pith helmet with mosquito netting hanging from it when something made the bees explode out of one of the hives.'

'From a distance she would have looked like you.' Something else occurred to her. 'What about those shots when we were walking from Kiryat Arba to that sacred cave – you told me two bullets from a high-powered rifle came pretty close to you.'

'Could have been Palestinians shooting at Jews,' Martin said. He didn't sound very convincing.

'Maybe the same people who killed Kastner and your Chinese friend Minh were shooting at you.'

'Uh-huh. The *Oligarkh* has a long reach. But we'll never know for sure.'

'Oh, Martin, I think I'm frightened . . .'

'Join the world. I'm never not frightened.'

The long shadows that materialize immediately before sunset were beginning to stretch their tentacles across the fields. Martin, following his own thoughts, said, 'You've changed the way I look at things, Stella. I used to think I wanted to spend the rest of my life boring myself to death.'

'For someone who wanted to bore himself to

death, you sure gave a good imitation of living an exhilarating life.'

'Did I?'

'Kiryat Arba, London, Prague, that Soviet island in the Aral Sea, that Lithuanian town rioting over who gets to keep the bones of some obscure saint. And then there's the whole story of Prigorodnaia and the seven-kilometer spur that leads to it. Some boring life.'

'You left out the most exhilarating part.'

'Which *is*?'

'You.'

Stella pushed herself away from the tree to crouch next to him and bury her face in his neck. 'Fools rush in,' she murmured, 'where angels fear to tread.'

The sun had vanished behind the hills to the west and a rose-gray blush had infused the sky overhead when they spotted the headlights coming down McGuffin Ridge Road from the direction of White Creek. Martin stood up and tugged Stella to her feet. The car appeared to slow as it neared the two farm houses. It swung away from them to climb the dirt ramp leading to the barn. The figure of a man could be seen pulling open the barn doors, and closing them after he'd parked the car inside. Moments later a porch light flicked on across the road in the nearest of the two houses. The man let himself into the house. Lights appeared in the ground floor windows. Martin and Stella exchanged looks.

'I don't want you to take any risks,' Stella said flatly. 'If he's armed, the hell with my sister's divorce, shoot him.'

Martin smiled for the first time that day. 'You sure you told jokes for the KGB? You sure you weren't one of their wetwork specialists?'

'Wetwork?'

'Hit men. Or in your case, hit women.'

'I told killer jokes, Martin. Hey, I'm more nervous now than I was last night. Let's get this over with.'

In the gathering gloom, they made their way on foot down the white stripe in the middle of the road toward the two houses. Somewhere behind them a dog barked and a quarter of a mile farther along McGuffin Ridge other dogs began to howl. Through the porch windows of the second house, Martin could see the Amish family sitting down to supper at a long table lit by candles; everyone bowed their head as the bearded man at the head of the table recited a prayer. Martin checked the Tula-Tokarev to be sure the safety was off, then climbed silently onto the porch ahead of Stella and flattened himself against the clapboard to one side of the front door. He motioned for Stella to come up and knock.

Speaking English with a thick Russian accent, the man who lived in the house could be heard calling, 'Is that you, Zaccheus? I told you to bring the meal over at eight. It is not civilized to sit down to supper at the hour you Americans eat.' The door opened and a gaunt man, his face

544

masked by a thick beard with only his seaweed-green eyes visible, regarded Stella through the screen. The porch light was above and behind her and her face was lost in shadows.

'Who are you?' he asked. 'What is it you're doing out here this time of day?'

Stella breathed, *'Priviet, Samat.'*

Samat gasped. *'Tyi,'* he whispered. *'Shto tyi zdes delaish?'*

Stella gazed directly into Samat's eyes. 'It's him,' she said.

Martin stepped into view, the antique Tula-Tokarev aimed at Samat's solar plexus. Stella opened the screen door and Martin stepped across the sill. Samat, white spittle forming at one corner of his thin lips, backed into the room. He held his hands wide, palms up, almost in greeting. 'Jozef, thanks to God, you are still among the living.' He started to pose questions in Russian. Martin realized that Jozef, like Stella and Samat, was a Russian speaker. He, Martin, could grasp words and phrases, sometimes the gist of a sentence, but an entire conversation in Russian was more than he could handle. He cut Samat off in mid sentence. *'V Amerike, po-angliiski govoriat* – in America, English is spoken.'

'What are you doing with *her*?' Samat looked from one to the other. 'How is it possible you know each other?'

Stella seemed as dazed as Samat. 'Don't tell me you two know each other.'

'Our paths have crossed,' Martin told her.

Samat sank onto a couch. 'How did you find me, Estelle?'

Martin pulled over a wooden chair and, setting it back to front, straddled it facing Samat, the handgun resting on the top slat in the high back and pointed at his chest. Settling onto a bar stool, Stella flipped the picture postcard at Samat's feet. Retrieving it from the floor, he took in the photograph, then turned it over to look at the post office cancellation stamp. 'Zaccheus was supposed to mail this from Rochester,' he whined. 'The son of a bitch never went farther than Belfast. No wonder you found the two houses on McGuffin Ridge.' He looked intently at Martin, then at the postcard. 'Jozef, you went back to Prigorodnaia. You saw my mother.'

'Why is he calling you Jozef?' demanded Stella, utterly mystified.

Martin kept his eyes locked on Samat's. 'I missed you by a day or two. The priest said you'd flown off in your helicopter after delivering the tiny cross carved from the wood of the True Cross.'

'Must you point that weapon at me?'

Stella answered for him. 'He definitely must, if only to make me feel better.'

Mopping his brow with the back of a sleeve, Samat asked, 'Jozef, how much do you remember?'

'All of it.' In his mind's eye Martin could visualize the first black-and-white photograph the Russian interrogator in Moscow had shown him;

an emaciated figure of a man, whom the Russian identified as Kafkor, Joseph, could be seen, stark naked with a crown of thorns on his head, wading toward shore from the row boat, the two guards in striped shirts following behind him. 'I remember every detail. I remember being tortured for so long I lost count of time.'

Stella leaned forward. She was beginning to grasp why Martin considered himself to be imperfectly sane. 'Who tortured you?' she asked in a whisper.

'The men in striped shirts,' Martin said. 'The ex-paratroopers who guarded the dacha in Prigorodnaia, who brought me across the river . . .' He eyed Samat. 'I remember the cigarettes being stubbed out on my body. I remember the large safety pin attached to a fragment of cardboard bearing the words *The spy Kafkor* being passed through the flesh between my shoulder blades. I remember being brought across the Lesnia with all the road workers gaping at me. I remember the guards prodding me up the incline to the crater that had been gouged into the spur of road.'

Samat started hyperventilating. When he could speak again, he said, 'I beg you to believe me, Jozef, I would have saved you if it had been within the realm of possibility.'

'Instead you gave Kafkor the spy a last cigarette.'
'*You do remember!*'

Stella looked from one to the other; she could almost hear her father instructing her that in the life of espionage operatives, questions would always outnumber answers.

Samat started to reach into a cardigan. Martin thumbed back the hammer on the handgun. The click reverberated through the room. Samat froze. 'I absolutely must smoke a cigarette,' he said weakly. He held the cardigan open and reached very slowly into an inside pocket and extracted a pack of Marlboros. Pulling one cigarette free, he struck a wooden match and brought the flame to the end of the cigarette. His hand shook and he had to grip his wrist with the other hand to steady it and hold the flame to the cigarette. Sucking it into life, he held it away from his body between his thumb and third finger and watched the smoke spiral up toward the overhead light fixture. 'What else do you remember, Jozef?'

Martin could almost hear the husky voice of the Russian interrogator, who went by the legend Arkhip Cheklachvili. He repeated what Cheklachvili had told him back in Moscow; at moments his own voice and that of the interrogator overlapped in his head. 'Prigorodnaia's tractor repairman drove me to Moscow in the village's tow truck. His intention was to take me to a hospital. At a red light on the Ring Road, not far from the American Embassy, I leaped from the cab of the truck and disappeared in the darkness.'

'Yes, yes, it all fits,' Samat blurted out. 'Mrs Quest sent us word . . . she told my uncle Tzvetan and me . . . that the FBI counterintelligence people stationed at the Moscow Embassy found you wandering in the back streets off the Ring Road. She said you couldn't remember who you were or what had happened to you . . . she spoke of a trauma . . . she said it was better for everyone if you couldn't remember. Oh, you fooled them, Jozef.' Samat started to whimper, tears glistening on his skeletal cheeks. 'If she had suspected you of remembering, you would not have been permitted to leave Moscow alive.'

'I sensed that. I knew everything depended on convincing her I was suffering from amnesia.'

'It was the *Oligarkh* who ordered them to torture you,' Samat said with sudden vehemence. 'He was convinced you had betrayed the Prigorodnaia operation. He needed to know to whom. Mrs Quest needed to know to whom. It was a matter of damage control. If rot had set in, we needed to burn it out, so my uncle said. I tried to reason with him, Jozef. I told him you might have denounced the operation when you came to realize what it consisted of – but only to people on the inside. Only to Crystal Quest. I swore you would never go to the newspapers or the authorities. I told him you could be brought around to see things from our point of view. After all, we all worked for the same organization, didn't we? We all marched to the same music. It wasn't our business to pass judgment on the operation. The CIA gave us a compass heading and off we went. You were a soldier like me, like my uncle; you were the link between us and Mrs Quest; between us and Langley.'

Martin had to lure Samat into filling in the blanks. 'It was the scope of the Prigorodnaia operation that sickened me,' he said. 'Nothing like that had ever been attempted before.'

Samat's head bobbed restlessly; words spilled out, as if the sheer quantity of them filling the air could create a bond between him and the man he knew as Jozef. 'When the CIA found my uncle Tzvetan, he was running a used-car dealership in Armenia. What attracted them to him was that his father and grandfather had been executed by the Bolsheviks; his brother, my father, had died in the camps; he himself had spent years in a Siberian prison. Tzvetan detested the Soviet regime and the Russians who ran it. He was ready to do anything to get revenge. So the CIA bankrolled him – with their money he cornered the used-car market in Moscow. Then, with the help of CIA largesse, I'm talking hundreds of millions, he branched out into the aluminum business. He made deals with the smelters, he bought three hundred railroad cars, he built a port facility in Siberia to offload alumina. Before long, he had cornered the aluminum market in Russia and amassed a fortune of dozens of billions of dollars. And still his empire grew – he dealt in steel and chrome and coal, he bought factories and business by the dozens, he opened banks to service the empire and launder the profits abroad. Which is where I came in. Tzvetan trusted me completely – I was the only one who understood how the *Oligarkh's* empire was configured. It was all here in my head.'

'Then, once Tzvetan had established himself as an economic force, the CIA pushed him into politics.'

'If my uncle ingratiated himself with Yeltsin, it was because he was following Mrs Quest's game plan. When Yeltsin wanted to publish his first book, Tzvetan arranged the contracts and bought up the print run. The Yeltsin family suddenly discovered that they held shares in giant enterprises. Thanks to the *Oligarkh*, Yeltsin became a rich man. When Yeltsin ran for president of the Russian Federation in 1991, Tzvetan financed the campaign. Tzvetan was the one who funded Yeltsin's personal bodyguard, the Presidential Security Service. It was only natural that when Yeltsin sought advice, he would turn to the leading figure in his inner circle, the *Oligarkh.*'

Martin began to see where the Prigorodnaia plot was going. 'Yeltsin's disastrous decision to free prices and willy-nilly transform Russia into a free-market economy in the early nineties unleashed hyperinflation and wiped out the pensions and savings of tens of millions of Russians. It threw the country into economic chaos—'

'The concept originated with Crystal Quest's DDO people. My uncle was the one who convinced Yeltsin that a free-market economy would cure Russia's ills.'

'The privatization of Soviet industrial assets, which looted the country's wealth and funneled it into the hands of the *Oligarkh* and a handful of insiders like him—'

Samat was scraping his palms together. 'It all came from the CIA's Operations Directorate – the hyper-inflation, the privatization, even Yeltsin's decision to attack Chechnya and bog down the Russian army in a war they couldn't win. You can understand where the Americans were coming from – the cold war was over, for sure, but America did not defeat the mighty Soviet Union only to have a mighty Russia rise like a phoenix from its ashes. The people at Langley could not take the risk that the transition from socialism to capitalism might succeed. So they got the *Oligarkh*, who detested the communist apparatchiki, who was only too happy to see Russia and the Russians sink into an economic swamp, to use his considerable influence on Yeltsin.'

Stella, watching Martin intently, saw him wince. For an instant she thought his leg must be acting up again. Then it dawned on her that the pain came from what Samat was saying: Martin had found the naked truth buried in Samat's story. She had, too. 'The CIA was running Russia!' she exclaimed.

'It was running Russia into the ground,' Martin agreed.

'That was the beauty of it,' Samat said, his voice shrill with jubilation. '*We paid the Russians back for what they did to the Ugor-Zhilovs.*'

Martin remembered what Crystal Quest had said to him the day she summoned him to Xing's Mandarin restaurant under the pool hall. *We didn't hire your conscience, only your brain and your body. And then, one fine day, you stepped out of character – you stepped out of all your characters – and took what in popular idiom is called a moral stand.*

At the time Martin didn't have the foggiest idea what she was talking about. Now the pieces of the puzzle had fallen into place; now he understood why they'd convened a summit at Langley to decide whether to terminate his contract – or his life.

Samat, drained, puffed on the cigarette to calm his nerves. Martin's found himself staring at the ash at the tip of Samat's cigarette, waiting for it to buckle under its own weight and fall. Life itself seemed to ride on it. Defying gravity, defying sense, it grew longer than the unsmoked part of the cigarette. Martin associated the ash with the naked man kneeling at the edge of the crater, the one who had been caught in the black-and-white photograph peering over his shoulder, his eyes hollow with terror.

Samat, sucking on the cigarette, became aware of the ash, too. His words slurring with dread, he whispered, 'Please. I ask you, Jozef. For the sake of my mother, who loved you like a son. Do not shoot me.'

'I'm not sure you should shoot him,' Stella said. 'Then again, I'm not sure you shouldn't. What is to be accomplished by shooting him?'

'Revenge is a manifestation of sanity. Shooting him would make me feel . . . *perfectly* sane.' Martin looked back at Samat, who was breathing noisily through his mouth, terrified that each breath would be his last. 'Where is the *Oligarkh*?' Martin asked.

'I do not know.'

Martin raised the Tula-Tokarev to eye level and sighted on Samat's forehead, directly between his eyes. Stella turned away. 'When you lived in Kiryat Arba,' Martin reminded Samat, 'you spent a lot of time on the phone with someone who had a 718 area code.'

'The phone records were destroyed. How could you know this?'

'Stella remembered seeing one of your phone bills.'

'I swear to you on my mother's head, I do not know where the *Oligarkh* is. The 718 number was the home phone of the American manufacturer of artificial limbs that I imported to London for distribution to war zones.' Tears welled in Samat's seaweed-green eyes. 'For all I know, the *Oligarkh* may no longer be alive. In the Witness Protection Program, these things are tightly compartmented, precisely so that no one can get to him through me. Or to me through him.'

Stella said, very quietly, 'He may be telling the truth.'

Samat clutched at the buoy Stella had thrown him. 'I never meant to harm you,' he told her.

'The marriage to your sister was a matter of convenience for both of us – she wanted to live in Israel and I had to get out of Russia quickly. I was incapable of sleeping with Ya'ara. You have to comprehend. A man can only be a man with a woman.'

'Which narrowed it down to Stella,' Martin said.

Samat avoided his eye. 'A normal man has normal appetites . . .'

Martin held the pistol unwaveringly for several long seconds, then slowly let the front sight drop. 'Your other uncle, the one who lives in Caesarea, claims you stole a hundred and thirty million dollars from six of his holding companies. He offered me a million dollars to find you.'

Samat glimpsed salvation. 'I will pay you two million not to find me.'

'I don't accept checks.'

Samat saw that he might be able to worm his way out of this predicament after all. 'I have bearer shares hidden in the freezer of the icebox.'

'There is one other matter that needs to be arranged,' Martin informed him.

Confidence began seeping back into Samat's voice. 'Only name it,' he said, all business.

Stella spent the better part of the next morning on Samat's phone trying to track down an Orthodox rabbi who would accommodate them. An old rabbi in Philadelphia gave her the number of a colleague in Tenafly, New Jersey; a recorded announcement at the Chabad Lubavitch Synagogue there suggested anyone calling with a weekend emergency try the rabbi's home number, which rang and rang without anyone answering. A rabbi at Beth Hakneses Hachodosh in Rochester knew of a rabbi at Ezrath Israel in Ellenville, New York, who delivered religious divorces, but when Stella dialed the number she fell on a teenage daughter; her father, the rabbi, was away in Israel, she said. He did have a cousin who officiated at B'nai Jacob in Middletown, Pennsylvania. If this was an emergency, Stella could try phoning him. It was the Middletown rabbi who suggested she call Abraham Shulman, the rabbi at the Beth Israel Synagogue in Crown Heights, Brooklyn. Rabbi Shulman, an affable man with a booming voice, explained to Stella that what she needed was an ad hoc rabbinical board, composed of three Orthodox rabbis, to deliver the scroll of the *get* and witness the signatures. As luck would have it, he was sitting down to Sunday brunch with two of his colleagues, one from Manhattan, the other from the Bronx, both of them, like Shulman, Orthodox rabbis. Oh, dear, yes, it was unusual but the rabbinical board could witness the signing of the *get* by the husband even if the wife were not physically present and then forward the document to the wife's rabbi in Israel for her signature, at which point the divorce would become final. Rabbi Shulman inquired how long it would take her and the putative husband to reach Crown Heights. Stella told the rabbi they could be there by late afternoon. She jotted down his directions: cross over from Manhattan to Brooklyn on the Manhattan Bridge, follow Flatbush Avenue down to Eastern Parkway, then follow Eastern Parkway until you reached Kingston Avenue. The synagogue filled the top three floors of number 745 Eastern Parkway on your left coming from New York, immediately after Kingston Avenue.

The three rabbis, looking somewhat the worse for brunch, were holding court in Shulman's murky book-lined study on the ground floor under the synagogue. Shulman, the youngest of the three, was clean shaven with apple-shiny cheeks; the two other rabbis had straggly white beards. All three wore black suits and black fedoras propped high on their foreheads; on the two older rabbis it looked perfectly natural, on Shulman it produced a comic effect. 'Which of you,' boomed Shulman, looking from Samat to Martin and back to Samat, 'is the lucky future ex?'

Martin, one hand gripping the Tula-Tokarev in his jacket pocket, prodded Samat in the spine. 'Who would believe,' Samat said under his breath as he shuffled across the thick carpet, 'you went to all this trouble to find me for a divorce.'

'Did you say something?' inquired the rabbi to the right of Shulman.

'It is me, the divorcer,' Samat announced.

'What's the mad rush to divorce?' the third rabbi asked. 'Why couldn't you wait until the shul opens on Monday morning?'

Stella improvised. 'He's booked on a flight to Moscow from Kennedy airport this evening.'

'There are Orthodox rabbis in Moscow,' Shulman noted.

In a bamboo cage set on a wooden stepladder next to floor-to-ceiling bookshelves, a green bird with a hooked bill and bright red plumes between its eyes hopped onto a higher trapeze and declared, clear as a bell, '*Loz im zayn, loz im zayn.*'

Rabbi Shulman looked embarrassed. 'My parrot speaks Yiddish,' he explained. '*Los im zayn* means *let him be.*' He smiled at his colleagues. 'Maybe *Ha Shem*, blessed be his Name, is trying to tell us something.' The rabbi turned back to Samat. 'I assume you wouldn't come all this way without identification.'

Samat handed his Israeli passport to the rabbi.

'You are Israeli?' Shulman said, plainly surprised. 'You speak Hebrew?'

'I immigrated to Israel from the Soviet Union. I speak Russian.'

'The Soviet Union doesn't exist anymore,' Shulman pointed out.

'I meant Russia, of course,' Samat said.

'Excuse me for asking,' the oldest of the three rabbis said, 'but you *are* Jewish?'

'My mother is Jewish, which makes me Jewish. The Israeli immigration authorities accepted the proofs of this when they let me into the country.'

Stella explained the general situation while Shulman took notes. Her sister, whose Israeli name was Ya'ara, daughter of the late Oskar Alexandrovich Kastner of Brooklyn, New York, currently lived in a Jewish settlement on the West Bank called Kiryat Arba. Ya'ara and Samat Ugor-Zhilov, here present, had been married by the Kiryat Arba rabbi, whose name was Ben Zion; Stella herself had been a witness at the marriage ceremony. Samat had subsequently abandoned his wife without granting her a religious divorce. This same Samat, here present, had had second thoughts about the matter and is now willing to put his signature to the document granting a religious divorce to his wife. She stepped forward and handed the rabbis a scrap of paper which spelled out the terms of the divorce. Samat's signature was scrawled across the bottom.

The resplendent parrot descended to the lower trapeze and cried out, '*Nu, shoyn! Nu, shoyn!*' Shulman said, 'That's the Yiddish equivalent of *Let's put the show on the road.*'

One of the older rabbis looked across the room at Martin. 'And who are you?'

'That's a good question, rabbi,' Martin said.

'Perhaps you would like to answer it,' Shulman suggested.

'My name is Martin Odum.'

Looking straight at Martin, Stella said, 'He has deeper layers of identity than a name, rabbi. Fact is, he's not absolutely sure who he is. But so what – women fall for men all the time who don't know who they are.'

Shulman cleared his throat. The three rabbis bent over Samat's passport. 'The photograph in the passport doesn't look anything like this gentleman,' one of the rabbis observed.

'I did not have a beard when I came to Israel,' Samat explained.

Stella said, 'Look carefully – you can tell by the eyes it's the same man.'

'Only women are able to identify men by their eyes,' Shulman remarked. He addressed Samat. 'You affirm that you are the Samat Ugor-Zhilov who is married to—' he glanced at his notes – 'Ya'ara Ugor-Zhilov of Kiryat Arba?'

'He does affirm it,' Stella said.

The rabbi favored her with a pained look. 'He must speak for himself.'

'I do,' Samat said. He glanced at Martin, leaning against the wall near the door with one hand in his jacket pocket. 'I affirm it.'

'Is there any issue from this marriage?'

When Samat looked confused, Stella translated. 'He's asking if you and Ya'ara had children.' She addressed Shulman directly. 'The answer is: You can't have children when you don't consummate the marriage.'

One of the older rabbis chided her. 'Lady, given that he is not contesting the divorce, I think you are telling us more than we need to know.'

Shulman said, 'Do you, Samat Ugor-Zhilov, here present, stand ready to grant your wife, Ya'ara Ugor-Zhilov, a religious divorce – what we call a

560

get – of your own free will and volition, so help you God?'

'Yes, yes, I will give her the damn *get*,' Samat replied impatiently. 'You guys use a lot of words to describe something as uncomplicated as a divorce.'

'Kabbalah teaches us,' Shulman noted as his two colleagues nodded in agreement, 'that God created the universe out of the energy in words. Out of the energy of your words, Mr Ugor-Zhilov, we will create a divorce.'

Stella smiled at Martin across the room. 'It doesn't come as a surprise to me that words have energy.'

Samat looked bewildered. 'Who is this Kabbalah character and what does he have to do with my divorce?'

'Let's move on,' Shulman suggested. 'Under the terms of the *get*,' he went on, reading from Stella's scrap of paper, 'your wife will keep any and all property and assets that you may possess in Israel, including one split-level house in the Jewish settlement of Kiryat Arba, including one Honda automobile, including any and all bank accounts in your name in Israeli banks.'

'I have already agreed to this. I signed the paper.'

'We must ascertain verbally that you understand what you have signed,' explained Shulman.

'That you were not coerced into signing,' added one of his colleagues.

'According to the terms of the divorce,' the rabbi

continued, 'you are putting on deposit with this rabbinical board one million dollars in bearer shares, with the intention that the said one million dollars, less a generous $25,000 donation to a Jewish program to relocate Jews to Israel, will be transferred to the ownership of your wife, Ya'ara Ugor-Zhilov.'

Samat glanced at Martin, who nodded imperceptibly. 'I agree, I agree to it all,' Samat said hurriedly.

'That being the case,' the rabbi said, 'we will now prepare the scroll of the *get* for your signature. The document, along with the $975,000 in bearer shares, will be sent by Federal Express to rabbi Ben Zion in Kiryat Arba. Ya'ara will be summoned before a rabbinical board there to sign the *get*, at which point you and your wife will be formally divorced.'

'How long will it take to prepare the scroll?' Martin asked from the door.

'Forty-five minutes, give or take,' Shulman said. 'Can we offer you gentlemen and the lady coffee while we prepare the document?'

Later, Martin and Samat waited outside the Synagogue while Stella brought around the Packard. Martin slid into the backseat alongside Samat. 'Where are we off to now?' Stella asked.

'Take us to Little Odessa.'

'Why are we going to the Russian section of Brooklyn?' Stella asked.

'Get us there and you'll see,' Martin said.

Stella shrugged. 'Why not?' she said. 'You certainly knew what you were doing up to now.'

She piloted the large Packard through rush-hour traffic on Ocean Parkway, past block after block of nearly identical gray-grim tenements with colorful laundry flapping from lines on the roofs. Twice Samat tried to start a conversation with Martin, who sat with the butt of the Tula-Tokarev in his right fist and his left hand gripping Samat's right wrist. Each time Martin cut him off with a curt *uh-huh*. Up front Stella had to laugh. 'You won't get far with him when he's in his one of his *uh-huh* moods,' she called over her shoulder.

'Turn left when you get to Brighton Beach Avenue,' Martin instructed her. 'It's the next traffic light.'

'You've been here before,' Samat said.

'Had two clients in Little Odessa before I became a famous international detective tracking down missing husbands,' Martin said. 'One involved a kidnapped Rottweiler. The other involved a neighborhood crematorium run by Chechen immigrants.'

Samat pulled a face. 'I do not comprehend why America lets Chechens into this country. The only good Chechens are dead Chechens.'

Stella asked Samat, 'Have you been to Chechnya?'

Samat said, 'Did not need to go to Chechnya to come across Chechens. Moscow was swarming with them.'

Martin couldn't resist. 'Like the one they called the Ottoman.'

The seaweed in Samat's eyes turned dark, as if they had caught the reflection of a storm cloud. 'What do you know about the Ottoman?'

'I know what everyone knows,' Martin said guilelessly. 'That he and his lady friend were found one fine morning hanging upside down from a lamppost near the Kremlin wall.'

'The Ottoman was not an innocent.'

'I heard he'd been caught doing fifty in a forty-kilometer zone.'

Samat finally figured out his leg was being pulled. 'Speeding in Moscow can be dangerous for your health,' he agreed. 'Also littering.'

'Turn left on Fifth Street, just ahead. Park on the left where it says no parking anytime.'

'In front of the crematorium?' Stella asked as she turned into the street.

'Uh-huh.'

'Who are we meeting?' Samat inquired uneasily as Stella eased the Packard alongside the curb and killed the motor.

'It's almost eight,' Martin said. 'We'll wait here until it's dark and the streets are empty.'

'I'm going to close my eyes for a few minutes,' Stella announced.

Stella's forty winks turned into an hour-and-ten-minute nap; all the driving she'd done that day, not to mention the worrying, had taken its toll on her. Samat, too, dozed, or appeared to, his chin sinking onto his chest, his shut eyelids fluttering. Martin kept a tight grip on the butt of the Tula-Tokarev. Curiously, he didn't feel bushed despite his having slept fitfully on Samat's couch the night before (woken every few hours by Samat calling from the locked closet that he needed to go to the toilet). What kept Martin alert, what kept the adrenalin flowing, was his conviction that revenge *was* a manifestation of sanity; that if he played this thing out, his days of being *imperfectly* sane were numbered.

As darkness settled over Little Odessa, the Russians began heading back to their apartments. Behind them, on Brighton Beach Avenue, traffic thinned out. Lights appeared in windows on both sides of Fifth Street; the bulb in the vestibule of the funeral parlor across the street came on. Two floors above the door with the gold lettering that read 'Akhdan Abdulkhadzhiev & Sons – Crematorium,' an elaborate chandelier fitted with Christmas tree bulbs blazed into life and the scratchy sound of an accordion playing melodies that sounded decidedly Central Asian drifted out of an open window. A lean man and a teenage boy dragged a pushcart filled with tins of halavah down the middle of the street and turned into one of the driveways near the end of the block. Two young girls skipping rope as they made their way home passed the Packard. An old woman carrying a Russian *avoska* filled with vegetables hurried up the steps of a nearby brownstone. When the street appeared deserted, Martin leaned forward and nudged Stella on the shoulder.

She angled her rearview mirror so that she could see Martin in it. 'How long did I sleep?'

'A few minutes.'

Samat's eyes blinked open and he swallowed a yawn. He looked up and down the street. 'I do not understand why we have come to the Russian section of Brooklyn,' he said anxiously. 'If it is to meet someone—'

Martin could hear a voice in his ear. *For once in your life, don't weigh the pros and cons – just act violently.*

'Dante?'

You don't want to shoot him, Martin – too noisy. Use the butt. Break his knee cap.

Stella said, 'Who are you talking to, Martin?'

Don't think about it, just do it, for Christsake!

'I'm talking to myself,' Martin murmured.

He was sorely tempted – to jailbreak, to set foot outside the Martin Odum legend; to become, if only for an instant, someone as impulsive as Dante Pippen. Clutching the Tula-Tokarev by the barrel, Martin slammed the grip down hard on Samat's right knee. The sharp crunch of the bone splintering filled the Packard. Samat stared in disbelief at his knee as a brownish stain soaked into the fabric of his trousers. Then the pain reached his brain and he cried out in agony. Tears spurted from his eyes.

Stella twisted in the seat, breathing hard. 'Martin, have you gone mad?'

'I'm going sane.'

Samat, cradling his shattered knee cap with both hands, thrashed in pain. Martin said, very softly, 'You killed Kastner, didn't you?'

'Get me a doctor.'

'You killed Kastner,' Martin repeated. 'Admit it and I will put an end to your suffering.'

'I had nothing to do with Kastner's death. The *Oligarkh* had him eliminated when the Quest woman told him you were trying to find me. My uncle and Quest . . . they wanted to cut off all the leads.'

Stella said, 'How did the killers get into the house without breaking a door or a window?'

'Quest supplied the keys to the doors and the alarm box.'

'You killed the Chinese girl on the roof, too,' Martin said.

Samat's nose began to run. 'Quest's people told the *Oligarkh* about the beehives on the roof. He sent a marksman to the roof across the street. The marksman mistook the Chinese girl for you. Her death was an accident.'

'Where is the *Oligarkh*?'

'For the love of God, I must get to a doctor.'

'Where is the *Oligarkh*?'

'I told you, I do not know.'

'I know you know.'

'We speak only on the phone.'

'The 718 number?'

When Samat didn't say anything, Martin reached

across Samat and pushed open the door on his side of the car. 'Read the name on the crematorium door,' he ordered.

Samat tried to make out the name through the tears blurring his vision. 'I cannot see—'

'It says Akhdan Abdulkhadzhiev. Abdulkhadzhiev is a Chechen name. The crematorium is the Chechen business that was accused of extracting gold teeth before cremating the corpses. If you don't give me the phone number, I'll push you out of the car and ring the bell and tell the Chechens sitting down to supper upstairs that the man who hanged the Ottoman upside down from a lamp-post in Moscow is on their doorstep. There isn't a Chechen alive who doesn't know the story, who won't jump at the chance to settle old scores.'

'No, no. The number . . . the number is 718-555-9291.'

'If you're lying, I'll break your other knee.'

'On my mother's head, I swear it. Now take me to a doctor.'

Martin got out of the Packard and came around to the other side of the car and, taking a grip on Samat's wrists, pulled him from the backseat across the sidewalk. He propped Samat up so that he was sitting on the sidewalk with his back against the door. Then Martin pressed the buzzer for several seconds. Two floors over his head a young woman appeared in the open window.

'Crematorium closed for the day,' she shouted down.

'Crematorium about to open,' Martin called back. 'You ever hear of a Chechen nicknamed the Ottoman?'

The woman in the window ducked back into the room. A moment later the needle was plucked off the record. Two men stuck their heads out of the window. 'What about the Ottoman?' an older man with a flamboyant mustache yelled down.

'The Armenian from the Slavic Alliance who lynched him and his lady friend within sight of the Kremlin is on your doorstep. His name is Samat Ugor-Zhilov. Your Chechen friends have been looking all over the world for him. There's no rush to come get him – he's not going anywhere on a shattered knee.'

Samat whimpered, 'For the love of God, for the sake of my mother, you cannot leave me here.'

Martin could sense the excitement in the room above his head. Footsteps could be heard thundering down the stairs. 'Start the motor,' he called to Stella. A current of pain shot through his game leg as he made his way around the car and climbed in next to the driver. 'Let's go,' he said. 'Don't run any red lights.'

Stella, biting her lip to keep from trembling, steered the Packard away from the curb and headed down the empty street. Martin turned in the seat to watch the Chechens drag Samat into the crematorium. Stella must have seen it in her rearview mirror. 'Oh, Martin,' she said, 'what will they do to him?'

'I suppose they will extract the gold teeth from his mouth with a pair of pliers and then put him in one of their cheapest coffins and nail the lid shut and light off the burning fiery furnace and cremate him alive.' He touched the back of her hand on the steering wheel. 'Samat left behind him a trail of blood – the Ottoman and his lady friend, your father, my Chinese friend Minh, the scavengers locked in cages on an island in the Aral Sea who died miserably when Samat used them as guinea pigs to test biowarfare viruses that he eventually gave to Saddam Hussein. The list is long.'

Using hand gestures, Martin directed Stella back into the heart of Brooklyn. When they reached Eastern Parkway he had her pull over to the curb. He retrieved the paper bag from the trunk and, taking her arm, drew her to a bench on one side of the parkway. 'There's a million dollars in bearer shares left in the bag,' Martin explained, handing it to her. 'Go to ground in a motel on the Jersey side of the Holland Tunnel for the night. Tomorrow drive to Philadelphia and go to the biggest bank you can find and cash these in and open an account in your name. Then drive to Jonestown in Pennsylvania. Not Johnstown. Jonestown. Find a small house, something with white clapboard and storm windows and a wrap around porch at the edge of town and a view across the corn fields. It needs to have a yard where we can raise chickens. There's a monastery not far away over the rise – you want to be able to hear its carillon bells from the house.'

'How do you know about Jonestown and the monastery?'

'Lincoln Dittmann and I both come from Jonestown. Funny part is we didn't know each other back then. My family moved to Brooklyn when I was eight but Lincoln was brought up in Pennsylvania. I'd almost forgotten about Jonestown. He reminded me.'

'Who's Lincoln Dittmann?'

'Someone I came across in another incarnation.'

'What do I do when I find the house?'

'Buy it.'

'Why don't you come with me?'

'I have some loose ends to take care of. I'll turn up in Jonestown when I've finished.'

'How will you find me?'

'Jonestown is a small town. I'll ask for the gorgeous dish with a permanent squint in her eyes and a ghost of a smile on her lips.'

Stella relished the coolness of the night air. The headlights streaking past led her to imagine that she and Martin were stranded on an island of stillness in a world of perpetual motion. 'Do you really remember what happened to you in Moscow?' she asked.

He smiled. 'No. A curtain screened off the fragment of my life that I lived under the legend Jozef Kafkor. But what I've lost won't change anything for us. The part of Martin Odum's life that I want to remember begins here.'

1997: LINCOLN DITTMANN CONNECTS THE DOTS

'U.S. Government Printing Office Annex. Harvey Cleveland speaking. How can I help you?'

'Do you recognize my voice, Felix?'

'Tell you the truth, no. Am I supposed to?'

'Does a hanger under the Pulaski Skyway ring a bell? A crazy Texan named Leroy was about to shoot you. You jumped a mile when you heard his wrist bone splinter.'

Felix Kiick could be heard chuckling into the phone. 'Speak of the devil,' he said. 'Lincoln Dittmann. How'd you get this number? It's supposed to be an unlisted hotline.'

'How are you, Felix?'

'Hang on – I'm going to scramble this call.' There was a burst of static, then Felix's voice came on line again, loud and clear. 'I'm almost but not quite retired. Six weeks, three days, four and a half hours to go and I'm out of here. What about you?'

'I'm more or less okay.'

'Which is it – more or less?'

'More, actually.'

'Your memory coming back?'

'Nothing's wrong with my memory, Felix. You're confusing me with Martin Odum.'

Lincoln's remark startled Felix. 'I guess I am,' he admitted warily. 'You *are* . . . Lincoln Dittmann?'

'In the flesh.'

'Why are you calling?'

'I'm connecting the dots. I thought you could fill in some of the blanks.'

'Tell me what you know,' he said guardedly. 'Maybe I'll hint at what you don't know.'

'I know what happened to Jozef Kafkor in Prigorodnaia, Felix. He was the cutout between Crystal Quest's operations folks at the CIA and the *Oligarkh*, Tzvetan Ugor-Zhilov. When Jozef figured out that Quest was part of the Prigorodnaia operation – when he figured out she *originated* the operation – he must have threatened to take the matter up with an assortment of congressmen or senators, at which point Jozef was tortured and starved by the *Oligarkh's* hired hands, and eventually buried alive.'

'I'm hanging on your every word, Lincoln.'

'You were a counterterrorism wonk before they put you out to preretirement pasture, changing diapers for clients in the FBI's Witness Protection Program. I seem to remember you'd been posted to the American embassy in Moscow at one point in your career. Were you in Moscow when they brought in Jozef Kafkor, Felix?'

Lincoln could almost *hear* Kiick smiling. 'It's within the realm of possibility,' the FBI man acknowledged.

'With your rank,' Lincoln said, talking rapidly, leaving precious little breathing space between sentences, 'you would have been the top FBI gun at the embassy. You would have picked up scuttlebutt about the DDO running a secret operation via a cutout. When Jozef turned up on your doorstep, it would have crossed your mind that he could be the cutout – his physical condition, the evidence of torture on his body, his mental state would have suggested that the DDO operation had gone off the tracks.' Lincoln came up for air. 'Why were the *Oligarkh* and Samat exfiltrated?'

Felix actually sighed. 'They'd been living on the edge for years – the Moscow gang wars, the Chechens, certain factions inside the Russian Federal Security Service, disgruntled KGB hands who found themselves out in the cold, Yeltsin's political enemies, wannabe capitalists whom the *Oligarkh* had ruined on his way up, take your pick. And then Jozef Kafkor comes on the scene – Jozef and his scruples. Quest would have assured the *Oligarkh* she was the only one who heard his qualms, but the Ugor-Zhilovs, Tzvetan and Samat, must have had their doubts. After all, Quest had a vested interested in lying to them to keep the operation up and running indefinitely. When Jozef was rescued from the grave the *Oligarkh* dug for him and ended up wandering the streets of

Moscow, the Ugor-Zhilovs didn't swallow Quest's story that he couldn't remember the Jozef Kafkor legend. Samat cracked first. He didn't like the idea of coming to the States. He thought he'd be safer tucked away in a Jewish settlement on the West Bank of the Jordan, so he got himself into Israel. The *Oligarkh* held on longer, but in the end he cracked, too, and they brought him in.'

'To the Witness Protection Program?'

'No way. He was too important for Quest to entrust to the FBI. Her DDO wallahs created a legend for the *Oligarkh* themselves and settled him somewhere on the East Coast of America.'

'Meanwhile you had Kastner and his two daughters in your protection program.'

'I liked Kastner.'

'If it's any comfort, given that you lost him, he liked you.'

'You're sprinkling salt in wounds, Lincoln.'

'And the day Kastner told you – he referred to you as his friend in D.C. – that he needed someone to track down Samat, you couldn't resist tempting fate, could you? I can imagine how the scenario played out after Moscow. Someone like you would have been fascinated by the man found wandering behind the embassy, his body covered with sores. You would have been intrigued by the CIA's immediate interest in him. You would have been curious to know what happened to Jozef Kafkor after he was smuggled out to Finland. You had friends at the CIA, you would have learned that the Jozef Kafkor exfiltrated to Finland on your watch had been reincarnated, so to speak, as Martin Odum; that this same Martin Odum wound up working as a private detective in Crown Heights. And so you gave Kastner Martin Odum's name.' When Kiick didn't confirm or deny this, Lincoln said, 'Why?'

'Why not?'

'Come clean, Felix.'

'This *Oligarkh* character and his nephew Samat rubbed me the wrong way. Crystal Quest rubbed me the wrong way – I still remember how arrogant she was when the FBI was obliged to turn the Triple Border action over to her. And there is no love lost between the FBI and the CIA in general. On top of that, there have to be limits. I mean, ruining the Russian economy—'

Lincoln said, 'How'd you figure it out?'

'All you had to do was look around you in Moscow. All you had to do was catch the smug smiles on the faces of the DDO wallahs assigned to Moscow station. Quest herself showed up several times – you couldn't miss the gleam of unadulterated triumph in her bloodshot eyes. They were involved in something very big, that much was apparent to everyone around. They were transforming the world, rewriting history. And we saw Yeltsin imposing these wild ideas that the newspapers said came from the *Oligarkh* – freeing prices overnight, which led to hyperinflation; privatizing the Soviet industrial base, which left Ugor-Zhilov and a few insiders fabulously rich and the rest of the proletarians dirt poor; attacking Chechnya, which bogged down the Russian military in the Caucasus. It didn't take a genius to put two and two together. Demolishing the Russian economy, impoverishing dozens of millions of people so that the United States wouldn't have to deal with a powerful Russia – holy mackerel, it was over the top, Lincoln. So I guess I saw a certain poetic justice for Martin Odum to be the one to track down Samat for the divorce. I guess, in the back of my head, I wondered if Martin's memory wouldn't be jogged if and when he caught up with Samat.'

'If Martin's memory was jogged, if he came to realize that he was Jozef, he would want revenge.'

Felix said, very carefully, 'Any sane man in his shoes would.'

'Kastner was murdered, wasn't he?'

'Probably. The CIA insisted on doing the autopsy. I didn't like the way it played out – it was too neat by half. Martin heads for Israel to pick up the trail of Samat. Kastner dies of a heart attack. And the Chinese girl wearing Martin's white jumpsuit winds up being stung to death by bees on the roof.'

'You noticed that.'

'I notice everything. So are you going to tell me, Lincoln – did Martin and Kastner's kid, Estelle, find Samat?'

'What makes you think Estelle is involved?'

'Because you phoned me on this unlisted number. It had to come from somewhere. My guess,' Felix added cautiously, feeling his way, 'is that Stella gave the number to Martin, and Martin passed it on to you.'

'Martin found Samat where you stashed him – upstate New York in the middle of Amish country. He persuaded him to give his wife a religious divorce. Some rabbis in Brooklyn did the paper work.'

'What happened to Samat after he signed on the dotted line?'

'He said something about wanting to see Russian friends in Little Odessa. That's the last anyone saw of him, flagging down a taxi and telling the driver to take him to Brighton Beach.'

'Now that Samat's been found, the case is closed.'

'There's still the *Oligarkh*. You wouldn't by any chance know where he hangs his hat these days?'

'I don't know. If I did I wouldn't tell you. On the off chance you can find him, don't. Remember what happened to Jozef. Touch a hair on the *Oligarkh*'s head, Quest and her wallahs will bury you alive.'

'Thanks for the free advice, Felix.'

'You saved my life once, Lincoln. Now I'm trying to save yours.'

1997: LINCOLN DITTMANN FEELS THE RECOIL IN HIS SHOULDER BLADES

The sanctum Lincoln had sussed out was as suitable as a sniper's blind gets. Most of the panes were missing from the window, which meant he could steady the Whitworth on a sash at shoulder height – Lincoln shot best standing up, with his left elbow braced against a rib. The window itself was covered with a canopy of ivy that had spread across the facade of the abandoned hospital across the street and slightly uphill from the U-shaped tenement at 621 Crown Street, off Albany Avenue. For a sharpshooter, weather conditions – it was sunny and cold – were ideal; humid air could slow down a bullet and cause it to drop, dry hot air could cause it to fire high. Lugging the rifle and a shopping bag up the stairs littered with broken glass and trash to the corner room on the fourth floor, Lincoln had removed the thick work gloves and coated all of his finger tips with Super Glue, then set out the bottles of drinking water, the Mars bars and the containers of liquid yogurts on a sheet of newspaper. He knotted Dante

Pippen's lucky white silk scarf around his neck before sighting in the Whitworth. He judged the distance from the front door of the hospital to the sidewalk in front of the tenement to be eighty yards, then calculated his height above ground and the length of the hypotenuse of the resulting triangle. He adjusted the small wheels on the rear of the brass telescopic sight atop the Whitworth, focusing on the crucifix hanging in a ground floor window giving out onto the street. Sighted correctly and fired with a firm arm, the hexagonal barrel of the Whitworth – rifled to spit out a .45-caliber hex-shaped lead bullet that made one complete turn every twenty yards – could hit anything the marksman could see. Queen Victoria herself had once gotten a bull's eye at four-hundred yards; she'd been so thrilled with the exploit that she had knighted Mr Whitworth, the rifle's inventor, on the spot. Lincoln tapped home the ramrod, working the hand-rolled cartridge into the barrel, then carefully fitted the primer cap over the rifle's nipple. Finally he removed the brass tampon on the barrel and stretched a condom over the muzzle to protect the barrel from dust and moisture. With his weapon ready to fire, Lincoln crouched at the sill to study the target building across the street from what had once been the Carson C. Peck Memorial Hospital.

Lincoln had made use of one of Martin Odum's old tricks to find the address that corresponded to the unlisted phone number 718-555-9291. He'd called the local telephone company from a booth on Eastern Parkway. A woman had come on the line. Like Martin in London, Lincoln had retrieved Dante Pippen's rusty Irish accent for the occasion.

'Could you tell me, then, how I can get my hands on a new phone book after my dog chewed the bejesus out of the old one?'

'What type of directory do you want, sir?'

'Yellow pages for Brooklyn.'

'We'll be glad to send it to you. Could I trouble you for your phone number?'

'You're not troubling me,' Lincoln had said. 'It's 718-555-9291.'

The woman had repeated the number to be sure she had it right. Then she'd asked, 'What kind of dog do you have?'

'An Irish setter, of course.'

'Well, hide the phone book from him next time. Will you be needing anything else today?'

'A new yellow pages will do me fine. Are you sure you know where to send it?'

The woman had said, 'Let me check the screen. Here it is. You're at 621 Crown Street, Brooklyn, New York, right?'

'That's it, darlin'.'

'Have a nice day.'

'I plan to,' Lincoln had said just before he hung up.

From his hideaway on the fourth floor of the abandoned and soon to be demolished hospital, Lincoln watched a black teenager balancing a ghetto blaster on one shoulder skate past 621 Crown Street. As dusk shrouded the neighborhood and the streetlights flickered on, what Lincoln took to be a group of Nicaraguans in dreadlocks and colorful bandannas piled out of a gypsy cab and filed into the building. Settling down to camp for the night, Lincoln examined the building across the street more closely through the scope on the rifle. All the windows on the first five floors had cheap shades, some of them drawn, some of them half raised; the people he caught glimpses of in the windows looked to be Puerto Ricans or blacks. The entire top floor appeared to have been taken over by the target; every window was fitted with venetian blinds, all but one tightly closed. The one where he could see through the slats turned out to be a kitchen, equipped with an enormous Frigidaire and a gas stove with a double oven. A stocky black woman wearing an apron appeared to be preparing dinner. Now and then men would wander through the kitchen; one of them had his sports jacket off and Lincoln could make out a large-caliber pistol tucked into a shoulder holster. The black woman opened the oven to baste a large bird, then prepared two enormous bowls of dog food. She seemed to shout to someone in another room as she set the bowls down on the floor. A moment later two Borzois romped into sight and were promptly lost to view under the sill of the window.

Cleaning away the debris, settling down on the

floor with his back against a wall, Lincoln treated himself to a Mars bar and half a container of yogurt. All things considered, he was relieved that he was the one doing the shooting and not Martin Odum. Marksmanship was not Martin's strong suit; he was too impatient to stalk a target and crank in one or two clicks on the sights for distance and windage and slowly squeeze (as opposed to jerk) the trigger; too cerebral to kill in cold blood unless he was goaded into action by the likes of Lincoln Dittmann or Dante Pippen. In short, Martin was too involved, too temperamental. When a born-again sniper like Lincoln shot at a human target, the only thing he felt was the recoil of the rifle. Staking out the target, taking your sweet time to be sure you got the kill, one shot to a target, Lincoln was in his element. He had owned a rifle since he was a child in Pennsylvania, hunting rabbits and birds in the woods and fields behind his house in Jonestown. Once, packed off to the Company's Farm for a refresher course in hand-to-hand combat and firearms, he'd impressed the instructors the first day on the firing range when they'd put an antiquated gas-operated semiautomatic M-1 in his hands. Without a word, Lincoln had screwed down the iron sights and fired off a round at the thirty-six-inch target hoping to spot a spurt of dirt somewhere in front of it. When he did he'd turned up the sights one click, which was the equivalent of one minute of elevation or ten inches of height on the target, and fired the second round into the black. He'd notched in a one-click windage adjustment and raised his sights and hit the bulls eye on the third try.

The cold set in with the darkness. Lincoln turned up the collar of Martin Odum's overcoat and, drawing it tightly around his body, dozed. Images of soldiers outfitted in white headbands charging a stone wall along a sunken road filled his brain; he could hear the spurt of cannon and the crackle of rifle fire as smoke and death drifted over the field of battle. He forced himself awake to check the luminous hands on his wristwatch and the building across the street. Falling into a fitful sleep again, he found himself transported to a more serene setting. Skinny girls in filmy dresses were slotting coins into a jukebox and swaying in each others arms to the strains of *Don't Worry, Be Happy*. The music faded and Lincoln found himself inhaling the negative ions from a fountain on the Janicular, one of Rome's seven hills. An elegantly dressed woman and a dwarf wearing a knee-length overcoat buttoned up to his neck were walking past. Lincoln could hear himself saying, *My name's Dittmann. We met in Brazil, in a border town called Foz do Iguaçú. Your daytime name was Lucia, your nighttime name was Paura.* He made out the woman's excited response: *I remember you! Your daytime name happens to be the same as your nighttime name, which is Giovanni da Varrazano.*

In his fiction Lincoln caught up with the woman as she continued on down the hill. He gripped her shoulders and shook her until she agreed to spend the rest of her life breeding baby polyesters with him on a farm in Tuscany.

Checking the building across the street again, Lincoln became aware of the first faint ocherous stains tinting the grim sky over the roofs in the east. Setting up the kill had been easier than he'd expected. He'd made his way through the alleyways behind Albany Avenue to the yard in back of Xing's restaurant. Using an old boat hook hidden behind a rusting refrigerator, he'd tugged down the lower rung of the ladder on the fire escape and climbed up to the roof. The bees had long since abandoned Martin's two hives, including the one that seemed to have exploded; stains of what looked like dried molasses were visible on the tar paper. Retrieving the key Martin had hidden behind a loose brick on the parapet, Lincoln had unlocked the roof door and let himself into Martin Odum's pool parlor. He made his way through the dark apartment to the pool table that Martin had used as a desk and took a single handrolled rifle cartridge from the mahogany humidor; Lincoln himself had fabricated the ammunition several years before, procuring high-grade gunpowder and measuring it out on an apothecary scale. Pocketing the cartridge, he picked up the Whitworth and blew the dust off of its firing mechanism. It was a surprisingly light weapon, beautifully crafted, exquisitely balanced, a delight to hold in your hands. This particular Whitworth had originally been his; he couldn't remember how it had wound up in Martin Odum's possession. He made a mental note to ask him one of these days. Wiping the weapon clean of fingerprints, he rolled it in one of Martin's overcoats and slung it across his back. Then, pulling on a pair of thick work gloves he found in a cardboard box, he retraced his steps down to the alley, recovered the shopping bag filled with nourishment that he'd prepared that morning and meandered through the deserted streets of Crown Heights to the massive building with 'Carson C. Peck Memorial Hospital' and '1917' engraved on its stone base. Breaking in turned out to be relatively uncomplicated: At the back of the hospital, on the Montgomery Street side, squatters had cut through the chainlink fence the demolition company rigged around the property and one of the ground floor doors was ajar. Crouching inside the building to get his bearings, Lincoln caught the muffled sound of a brassy cough rising from the stairwell, which suggested that the squatters had installed themselves in the basement of the building.

The ocherous streaks had dragged smudges of daylight across the sky, transforming the rooftops into silhouettes. Massaging his arms to work out the coldness and the stiffness, Lincoln pushed himself to his feet and padded over to a corner of the room to relieve himself against a wall. Returning to the window, kneeling at the sill, he noticed a light in the top-floor kitchen window across the street. The black woman, wrapped in a terrycloth robe, was brewing up two large pots of coffee. When the coffee was ready she filled eight mugs and, carrying them on a tray, disappeared from view. Below, at the entrance to 621 Crown, two Nicaraguan women wearing long winter coats and bright scarves and knitted caps pulled down over their earlobes emerged from the building and hurried off in the direction of the subway station on Eastern Parkway. Twelve minutes later a black BMW pulled up to the curb in front of the tenement. The driver, a tall man in a knee-length leather overcoat and a chauffeur's cap, climbed out and stood leaning against the open door, clouds of vapor streaming from his mouth as he breathed. He glanced at his watch several times and stamped his feet to keep them from growing numb. He checked the number over the entrance of the building against something written on a scrap of paper and seemed reassured when he spotted the two men shouldering through the heavy door of 621 into the street. Both were dressed in double-breasted pea jackets with the collars turned up. The men, obviously bodyguards, greeted the driver with a wave. One of the bodyguards strolled to the corner and looked up and down Albany Avenue. The other walked off several paces to his left and checked out Crown Street. Returning to the BMW, he eyed the windows of the deserted hospital across the street.

The security arrangements were clearly casual;

the bodyguards were going through the motions but there was no urgency to their gestures, which is what often happened when the individual being protected has been squirreled away and the people responsible for his safety assumed that potential enemies wouldn't be able to find his hole. Back at the BMW, the two bodyguards and the driver were making small talk. One of the bodyguards must have detected a signal on his walkie-talkie because he hauled it from a pocket and, looking up at the closed venetian blinds, muttered something into it. Several minutes went by. Then the front door of 621 swung open again and another bodyguard appeared. He was straining to hold back two Borzois attached to long leashes. To the amusement of the men waiting near the BMW, the dogs practically dragged the man into the gutter. Behind him a stubby hunch-shouldered man with a shock of silver hair and dark glasses materialized at the front door. He had a cigar clamped between his teeth and walked with the aid of two aluminum crutches, thrusting one hip forward and dragging the leg after it, then repeating the movement with the other hip. He paused for breath when he reached the end of the walkway in front of the building's entrance. One of the bodyguards opened the back door of the car. In the corner room across the street, Lincoln rose to his feet and in one flowing motion jammed his left elbow into his rib cage as he steadied the rifle on a window sash. Closing his left eye, he pressed his right eye to the telescopic sight and walked up the muzzle of the Whitworth until the cross-hairs were fixed on the target's forehead immediately above the bridge of his nose. He squeezed the trigger with such painstaking deliberation that the eruption of flame at the breech's nipple and the bullet rifling out of the barrel and the satisfying recoil of the stock into his shoulder blade all caught him by surprise. Sighting again on the target, he saw blood oozing from a ragged-edged tear in the middle of the man's forehead. The bodyguards had heard a sound but not yet associated it with gunfire. The one holding open the back door of the car was the first to notice that their charge was collapsing onto the pavement. He leapt forward to catch him under the armpits and, shouting for help, lowered him to the ground.

By the time the bodyguards realized that the man they were protecting had been shot dead, Lincoln, oblivious to the spasms in his game leg, was well on his way to the breach in the chainlink fence.

1997: CRYSTAL QUEST COMES TO BELIEVE IN DANTE'S TRINITY

Dante Pippen, a maestro of tradecraft, had positioned himself in a booth at the rear of Xing's Mandarin Restaurant with his back to the tables, facing a mirror in which he could keep track of who came and went. He sized up the two figures in trenchcoats who entered the restaurant at the stroke of noon. Both had the deadpan eyes that marked them as flunkies for the CIA's Office of Security. The one with the cauliflower ears of a prize-fighter ducked behind the bar to make sure that Tsou Xing, who was holding fort on his high stool in front of the cash register, didn't have a sawed-off shotgun stashed under the counter. Ignoring Dante, the second man, who had the shoulders and neck of a weight lifter, pushed through the swinging doors into the kitchen. Moments later he reappeared and planted himself in front of the doors, his arms folded across his barrel chest.

It wasn't long before Crystal Quest turned up at the door of the restaurant. Coming into the murky interior from the dazzling sunlight of Albany

Avenue, she was momentarily blinded. When she could see again, she spotted Dante and started toward him, the thick heels of her sensible shoes drumming on the linoleum floor. 'Long time no see,' she said as she slid onto the banquette opposite him. 'As usual you look fit as a flea, Dante. Still working out on that rowing machine?'

Dante managed a half-hearted laugh. 'You're confusing me with Martin Odum, Fred. He's the one with a rowing machine.'

Quest, who knew a joke when she heard one, grinned nervously.

Dante said, 'How about treating your bloodstream to a shot of alcohol?'

'Alcohol's just what the doctor ordered. Something with a lot of ice, thank you.'

Dante called for a whiskey, neat, and a frozen daiquiri, heavy on the ice. Tsou waved his good arm in acknowledgement. Waiting for the drinks, Dante watched Quest toying absently with the frills down the front of her dress shirt. He noticed that the jacket of her pantsuit, like the skin around her eyes, was wrinkled; that the rust-colored dye was washing out of her hair, revealing soot-gray roots. 'You look the worse for wear, Fred. Job getting you down?'

'Being DDO of an intelligence entity that has recast itself as a risk-averse high-tech social club is not a cake walk,' she said. 'There are people at Langley who do nothing but stare at satellite down-loads from morning to night, as if a photograph could tell you what an adversary *intends* to do with what he has. Hell of a way to run an espionage agency. They've slashed our budget, the president doesn't have the time or the curiosity to read the overnight briefing book we prepare for him, the liberal press climbs all over us for our occasional fumbles. It goes without saying we can't gloat about our occasional successes—'

The Chinese waitress wearing a tight skirt slit up one thigh set the drinks on the table. Watching the girl slink away in the mirror reminded Dante of Martin's late lamented Chinese girlfriend, Minh. 'Do you have any?' he asked Quest.

Crunching on chips of ice, she'd lost the thread of the conversation. 'Have any what?' she inquired.

'Successes.'

'One or two or three.'

'Like the Prigorodnaia business,' Dante murmured.

Quest's eyes hardened. 'What Prigorodnaia business are you talking about?'

'Christsake, Fred, don't play the innocent,' Dante snapped. 'We know what happened to Jozef Kafkor. We know the DDO provided seed money to the Armenian used-car dealer so he could corner the Russian aluminum market. We know how Ugor-Zhilov, a.k.a the *Oligarkh*, ingratiated himself with Yeltsin, arranging for the publication of his book, organizing his personal bodyguard, replenishing his bank account. Once installed in Yeltsin's inner circle, the *Oligarkh* nudged him into freeing up prices and privatizing the industrial base of the defunct Soviet Union. We know he lured Yeltsin into attacking Chechnya just when the Red Army was recovering from the Afghanistan debacle. We know that for a period of years in the early nineties the individual running Russia from behind the scene was none other than . . . Fred Astaire. We know she was running it into the ground so that the new Russia rising from the ashes of the Soviet Union couldn't compete with America.'

The blood seemed to seep from Quest's cheeks until the only color remaining came from the smears of blush she'd applied during the shuttle flight from Washington. She spooned another chunk of ice into her mouth. 'Who's *we*?' she demanded.

'Why, I would have thought that was obvious. There's Martin Odum, the one-time CIA field agent turned detective who specializes in collecting mahjongg debts. There's Lincoln Dittmann, the Civil War buff who actually met the poet Whitman. And last but certainly not least, there's yours truly, Dante Pippen, the Irish dynamiter from Castletownbere.'

Quest snickered bitterly. 'That business of Lincoln claiming to have been at the battle of Fredericksburg – it was a brilliant piece of theater. It had us all fooled – the shrink, me, the committee that met from time to time to review the situation, to decide whether to terminate your contract or your life. We all assumed that Martin Odum was off his rocker. Teach me to give someone the benefit of the doubt.'

Nursing his whisky, Dante shrugged a shoulder. 'If it's any consolation, Lincoln *was* at the battle of Fredericksburg.'

Quest raised an eyebrow; she didn't appreciate having her leg pulled. 'Why'd you need to see me, Dante? What's so important that it couldn't wait until you had a chance to come down to Langley?'

'We've taken out life insurance, we've taped what you don't want the world to know – the Prigorodnaia operation; how you provided the keys to Kastner's safe house so the *Oligarkh's* people could break in and murder him; how you told them about Martin's beehives, which led to the death of the Chinese girl, Minh. Add to that the sniper who tried to kill Martin in Hebron. Not to mention the Czechs who gave Martin a car and a pistol in Prague and told him to run for it. These attempts on Martin's life had your prints all over them.'

'That's nonsense. Knowing what I know, the last thing I would have done is charge a pistol with dummy Parabellums.'

Dante said, 'How did you know the handgun was loaded with dummy Parabellums?'

Quest smudged a fingertip dabbing at the mascara on an eyelid. Dante took her failure to answer for an answer. 'Listen up, Fred, if any one of us dies of anything but old age, the tapes will be duplicated and distributed to every member of the Congressional Oversight Sub-committee, also to selected journalists in the liberal press who report on your *occasional* fumbles.'

'You're bluffing.'

Dante raised his chin and looked Quest in the eye. 'If you think that, all you need to do is call our bluff.'

'Listen, Dante, we all came of age in the cold war. We all fought the good fight. I'm sure we can work something out.'

'There's one more item on our agenda. We held a meeting to decide whether to terminate your life or your career. Career won, two to one. Within one week we want to read in the newspapers that the legendary Crystal Quest, the first woman Deputy Director of Operations, a veteran of thirty-two years of loyal and masterful service to the Central Intelligence Agency, has been put out to pasture.'

Sucked against her will into Dante's trinity, Quest asked, 'Who was the one who voted to terminate my life?'

'Why, Martin, of course, though being the more squeamish of the three, he wanted me or Lincoln to make the hit.' Dante smiled pleasantly. 'Some people forgive but don't forget. Martin's the opposite – he forgets but doesn't forgive.'

'What does he forget?'

'Whether Martin Odum is a legend or the real him.'

'It's the original him, the first legend. You worked for Army Intelligence—'

'You mean, *Martin* worked for Army Intelligence.'

Quest nodded carefully. 'Martin's specialty was East European dissidents. I stumbled across a paper *he* published in the *Army Intelligence Quarterly* identifying two veins of dissidence: the anticommunists, who wanted to do away with communism altogether, and the pro-communists, who wanted to purge communism of Stalinism and reform the system. *His* article, which turned out to be far sighted, predicted that in the end the pro-communists were more likely to have an impact on East Europe and, ultimately, the Soviet Union itself, than the anticommunists. I remember . . . *Martin* citing the trial of Pavel Slánský in Prague, claiming he was the precursor of the reformers who came after him, Dubeck in Czechoslovakia, eventually Gorbachev in the Soviet Union.'

'And you lured him away from Army Intelligence into the CIA?'

'The Legend Committee worked up a cover for him using his real name and as much of his actual background as they could. He'd lived in Pennsylvania until his father moved the family to Brooklyn. Martin was something like eight at the time. He was raised on Eastern Parkway, he went to PS 167, Crown Heights was his stamping ground, he even had a school chum whose father owned a Chinese restaurant on Albany Avenue. When we discovered he could handle explosives, for a while we had him making letter bombs or rigging portable phones to explode from a distance.

Martin was the last agent I personally ran before they kicked me upstairs to run the officers who run the agents. The Odum we concocted wasn't a detective. That's something you . . . that's something *Martin* added to the cover story when his Company career came to an end.' Quest, shaken, began gnawing on a chip of ice.

Dante tucked a ten dollar bill under the ashtray and stood up. 'I'll pass all this on to Martin if I see him. I suspect he'll be relieved.'

Quest looked up at Dante. 'It was you who shot the *Oligarkh*.'

'Christsake, Fred.'

'I know it was you, Dante. The kill had your M.O. on it.'

Dante laughed lightly, his shoulders shuddering with pleasure. 'You're losing your touch, Fred. I have nothing to gain by lying to you – it was Lincoln who made the hit on the *Oligarkh*. Newspaper accounts said the police couldn't identify the bullet or the murder weapon, which means Lincoln must have used that old Civil War sniper rifle you found for him when you were working up the Dittmann legend. Jesus, that's really humorous. Martin or I wouldn't know how to load the damn thing.'

Snickering in satisfaction, Dante headed for the front of the restaurant. The weight lifter came off the kitchen doors and started after him. The prize-fighter edged around the bar to block his path. Tsou Xing called in a high pitched voice, 'No violence inside, all-light.'

Dante's Irish temper flared. Glancing over his shoulder at Quest, he said, very softly, 'Am I to understand that you'll be calling our bluff, Fred?'

Quest locked eyes with Dante, then looked away and took a deep breath and wagged a forefinger once. The two flunkies from the Office of Security stopped in their tracks. Dante nodded as if he were digesting a momentous piece of information, something that could transform his legend and add to its longevity. Humming under his breath one of Lincoln's favorite tunes, *Don't Worry, Be Happy*, he pushed through the door into the blinding sunlight.